PRAISE FOR MARSHALL KARP

"Marshall Karp is a genius storyteller!"
—HANK PHILLIPPI RYAN, *USA TODAY* BESTSELLING AUTHOR

"Marshall Karp knows how to keep a story running full speed, full time."
—MICHAEL CONNELLY, #1 *NEW YORK TIMES* BESTSELLING AUTHOR

"Brings to mind Robert B. Parker, Janet Evanovich, Dean Koontz, Stuart Woods, and a lot of other fast-paced authors."
—JANET MASLIN, *THE NEW YORK TIMES BOOK REVIEW*

"Marshall Karp is up there with Carl Hiaasen and Donald Westlake and Janet Evanovich—smart, fast-paced, clever, and really, really funny."
—JOSEPH FINDER, *NEW YORK TIMES* BESTSELLING AUTHOR

"Rousing...Shocking plot twists, clever dialogue, and dead-on characterizations keep the pages turning. Readers will agree that his happy welding of police procedural and sly humor is the best yet in the series."
—*PUBLISHERS WEEKLY* (STARRED REVIEW) ON *NYPD RED 7*

"*NYPD Red 7: The Murder Sorority* is one of the most engaging thrillers of the year. James Patterson could not have passed down the torch to a more suited author than Karp."
—KASHIF HUSSAIN, BEST THRILLER BOOKS

"Totally original, a sheer roller-coaster ride, packed with waves of humor and a dynamic duo in Lomax and Biggs. Karp shows a master's touch in his debut."
—DAVID BALDACCI, #1 *NEW YORK TIMES* BESTSELLING AUTHOR, ON *THE RABBIT FACTORY*

"Smart, funny, and intuitive, Lomax and Biggs glide through the overlit shoals of Los Angeles like sharks through ginger ale."
—**DONALD WESTLAKE ON *FLIPPING OUT***

"Marshall Karp could well be the Carl Hiaasen of Los Angeles—only I think he's even funnier. *The Rabbit Factory* will touch your funny bone and your heart."
—**JAMES PATTERSON, #1 *NEW YORK TIMES* BESTSELLING AUTHOR**

"Marshall Karp needs a blurb from me like Uma needs a facelift. This guy is the real deal, and *Bloodthirsty* is a first-class, fast, funny, and fabulous read by a terrific writer."
—**JOHN LESCROART, *NEW YORK TIMES* BESTSELLING AUTHOR**

"Blending the gritty realism of a Joseph Wambaugh police procedural with the sardonic humor of Janet Evanovich, Karp delivers a treat that's not only laugh-out-loud funny but also remarkably suspenseful."
—***PUBLISHERS WEEKLY* ON *FLIPPING OUT***

"Better than mostly anything on the market… *The Rabbit Factory* is, quite simply, stunning."
—**CHRIS HIGH, *TANGLED WEB* AND *SHOTS MAGAZINE***

"Wickedly funny…this quirky, off-kilter novel also has a really big heart…[and] an emotional core that will make readers care about these tough but vulnerable crime fighters and keep them hoping for a sequel."
—**BOOKREPORTER.COM ON *THE RABBIT FACTORY***

NYPD RED 8
THE 11:59 BOMBER

BOOKS BY MARSHALL KARP

THE NYPD RED SERIES

NYPD Red 8: The 11:59 Bomber
NYPD Red 7: The Murder Sorority

COAUTHORED WITH JAMES PATTERSON

NYPD Red 6
Red Alert (a.k.a. *NYPD Red 5*)
NYPD Red 4
NYPD Red 3
NYPD Red 2
NYPD Red

THE LOMAX AND BIGGS MYSTERIES

Terminal
Cut, Paste, Kill
Flipping Out
Bloodthirsty
The Rabbit Factory

DANNY CORCORAN AND THE BALTIC AVENUE GROUP

Snowstorm in August

STANDALONE NOVELS

Don't Tell Me How to Die
Kill Me if You Can (with James Patterson)

NYPD RED 8
THE 11:59 BOMBER

MARSHALL KARP

BLACKSTONE
PUBLISHING

Copyright © 2025 by Mesa Films, Inc.
Published in 2025 by Blackstone Publishing
Cover design by Sarah Riedlinger
Book design by Kathryn Galloway English

All rights reserved. This book or any portion
thereof may not be reproduced or used in any manner
whatsoever without the express written permission
of the publisher except for the use of brief quotations
in a book review.

The characters and events in this book are fictitious.
Any similarity to real persons, living or dead, is coincidental
and not intended by the author.

Printed in the United States of America

First edition: 2025
ISBN 979-8-212-87651-3
Fiction / Thrillers / Crime

Version 1

Blackstone Publishing
31 Mistletoe Rd.
Ashland, OR 97520

www.BlackstonePublishing.com

*For Danny Corcoran,
Detective First Grade, NYPD (ret.)
my friend, my anchor, my partner in crime*

PROLOGUE

THURSDAY, 11:03 A.M.
ASTORIA, QUEENS

IT WAS SUPPOSED TO be one of the happiest days of their lives.

The grandmother, the mother, and the bride-to-be heading to the city to find The Dress.

"We should go to Macy's," the grandmother said.

"They don't sell wedding gowns, Yaya," Karissa said.

"They should," the old woman said.

"We can go there for the bridesmaids' dresses. Maybe you can find Mr. Macy and tell him how to run his business."

The mother tried to stifle a laugh.

The grandmother remained stone-faced. "So where *are* we going?" she demanded.

"A little bridal boutique on Broad Street in the financial district."

"It sounds expensive," Yaya said. "Can't you find a nice store in the People Who Don't Have a Lot of Money District?"

Karissa exhaled heavily. "Mom?"

"My grandmother did the same to me when I was looking for my wedding dress," the mother said. "It's a family tradition."

"A trad—what's the tradition?" Karissa said. "To make me even more crazy than I already am?"

"Don't worry about it. It's a superstition. She's planting a seed."

"What seed?"

"Dysphoria," the mother said.

Karissa shook her head. "Never heard of it."

"Dysphoria is the opposite of euphoria. It's a state where you're not too happy. You're uneasy. You're uncomfortable."

"Ma, I don't get it. I'm shopping for my wedding dress. Why shouldn't I be happy?"

"Because what you're doing today should be done once in a lifetime," the mother said. "And if you're too happy, then you might want to do it again."

Karissa put her hands to her face and felt the tears trickle down her fingers. Then she wrapped her arms around her grandmother. "I love you, Yaya."

A smile spread across the old lady's face as she hugged her granddaughter. "*S' agapó, glykiá mou.*"

At 11:18, the three women left Yaya's house on Thirty-Second Street in Astoria and made the four-minute walk to the subway.

At 11:29, they boarded the W train to Manhattan.

At 11:43, they arrived at the Fifty-Ninth Street / Lexington Avenue station and transferred to the downtown 5 train.

At 11:58, they arrived at the Wall Street station.

At 11:59, the bomb exploded.

They died instantly.

CHAPTER 1

THURSDAY, 11:54 A.M.
CENTRAL PARK

HE HAD DONE HIS research. The Sheep Meadow in Central Park was the best place in New York City to make an untraceable phone call.

Almost every incoming call to a city agency could be triangulated to within ten or twenty yards of the point of origin. And since there were cameras everywhere, as soon as they zeroed in on your location, they'd have a high-res picture of your face. And once they had that, how long would it take for them to have you in cuffs?

Even if he called from the Staten Island Ferry in the middle of the Hudson River, the ubiquitous eyes in the sky would pick him up boarding at the Whitehall Terminal or getting off at St. George on the other side.

But the Sheep Meadow, a sprawling fifteen-acre lawn on the south side of the park, was one of the few remaining places in the city of nine million people where a person had a shot at remaining invisible. On a normal sunny July day like this, there would be hundreds of people stretched out on the grass, reading, relaxing, or simply reveling in the elegantly conceived, brilliantly executed pastoral sanctuary in the middle of the urban madness that was New York City.

Sure, the cops would know where the call came from, but there were no cameras close enough to identify him. Not only was this the best place to hide in plain sight, but today was the perfect day. There was a concert tonight, and by 11:30 this morning, thousands of music lovers had already staked their claim to a blanket-size patch of ground.

He was giddy as he watched them pour onto the meadow from all sides. He could have worn a red-and-white striped shirt and bobble hat like the *Where's Waldo?* guy, and he'd still be lost in the crowd.

He waited until 11:54 to make the call. Five minutes wouldn't give them enough time to do anything, and he needed to go on record that he was the one punishing the city for what they had done. After the bomb went off, every glory-seeking asshole in five boroughs would be calling in and taking credit.

He had vacillated about whether to call 911 and talk directly to the cops, or call the nonemergency number, 311. He finally decided on 311. He wanted the person on the other end of the phone to be smart but not cop smart. Calling a civilian was a safer bet.

He knew that the call would be recorded, so he bought the most sophisticated voice-changing software he could find. He dialed, wondering who would answer. Whoever did would remember this call forever.

The call went through. "Hello, and thank you for calling 311 in New York City," a robotic female voice said. "We're here to help, but if this is an emergency, please hang up and dial 911. Today, Thursday, alternate-side-of-the-street parking and parking-meter rules are in effect. Tomorrow, Friday, alternate-side-of-the-street parking and parking-meter rules are in effect. To continue in English, please press one. All other callers, please remain on the line."

He hadn't expected this. It never dawned on him to test-call a hotline. What the hell happened to operators who just picked up the damn phone?

"*Para español, presione tres,*" a different automaton said. The next voice sounded Russian, but he didn't wait. He scrambled for his keypad and pressed "1."

"For assistance with parking tickets, including bus lane, red light, or speed camera violations," the original robot said, "please press one. To report illegal fireworks or to make a noise complaint, please press two. To report trash, recycling, or compost that was not picked up on your collection day, please press three."

This was why he hated the city. It didn't matter if you called begging for help; they'd figure out a way to avoid you.

He cursed at the virtual dispatcher as she droned on with prompts for New Yorkers who had issues with damaged street signs, abandoned vehicles, rodents, food assistance, or property taxes. He looked at his watch: 11:55.

Finally, the bot ran out of options. "All other customers, please remain on the line."

"I'm not a *customer*, bitch," he said into the ether. "I'm your worst nightmare."

Silence. 11:56.

"Now, briefly tell me what I can help you with this morning," the bionic woman said. "You can say things like 'report a noisy neighbor' or 'my apartment needs repairs.' Go ahead."

"Hi," he said. "Can I just talk to an agent, please?"

"You want to speak to a 311 representative, right?"

"Yes!" he snapped.

"All right, a representative. Before I connect you," she said, her voice as perky and promising as an android can get, "tell me a little bit about why you're calling."

He buried his face close to the screen, not that the couple smoking a joint on the blanket next to him gave a rat's ass. "Agent! Representative! Human fucking being!" he said, spitting the words into the phone.

But the sadists who designed the 311 system knew their audience. New Yorkers want what they want when they want it. The robot was programmed to be equally pigheaded.

"I understand you want to speak with someone who can help you, but before I can direct your call, I need to know—"

He hung up as the time on the phone jumped to 11:57. He had no choice. He dialed 911.

"New York City 911. Do you need police, fire, or medical?" a real, live human female voice asked.

"I want to leave a message for the mayor," he said.

"Sir, this number is for emergencies only," the dispatcher said. "Is this an emerg—"

"Listen to me," he said. "I have a message for the mayor. Tell her I am going to destroy New York City the way it destroyed my family. You got that?"

You bet she did. He was being recorded.

"Sir, what is your name?" she asked. He could hear computer keys click-clacking as she talked. She probably got bullshit calls all day long. She knew he was the real deal.

"Did you hear what I said?" he replied. "Tell the mayor I am going to do to this city what it did to me."

"Sir, what are you planning on doing?"

He grinned. She had to know he wasn't going to answer that one, but you had to give her credit for trying.

"Do you know what time it is?" he asked.

"It's 11:58," she said calmly. "Sir, please tell me exactly what you're planning to do."

He laughed. "You'll know in sixty seconds."

He hung up, folded his blanket, inhaled as much of the secondhand cannabis in the air as he could, and slowly sauntered out of the park.

CHAPTER 2

THURSDAY, 11:56 A.M.
FINANCIAL DISTRICT

I BROKE ONE OF my chopsticks in half and tossed the pieces on the table.

"*Someone* is in a pissy mood this morning," my partner, Kylie MacDonald, said, popping a piece of General Tso's chicken into her mouth.

"What makes you say that?" I asked, pointing my remaining chopstick at her.

"I don't know, Zach. Woman's intuition? Or maybe it's just the fact that I've spent a third of my life working as a cop. I have a Spidey sense for simmering violence."

"I'm not violent," I said. "However, it's possible that being dragged to court on my day off, getting jerked around by the criminal justice system, and then winding up eating Chinese food for breakfast may have left me a little . . ." I destroyed the second chopstick with a loud snap. "Peevish."

"Maybe next time you should order the beef chow fun instead of the hot-and-cranky soup."

I gave her the finger and checked my phone: 11:56. "Four more minutes," I said, "and we'll have wasted our entire morning."

"Look on the bright side, Zach. We just closed a case that's been dogging us for a year and a half."

"Closed" was an overstatement. Eighteen months earlier, Captain Cates had called us into her office. "Someone stole a wristwatch from a locker in a gym on West Eighty-Second," she said. "The chief of D's wants us take care of it."

"Someone stole a watch from a locker, and the chief wants *Red* to handle it?" Kylie said. "I'm guessing it's not a Timex."

It was one of those days when the boss wasn't in the mood for cop snark. "The watch is a three-million-dollar Richard Mille," she said, "and the owner is a thirty-million-dollar-a-year soccer star from Spain. Is that Red enough for you, MacDonald, or should I call the chief and tell him we're not interested?"

Kylie and I got to the gym in ten minutes and had the watch in hand and the towel guy under arrest twenty minutes later.

Since then, the trial had been scheduled and postponed half a dozen times. Late last night we were notified to be in court and ready to testify by 9:30 a.m. We were there by 8:30 and sat on our hands until 10:55, when the DA shot us a text: *Defendant pled out. You're free to go.*

Go where? I thought. It was my day off. By now, I was supposed to be on a fishing boat a hundred miles away.

Kylie, who was happy to put the case behind us, immediately decided we should celebrate the win at Lily Chu's. The food is so-so, but Lily is a total sweetheart who caters to cops. Plus, it was one of the few Chinese restaurants in the financial district that opened before noon.

At 11:58, the waiter came over to our table with two fortune cookies. Kylie broke one in half and began reading from the tiny slip of paper inside.

"You are a superior lady detective, not crabby like your man partner."

"I'm not crabby," I said. "You got a faulty cookie."

"Cookies never lie. Let's take a look at yours," she said, cracking open the second cookie. "Man cop thinks he's smart, but the longer he keeps a secret, the harder it will bite him in the ass."

I'd been conned. "Jesus, Kylie. Give me a break, will ya?"

"Oh, wait. There's more," she said, turning the fortune over. "Theo deserves to know the truth. Stop dicking around and tell him you're his father."

I took the paper from her hand, rolled it into a ball, and flicked it in her face. "So you *do* know what's bothering me," I said.

"Of course I know what's bothering you. You've been a total mope ever since the day you got back the DNA results. What I *don't* know is why you're even mopier today than you've been for the last three weeks."

"Because I was supposed to drive out to Montauk this morning and go fishing with Theo."

"You never told me that."

"Right. Because if I told you, the first thing you'd say is, 'Are you planning on telling him you're his father?'"

A few weeks ago, I stumbled onto the fact that I have an eighteen-year-old biological son who I never knew existed. Theo Wilkins is an amazing young man. If the universe was going to drop a surprise kid into my life, it couldn't do better than Theo. But I wasn't ready to tell him. The only people I told were my psychologist girlfriend, Cheryl, who I knew would give me time to sort it out in my head, and Kylie, who would, of course, meddle.

"Well?" Kylie said. "Are you planning to tell—?"

She was cut off in mid-meddle when both our radios crackled with a series of piercing beeps that turned heads even in this age of digital cacophony. Whatever it was, it was high priority.

The dispatcher's voice was calm but urgent. "Ten-thirteen. Officer needs assistance. Confirmed explosion at the Wall Street transit station. The five train, downtown platform, Wall Street at Broadway. Numerous persons down. FD, ESU notified and en route."

The station was two minutes away. We bolted from our chairs. Kylie keyed her mic. "Red Portable responding."

We hadn't settled the bill, but Lily Chu, who had heard the call, shouted, "Go, go, go, go, go!"

As soon as we hit the street, we could see the ashy gray haze rising up through the canyon of office towers along Broadway. We could hear the blaring air horns of fire engines as they tried to plow their way through the financial district's notoriously narrow streets, some no wider than the cow paths that preceded them hundreds of years ago.

And as we raced toward the scene, we could smell the panic emanating from the swarm of humanity stampeding toward us.

Decades after 9/11, Lower Manhattan was once again under attack, and its citizens, caught in the grip of PTSD, were running for their lives.

CHAPTER 3

I WAS STILL IN high school on September 11, 2001, but I've worked with enough veteran cops to hear stories about Trinity Church, the parish that has been part of the fabric of New York City for over three hundred years.

Standing in the shadow of the World Trade Center, the church miraculously survived the more than a million tons of debris that rained down on Lower Manhattan that historic Tuesday morning.

In the months after the attack, Trinity opened the doors of its St. Paul's Chapel to the thousands of rescue and recovery workers who arrived to search for survivors and sift through the ruins.

And now, through a strange twist of fate, the church, only steps away from the subway station at Broadway and Wall Street, once again became a refuge for first responders at New York's latest ground zero.

When we arrived, the street was a beehive of cops, firefighters, EMTs, and transit workers who were evacuating the hundreds of passengers caught in the blast.

This wasn't our first bomb scene, so when we got to the station entrance, Kylie and I braced ourselves to hit a wall of thick smoke. But the MTA's ventilation system is designed to continuously expel air through a network of grates in the sidewalk above, so the stairs reeked, but they were navigable.

Wall Street is a high-volume station. Normally, it's packed with people staring at their phones and occasionally leaning over the platform, craning their necks, hoping to spot their train's headlights emerging from the end of the tunnel.

But all signs of normality had been obliterated. The station looked like a scene out of a disaster movie. The crippled train sat there, its doors open, as first responders shepherded the walking wounded to safety. But not everyone could walk. Bodies littered the platform, some bleeding, some crying in shock or pain, some not moving at all.

Kylie and I weren't there to help them. Our job was to find out what happened.

It wasn't difficult to know where to start. The first three cars of the train were relatively unscathed, but the sixth—number 5202—had taken the brunt of the blast. The cars on either side, their windows blown out, their steel chassis peppered with shrapnel, were collateral damage.

I sniffed the pungent air. It smelled like tar. "C4," I said to Kylie.

Directly opposite car 5202 were the smoldering remains of whatever had been there when the bomb went off.

Several cops and an orange-vested transit worker were clustered in front of it when one of them, a silver-haired sergeant, spotted us.

"Detectives," he called out, and hustled over. His nameplate said *Sullivan*, the pin with the *XXX* on his shirt said he'd been on the job for at least thirty years, and his lean, angular body and the keen, determined look in his eyes said he wasn't even thinking about retirement.

"Five dead so far, another three likely," he said. "The surviving victims aren't much help, but you're gonna want to talk to the station manager. He saw it go off."

We walked up to the man and introduced ourselves.

"Pete Maltese," he said.

"What can you tell us, Pete?"

"I was at the uptown end of the station. It was a normal day, normal lunch crowd—busy, but no issues. The number five pulls in, stops, the doors open, people get off, people get on, and then *boom*! Just like that, the shed explodes."

"What shed?"

"A work crew shed. It was right here." He pointed at the pile of rubble. "Some wacko must've gotten in and planted a bomb inside."

"What was in the shed?" I asked.

"Tile. It's typical MTA bullshit. They hire someone to replace all the cracked tiles in the station. As soon as the contractor gets the job from the city, he stakes his claim by setting up a makeshift work shed, and then he gets around to doing the job whenever he gets around to it.

"These sheds are slapped together in a hurry. Four-by-eight plywood sheets on a two-by-four frame. It's a major pain in the ass for the customers. A lot of them like to stick close to the wall, but this thing eats up more than half the platform, so they've got to get close to the tracks to get around it."

"Was the shed locked?" Kylie asked.

"Technically, yeah," Maltese said. "It's the contractor's way to cover his ass. But in reality, no. The door—if you even want to call it a door—is just another piece of plywood, secured by a chain and a cheap lock. Any idiot could jimmy it, hide a bomb in there, lock it up again, and it wouldn't get noticed until one of the workmen saw it."

"How long has the shed been here?"

"They put it up March eighteenth, right after Saint Patrick's Day."

"And when was the last time the repair crew used the shed?"

"March eighteenth."

"So, the bomber could have planted it there last night. Or last week. Or three months ago," Kylie said.

The station manager lowered his face into his hands, raked his fingers through his hair, and shook his head. "The damn city makes it too easy for these terrorists. You'd think, of all the cities in the world, we'd know better."

"How many cameras do you have covering the—"

Kylie's question was cut off by a loud yell coming from the front of the station. It sounded like "Yes, sir!"

We looked up. It came again. "Yes, sir!"

It was a man's voice, booming, wailing, filled with anguish. He got closer, and I could make it out now over the din. It wasn't *yes, sir*. It was *Karissa*.

"Karissa! Karissa! Karissa!"

He was a big man, burly, about six four. The emergency doors next to the turnstiles were open, and he barreled onto the station. Two uniformed cops tried to stop him, but he bowled them over like duckpins as he raced along the platform bellowing. "Karissa! Elena! Mama!"

As he got closer, I could see a strip of yellow crime scene tape clinging to his shirt. Instinct told me that he was a desperate man who had broken through the barrier and bounded down the steps in search of his loved ones. But training told me that he could be a suicide bomber intent on killing as many first responders as possible. He had to be stopped.

As Sergeant Sullivan, Kylie, and I raced toward him, the big man saw what he no doubt prayed wouldn't be there: the bodies of three women sprawled on the platform. He dropped to his knees and wailed as a cluster of cops dogpiled him.

He didn't give up. "My daughter, my wife, my mother," he cried, thrashing. It took six cops to pin him to the floor and cuff him.

Sergeant Sullivan dropped to one knee. "Settle down!" he barked over the din. "Do you hear me? Settle down, and we'll let you up."

The man stopped trying to break free and lowered his cheek to the pool of blood on the concrete. "Okay. Okay," he whimpered. "My daughter, my wife, my mother. They're hurt. Please, take them to a hospital."

The Wall Street station was now a triage center. All those who needed medical attention were being evacuated to area hospitals as quickly as possible. Only when that had been accomplished would the three lifeless women on the platform be taken to the morgue.

"I told them not to take the subway. I told them to take an Uber," the man said, his body still pressed to the floor. "They were shopping for a wedding dress."

Sullivan, Kylie, and I looked at the youngest of the three dead women. She had a diamond engagement ring on her left hand. Two bridal magazines rife with Post-it notes had spilled from her tote bag.

The man on the platform wasn't a terrorist.

"Help him up," Sullivan said.

The cops helped him struggle to his feet. Four of them stood behind him so that they blocked his view of the bodies. He was about fifty-five years old. His salt-and-pepper hair and the left side of his face were spattered with his daughter's blood. And then our eyes met.

"Zach," he said.

And in that single moment, the horrific event that would jolt a city of nine million people became deeply and irretrievably personal.

"Nico," I said. "I'm sorry, Nico. They're gone. All three of them. I am so sorry for your loss."

CHAPTER 4

I WASN'T THE ONLY cop who knew Nico Patrakis. Thousands of us, from the greenest rookie all the way up to the police commissioner himself, knew and admired him. Nico and his family had been feeding us for more than fifty years.

It started in the late sixties, when Dmitri Patrakis emigrated from Greece, his wife pregnant with Nico and his pockets bare except for thirty dollars and his grandmother's prized recipe for souvlaki. The young couple moved in with cousins in Queens, and a month later Dmitri had earned enough money as a laborer to rent a food cart.

Five minutes after he opened for business on Liberty Avenue in Ozone Park, a beat cop had strolled by and asked to see his permit. Dmitri assured him that he intended to get one as soon as he earned enough money to pay for it.

The cop explained that that's not how it works. "It's illegal to sell food in the city without a permit. I'm going to have to shut you down."

And then Dmitri Patrakis uttered the words that would change his life. "Is it illegal to give away food?"

The cop shook his head. It wasn't.

"In that case, Officer," Dmitri said, lifting a skewer off the grill and handing it to him, "be my guest."

The cop was hungry. The aroma was tantalizing. He took a bite. "Damn!" he said. Another bite. "*Damn!*"

The meat had been grilled to perfection—crispy on the outside, tender and juicy on the inside, rich with the flavor of the marinade Dmitri's yaya had created decades ago back in Livadeia.

The cop took another bite. "Damn!" he said, the heavenly juice dribbling down his chin.

"You like it?" Dmitri asked, handing him a napkin.

"Are you kidding? This has got to be the best damn street meat in the entire city," the cop said, wiping his face. "But you still can't sell it."

Dmitri shrugged. "Then call your friends and tell them lunch is on me."

Ninety minutes later, every last morsel on the cart was gone. Dmitri didn't have a penny to show for it, but his reputation was gold. His food was addictive. And by the end of the day, the men and women of the 106th Precinct had collected enough money not only to pay for what they'd devoured, but for Dmitri to buy the permit.

Three years later, when the NYPD moved to its new headquarters, Dmitri was awarded a coveted spot in front of 1 Police Plaza. He'd been there ever since, feeding countless cops, judges, and lawyers, and eight mayors. His son Nico was a regular fixture at the cart since he was five.

When Nico was eighteen, Dmitri and his wife went back to Greece, leaving their son to man the cart for the busy summer months. Nico was hooked from the get-go. He loved the social interaction with people—some of them strangers, many of them regulars—and, of course, his location at the heart of the city's justice system gave him a front-row seat to the greatest show on earth.

By the time Dmitri returned in September, Nico had a passion and a business plan. Today, the Patrakis family has multiple carts and food trucks throughout the city, many of them in high-traffic areas. Their contribution to New York City is legend, told and retold by the local press, because who doesn't love a feel-good story about an immigrant who came to our shores and lived the American dream?

But on that mournful afternoon, as Nico Patrakis sat in an

interrogation room at the 19th Precinct, his face, his hair, his clothes still matted with the dried, cracking blood of his murdered daughter, the dream was shattered, the man was crushed.

Kylie and I entered the room and sat across from him.

"You're not being charged with anything," I said.

"Thank you," he whispered.

"We're going to find who did this, Nico, and you can help. Do we have your permission to record the conversation?"

"Of course."

"This has the markings of a terrorist attack, but is there any remote possibility that it was your family who was targeted?"

The question caught him by surprise, but he considered it. "No. Who would do that? Everyone who knew them loved them."

"But is there anyone who doesn't love *you*?" Kylie asked. "Someone who would do this just to hurt you?"

"Kylie, Zach, you know me. You know my father. You know our credo, our values. We donate food to charities. We feed the homeless. We don't just have customers. We have friends."

"I know," Kylie said. "I'm sorry I had to ask. We just need to explore every possible motive."

"Even if I did have enemies," Nico said, "nobody could possibly know my family would be on that subway, at that station, at that time. It wasn't a regular outing. It was a once-in-a-lifetime . . ." His voice cracked, his ability to go on crippled by the words *once-in-a-lifetime*.

He put his face to his hands and pressed his blood-crusted fingernails to his temples.

We gave him time.

Finally, he spoke. "Am I done? I have to get to the airport."

"Are you going somewhere?" I said.

He shook his head. "Karissa's fiancé, Kostas, doesn't know yet. He's a man of influence, respected in his circle. Always treats my daughter like a queen. He's flying home from a business trip to San Diego. It falls on me to break this news to him—no one else."

"We'll have someone drive you there," Kylie said.

"No," he said. "Thank you. By now my family will know I'm here. I'm sure they'll be waiting downstairs."

Of course they would. In times of crisis, Nico wouldn't reach out. He would close ranks. His inner circle would get tighter. He would look only to the people who would bring him nurturance. Definitely not the cops.

He stood up. "Thank you," he said softly.

I stood and put my hand on his shoulder. "We will hunt the killer down, Nico," I said. "Whoever did this, we will find them and bring them to justice."

"I know that's your job, Zach," he said. "But justice won't bring them back."

My eyes turned and locked on to Kylie's. She'd heard it too. It was an alert.

Nico extended his right hand to me, his left to Kylie. He had refused to wash, so as the blood oxidized, his skin had become the color of rusted iron. We each clasped a hand without hesitation. It was a silent blood oath, an unspoken promise: *We will find the killer.*

He held us each firmly in his grip. "*To aíma férnei aíma*, Zach. *To aíma tha férnei aíma*, Kylie," he said.

And then, without uttering another word, he left the room, steeled for a life of unfathomable loss and unbearable sorrow.

A few minutes later, we played back the interview and ran his final words through a handheld translator.

"Blood will have blood," he'd said. "Blood will have blood."

Nico Patrakis was old school. He wouldn't be satisfied with justice. He wanted revenge.

CHAPTER 5

THERE WERE SIXTEEN OF us sitting around the table, including four chiefs who answered directly to the police commissioner.

Captain Cates was standing at the head of the table. All eyes were on her.

"This call came in at 11:57 this morning," she said. "An alert 911 operator flagged it immediately. The caller used a voice changer that was so realistic, the operator never suspected that every word he said was being altered. So disregard what he sounds like. Just listen to what he has to say."

She tapped the space bar on her laptop, and the recording filled the room.

"New York City 911. Do you need police, fire, or medical?"

"I want to leave a message for the mayor," a man's voice responded.

"Sir, this number is for emergencies only. Is this an emerg—"

"Listen to me. I have a message for the mayor. Tell her I am going to destroy New York City the way it destroyed my family. You got that?"

I looked around the room. *Destroy New York City*. Everyone got that.

"Sir, what is your name?" the 911 operator asked.

"Did you hear what I said? Tell the mayor I am going to do to this city what it did to me," the man spat out.

I'd heard the tape twice before, but that threat—cold, dispassionate, filled with conviction—convinced me every time. That was our bomber.

"*Sir, what are you planning on doing?*" the operator asked calmly.

"*Do you know what time it is?*"

"*It's 11:58. Sir, please tell me exactly what you're planning to do.*"

He laughed. "*You'll know in sixty seconds.*" He hung up.

Cates flipped the laptop shut. "The bomb at the Wall Street station went off exactly sixty seconds later, at 11:59," she said.

"Delia." It was Harlan Doyle, the chief of detectives, one of the few people in the room who could call Captain Cates by her first name. "Did we get anyone else claiming responsibility?"

"Yes, sir. We got a call from the usual cast of glory hounds, all eager to take credit," Cates said. "We're checking each one out, but they all came in after the fact. This is the only one that was called in before the bomb."

"But he didn't say 'bomb,'" a voice chimed in.

It was a dumbass thing to say, and of course it came from the dumbest cop in the room. Lieutenant Pete Peterson worked for the office of the deputy commissioner, public information—the department's liaison to the press. But the DCPI, Vera Parnell, was out of the country on a fact-finding mission for the PC, and somehow Peterson had been assigned to sit in for her.

But he was no match for Cates. "You're right, Lieutenant," she said. "The caller did not say 'bomb,' but he did say he was going to destroy the city at 11:59, which makes him an extremely credible suspect in my book."

The chief of D's smirked. He was one of Cates's biggest champions, and he enjoyed watching her chew up and spit out jerks like Peterson.

"Captain . . ." It was Tonya Foye, chief of intelligence and counterterrorism, and the highest-ranking woman in the room.

"Yes, ma'am," Cates said immediately.

"What's the current count on fatalities and injuries?"

"Ma'am, as of sixteen hundred hours, we have six dead, and another five are considered likely," Cates said. "We also have thirty-two additional victims with varying injuries, mostly from shrapnel."

"Any victims of note?" Peterson asked, not bothering to look up from the pad he was scribbling on.

Victims of note. If Tom Cruise, Martha Stewart, and Lil Wayne had all been on that subway, the press would grill Peterson about them, and he'd have to be ready with answers. In theory, he had asked a fair question. But the way he asked it made me cringe. *Victims of note.* It was reminiscent of the paparazzi who swarmed to crime scenes so they could capitalize on the tragedy.

And then it dawned on me. Peterson had been given the same list of victims that Cates had. There was only one reason why he asked her a question he already knew the answer to: He wanted to trip her up, to embarrass her in her own house.

"Lieutenant, there were no boldfaced names on the list," Cates said. "But three of the deceased hit home for us. Nico Patrakis and his food cart have been a fixture on the plaza at One PP for decades. Sadly, Nico's mother, his wife, and his daughter were all killed in the blast."

Peterson's mouth curled into a sardonic smile—the condescending professor pitying the clueless student who just came up with the wrong answer. "Thanks, Captain," he said, "but this bomb just went off at the heart of the financial district. I don't think the media is going to want to play up the fact that some guy who sells hot dogs lost his—"

"Souvlaki!" the chief of detectives bellowed.

Peterson froze. "Sir?"

"He didn't sell hot dogs," Doyle said. "He made the best fucking Greek food from here to Athens."

"I stand corrected, sir," Peterson said.

"How long have you been with DCPI?" Doyle asked.

"Coming up on two years in January, sir."

"So the answer to my question is, you've been with DCPI for eighteen months."

"Yes, sir."

"And when you got transferred to DCPI eighteen months ago, did anyone explain to you what your job actually is?"

Peterson knew enough not to answer.

"It's a lot more than giving the press a body count," Doyle said. "It's your responsibility to monitor how the department is portrayed by the media. When you heard that we are all genuinely devastated by Nico Patrakis's loss, did you ask how we're going to pay our respects, or what we're going to do to help the family? No! Instead you just pissed on the opportunity to shine a light on the fact that cops are as human and compassionate as the people we're sworn to protect and serve."

"It's good advice, sir," Peterson said. "Thank you."

"Don't thank me. I was just repeating what Captain Cates told you."

Doyle nodded at Cates, and she took command of the room again. "I have a preliminary report from the bomb squad," she said.

The report was thin. The explosive was C4, which is surprisingly easy to get if you know your way around the dark web, and the device was rudimentary. "It's right out of Bomb Building 101 on YouTube," Cates said, "but the bomb squad is still sifting through the rubble, looking for components that might narrow it down.

"The bomb was left in a work shed on the platform. The shed is out of camera range, so we have a team of detectives combing the footage at the turnstiles and running it through facial recognition, looking for possible suspects who *might* have put it there. But it's going to take time. The shed has been unattended for months, so we have to start with the footage from this morning and slowly work our way backward—possibly all the way back to March eighteenth."

"Jesus," Chief Doyle said. "What about the 911 caller? Have we pinpointed where he called from?"

"We did, sir. He called from the Sheep Meadow in Central Park. But the only cameras are on the perimeter, and because there's a concert scheduled for tonight, there were probably more than five thousand people on the lawn when the call came in."

"And five thousand potential witnesses are just as bad as none," Doyle said. "This guy may be an amateur at making bombs, but don't underestimate him. He's smart. He's a planner. He is in our city, and he is definitely not done. If you have a beef with one guy, you kill him and it's over. But if you have a beef with a city of nine million people, killing six of them is only the beginning.

"I'm going to order a top-to-bottom search of every single corner of every piece of major infrastructure, subway station, and transportation hub across the city. We'll work with the MTA, the feds, the state police, and I'll ask the governor to call in the National Guard if I have to.

"Delia, I'll assign forty detectives to the task force for you to use as you see fit. But it's your job to catch this bastard."

"We'll find him, sir," Cates said. "You have my word."

"Good. And when you do," Doyle said, his eyes homing in on Peterson, "the first person I'm going to call is Nico Patrakis."

The room went silent, and I sat back and scanned the men and women sitting around the table. In theory, we're all on the same side. But in reality, we don't all share the same agenda.

Kylie, Cates, and I, along with a few others, were dead set on finding the person who planted the bomb and stopping them from doing it again. The brass was focused on how to deal with the blowback if we didn't find the bomber. Pete Peterson cared only about what was in it for Pete Peterson.

It felt good to watch him get caught and spanked, but I knew he didn't have the character to own his own shit. He'd blame Cates, which meant that on top of running the department's most visible investigation, she would have a target on her back.

And the shooter would be one of our own.

CHAPTER 6

WHEN THE RED TEAM was formed a few years back, Mayor Stanley Spellman had his doubts whether it would work.

"I'll give it a shot, but I'll be damned if I'm going to piss away a nickel of the taxpayers' money building another fucking police station," he had said with all the charm that made him a one-term mayor.

Which is why the new elite task force created to protect and serve the city's most prominent citizens started out in a century-old red-brick building on East Sixty-Seventh Street. It was, and still is, the home of the 19th Precinct, and we set up shop on the third floor. It looked as though it had been renovated back in the day when cinder-block walls, vinyl floor tiles, institutional desks, very few partitions, and even less privacy were all the rage.

Earlier this year, our new mayor, Muriel Sykes, who is a big fan of Red, gave us some money to upgrade. Not a bundle, but enough to propel us from the World War II look to the mid-nineties: modular furniture, desks that could actually accommodate computers, and two rather trendy glass-walled offices—one that served as a conference room, the other belonging to Captain Cates.

She hated it from day one. Called it a fishbowl. "Creeps me out," she told us once. "Like I'm a dummy in a department store window."

"I think Lieutenant Peterson proved which one of you is the dummy,"

Kylie said as we followed her into the fishbowl. "Is he just a total jerk, or is he out to get you?"

"Both," Cates said.

"Fill us in," Kylie said, closing the door. We'd be seen but not heard.

Cates sat at her desk, and we each grabbed a chair. "Remember a few months ago I called my friend Captain DeLeón at DCPI, and she had one of her people dig out the name of every American journalist who applied for a Canadian press pass at the Lords of Agony trial in Vancouver?"

"Do we remember?" Kylie said. "Boss, it helped us bring down the assassins who murdered the Hellman brothers."

"Oh, really?" Cates said. "Are you sure *you're* the cops who brought them down? Because I was at a wedding a few weeks later, and Lieutenant Peterson was regaling several bridesmaids with the details of how *he* cracked the case."

Kylie shrugged. "Stolen valor," she said. "Some guys will say anything to get laid."

"Maybe so," Cates said, "but I overheard him, and I called him on it."

"No wonder he's trying to sandbag you."

"He's a total fraud," Cates said. "Taking credit for other people's success is his MO."

"Looks like we're stuck with him," I said. "At least till he pisses off enough brass to get himself kicked off the task force. What else should we know about him?"

Cates shook her head and gave us one of those where-do-I-start? smiles. "First of all, he's connected. His mother is State Senator Dorothy Peterson, so when her baby boy got out of the Academy, she called the mayor, and young Peter's first assignment was at the Seven-Eight in Park Slope, Brooklyn."

"The crime is rampant there," Kylie said. "Jaywalking, bingo-night cheating scandals, pigeon feeding, library books overdue for weeks on end."

"I know," Cates said. "That made Senator Mommy happy, but it had its downside. Peterson wasn't the only young stud at the precinct. There were at least a dozen pretty boys there, all out to prove they were God's gift to law enforcement and women—not necessarily in that order.

In fact, the place was so lousy with wannabe players that the older cops started calling the precinct Fort SwipeRight. But it's not easy to impress the girls with 'Guess how many illegal lemonade stands I shut down this summer?' So what do you do when you have nothing to brag about?"

"You start taking credit for other people's collars," Kylie said.

"Exactly. He loves to dazzle the ladies by saying things like, 'Derek Jeter was so happy when I recovered his stolen World Series rings that he invited me to hang with him at his castle on Greenwood Lake,'" Cates said.

"That's bullshit," Kylie said. "Tara Cruz and Ann Mancini cracked that case."

"I know. But Cruz and Mancini aren't the kind of cops who drop celebrity names. Did you notice how disappointed he was that there were no A-listers among the dead? For guys like Pete Peterson, classified information is currency. The press pays him off with tickets to sporting events, concerts, or Broadway shows. And when I say tickets, I'm talking about the kind of primo seats you can't buy on a cop's salary. It's also his go-to aphrodisiac to win the hearts, minds, and libidos of women. He's as dirty as they come. If he sees something he wants, he has no problem selling department secrets to get it," Cates said. "Which is why he is known in some circles as Re-Pete Peterson."

"How could they assign a guy like that to be our liaison to the media?" I said.

"Did you miss the part where I said his mother is a state senator?" Cates asked. "There's not a precinct commander in the city who wants him, so they squirreled him away at One PP."

"But he's dangerous," Kylie said. "Not only does he want to sandbag you. His big mouth can sabotage this entire investigation."

"You asked me to fill you in," Cates said. "I did. Now that you know, don't tell him anything you don't want to see on the eleven o'clock news."

Kylie and I spent the next two hours checking in with the bomb squad and with the team of detectives who would be going through the more than 2,500 hours of security footage from the Wall Street station. Their job was daunting: Find the one person who pushed their way through the turnstiles in a few seconds, walked out of camera range, and planted the bomb.

It was about seven p.m. when my text alert beeped. The name on the screen said Theo, and this inexplicable surge of joy filled me. Theo. My son. I read the text.

> Fishing rocked. Caught 4
> stripers and a bluefin.

I responded.

> Overachiever.

I watched the three dots on my screen dance. The kid was just warming up.

> If you want to redeem yourself for
> bailing on me this morning, come
> witness my name on the big screen.
> Silvercup @ 8:30.

A second surge of joy went through me, this one laced with pride. He'd met me only a few months ago, had no idea I was his father, but was quick to toss me a lifeline to be a permanent part of his world.

Theo is a dream chaser. Wise beyond his eighteen years, he's hell-bent on becoming the best director to come down the pike since Spielberg.

> Bring Cheryl and tell Kylie
> she's my plus one.

Theo had known and adored Kylie ever since he was a kid. The feeling was mutual.

"Theo just invited us to a screening of his movie tonight," I said to her.

She grinned. "*His* movie? He's an assistant to somebody's assistant."

"Hey, give the kid a break. His mom's dead, the father who raised him is on the other side of the world, and this is the first time his name is going to be in the end credits of a real movie. Right now we're the only people in the Western Hemisphere who can show up and say, 'Way to go, Theo!'"

"Ordinarily, I'd say we can't go anywhere till we lock this guy up," she said. "But until we have something more to go on, there's nothing we *can* do."

"I was hoping you'd say that," I said.

"Then we're going," she said. "And since this is likely to be the last free night we have till we catch the bomber, let's do dinner at a fantastic restaurant afterward!"

Her face lit up with that familiar look that lets me know she's taking charge. "Don't worry, Zach." She winked. "I know a guy."

CHAPTER 7

"I KNOW A GUY" was an understatement. Kylie's current significant other was Shane Talbot, whose new restaurant, Farm to Fork, is one of the hardest-to-get-into, impossible-to-forget dining experiences in the city.

I like Shane a lot. In fact, I'd say he's the second-best relationship Kylie has ever had. The first, of course, was me. It was a dozen years ago, back when we were at the Academy. We met, couldn't get enough of each other, but it fizzled like a Roman candle twenty-eight days later when Kylie's ex-boyfriend, Spence Harrington, got out of rehab.

A year later they were married.

A decade after that, Spence fell off the wagon, almost died of a heroin overdose, and then disappeared. He'd been gone a couple of years by now, and Kylie didn't know if he was dead or alive, which kind of threw a monkey wrench into the possibility of taking her relationship with Shane to the next level.

By eight p.m., Kylie and I were driving across the Ed Koch Bridge on our way to Silvercup Studios. By choice, neither of us had said a word since we left the precinct. As any kindergarten teacher can tell you, structured quiet time is the best way to restore the mind and body from the sensory overload of the day. And what works for five-year-olds who are about to lose their shit because "Johnny knocked my block tower down" also works for two cops who charged into the chaos of a devastated subway station, shared in the grief of a man whose entire family was wiped out in an instant, and endured an excruciating battle of egos at 1 Police Plaza.

We were only a few minutes from our destination when Kylie broke our little decompression bubble. "It's a total bummer that Travis can't be there for Theo's big night," she said.

I know she didn't mean to do it, but that simple statement jump-started the hamster wheel in my brain. *Travis can't be there for Theo's big night.*

Travis. The man who became the father to the son I never knew I had.

My mind flashed back to the summer after I graduated from high school. I was working as a gofer for a construction crew in the Hamptons. The pay was paltry and the days were long, but the nights were a series of spontaneous beach parties fueled by music, beer, weed, and who-gives-a-fuck.

And then I met her. Sylviane LeBec. She was totally out of my league. I was eighteen, a kid from Staten Island playing at being an adult. She was twenty-three, with a sultry French accent, a taste for wines I couldn't even pronounce, let alone pay for, and stories of European cities I'd seen only in the movies.

But we had one thing in common: raging hormones.

She never told me she was pregnant. When the summer was over, I went off to freshman orientation, and Sylviane went off to have my baby. That's when she met Travis Wilkins. He was twenty-eight. A grown-up. They fell in love and got married when Theo was two months old.

The boy was only six when Sylviane died. By then, he knew that the man he'd always called Daddy wasn't his biological father. But it didn't matter. With the love of their lives gone, Travis and Theo had each other to cling to, and the bond between them grew stronger.

Twelve years later, the universe decided to mess with their lives. Kylie introduced me to her old friend Travis and his teenage son, Theo. I remember my first thought when I met him. Great kid. Hard not to like. He'll go far.

It was only by happenstance that I saw the framed picture of Theo's dead mother, but I recognized her instantly. It was Sylviane. I did the math, swiped Theo's toothbrush from his bathroom, and waited for the lab to tell me what I'd already figured out. He was my son.

He didn't know it. Travis didn't know it. Nobody knew. That had been Sylviane's decision, and I found myself agreeing with her. Why would a caring, loving mother want to tell her son about some random teenage sperm donor from her past?

The hamster wheel in my head spun faster. Who was I to drop a bomb on Theo's lifelong relationship with Travis? What damage might I cause by—

"Stop!" Kylie barked. The command was followed by a sharp jab to my left shoulder.

"Jesus, Kylie," I said. "What the hell was that for?"

"I know you. I said it sucks that Travis can't be there for his kid, and you immediately started ruminating about all the reasons why you should never tell Theo that he's your flesh and blood. Just get it over with, Zach. The truth never hurt anyone."

"Are you sure about that? Because I told *you* the truth," I said, rubbing my shoulder, "and look what that got me."

CHAPTER 8

WE ARRIVED AT SILVERCUP at 8:15, which is fashionably early for most people, unheard of for the two of us.

Shelley Trager knows how to host a party, especially when his guest list is heavy with members of the trade press. He built a thirty-by-forty-foot area directly outside the screening room, which his production designers can easily convert into a setting that plays off the theme of the film.

As soon as we entered the space, we found ourselves on a Caribbean beach. Exotic flowers, potted palms, reggae music, conch shells, and strings of lanterns overhead that brought a warm tropical-sunset glow to the room.

A sign hand-painted on corrugated steel welcomed us to *Last Call in Barbados*, which of course was the name of the film.

It probably cost tens of thousands of dollars just to put fifty people in the mood to watch a movie. But for a big studio, it was chump change.

"Whaddya think?" It was Shelley Trager.

"Me?" Kylie said, giving him a quick hug. "I think it's a hell of a lot of money to spend on foreplay. It probably would have been cheaper to fly the whole lot of them to Barbados."

"True," Shelley said, "but then I'd have to keep smiling at them for two days. Three hours is my limit."

He spread his arms and gave me a bear hug. "So glad to see you both."

"It's a command performance," I said. "Theo wanted us to be here to witness his first major screen credit."

"That kid is something else," Shelley said. "This time around, his name is going to scroll by in a heartbeat while most of the audience is already out the door. But one of these days, he's going to be above the title. Grab yourselves a drink. I've got hands to shake, backs to pat, egos to stroke. Stick around after the screening. I'd love to catch up."

There was a bamboo bar set up in one corner. The bartender offered us a choice of tropical cocktails, but Kylie opted for sauvignon blanc, and I was happy with a beer.

A waiter stopped by and held out a tray of hors d'oeuvres. I was about to take one when a man reached out from behind me and smacked my hand.

"I saw that one first," the man said as he plucked a shrimp off the tray.

I not only recognized the voice, but I damn well know cop humor when it rears its adolescent head.

"Reitzfeld!" I said without even turning around.

"Busted," he said, popping the shrimp into his mouth.

Bob Reitzfeld was a retired NYPD lieutenant and now the head of security at Silvercup. Cops have one thing in common with the Hollywood crowd. We hug. Only we mean it.

"It's been a while," I said. "Everything good?"

"Fantastic. I'm off duty right now," Reitzfeld said, holding up a bottle of Heineken. "Surprised to see you here. I figured you'd be at One PP, working through the night looking for this bomber."

"We would be if we had something to go on," Kylie said.

We caught up briefly, then grabbed our drinks and found Theo, who was sitting at a high-top cocktail table with my girlfriend, Cheryl Robinson. I gave her a quick kiss, and Kylie and I joined them.

"Congratulations," I said, toasting Theo with my beer.

"Don't congratulate me," Theo said. "I'm just an intern with big dreams. Preston Balfour is the rock star tonight."

"Never heard of him," Kylie said.

"I'm not surprised. His first two films tanked. I saw them. Stock characters, wooden dialogue, but then two years ago, he did *The Healing Exchange*."

"Never heard of that one either."

"You should get out more," Theo said. "The critics gave it lukewarm reviews, but it struck a nerve with audiences, so it made a lot of money. And you know how studios feel about money. When they saw the script for his new one, they put up forty mil."

A burst of high-pitched laughter from the other side of the room.

A tall, dark, and not remotely handsome man was holding court with a cluster of people, most of them women. He had an angular face, too-thick eyebrows, too-thin lips, and a smile that was more arrogant than engaging.

He was wearing a tight white T-shirt and linen pants that were basically tan but that he probably paid extra for because the label said they were ecru, and a look-at-how-cool-I-am pink blazer. His feet were encased in a pair of rope espadrille sandals that screamed, "I care deeply about the planet!" although I'd bet his ride was a Beemer, not a Prius.

"Let me guess," Kylie said. "He's the director."

"Writer-producer-director," Theo said. "Preston Balfour. I'm a peon, so I haven't met him, but the word is, he's kind of an asshole."

"You should form your own judgment," Kylie said. "He could turn out to be a great guy who just dresses like an asshole."

The lights dimmed and brightened several times—the time-honored tradition announcing that the show was about to start.

Someone tapped on a glass, and Shelley stood up. "Welcome to the first advance screening of *Last Call in Barbados*," he said. "The film will be followed by a Q and A with our visionary writer-director, Preston Balfour. So refill your drinks or empty your bladders, and make your way into the screening room so we can—"

A loud crash as a man burst into the room and kicked over a turquoise beach chair. "You motherfucker!" he bellowed, charging straight at Preston Balfour. "That's my story! That's my life you stole! I'm going to fucking kill you!"

The petrified director tried to scramble out of the way, but he backed into a wall, and the intruder, coming in red-hot, gut punched him.

Balfour doubled over, and the attacker threw a left jab at his nose. A splodge of blood spread across his face and spilled down onto the pink blazer.

The maniac followed up with a fierce right hook to the jaw.

His left arm was about to come around again when Bob Reitzfeld, no longer off duty, came out of nowhere and tackled him. They both went down. Thrashing and cursing, the assailant put up a fight, but Reitzfeld had forty pounds and thirty years of training on him. Less than a minute into the melee, the party crasher was cuffed and hauled to his feet.

That's when we could finally get a good look at his face.

Kylie reeled. "Spence!"

Her long-lost husband was finally back in her life.

CHAPTER 9

REITZFELD LED HIS PRISONER from the tropical serenity of the faux beach bar into the no-nonsense corridors of commerce.

"My office," Shelley said, leading the way. Phone in hand, he began making calls. When you're in crisis management, speed is critical. Corporate reputations that took decades to build can crumble overnight.

Kylie and I followed. "Are you okay?" I asked her. It was a dumb question, but it was the best I could do on such short notice.

She responded with a look that said nobody was okay and she was at the top of the list. Kylie can lose her cool in a Zen garden, so I tried to temper the inevitable burst of fury she was about to unleash.

"At least you know he's alive," I said.

"It appears he is, Zach. But the night is young," she said, pounding a fist into her palm.

As soon as we got to Shelley's office, Reitzfeld sat Spence in a chair, and with a single nod from the boss, he took off the cuffs.

"Bob," Shelley said, "I've got a team heading to the screening room to do damage control with the press. You handle Preston Balfour."

"On it," Reitzfeld said, bolting from the room.

"He's all yours, Kylie," Shelley responded.

Kylie wheeled around and erupted at Spence. "Where the fuck have you been for the past two years?"

Spence looked up at her, his eyes filled with regret, his rage dissipated. "Barbados," he said.

"Barbados?" Kylie said. "Barb—" She stopped, and I could sense her putting the pieces together, just as I was doing.

"Yeah. Barbados," Spence said. "Like in Preston Balfour's movie. Only it's not his movie. It's my life story. You want to know where I've been since I last saw you? Read the script."

"Oh, shit," Shelley said. "Spence, are you Nick Hildebrandt?"

Spence nodded. "It's not the name I would have picked for myself, but yeah, I'm Nick."

"And I'm lost," Kylie said. "Shelley, what's going on?"

Shelley's body language told me that he too was still trying to figure out what was going on. And he didn't like where his thinking was taking him.

"Shelley!" Kylie snapped when he took too long to answer her question.

"The movie, *Last Call in Barbados*," Shelley said. "It's about a screenwriter who's been clean and sober for ten years. He gets hooked on drugs again, and his life spirals out of control."

"And you think that's your story?" she said to Spence. "Like you're the only show-business asshole whose career crashed and burned because of drugs and alcohol? Well, guess what. You're not the first, and I guarantee you won't be the last."

"Do me a favor, Kylie," Spence said. "Stop asking so many questions and shut up long enough to listen to some answers." He nodded at Shelley to go on.

"Nick's wife in the film is an NYPD detective," Shelley said, looking directly at Kylie. "At one point, he disappears, and she tracks him to a seedy hotel. When she gets there, he's already OD'd, but she's a cop and she carries Narcan, so she saves his life."

"Tell her where the seedy hotel is," Spence said.

"Atlantic City."

"Oh, God," Kylie said in a barely audible whisper.

"Is that where it happened in real life?" Shelley asked. "Atlantic City?"

Kylie nodded.

"I didn't know," Shelley said. "Maybe if I'd known that, I might have made the connection, but a cop and a screenwriter . . . And that's only the first ten pages of the script. The rest is all about Nick in Barbados. The film is about the redemption of someone who was written off as unredeemable."

"When I left the hospital in Atlantic City, I took a bus to New York," Spence said. "I really didn't want to live anymore. I went to the apartment, took whatever drugs and money I had stashed away, grabbed every watch, ring, and anything else of value that I could hock, and left. I figured, with enough booze and drugs, I'd be dead in a month. The cops would find me, and I had an I'm-sorry-I-ruined-your-life letter in my pocket addressed to you. But I didn't die."

"How did you wind up in Barbados?" Kylie asked.

Spence laughed. "Beats the shit out of me. Apparently, I was on a cruise ship, and Barbados was one of the ports. It looks like I got off the boat, found a friendly neighborhood drug dealer, and the ship sailed without me. I didn't care. There's some beautiful public beaches in Barbados. It seemed like a nice place to cash in my chips."

"But you didn't."

"No. I met Mia. She owned a beach bar. She'd been sober for eighteen years herself, and she was on a mission to help any hopeless drunk that was willing to listen." He grinned. "But you know me, K-Mac. Listening to good advice is not my strong suit."

"I know you well, Spence," Kylie said. "And you're right. You suck at listening. But I also can tell when you're drunk or high, and right now you're neither. You may be crazy as a shithouse rat, but that's genetic, not substance abuse. Mia got you clean and sober, didn't she?"

He nodded. "Haven't had a drink or a drug for twenty-one months."

"Congratulations. And you fell in love with her, didn't you?"

"I did," he said softly.

His eyes welled up, and I could almost feel him reliving that moment in time when this woman, Mia, became the most important person in his life.

"And then . . ." he said, his lip quivering. "And then I married her."

CHAPTER 10

"YOU *MARRIED* HER?" Kylie said.

"Yes," Spence said.

"Did she know that you are currently married to me?"

"Yes, but she didn't care."

"Classy. So when do I get to meet the *other* Mrs. Spence Harrington?"

"You can't. She died three days after we were married."

Kylie inhaled sharply and put her hand to her mouth. "Oh, God, Spence. I'm so sorry."

"It's okay. We knew she was dying. Our wedding was in her hospital room. She knew we were violating the law in two countries, but she wanted to leave me everything she owned, and she . . ." He squeezed his eyes shut, as if that might block the pain. But, of course, it didn't. He opened them again. "She wanted her tombstone to say, 'Mia Hancock Harrington, beloved wife,' because she said 'hot girlfriend' was too tacky."

"Jesus," Shelley said. "Those are the exact words Balfour used in the movie. How could he possibly know all the details of your life?"

"When Mia died, she left me her house, the beach bar, and a fifty-foot charter fishing boat that had belonged to her father. It's really sweet. Two staterooms, state-of-the-art electronics, cruises at thirty-five knots. About a year and a half ago, Balfour showed up at the bar, and we got to talking. By the end of the night, he tells me he wants to charter the boat for four days and nights.

"He wanted to go out about seventy, eighty miles, hoping to land a blue marlin. I told him I've got some navigational chops, but I don't have the kind of maritime knowledge for a trip like that. But I do have my guy Grantley, who's the most experienced pilot on the island. Balfour says, 'Great. Grantley can drive the boat while you and I sit in the sun and get to know each other better.' I didn't see it at the time, but now I realize that little by little, he was hijacking my story so he could sell it to a studio."

"He had a pretty good-sized hit two years ago," Shelley said. "I'm surprised you didn't know he was in our business."

"*Our* business? You mean *your* business. I'm a fishing boat captain. I canceled my subscription to *The Hollywood Reporter* years ago. Now I spend my time learning how to read charts, use a compass, and navigate by the stars if my equipment craps out. Maybe if I lived in New York, I'd have Googled the guy, but we're a little more laid-back in Bridgetown. He paid in cash, his passport said he was who he said he was, and he gave Grantley a hefty tip. That's all I knew about him, and that was enough."

"But you showed up tonight threatening to murder him, in front of fifty people," Kylie said. "How did you know about the screening?"

"Great question, Detective MacDonald." Spence is a master at dropping bombshells, and I could see he was winding up to blitz her again. "He emailed me and told me about it."

He waited for the *holy shit* reaction he'd been angling for, got it, and went on. "It turns out that Balfour is not only a heartless, conniving plagiarist, he's also a candidate for dumbest criminal ever. A few days ago, he sent an email to everyone in his address book telling them about tonight. You'd think he'd eliminate *unwitting victims* from his mailing list, but apparently, he's not as crafty as most con men.

"I went to his website and read the synopsis. I was floored. And then he posted a giant fuck-you to all the losers who didn't recognize his genius. He actually listed every studio that turned him down. I may not be in the business anymore, but I still know plenty of people who are. It took me less than five minutes to track down someone willing to send me a PDF.

"At first, I was afraid to even look at the file. I've relapsed enough times to know that if I read that script, I could wind up drinking myself into a coma in my own bar. But I had to open it. It was more painful than I could have imagined. It was my story. Mia's story. Mia's life. He was profiting off Mia's death!"

His hands were trembling. He pressed them to his face to quiet them.

Kylie took a carafe of water from Shelley's desk, poured a glass, and handed it to Spence. He downed it, asked for another, and drank that too.

"Shelley," he said, "I'm sorry to sabotage your screening. I woke up in Barbados this morning and decided to fly to New York and ask you not to release the movie. But when I walked into that room and saw Balfour preening around in his titty-pink jacket and his condescending phony smile, I totally lost it. I'm sorry. It's not sober behavior, but at least I didn't drink, which is kind of a miracle."

"Have you eaten?" Kylie asked.

"Not since this morning," he said. "Food wasn't high on my list."

"We're going to dinner. Me, Zach, his girlfriend, Cheryl, and do you remember Theo Wilkins?"

His face lit up. "Theo? Travis's son. He was, what, ten years old when he told us he wanted to be a director."

"He still does. He's eighteen now, and he's working here for the summer. He'd love to see you again. Come to dinner with us."

There was a knock on the door, and Bob Reitzfeld walked in without waiting for a response. "I just had a long talk with Preston Balfour," he said.

"Am I going to jail?" Spence asked.

"No. I shitcanned it."

Spence exhaled a sigh of relief. He had been married to Kylie long enough to know copspeak. Reitzfeld had somehow sweet-talked Balfour into not pressing charges.

"I have three paramedics on my security team," Reitzfeld said. "I grabbed one, and she patched Balfour up. The guy's a bleeder, so it looked worse than it was. But his nose isn't broken, and once she cleaned up the blood, all he's got is some swelling and some discoloration, but that'll clear up fast.

"Then I told him he had two options. The first was to call NYPD, in which case he'd have to go down to the station, be photographed, give a statement, explain his prior relationship with Spence, and tell them that Spence accused him of plagiarism before he clocked him. Option two would be to just let it go. He grabbed it in a heartbeat."

"What about the press?" Shelley asked.

"They're watching the movie as we speak. But first, Madeline from the DC team apologized for the outburst. She told them that someone from the film crew had too much to drink. Then she topped it off by apologizing for how lame the fight was. She promised we'd bring in professional stunt fighters at the next screening. Big laugh. None of them gave a rat's ass. It's all under the rug."

"So I can go?" Spence said.

"Absolutely," Shelley said.

"Can I convince you to hold off on releasing the movie?"

When they worked together, Shelley and Spence had been the best of friends. But this was business.

"Spence, you know I can't do that. I'm a partner in this production with three other studios. They've spent millions already."

"That's their fucking problem, Shelley."

"The hell it is!" Kylie said, her earlier anger kicking back in, her compassion for his dead wife gone. "Your beef is with Balfour. You can sue him for plagiarism, and if you get a good legal team, every nickel he earns should and probably will go to you. But beating the crap out of Balfour won't solve anything. Why don't you start by calling a lawyer."

"I don't want a lawyer, I don't want any money, and I don't want Mia's memory exploited. She's the one who convinced me that living in the spotlight fed my addiction. And now Balfour wants to put my misery on the screen. I can't let him do that. I have to stop him. I'm going to stop him. And for the record, beating the shit out of that evil prick was probably the best idea I had."

He shoved his chair back and stood up. "It's been a hell of a reunion, Kylie. One more favor before I go. Tell Theo I said he should think long and hard about jumping into this snake pit known as the entertainment industry."

He stormed out of the room. I looked at my watch. It was 10:15.

Six hours later, my phone rang. I looked at the caller ID. It was Kylie.

"What?" I said.

"Zach . . ." she said, a hitch in her voice.

Kylie's middle-of-the-night calls are always crisp, clean, and dispassionate. We're cops. There's a crime. Get out of bed. This was different.

"Preston Balfour was killed last night," she said.

I swung my legs off the side of the bed, planted my feet on the floor, and braced for what I knew was coming even before she said it.

"Spence was arrested. They're charging him with murder."

CHAPTER 11

"DAMN!" I SAID, IMMEDIATELY taking responsibility. "We never should have cut him loose. He warned us. He said he was going to stop Balfour, and he did."

"Jesus, Zach. It's a good thing you're not on the jury. Usually, people listen to the evidence before they convict."

"I know. But you know who also looks at the evidence? The District Attorney's Office. They must have something pretty solid if they locked him up. Who called you?"

"The Warlock," she said. "As soon as they read Spence his rights, he lawyered up."

"That's the first smart thing he's done since he showed up in New York."

The Warlock was a legend in the criminal justice system. His real name was Dennis Woloch, but he had such an uncanny ability to cast a spell over juries that one newspaper columnist dubbed him Woloch the Warlock.

The name stuck, and with every not-guilty verdict, Woloch's reputation for being the best defense counsel money can buy intensified. Fortunately for Spence, a client didn't always need deep pockets to procure his services.

The Warlock thrived on juicy tabloid fodder, and it didn't get any juicier than the murder of an award-winning writer-director by the recently resurfaced drug-addict husband of NYPD Red Detective Kylie MacDonald.

"Did the Warlock give you any details?" I asked.

"No. There's nothing you or I can do till Spence is arraigned in the morning."

"Then get some sleep."

"Fat chance," she said.

"Listen to me, damn it! Spence is in custody, and there's nothing we can do right now to help him. What we can do is hunt down a sociopath who's got a grudge against the city and God-knows-how-much C4 to settle it. But we're not going to catch him if we're running on empty. Get some sleep."

She exhaled long and loud—the only indication I would get that she had heard me and would at least consider my suggestion.

"The arraignment is at nine thirty," she said. "I reminded the Warlock that you and I can't go anywhere near 100 Centre Street, or IAB will be all over us for being involved with a murder suspect. He said to go to Columbus Park in Chinatown at about ten, and he'll meet us there as soon as he leaves the courthouse."

"I'll be in the office by seven thirty," I said.

"I'll bring coffee . . ." She hesitated. "Hey, Zach, I'm sorry to wake you up. I just needed to—"

"Knock it off, MacDonald. The only way you'd owe me an apology is if you *didn't* call me in the middle of the night."

"Thanks." She hung up, and I sat there staring at my phone.

Cheryl slid over to my side of the bed and put her arm around me.

"Preston Balfour was murdered," I said. "Spence was . . ."

"I know. I heard enough to put two and two together," she said.

She took her arm from around my neck and transformed effortlessly from the love of my life to Dr. Cheryl Robinson, NYPD psychologist.

"I also heard you take the blame for letting Spence walk after he attacked Balfour," she said. "But Balfour didn't press charges. You *had* to let Spence go."

"I know," I said. "But I should have dragged him to dinner with you, me, Kylie, and Theo. That might have tempered some of his rage."

"Zach, how many years have you known Spence?"

"About twelve."

"And how many times in twelve years have you been able to drag him anywhere? Two years ago when he was falling apart, you did everything you could to get him off the drugs and alcohol. Did he listen to you then?"

"He doesn't listen to anybody. He's a stubborn son of a bitch."

"So are you. But Spence is an addict. And two years ago, he was an addict in total denial. There was no way he was going to listen to you then."

"But he's sober now."

"He may not be drinking, but I doubt if that man has a sober thought in his head," she said. "I saw him go ballistic at the screening. I wasn't in Shelley's office, but from what you and Kylie told me last night, Spence is filled with rage. The woman who helped him get back on his feet is dead, and Preston Balfour wants to turn her selfless act into his own personal cash cow. And for the record, taking Spence to dinner where he could meet Kylie's fantastic new boyfriend would not have helped defuse his fury one iota."

"So do you think he did it?" I said. "Did Spence kill Balfour?"

She shook her head. "I don't know. But what you said to Kylie—the fact that the DA arrested him so quickly—has to mean that there's some damning evidence we don't know about yet."

"Kylie's already out of her mind," I said. "It's only going to get worse. I don't know what to do."

"Bullshit! You know exactly what to do. She's your partner. You stand by her. You support her. You know her better than anyone, Zach. Kylie is a control freak locked in an inflexible, go-by-the-book system, and I wouldn't be surprised if the department restricts her to the point that one day she flies off the rails and decides to do whatever it takes to save Spence, even if she has to throw her career down the toilet."

"I won't let that happen," I said. "I promise."

She smiled. "Then you *do* know what to do."

"Yeah, but what I know and what I can accomplish are two different things."

"What does that mean?"

"It means I'll do everything in my power to keep Kylie from blowing up her career," I said. "I can't promise I'll be successful, but I can tell you this. We're partners. And if she goes down in flames, I'm going down with her."

Cheryl slipped off the bed and straddled my legs.

"You are the best partner ever," she said, kissing me softly on the lips.

I grinned. "Is that your professional opinion, Dr. Robinson?"

"Hell, no, Detective Jordan," she said, pressing me back onto the mattress. "That opinion is very, very personal."

CHAPTER 12

KYLIE AND I GOT to Columbus Park at ten. A crowd had already gathered around two elderly Asian men who were playing *xiangqi*, Chinese chess. I watched from a discreet distance while Kylie got lost in her phone.

Most of the onlookers were seniors themselves—some born right here, others who had escaped the political turmoil of China or Hong Kong. No matter what their stories, they had one thread in common. They had discovered a piece of their heritage right here in Lower Manhattan. The park was their second home, a welcoming community center without walls or membership fees.

For the next ten minutes, I soaked up their energy, their joy, their camaraderie. It was calming—the flower I never have time to stop and smell, a swath of the cultural tapestry that has always been the essence of New York.

"Zach!" Kylie said, snapping me out of my reverie. "There's the Warlock!"

The man strode purposefully toward us. He was fortysomething, six two, with a thick, wavy mane of salt-and-pepper hair that framed his face so perfectly, it made other men wonder how lucky one guy can get.

Dennis Woloch doesn't care whether his clients are guilty or innocent. He cares only about winning. So of course, Kylie went right to the heart of it.

"What have they got on him?"

"The victim, Preston Balfour, was stabbed to death in his apartment," Woloch said. "Three eyewitnesses saw Spence hovered over Balfour's body with a bloody knife in his hand. Spence's fingerprints are all over the murder weapon, and he has defensive wounds on his arm and wrists. The judge remanded him. No bail."

"What did Spence say?"

Woloch took out his phone. "Let's find a quiet spot and you can hear it for yourself."

We walked over to Bayard Street, found a tenement building, and crammed into the vestibule, where Woloch made sure no one was within earshot, and hit play.

"*Oh God, Dennis, thanks for coming,*" Spence said, his voice a mix of relief and fear. "*You've got to get me out of here.*"

"*I'll do my best.*"

"*It's insane. They arrested me for murder. I know it looks bad. I mean, I was covered with blood, but I didn't do it. I swear I—*"

"*Spence, who's dead?*"

"*Preston Balfour. He's a writer and director. He has a new movie coming out, but it's not his story. He stole it from me. He, he—*"

"*So you had a beef with him.*"

"*Fucking-A right I had a beef with him. Wouldn't you? There was a screening at Silvercup last night, so I crashed it. I got a little carried away and punched him a couple of times, but then I cooled down. I had a talk with Kylie. Balfour didn't press charges, so I left.*"

Woloch hit pause and looked at Kylie for corroboration.

"That's kind of the PG version of what happened," she said. "He left out the part where he said he was going to kill Balfour in front of fifty witnesses."

"Good to know," he said, and hit play.

"*After I left Silvercup, I started walking. Wherever I turned, there was a bar. I've been sober twenty-one months, but it's like the universe wanted me to pick up a drink.*"

"*Did you?*"

"No. I called my sponsor in Barbados. He said he wanted me to find the guy I punched out and make amends, and then I should get on the next flight back to Bridgetown. I asked if I could skip the first part and just fly home, and he said, 'Not if you want to stay sober.'

"I still had Balfour's number, so I sent him a text asking if we could talk in person. I promised I wouldn't get physical. He sent me the address, and I took a train to Lower Manhattan.

"He has a condo on Baxter, right in the heart of that Little Italy–Chinatown–Soho vibe. I got there about eleven p.m., and the place was popping. People, music, laughter. I've been in Barbados so long, I forgot how much energy this city has at night. Anyway, his building has no doorman, so I checked the panel for Balfour's apartment number. It was 4B, but before I can even ring the bell, a food delivery guy on his way out opens the door and holds it for me. I take the elevator to the fourth floor, find his apartment, and I'm about to knock when the front door flies open. It's a guy, and he's got this huge bloody knife in his hand. I'm like, 'Holy shit!' And then I see Balfour. He's on the floor, writhing, covered in blood. The guy tries to push past me, so I instinctively grab his wrist."

Woloch interrupted. "What were you planning to do?"

"What do you think? Stop him. Get the knife before he used it on me. And he did. Look at me, Dennis."

Woloch hit pause. "His hands were all sliced up," he said to us. "Exactly what you'd expect to see if he was struggling to get the knife away from the killer."

Kylie gave him one of those I-ain't-buying-it frowns. "Or if he was in a rage and stabbing the man who stole his life story," she said.

Woloch smiled. "I guess I just think like a defense attorney, and you think like a cop."

Kylie smiled back. "So it's a standoff."

"I don't think so, Detective. The burden of proof is on you."

He pressed play.

"I'm not a fighter," Spence said, "but I've done a shitload of fight scenes in my day. Plus, my adrenaline is pumping. I slam the guy against the doorjamb. I pin his arm to the wall—the one with the knife. I grab his other wrist, and then, wham—I head-butted him smack on the bridge of the nose. He lets out a yelp, and the knife hits the floor. I dive for it, turn around to make sure he's not going to come up swinging, but he's already on the run, headed for the stairwell.

"And then I hear Balfour. He's gurgling, coughing up blood, like you see in a war movie. I dropped down next to him. I could see the stab wounds, blood pouring out every one of them. He grabs my arm, and he goes, 'Doctor, doctor.' I said, 'Hang in there. I'm calling 911.' Before I can even get my phone out of my pocket, he lets out one more long exhale. It's like the classic guy-dying-on-camera scenes. But this one is real. His hand falls. His eyes go blank. It was surreal. I used to hang out with this guy in Barbados, and now I'm in New York and he's dying in my arms. I couldn't believe it. I just froze."

Ten seconds passed before Spence spoke again.

"And then I heard the screams. Three women—young, in their twenties—were standing outside the open apartment door. They saw the body, the blood, and they started shrieking. I stood up, and I realized I still had the knife in my hand. But they saw it, and they ran screaming. I heard the door to their apartment lock. One of them must have called 911 as soon as she saw Balfour all butchered up, because I could already hear the sirens. A minute later, I'm facedown on the rug, my wrists in cuffs, with two cops kneeling on my back, and I could hear another cop yelling, 'We got him, we got him!'

"I thought he meant they caught the guy running out of the building. But no, they meant me. I started screaming, 'I didn't do it. The guy who did it is getting away. He tried to kill me with the same knife. I'm the one who took it from him.' But they're not listening. They yank me to my feet, and someone says, 'Get him out of here. This is a crime scene. Get him back to the base.'

"By now I know I'm fucked, so I don't say another word until I'm at the precinct, and this detective reads me my rights. And then all I say is, 'I want a lawyer.'"

Woloch hit stop and put the phone in his pocket.

"Do you believe any of his story?" I asked.

"Zach, you know me. It doesn't matter if I believe it. My job is to get twelve people to buy it. But in this case, I believe every word of it. Spence didn't kill him."

An elderly Chinese woman carrying a weathered mesh tote bag filled with groceries opened the outer door to the vestibule. As soon as she saw the three of us, she backed out. She didn't care how respectable we may have looked—she knew better than to unlock the inside door with three strangers standing there.

"We've overstayed our welcome," Woloch said.

We smiled politely at her, left the building, and kept walking.

"You think Spence didn't kill him?" Kylie said as soon as we rounded the corner to Mulberry Street. "You bought his story?"

"I wouldn't expect you to buy it just listening to a recording," Woloch said. "But I looked him in the eyes. I watched his body language. I felt his outrage, his disbelief, his sheer dread, at the arraignment. You can't fake that kind of innocence. It was visceral."

"You know he wrote cop shows," Kylie said. "He got paid to make shit like that up."

"I know it, the prosecution knows it, and they will make sure the jury knows it, which is going to make it damn near impossible for me to plant the seed of reasonable doubt in the mind of even just one of them. The way I see it, there's only one way to get a not-guilty verdict."

"What's that?" Kylie said.

"Find the real killer."

"Who caught the case?"

"Charlie Elliott at the Fifth Precinct."

"He's a damn good detective," Kylie said. "If there's any substance to Spence's—"

"You want substance?" Woloch said. "Elliott talked to the three witnesses. They didn't see this mystery man. What they did see was Spence with the bloody knife in his hand, hulking over the recently deceased Mr. Balfour. And when forensics is done, the DA will have enough *substance* to put your husband away for life."

Kylie winced. I'm not sure whether it was because she thought Detective Elliott had made the right call, or because Woloch had referred to Spence as her husband.

"They've closed the case, Kylie. Nobody from NYPD is going to chase Spence's alibi. I, of course, will castrate them in court for their negligence, but that won't sway the jury. I believe that the real killer is out there, and the only one smart enough—and dedicated enough—to find him is you."

"*Me?* Jesus, Dennis, you know that I am absolutely forbidden to get anywhere near this case. It's against every rule in the book."

The Warlock ran his fingers through his signature mop of hair. "Against the rules?" he said in the same honeyed baritone that won the hearts of countless juries. "And since when has that ever stopped you?"

CHAPTER 13

IT WAS CLOSE TO noon when we got back to the precinct. We headed straight to Cates's office. As much as she hates that fishbowl, it does have one advantage. She can see who's coming long before they get there.

"No!" she said as soon as Kylie and I stepped through the door. She didn't even bother looking up from her computer.

"No?" Kylie said. "No to what?"

"No to what you're about to ask me."

"How do you know what I was going to ask you?"

Cates swiveled her chair around and penetrated us with a look that would make a drill sergeant shiver.

"Your husband was just arrested for murder. As soon as I saw you making a beeline for my office, I knew that the first thing you were going to ask me was for permission for you to prove him innocent." She paused. "On job time! Am I right or am I wrong?"

"You were close," Kylie said. "That was the third thing. The first thing I was going to tell you was that Zach and I talked to Spence's lawyer, Dennis Woloch."

Cates grimaced. There's not a cop in the department who wants to be grilled by the Warlock.

"Spence swears he didn't do it, and Woloch believes him. He believes that the real killer is still out there."

"The *real* killer? Where have I heard that before? I just spoke to Captain Tuttle, the zone captain for the fifth squad. He said Detective Elliott, who caught the case, is a total pro. He canvassed Balfour's apartment building and the neighborhood. He can't find a single witness who can back up Spence's story. The DA believes they have a rock-solid case, and Tuttle is one hundred percent behind his detective. He made it clear to me that he doesn't plan on wasting valuable resources looking for anyone else. No further investigation is required. So even before you ask the question, the answer is still no."

"But what if Spence is telling the truth?" Kylie said. "What if other people are at risk? The department is going to have egg on its face if Spence is locked up and this guy kills somebody else connected to the film."

Kylie tossed me a look. My turn to jump in.

"Captain," I said, "we have a genuine concern for Theo Wilkins and for everyone else connected with Balfour or his film. If Spence is right, they're all at risk."

"That's Captain Tuttle's problem," Cates said. "Is that clear, Detective?"

"Crystal, Captain," I said. "However, it's . . . um . . . a little too late for that."

"And just what the hell is that supposed to mean?"

"The blowup at Silvercup Studios last night. Kylie and I were both there."

"What blowup?"

"There was a screening last night of Preston Balfour's new movie. Just before it started, Spence charged in and accused Balfour of stealing the material. It seems like a valid claim, and Woloch will easily prove that in court."

"So Balfour hijacked someone else's story. It doesn't matter. He's not on trial. He's the victim."

"Yes, but Spence did more than accuse Balfour. He assaulted him and screamed, 'I'm going to fucking kill you' in front of a roomful of people, including the two of us."

Cates put a hand to her head. She knew what was coming next.

"Of all the people who heard Spence threaten to kill Balfour, who do you think the prosecution is going to call to the stand to testify as eyewitnesses for the state?" Kylie said.

"The two most reliable, most perceptive people in the room," Cates said. "And the DA gets bonus points because one of them is the defendant's wife."

"Which brings me around to the third thing," Kylie said. "Zach and I are involved in this case up to our eyeballs. If Woloch mesmerizes the jury into believing that NYPD did absolutely nothing to prove or disprove Spence's story, the humiliation will spread all the way up to the thirteenth floor of One PP."

Cates looked at Kylie. "So you want to chase down your husband's alibi," she said. "Dedicated cop that you are, you—Mrs. Spencer Harrington—want to hunt high and low for this phantom killer so that no one will be able to fault the department for taking the easy way out."

"Exactly."

"One question," Cates said.

"Yes, ma'am."

"Do you really think I am dumb enough to remotely believe that you're willing to go out there and shoot your husband's alibi full of holes?"

"No, ma'am. You know my agenda. But you also know how bad we'll look if nobody checks out his story. So as long as you need a team of investigators to prove how diligently this case was handled, and since Zach and I are already involved, you may as well give the assignment to a team with a stellar track record."

A half smile crossed Delia Cates's lips. If nothing else, she respects a worthy adversary, and Kylie always gives her a run for her money.

"Fine!" Cates said. "Do it, and do it by the book. I'll call Captain Tuttle and let him know that you'll be—"

All three of our radios erupted with a series of demanding beeps that signaled a high-priority job.

"In the confines of the Nineteenth Precinct, we are receiving numerous calls for an explosion at One Thousand Third Avenue," the dispatcher announced.

New Yorkers know landmarks. Cops know street addresses. 350 Fifth Avenue is the Empire State Building. The Dakota, where John Lennon was assassinated, is at 1 West Seventy-Second Street.

And 1000 Third Avenue is the city's quintessential department store, a nine-story shopping mecca for New Yorkers and tourists from around the globe who enjoy the finer things in life and don't mind paying for them.

Bloomingdale's.

I had a flash of instinct, and I immediately pulled up the 911 log on my phone to see when the first call came in.

One look, and the flash turned into a sick feeling in the pit of my stomach.

Our bomber had not only struck again, he struck at precisely the same time of the morning as he had the day before.

11:59.

CHAPTER 14

BLOOMINGDALE'S OCCUPIES AN ENTIRE square block—from Fifty-Ninth Street to Sixtieth, and Third Avenue to Lexington.

Our office on Sixty-Seventh Street is less than half a mile away. If the traffic gods were smiling, we could shoot down Lex in twenty seconds flat.

But as soon as Kylie, Cates, and I sprinted down the stairs and hit the street, we knew that wheels were not an option. The normal Friday noon stop-and-go traffic had ground to a halt and wasn't going anywhere.

We took to the sidewalk, pushing our way through the crowd, some of whom were heading south to get a closer look at the disaster, and others who were scrambling uptown, terror in their eyes, phones pressed to their ears.

Cops had set up a barrier at Sixty-Second Street to keep the morbidly curious from getting any closer. They waved us through, and a few minutes later we were at Sixtieth, which was clogged with emergency vehicles.

On the Lexington Avenue side, a stream of shoppers was still exiting the store, their faces a mix of fear and relief as they were led to safety.

Cates had radioed ahead, and a uniformed sergeant flagged us down.

"Loading dock," he said, leading the way. "The bomb went off on the first floor. Six confirmed dead. At least two dozen injured. We're about ninety-nine percent evacuated. We're still collecting the stragglers.

Two of them practically had to be dragged out because they weren't finished shopping."

It sounded like a lame joke, but having spent the past few years at Red catering to the rich, the spoiled, and the entitled, I had no doubt that the sergeant was dead serious.

From the loading dock, the sergeant led us to the nerve center of the Bloomingdale's Asset Protection and Risk Management Department—a well-guarded fortress on the second floor. Very few people ever get to see the inside. There are cameras, both stationary and moving, throughout the store, watching every customer, every employee, and all that data is instantly transmitted to the wall of monitors and about a dozen security people inside the command center.

Cy McAllister, a retired NYPD deputy inspector, was in charge of the entire operation. McAllister is not your stereotypical unassertive tech-head who hides behind a computer all day. He's a large, outgoing, garrulous man with a toothy smile set behind a thick ginger beard that is well on its way to white. Meet him for a beer, and he'll regale you with tales of the trade, always kicking it off with his go-to opening line: "American business loses a hundred billion-with-a-capital-*B* dollars to shoplifters every year, and most of them shop at Bloomingdale's."

It's a bit of a stretch, but the fact is, for a lot of thieves, Bloomingdale's is the Mount Everest of department stores. Young, old, experienced, or just starting out, the temptation of walking away with all that high-end merch is a rush. So they trek to the mountain, and thanks to Cy McAllister and his team, hundreds of them get caught every year. And because the store has a zero-tolerance policy, every one of those light-fingered idiots winds up getting photographed, fingerprinted, and charged at the 19th Precinct.

Even though Cates, Kylie, and I had all worked with McAllister, we still had to be ID'd and vetted before we were buzzed through. He skipped the pleasantries.

"The perp entered the store through the northernmost door on the Lexington Avenue side at 11:54," McAllister said. "Here he is."

We looked at the center screen, where the agent at the console had freeze-framed a man in midstride. The man's age was difficult to determine, but he was medium height, medium build, wearing black baggy pants, a loose-fitting black sweatshirt, a black bucket hat, and sunglasses.

The camera zoomed in on his face. He was wearing a black mask. Not the old-fashioned empty-your-cash-drawer-and-put-the-money-in-the-bag mask you see in the movies, but a please-keep-your-distance-I'm-still-paranoid-about-Covid perfectly socially acceptable mask.

A finger flick from McAllister, and the camera angle reversed.

"And there's your bomb," he said, pointing at the black knapsack on the man's back. "I wish we had seen something that would alert us to approach this guy, but backpacks around here are as common as teacup poodles in Tory Burch tote bags. He fits right in."

The camera followed the man walking through the first floor, much of which is sectioned into free-floating branded boutiques—Chanel, Lancôme, Ralph Lauren, and dozens of other high-end companies selling overpriced fragrances, cosmetics, and personal grooming products.

Another flick of the finger, and the picture froze on the Yves Saint Laurent counter.

"Look at this." McAllister tapped on the gleaming waist-high showcase. "Glass." He tapped on one mirror, then a second, and a third. "Glass, glass, glass."

His finger moved to a display of dozens of crystal bottles, then to video screens of elegant women, then to the bold backlit translucent sign with the YSL logo. "Glass, glass, glass, glass, glass wherever you turn. The whole fucking first floor is made up of tons of razor-sharp shrapnel waiting to explode and slice people to ribbons. This butcher didn't go to bedding, or carpeting, or loungewear. He came here to where every item, every fixture, every single customer amenity is a deadly missile ready to be launched. He came here for maximum carnage."

The time code on the video read 11:55:23. It was three minutes and thirty-seven seconds shy of 11:59.

The video resumed. "He knows exactly where he's going," McAllister said. "Luxury bags. Gucci, Louis Vuitton, Prada."

The man stopped to look at a display of three suitcases—one leather, one canvas, and one silver hard-shell case. He admired them for a few seconds and calmly made his way behind the display. Just before he dropped out of sight, we could see him shrug his left shoulder and reach for the strap.

It took only a few seconds, but when he came back around to the front of the display, the knapsack was gone.

The time code said 11:57:02. He had less than two minutes to leave the blast zone. He strode purposefully back toward the Lexington Avenue exit. As he walked, he reached into his pockets, then put a hand to each ear.

"Earplugs," Cates said.

McAllister nodded. He hadn't caught that. He turned to the operator sitting at the console. "Stay on camera one-one-four and play it out."

The video resumed. Life at the store went on. Shoppers walked past the suitcase display. I watched as they moved in and out of camera range.

At 11:57:43, a girl, about five, entered the frame. She just stood there, her back to the suitcases, no mother or father in sight.

We're cops. We deal with death every day. We've seen it all. We're tough as nails. Bullshit. People have no idea how emotionally involved we can become over the deaths of innocent people. Staring at the child no more than five feet from the abandoned knapsack, watching the time code tick away the seconds, and knowing what was to come at 11:59:00 and that there was *nothing* I could do to save her was torturous.

And then, at 11:58:27, a woman entered the frame and took the girl by the hand. As she scampered off, I could see Cates and Kylie exhale slowly.

"I checked the other cameras," McAllister said. "The kid and her mom were out of harm's way when the bomb went off."

At 11:58:59, no one was standing in front of the suitcases. But we could see two salespeople at a counter ten feet away, each talking to a customer.

A second later, the screen went white and then a smoky gray as the aftermath wreckage gradually came into view.

"Camera one-zero-three," McAllister said.

In an instant, every monitor in the room lit up with the first picture we had seen.

"There's your killer," McAllister said, pointing at the lone man, so perfectly shrouded in black that there wasn't a facial-recognition program on the planet that could identify him.

One of McAllister's security people handed him a sleek black external hard drive, and he passed it over to Cates. "This is everything we have on him from the moment he entered the store till the first responders showed up. Whatever else you need, let me know and I'll send it over."

"Thanks," Cates said.

"I wish I could do more," McAllister said, "but this bastard is smart. Two bombs in two days, a store full of high-tech surveillance equipment, and we know nothing about him."

"We do know one thing," Cates said.

McAllister looked at her. "What's that?"

"We know what time his next bomb is going off."

CHAPTER 15

WE SPLIT UP.

Cates hustled over to Fifty-Seventh Street, where the chief of detectives, the police commissioner, and the mayor were waiting for her in a command vehicle.

Kylie and I hit the streets. Criminals often return to the scene of the crime—especially arsonists and bombers, who get off on soaking up the chaos and destruction they've caused.

"Our guy's not going to be that stupid," Kylie said. "He's too good at covering his tracks. He knows we'll be filming everyone in the area and looking for a match with the crowd from yesterday's . . . Holy shit, Zach, look over there."

It was Nico Patrakis.

"Nico!" I shouted.

He looked up, not happy to see us. And when Nico wasn't happy, his entourage wasn't happy. Eight men stepped in and formed a wall around him.

I walked right up to the biggest one among them and stood there, chest to chest, eyeball to eyeball, sneer to sneer.

"If you don't mind," I said.

Apparently, he did mind. He didn't budge.

I felt for Nico. Yesterday he was a victim, but today he had drawn the line. Them versus us. So be it. I was about to move the big guy myself when Nico spoke.

"*Fóti! Afíste ton na perásei.*"

Fóti, his eyes still burning into mine, took a half step back.

"Nico," I said, "haven't you been through enough pain? Do you really need to be here?"

"I'm here for the same reason you're here, Zach," he said. "I'm looking for the *maláka* who murdered my family."

"Nico, finding the people who did that is our job."

"From what I see here," he said, his hand sweeping across the madness in front of us, "I'd say you're not doing such a great job."

"I promise we will find him," I said, "and when we do, you'll be the first one I call."

"So you want me to sit by my phone and wait, hoping that you do *your* job? What about *my* job, Zach? It is my God-given duty to avenge my family."

"You think your daughter, your wife, and your mother want you to spend years in prison for doing something reckless?"

"I don't think what I've done is reckless. In fact, I think it's very constructive."

"What you've *done*? What do you mean, what you've done?"

"I've offered a reward. One hundred thousand dollars to the person who can help me find the killer."

"Damn, it, Nico, that's the worst thing you can do," I said. "Nothing muddies up an investigation more than a bunch of treasure hunters calling us with bullshit leads and crazy theories."

"Don't worry. They won't be calling you. They'll be calling us." He looked around at his little Greek army. "We'll follow up on the leads."

"*You'll* follow up on the leads? You think you can tell the difference between an honest good Samaritan who might actually know something, and some lying scumbag who would pin it on his own mother for a hundred thousand dollars? There are some world-class liars out there, and you could wind up with a dozen suspects. What are you going to do then? Kill them all and let God sort them out?"

"Detective Jordan," Nico said, his eyes cold, his body language defiant, "the person who murdered my family may be able to hide from you and me, but he can't hide his evil from the world. Someone out there knows him. Do you think that person is going to pick up the phone and call you? No. So I'm going to give them a hundred thousand reasons to call me."

"Nico," I said, "I'm warning you. If you step over the line, if you turn your friends and family into a band of vigilantes, I will lock you up myself."

"You do what you have to do, Zach. And I'll do what I have to do. Now, if you'll excuse me, I have to go. A lot of people died here today. I want to get their names, so I can pay my respects to their families."

The ranks closed around him. I stepped back and walked away with my partner.

"The one thing we know about Nico," Kylie said, "is that he's just like his father: a shrewd businessman. He knows he doesn't have the skills to find the bomber, but you heard him. Somewhere out there, somebody knows who the guy is and where he's hiding out. And a hundred thousand dollars—straight from Nico, no cops, no questions asked—might be all it takes to get that somebody talking."

"I know," I said. "So now not only do we have to find him, we have to get to him before Nico does."

CHAPTER 16

THE BOMB HAD EXPLODED just as Ramón made it to Fifty-Ninth and Lexington. Leaving the knapsack and getting out of the store, he reminded himself, was the easy part. Getting away undetected would be a hell of a lot more complicated.

The cops had eyes everywhere. Not only did they have their own vast network of surveillance cameras, they also could turn to the tens of thousands of businesses and private residents who had installed their own security systems. Add to that all the license plate readers that were strategically placed throughout the city, and you could gun someone down in the Bronx, and the NYPD could track you all the way to JFK and then be waiting for you when you landed in Miami.

The cops might be smart, Ramón thought to himself. But Arthur was smarter. He knew how to beat the system.

"Walk east on Fifty-Ninth," Arthur had instructed him. "When you get to Third, people will be pouring out of the store. Join the crowd. You'll be on camera, but don't worry. Just keep your mask on and keep walking toward Second. There's a parking garage in the middle of the block that's covered with scaffolding. It's a blind spot. And just like that, you're gone."

"Won't the cops check the cameras at the garage and see me drive out?"

"You're not going into the garage," Arthur told him. "We'll buy a scooter from the no-questions-asked section of Craigslist. It will be chained to one of the scaffold support poles. As soon as you duck under, you'll reverse your black hoodie to the orange side, put on your helmet, and when a truck rides by, you'll pull out to his right. The cops may spot you; they may not, but they won't be looking for a biker in an orange sweatshirt."

"And then what?" Ramón asked.

"Then you'll shoot up First to the Willis Avenue Bridge. From there, it's less than ten minutes to Oak Point."

Ramón nodded. Oak Point Avenue was at the heart of a huge industrial area in the Bronx where there were millions of square feet of warehouses to rent. The roads were wide to accommodate the trucking traffic, and once you got past Tiffany Street the cameras were few and far between, which is why the area became known as "the place where stolen cars go to disappear."

Arthur may have had the brains, but Ramón had the connections. He knew the neighborhood well. More importantly, he knew the people who could keep their mouths shut.

Forty-two minutes after his latest terror attack, he pulled the scooter into the four-bay garage of a busy salvage yard where, in only a few minutes, the seven-year-old Honda would be completely disassembled and stripped of all identifying markings so that it could begin its new life, living up to the sign painted on the front of the building: Auto Parts.

Ramón shucked the sweatshirt, the baggy black pants, and the helmet and walked out a rear door wearing camo shorts, a khaki T-shirt, and a fashion accessory that was more popular in the Bronx than in any other place on the planet—a New York Yankees baseball cap.

He walked south to Barretto Point Park, disappeared from any possible camera in the sky into a thick clump of trees, emerged wearing a final change of clothes, and backtracked to where his car was parked on Leggett Avenue.

Then he headed toward Larchmont, where Arthur would be waiting with a cold beer and the next bomb.

When he got to I-95, he flipped on the radio and tapped the button for Yacht Rock 311 on SiriusXM.

The rest of the ride was a smooth cruise to soft rock from the late seventies and early eighties.

Just music.

Ramón didn't need the news.

He *was* the news.

CHAPTER 17

THEY WERE AN UNLIKELY pair, the two men who conspired to bring the city of New York to its knees.

Arthur had been born forty-two years earlier in the Gravesend section of Brooklyn. For almost twenty years before his arrival, his parents, Anna and Stefan Harmati, had tried valiantly to conceive. Eventually, they accepted what they deemed was God's will. Anna was infertile.

And yet, on the morning of her fiftieth birthday, Anna gave birth to a healthy, hardy baby boy. From the moment he took his first breath, Arthur was loved, adored, and treasured. After all, he was a miracle baby.

Ramón Reyes was not nearly so blessed. Born in Havana, Cuba, the fifth of eight children, he might well have gotten lost in the shuffle. But the boy had a gift. He could hurl a baseball over the plate with unerring accuracy.

Tall for his age, he was only seven when he started playing baseball in the streets and immediately caught the eye of local coaches. By age eleven, he had joined a youth league, and scouts from the Cuban National Series were already keeping tabs on him.

At sixteen, he was a rising star whose reputation had reached Major League Baseball scouts in the States, but the US embargo and the Castro regime's strict laws made it impossible for him make the jump. By his twenty-first birthday, Ramón was the top pitcher in the Cuban National Series, drawing crowds wherever he played.

But it wasn't enough. Yearning for a bigger stage, he made the decision to defect. He found a trafficking ring that guaranteed him safe passage to the Dominican Republic and then on to Miami. He thought he had paid them well, never realizing that they could get a bounty ten times that amount by turning him over to the secret police. He was less than an hour out to sea when the boat he was escaping on got intercepted by the Cuban Coast Guard. For the next forty-eight hours, he endured government-sponsored torture that ended only when a pair of bolt cutters viciously amputated the thumb and index finger from his pitching hand.

Then, on a bustling Saturday afternoon, a government-owned, Russian-made Lada rolled onto the Plaza de Armas in Old Havana, and Ramón was tossed to the curb, beaten and bloodied—a cautionary tale to would-be defectors.

Six days later, with the bandages still on his hand, and the heartbreak of a shattered dream still painfully fresh in his soul, he set out again to abandon his homeland.

This time, he snaked his way to Mexico, then paid a coyote to smuggle him across the border into Laredo, Texas. But Miami was no longer an option. There were too many Castro loyalists who would recognize the tall, athletic, eight-fingered young man and target him for assassination.

He set out for New York, *la ciudad de las segundas oportunidades*—the city of second chances.

Sixty-one hours and 1,957 miles later, he stepped off a Greyhound bus at the Port Authority Bus Terminal and turned himself in to the first cop he saw.

It took another ten months, but having documented his persecution and mutilation, he convinced the United States government that he would be killed if they deported him to Cuba, and they granted him asylum.

A week after his new life in America began, Ramón applied for a job as a dishwasher at an unpretentious neighborhood restaurant on Second

Avenue in Manhattan, where he was immediately hired by the manager, a feisty octogenarian named Anna, and her talented, soft-spoken chef husband, Stefan.

Two nights later, one of their regulars stopped in for dinner. Anna introduced them.

"Ramón," she said, "I want you to meet my miracle baby boy, Arthur."

The two men shook hands. It was the beginning of a lifelong friendship.

CHAPTER 18

RAMÓN TURNED INTO ARTHUR'S driveway on Bay Avenue and pulled behind the house, out of sight from the road.

Not that it mattered. He was here often enough, doing odd jobs for Arthur and Gwen, but keeping the car out of view was safer than having some do-gooder neighbor say, "I didn't see his car all morning, but I know it was parked there that Friday afternoon while I was watching the TV about the Bloomingdale's explosion."

Arthur's workshop was also in back. A minimalist ninety-six-square-foot shed, it was more hidey-hole than man cave and held zero interest for his wife or his two daughters. "On the other hand," he once told Ramón, "if a bomb-sniffing dog lived in the neighborhood, he'd go batshit in here."

Ramón tapped in the security code, stepped into the workshop, and changed his clothes one last time, putting on the overalls, T-shirt, work boots, and baseball cap people were used to seeing him wear.

Then he locked up and went to the back door of the house. He didn't knock. He knew he'd been on four of Arthur's sixteen security cameras since he made the turn onto Bay Avenue. He stood outside and listened to the click-snap of the dead bolt being unlocked. The door opened, and he stepped inside.

"Any problems?" Arthur asked, click-snapping the lock back in place.

"None that I'm aware of," Ramón said, "but you know me. Once I leave the package, I don't listen to the news."

"Too bad. You missed hearing the president of the United States call you a depraved, inhumane coward."

"*Pendejo*," Ramón said. "Did he forget how many bombs *he* dropped?"

Ramón followed Arthur to the kitchen, opened the left-hand door on the oversize recessed wood-paneled refrigerator, and grabbed a beer. He popped the top, took a swig, and surveyed the room.

The two men had been planning the attacks for the better part of a year. The first requirement was to get everybody out of the house. The kids were easy. They left for summer camp at the end of June. Getting rid of his wife took a little more finesse, but Arthur convinced his brother-in-law to split the cost of a seventeen-day Mediterranean cruise for Gwen and her sister.

Arthur had had the house to himself for only six days, but the charming magazine-perfect country kitchen had rapidly lost its charm—dishes in the sink, takeout containers on the countertop, flies hovering above the overflowing garbage can.

Ramón was a man of few words, but in this case, he didn't need any. His look said it all.

"Don't judge me," Arthur said.

Ramón smiled. "I'm not judging, boss. I'm just wondering who I'm going to work for after Gwen comes home and puts a knife through your heart."

"You don't understand, pal. After twenty-two years of living with a neat freak, it feels fantastic not to live in Barbie's goddamn Dreamhouse. As soon as Gwen and the girls left, I put the toilet seat up in every bathroom in the house, and for the next two weeks, I don't have to mop up every drop of piss that misses the bowl. Besides," he added, "Gwen will never know. I have a cleaning crew coming in the day before she gets back."

Ramón held up a hand. "I don' clean sheet up, boss," he said in a cartoonish Spanish accent. "I blow sheet up."

"And blow shit up you did," Arthur said, putting his arm around his friend and leading him into the living room.

Ramón did a quick scan. Happily, the living room was still livable. The TV was on but muted, and the screen was split between a stone-faced anchorman and footage of customers and employees streaming out of the store, which by now was old news but still as close as the cameras could get to the carnage inside.

"The media is calling you the 11:59 Bomber, which, of course, is blatantly obvious," Arthur said, easing himself down into a leather armchair. "But someone on social media came up with *hashtag Ka-Boomingdale's*, so there's still hope for originality."

Ramón didn't give a shit about what they were saying, original or otherwise. He was exhausted—physically, mentally, and emotionally drained. He plopped down on the cushy sofa and settled in. The soothing forest-green fabric was a soft crushed velvet, and the floral throw pillows were plump and inviting. Gwen, who had studied art history in college, had a knack for making the house welcoming and comfortable.

"Take me through it," Arthur said. "From the top. Every detail."

That was Arthur for you, Ramón thought. Always analyzing. His clinical mind hashing and rehashing every detail.

It took Ramón twenty minutes to take Arthur through his day, from the time he chained the scooter to the scaffolding on Fifty-Ninth Street to the minute he pulled into the driveway in Larchmont. Step by step by step. Arthur not saying a word, just taking mental notes, trying to figure out how to do it better the next time. And, of course, there would be a next time.

When he was done, Arthur leaned forward in his chair, his jaw tight, his eyes lasered in on his coconspirator.

Ramón clenched his jaw as he waited for the verdict.

Arthur's face opened into a warm and approving toothy smile. "Perfect," he said. "Flawless. Brilliant. You, my friend, make Ted Kaczynski look like a bumbling amateur. *Gracias, amigo.*"

Ramón sank deeper into the sofa and let out a long, slow exhalation.

Arthur reached into his pocket. "Here's your cell phone," he said, handing it to Ramón.

It was all part of the plan. If, for any reason, the cops pinged Ramón's iPhone, they would have electronic evidence that he was in Larchmont all day, checking his email occasionally in the morning and then hastily scrolling through the news websites and social media shortly after 11:59.

A flicker from the TV screen caught Arthur's eye, and he realized that the news anchor was gone and the station had cut to a press conference. Police Commissioner Colin Radcliffe was standing at the podium. Mayor Sykes was at his side.

Arthur picked up the remote, unmuted it, and caught the PC in mid-sentence. "*. . . continued sweeps of the transit system, as well as iconic New York landmarks and other symbolic targets like the one the bomber chose today. The entire effort will be spearheaded by our elite NYPD Red team, commanded by Captain Delia Cates.*"

Arthur inhaled sharply and moved closer to the TV as Cates stepped up to the microphone.

"*Just before noon today,*" she said, "*a person walked into Bloomingdale's department store wearing a knapsack, abandoned it in the cosmetic section on the main floor, and exited the building. Within minutes, the knapsack exploded, killing six people and injuring dozens more. It was the second bombing in two days, both of which were timed to go off at 11:59 a.m. We have the vast resources of the NYPD at our disposal, including help from the state and the federal government, and we have undertaken the most comprehensive manhunt in the history of our city. I won't be taking any questions now, but—*"

He muted her. *Cates. Lieutenant Delia fucking Cates.* He grinned. *Oh, excuse me. It's* Captain *Delia fucking Cates now, isn't it?* The very same bitch cop who had driven him to the point of waging this war against the city was now in charge of bringing him down.

He laughed out loud, savoring the irony. "Just when you think it can't get any better," he said, his eyes still glued to the image of the person he hated most in all the world. "How about that, Ramón? We not only get to settle the score with the city, but we get to put Delia Cates in the fucking ground where she belongs."

Ramón didn't respond.

Arthur turned around. His partner in crime was curled up on the sofa, a pillow to his chest, fast asleep.

"Rest easy, my friend," Arthur said. "You earned it."

Then he turned his gaze back to the TV. "As for you, Delia Cates," he sneered, "the man you fucked over to get those captain's bars is coming after you, and I am . . ." He paused to savor the word on his tongue.

"Invincible."

CHAPTER 19

DELIA CATES IS NYPD to the bone—a third-generation cop, a Marine veteran, with a bachelor's from Columbia and a master's in criminal justice. A lot of us know that she's a favorite of Chief of Detectives Harlan Doyle, but no one realized how much of a favorite until he put her front and center at the press conference.

Chiefs love the limelight. They bask in it. So the fact that Doyle stepped aside and gave his face time with the public to Cates was a loud and clear message to the department. *Keep your eyes on this cop. She's a rising star.*

Her speech was short and ticked all the right boxes.

"*We have the vast resources of the NYPD at our disposal.*" Check.

"*Including help from the state and the federal government.*" Check.

"*We have undertaken the most comprehensive manhunt in the history of our city.*" Check.

They were all reassuring words that the public needed to hear, and she had delivered them with less than two minutes' notice that she'd be stepping up to the podium.

And she wisely closed with "I won't be taking any questions now," because she knew that she didn't have any answers. We'd only just started looking for the subway bomber, and we still had very little to go on. Twenty-four hours later, he'd doubled down, going from madman to serial bomber with a dozen deaths on his hands, and Cates was the cop chosen to lead the effort that would bring him down.

The weight of the world may have been on her shoulders, but she didn't show it. In the squad car going back to the station, she sat motionless, as if she were meditating. Kylie and I remained silent, giving her plenty of space.

Just as we turned onto Sixty-Seventh Street, she spoke.

"George Metesky," Cates said, her cadence slow so that we heard each syllable clearly.

It didn't help. We were clueless.

"Who?" Kylie asked.

"George Metesky," Cates repeated. "He was an electrician at Con Edison back in the 1930s. He was working in one of their power plants when a boiler exploded and left him disabled. He got some sick pay, but his claim for workers' comp was denied. He was bitter, and rightfully so in my opinion. The resentment festered, and in November of 1940, he decided to get even with the company. He left a bomb at a Con Ed plant on the west side."

She had our undivided attention.

"It fizzled," Cates said. "But he didn't give up. He planted almost three dozen more bombs in public places—movie theaters, subway stations, phone booths, the restrooms at Grand Central and Penn Station. The bombs were rudimentary, so no one was killed, but innocent people were injured, some quite seriously. The press called him the Mad Bomber. My grandfather was one of the detectives assigned to the case."

"But you know his name, which means the cops caught him," Kylie said.

"Not until January of 1957. He terrorized the city for over sixteen years."

"*Sixteen years?*" Kylie said.

"And they didn't catch him in the act of planting a bomb. He kept writing to the newspapers, venting his rage about the injustices he'd suffered at the hands of Con Edison. A clerk at the company dug into the files until she finally came up with a disgruntled employee from two decades back." She paused to let it sink in. "Our bomber is also nursing a grudge," she said.

"I can play back his 911 call in my sleep," Kylie said. "'Tell the mayor I'm going to destroy New York City the way it destroyed my family.'"

"Right," Cates said. "That's the one sure thing we know about our bomber. He is fixated on getting even with the city. Which probably means he took them on at some time. And that could mean he sued them."

"And lost," Kylie said.

"Do you know how many people sue the city and lose every year?" I said.

"I have no idea," Cates said, "but I know two things. We have the vast resources of the NYPD at our disposal to help us find out. And it sure as hell is not going to take sixteen years."

CHAPTER 20

BY THE TIME WE got back to the office, someone had installed two large digital clocks in the squad room. One displayed the time of day in bright green numerals. The other was a countdown clock, ticking off the seconds until 11:59 a.m. on Saturday.

We had twenty hours and thirty-seven minutes left to do what our predecessors had taken forever to figure out.

Kylie and I scoured the security footage Cy McAllister sent from Bloomingdale's. The man in black had hidden his face well, but we had gait analysis software that allowed us to document the way he walked, which might later connect him to the subway bombing.

A second team tracked him from the time he'd left the store through the Lexington Avenue door. They followed him to Fifty-Ninth Street, where he disappeared under some scaffolding. They caught the fact that he changed his hoodie from black to orange, picked him up driving away on a scooter, and then completely lost him in the Bronx.

Dialect specialists continued to analyze the audio recording of yesterday's 911 call. The caller had spoken only seventy-two words, none longer than two syllables. Even though he used voice-changing software, they were able to determine that he was male, middle-aged, and educated, and his accent said that either he had been born and raised in New York City or he was a damn good actor.

The veteran 911 operators—the ones with the most experience—were all called in. A voice profile of the man who made the first bomb threat had been embedded into the system. If the same man called again, there was a good chance the system would recognize him, and a linguistics expert would review it immediately and verify whether it was a match.

Another team, led by an old friend of mine, Detective Efrain Curet, was cataloging and analyzing the CCTV at the Wall Street station. They had the monumental task of wading through more than 2,500 hours of footage and pinpointing those few seconds in time between mid-March and early July when someone slipped into the station and left a deadly bomb in the work crew shed.

I touched base with Efrain several times during our twenty-four-hour countdown. I got the same response every time.

Plenty of haystack. No needle. Yet.

Word filtered in from the world outside the station house. Traffic was exceptionally light for a Friday night in July. Restaurants were flooded with cancelations. DoorDash, Grubhub, and Uber Eats food deliveries were swamped. New Yorkers were staying home.

Night turned into day, and by Saturday morning, the city that never sleeps was afraid to get out of bed. Subway and bus ridership was down dramatically. "Closed" signs hung in store windows, especially the small mom-and-pop businesses. The ubiquitous food carts of summer were noticeably absent. Street fairs were canceled. The Department of Environmental Protection reported that ambient noise—the sounds of a vibrant city—was at the lowest decibel level since the early ghost-town days of Covid in 2020.

Once again New Yorkers were caught up in the familiar grip of a terrorist in their midst. Millions of people, citizens and visitors alike, abandoned their plans and waited for the next bomb to go off at exactly one minute before noon.

Kylie, Cates, and I were also waiting, along with two dozen other senior cops, as the countdown clock stopped at 00:00:00 and the digital clock hit 11:59:00.

Another sixty seconds slowly slogged by. Then another. If a bomb had gone off at 11:59, we would know it by now.

12:02. 12:05. 12:07. Nothing.

At 12:10, Cates stood up. You'd think her face might show some sign of relief that the devastation we'd feared had not happened. But there was only fury in her eyes, anger in her voice.

"He's fucking with us," she said. "He's fucking with the entire city."

CHAPTER 21

"WE NEED TO GET out of here, Zach," Kylie said, bounding down the stairs as soon as the meeting broke up.

"We?" I said, following her. "Where are *we* going?" Of course, I knew where *she* was going—with or without me—but I wanted to remind her that this was a partnership, not a monarchy.

"Fifth Precinct," she said, ignoring the dig. "We're going to sit down and talk to the detective who collared Spence."

"Charlie Elliott," I said, getting into the car. "I don't know him, but I asked around. He's been on the job for twenty-six years, and he's hands down the best detective they've got."

"Yeah, well, even the best can make a monumental mistake."

"If that's going to be your approach," I said, "I think you'd better let me do the talking."

"What is that supposed to mean?" she said, turning onto Lexington Avenue.

"It means that if you walk into Detective Elliott's house and tell him he bungled the investigation and now you're going to jump in and get it right, he will shower you with a string of expletives and show you to the front door, and any cooperation you were ever hoping for will be gone forever."

"Fine," she said—her go-to response when she knows she's in an argument she has no chance of winning. "So how *should* I handle it?"

"Let me deal with Elliott. He's not going to be happy no matter who does the talking, but given the choice between me and you . . ."

She gave me a sideways glance, contorting her face into a scowl. "You're making it sound like I'm some sort of hothead."

"Let's just say you have a reputation for spontaneously combusting whenever you open your mouth."

"Fine," she said again. "But just remember this: Spence's life is on the line. He swears he didn't kill Preston Balfour, and I believe him. Cates gave us the green light to talk to Elliott, and that's exactly what we're going to do."

"For the record," I said, "Cates gave us the go-ahead before this modern-day Mad Bomber stepped up his game."

"*For the record*, Zach," Kylie said, spitting my words back at me, "there are almost a hundred detectives working this case around the clock, with a hundred more ready to jump in. The machine is humming along, but right this very minute there's not much for the two of us to do, and I'm not going to just sit around waiting for this asshole to blow something up."

She hit the gas, swerved around a bus, and darted from lane to lane, because putting our lives at risk always seems to calm her down.

"I'm assuming you didn't call Elliott to tell him we're coming," I said.

"You know how it works, Zach," she said. "You try to schedule a meeting, and it takes forever, but if you show up unannounced, most of them are likely to bite the bullet and just get it over with."

"Great," I said. "So on top of everything else, we'll be ambushing him."

The 5th Precinct is in Chinatown and extends into Little Italy. If you like to eat, it's one of the best precincts to be assigned to. We ID'd ourselves to the desk sergeant, and he waved us upstairs to the squad room.

"Shit!" a cop I never saw before in my life said. He got up and handed a twenty-dollar bill to a weary-looking detective who was eyeball deep behind a stack of paperwork. The sign on his desk said *Detective Charles Elliott*.

"Detectives," Elliott said. "I was expecting you. In fact, I bet twenty bucks that you'd be here before one o'clock."

I looked at my phone. It was 12:54. "How did you . . ."

"When that bomb didn't go off at 11:59, I figured you'd tear ass straight down here and tell me how to do my job."

"That's definitely not why we're here," I said. "In fact, anyone who can predict where I'll be before I even know I'm going there doesn't need my help with their detective skills."

He folded the twenty lengthwise, held it up to his face, ran it through his fingers, and took a deep breath. He was quietly inhaling victory. I couldn't help but like this guy.

"Then why are you here?" he asked, enjoying the fact that I was now playing defense.

"At the arraignment, Harrington's attorney challenged the DA. He said his client was a fall guy. He said that Harrington described the real perpetrator to the investigative team, but they didn't look hard enough to find him."

Both Elliott and his partner cracked up laughing. "That is total bullshit," Elliott said.

I held up both hands. "Hey, I agree, but don't shoot the messenger. It's just that, Balfour being the high-profile victim that he is, the DA asked the Red team to work with you and cancel out any possibility of another perp."

That too was bullshit, but instead of rubbing our noses in it, Elliott sat back in his chair.

"We've got a lot of gangs in Chinatown," he said. "I'm not complaining. They give us job security. One of them, the Golden Snakes, operates the bus routes that run back and forth between Chinatown and the casinos in Connecticut. They rake in so much cash that another gang, the Manchu Qing, has been trying to muscle in on it. Last night, it got ugly. A shootout on Pell Street. Three in the morgue and three more on life support.

"It is now one o'clock on Saturday afternoon. My partner and I got here at seven yesterday morning, and we haven't slept a wink since, which is why I look like the walking dead and he looks even deader. So first off, let me say that I will not be working with you. As soon as you leave, I will grab two hours' sleep and then head straight to the morgue and watch them slice and dice three, maybe more, gangbangers.

"What I will do is set you straight on this so-called real-perpetrator alibi I'm accused of not looking into. Three eyewitnesses saw Harrington standing over the victim, the murder weapon in his hand, covered in blood that I will bet my pension turns out to be Balfour's. And Harrington's *explanation* for this rather incriminating tableau was, 'I didn't do it. I wrestled the knife away from the man who did.'"

"Did he describe the man?" I asked.

"I don't know," Elliott said. "Is 'average height, average weight' a description? I asked if he was white, Black, Asian, or Hispanic, and he responded with 'I'm not sure.' I tried to pin him down, and he said the guy wasn't 'white-white. He was kind of swarthy.' His word—*swarthy*. That's all he gave us. So we looked at all the CCTV footage in the area. It was a busy Friday night. Harrington had described half the men on the street, and at the same time, he didn't describe anybody. As far as I could tell, he didn't really have an alibi of any substance."

There was no holding Kylie back. She jumped in. "Detective Elliott, my husband was a writer-producer on dozens of TV cop shows. If he wanted to lie to you, he'd have come up with something much more dramatic. Maybe the reason his alibi lacks more detail is because he was in shock and all he could do was tell you the truth."

Elliott looked at Kylie. "The *truth*, Detective MacDonald, is that your husband crashed a private screening and threatened to kill Preston Balfour in front of a roomful of people. A few hours later, Balfour is murdered, and I interviewed multiple eyewitnesses who described in vivid detail a picture of one man who stabbed another man to death. I'm sorry, but I know more than a few cops whose family members crossed over to the wrong side of the law. It's painful to see, but it doesn't change my mission. I stand behind my call, but if you've been assigned to take a deeper dive into his alibi and look for this swarthy phantom, be my guest."

"Detective Elliott," I said, "we'll be happy to work with you on this—"

Elliott shook his head. "At the risk of repeating myself, Detective Jordan, we will *not* be working together. I have no desire to put an innocent man in prison, but as far as I'm concerned, my work is done, and I'm happy to pass the torch. I'll give you access to the Balfour files, and you can take it from there. Good luck."

He stood up. "And now I'm going to get some much-needed sleep." He left the squad room, his partner right behind him.

Kylie didn't say a word. But I know her well. The case I thought we wouldn't even be able to go near was dumped right in our laps. It was all ours. All hers. She didn't just exit the building. She emerged triumphant.

I, on the other hand, was nervous as hell. I didn't share her blind faith. I had seen the dark side of Spence Harrington in the past. Detective Elliott may have gotten it right. My partner might well be married to a stone-cold killer.

CHAPTER 22

"FIRST STOP: CHUCK DRYDEN at the lab," Kylie said, turning onto Canal Street and heading toward the Manhattan Bridge.

The NYPD Forensics Lab is on Jamaica Avenue in Queens. It would have been a forty-five-minute drive on a good day. But, of course, there are no good days in New York City traffic, and we crawled for over an hour. And unlike in the movies, where cops have no trouble finding parking spaces directly in front of the building they're going to, we had to park on 148th Street and walk four blocks.

So I was road-weary and cranky when we finally got to the lab. Security had just buzzed us through when a familiar voice called out.

"Yo, Zach. Kylie."

It was Theo, the eighteen-year-old wannabe writer-director who meant more to me than he could possibly imagine.

"What are you guys doing here?" he chirped.

"It's a police lab," I said, my voice flat, my expression deadpan, doing my best to cover up the fact that just seeing him had completely turned my day around. "Have you ever watched CSI? This is where all the cool cops come in the beginning of the show to get clues that will help them catch the bad guy just before the final commercial. The real question is, what are *you* doing here?"

"I'm shooting the documentary for the DCPI," Theo said. "I

can't believe you forgot. You and Kylie are the ones who helped me get the job."

"First of all, I didn't forget," I said. "It's just that I've had a lot more on my mind than your career. And second of all, we did not get you the job. All we did was introduce you to Commissioner Parnell. You're the one who pitched the idea and sold it to her."

"True," he said, his smile lighting up the space around us. "But I'll still thank you in my acceptance speech at the Oscars."

Theo's idea was simple and timely. The documentary was called "Commanding Respect: The Women Leading the NYPD," and it featured bios and interviews with the best and brightest female cops in the department.

"How's it going so far?" Kylie asked.

Theo pressed his hands to his temples. "My mind," he said, flinging his hands upward and mimicking the sound of an explosion, "has been blown."

"Details," Kylie said.

"Okay, let's see . . . So far, I met three amazing women. Inspector Lisa Demberg, CO of the Harbor Unit—we shot a lot of stuff on a police boat. Lieutenant Lauren Sholder, CO of Missing Persons, and I just spent two hours with Inspector Francine Ventura, who runs this forensic unit. I was supposed to meet up with your boss, Captain Cates, tomorrow, but I just got a text that she has to cancel. Apparently, this guy who's trying to blow up the city is more important than my dreams of being a filmmaker."

"Bummer," Kylie said.

Theo's face got serious. "What's the latest on Spence?"

We caught him up on everything that happened since the arraignment, and ended with the outcome of our meeting with Detective Elliott.

His head exploded again. "Are you kidding? This is *your* case now? Can I help?"

"Yes, it is," I said. "And no, you can't."

"No problem," Theo said. "I'll just hang around and watch." He tapped the visitor badge hanging around his neck. "I'm totally legal."

"We're going to talk to Chuck Dryden," Kylie said. "He's a crime scene analyst who will take us through the forensics. You can tag along, but do not say a word."

Theo pantomimed a zip across his lips and followed us to Dryden's office.

It was totally against protocol, but, hey, I loved having him along. Besides, if Captain Cates ever chewed us out for doing it, I'm sure Kylie would just shrug and say, "Sorry, boss, but the kid had a badge."

CHAPTER 23

WHEN I ENTERED HIS lab, Chuck Dryden looked up from his workstation and nodded politely. "Zach, I wasn't expecting you," he said, his voice modulated to library levels.

Then Kylie walked in, and I could almost hear his heart crashing against his rib cage. "De-De-Detective MacDonald," he stuttered.

Chuck is awkward around people, especially women, and his infatuation with Kylie was as obvious as it was hopeless. To him, she was a celestial body, and he was just some poor schlub on the ground with a telescope.

"Hey there, Chuck," she said, our budding young director at her side. "This is my friend Theo. He's just going to watch. Okay?"

"Sure. Absolutely. Yes. Hello, Theo." He looked back at Kylie. "But what is he going to watch? I don't have anything new on the bombings."

"Zach and I are helping Detective Elliott dig a little deeper into the Preston Balfour homicide."

"Really? I thought your husb—" Chuck stopped himself cold. "Let . . . let me get my files."

Chuck is thorough, precise, meticulous. What he lacks in social skills he more than makes up for in crime-solving abilities.

He produced a cardboard box. Its pedigree was hand-scrawled in black marker on one side.

"The murder weapon," he said, carefully opening the box. And there it was: a bloodied kitchen knife secured to the bottom with zip ties.

"It's a classic eight-inch Wüsthof chef's knife," Dryden said. "It belonged to the victim. It came from a slot in the knife block on his kitchen counter. It was swabbed for DNA, and we anticipate that the blood will match that of the victim and that of Mr. Harrington, from whom the weapon was retrieved and who, as you know, is under arrest."

"Yes, Chuck," Kylie said. "I am well aware that my husband has been incarcerated."

Dryden stood there, his discomfort apparent. Her words had taken their toll. In the silent movie of his life, Kylie was the only sound, and now he was admitting to her that he was part of the team that would put Spence in prison for decades.

"Chuck, please," she said. "Is this all? Do you have anything else we can look into?" Her eyes were soft, vulnerable, pleading.

"Well, I don't know if it will help, but I . . . I did find one thing that seemed rather strange. You know, unusual."

It felt as though Dryden had tossed her a life preserver, and as soon as he said it, Kylie grabbed hold. "What? What have you got?"

"The blood—the victim's and your husband's—was commingled with *Sida cordifolia*."

"With what?"

"*Sida cordifolia*," Dryden said. "It's more commonly known as bala. It's an ancient antiseptic, antifungal elixir traditionally used in Ayurvedic folk medicine."

"Ayur—" Kylie said. "Chuck, please. Keep it simple."

"Of course," he said. "Ayurvedic is the oldest and probably one of the most accepted forms of medicine practiced in India. The bala subshrub is indigenous to the Indian subcontinent, and it has all kinds of magical, mystical healing powers. They say it purifies the blood, controls respiratory problems, helps with constipation, urinary tract infections—"

"Chuck!" Kylie barked.

He smiled sheepishly. "TMI?"

"You had me at constipation," Kylie said. "But what I'd really like to know is how that magical Indian elixir got on the murder weapon."

If she were any other cop, Dryden might well have looked at his worktable covered with dozens of evidence bags waiting to be inventoried, every one of which was marked PRIORITY, and said, "I have no idea. I just identify, document, and collect the evidence. You're the detective. You figure it out." But, of course, when Kylie does the asking, Chuck Dryden does his best to go the extra mile and come up with an answer.

"Excellent query, Detective," he said. "There was probably a time when, if you wanted bala, you had to travel to India. But like everything else, the ability to acquire exotic products from faraway places has evolved. You can now buy just about anything on the internet if you know where to look. However, since there was no other trace of *Sida cordifolia* in the victim's apartment, I would say it may well have been transferred from the killer."

"Well, they accused Spence of the killing, but I can guarantee you that he has never even heard of this stuff," Kylie said.

"That may well be true," Dryden said. He started to say something else, then hesitated.

"Chuuuuuck? Chuck Drydennnn?" Kylie said, her inflection bordering somewhere between friendly and seductive. She put her hand on his shoulder, and I could see the look in his eyes. Utter joy, commingled with sheer terror.

"You and I go back a long way, Chuck. I just said I guarantee you that Spence has never even heard of this bala, and you were about to say something. Whatever you know, whatever you think might help, please don't hold it back."

Chuck crumbled like a taco in a food fight. "Sure. Right. Okay," he said. "This is strictly off the record, mind you, but when I told Detective Elliott about the bala, he sent a team from the fifth squad to check Mr. Harrington's hotel room. Afterward, I spoke with the detectives who did the search, and they informed me that they found nothing."

"Let me repeat what I just heard," Kylie said. "The blood on the knife had traces of this bala, but except for the trace that was on the murder weapon, there was none to be found in Balfour's apartment or in Spence's hotel room."

"You didn't hear that from me, but yes."

"So that trace could have come from a third party," Kylie said.

"I didn't say that, but it's entirely possible."

"Chuck, you are a gem," Kylie said. She leaned over and gave him a quick hug. Then she turned and left the room. Theo and I followed. Dryden just stood at his workstation, most likely lost in fantasy.

"Did you hear that, Zach?" Kylie said. "That bala shit was on the knife but not in Spence's room. The Warlock can create a lot of reasonable doubt in the minds of the jury with that little piece of evidence."

"I'm sure he can," I said.

It didn't negate the fact that Spence was seen covered with the victim's blood and holding the murder weapon. But, of course, I'm smart enough to know that that was better left unsaid.

CHAPTER 24

RAMÓN COULDN'T SLEEP. He had set his alarm for two a.m., but after hours of tossing and turning, he got out of bed just after midnight, showered, put on the board shorts, the rashguard shirt, and the NRS Kinetic water shoes, and made himself a pot of coffee.

Not sleeping was not like him. Sleep was his defense mechanism, his way of coping with the choices he'd made. He'd been able to rationalize the killings. He was a mercenary, a gun for hire, a soldier of fortune. Arthur made the life-and-death decisions. Ramón was just the messenger. But he knew better than most what it was like to be a victim.

As a young baseball phenomenon, he had been idolized. And then, out of nowhere, he was brutalized, his hand mutilated, his dreams crushed. That was life. One day, you're on top of the world; the next day, you're six feet under.

No, it wasn't guilt or remorse for taking innocent lives that kept him awake. It was Arthur. The two of them had spent the afternoon together yesterday, and all Ramón wanted to do was hang out, sip a few beers, and watch a ball game. But all Arthur could do was rant. He raged on about the mission, about payback, about justice for his mother and father, about the Nazis who were running the city, about his need to inflict more damage, and about *killing that bitch cop who ruined my life*.

The truth was that nobody had ruined Arthur's life. He had

self-destructed. It started when his parents died. He blamed the city for their deaths. Against his lawyer's advice, he sued them for millions, and after years of postponements, trial delays, and an unsympathetic judge who consistently turned down his motions, he lost.

Instead of accepting the verdict, Arthur decided to get even. He'd start with the judge. It was easy enough to find out where the man lived. He canvassed the neighborhood until one afternoon he spotted the judge coming out of a supermarket, a shopping bag in each hand.

Arthur rushed him, threw him to the ground, and began pummeling him. It was broad daylight. They were on a busy street. People began to gather, but of course, nobody tried to break it up. New Yorkers know better. They've seen too many stories about good Samaritans who wind up with a knife in their chest or a bullet through their brain.

A few of the bystanders pulled out their phones and dialed 911, but the judge, a small man in his seventies, might well be dead before help arrived.

And then a figure barreled through the crowd, grabbed the back of Arthur's collar, pulled him off the judge, and smashed him to the sidewalk, nose first. Within seconds, his face was bloodied, and he was pinned to the ground by the heroic off-duty cop who had intervened. Her name was Lieutenant Delia Cates.

People cheered, squad cars came to a screeching halt, uniformed officers yanked Arthur to his feet and arrested him, and, of course, dozens of onlookers recorded his humiliation and posted it to social media. He copped a plea to misdemeanor assault and served six months on Rikers Island.

Ramón had trekked out to see him every other week. With each visit, he became more aware of Arthur's downward spiral. Living among the city's most violent criminals in that squalid complex of jails, his anger festered, and his need for revenge consumed him. As soon as he got out, he sat down with Ramón and laid out his plan to get even.

"I've learned how to make bombs," Arthur informed Ramón. "We are going to blow the shit out of this city until the mayor gets down on her hands and knees and begs for mercy."

We? Ramón was horrified. He tried to say no, but Arthur steamrolled him.

"How can you not help me?" Arthur had said, his eyes drilling into Ramón's in disbelief. "You came to this country a broken man, driven from your home, cut off from your family. You reached out to my mother and father, and they took you in. They embraced you. They gave you a job, a future. They gave you a *life*. You became a brother to me. What kind of an ungrateful man are you that you would refuse to help me avenge their deaths?"

Arthur had always had a Svengali-like effect on him, and Ramón tried desperately not to collapse under the weight of all that guilt.

"Help you?" he said meekly. "You're not asking me to *help* you. You're asking me to put my life on the line. You're asking me to take monumental risks that could get me killed. Or, even worse, land me in prison for the rest of my life."

And then, without warning, Arthur changed the rules of the game. "I'll pay you," he said.

"Thanks," Ramón said, "but I've only got eight fingers left, and I'm not risking any more for thirty bucks an hour."

"You're right," Arthur said. "This is high risk. You should get more for planting a bomb than you do for cleaning the gutters or pressure-washing the patio. You should get at least . . ." Arthur stopped abruptly, letting the unfinished thought hang in the air. The silence, of course, only served to draw Ramón in deeper.

Arthur flicked his index finger rapidly between his lower lip and his chin. He was thinking, calculating. Finally, the finger stopped, and he looked back at Ramón. "How much did I pay you last year?"

Not enough, Ramón thought. *Not by a long shot*.

"Last year?" he said. "I can't say to the penny, but with the Christmas bonus, it came to around sixty-eight thousand dollars. Maybe a little more."

"Let's round it up to seventy-five thousand dollars," Arthur said. "Does that sound fair?"

"Seventy-five thousand dollars for what?" Ramón said cautiously.

"Seventy-five thousand dollars for every bomb you plant," Arthur said.

Ramón felt his throat constrict. Was Arthur really that insane, that obsessed? Hell, he had the money. His house was worth what? Eight million? Ten? His income, with its staggering year-end bonuses for playing with other people's money, was unconscionable. Gwen's decorating clients were all überrich, willing to shell out as much for a lamp as other people would for a Porsche. Ramón had been an hourly worker since the day he came to America. Arthur's offer meant freedom, a way out.

Everyone has their price. And seventy-five thousand dollars for a few hours' work was Ramón's. He made the life-altering decision on the spot.

"I'm in," he said. "What do you want me to do?"

CHAPTER 25

ARTHUR LAID OUT the plan. He would build the bombs; Ramón would leave them exactly where Arthur instructed him. Within minutes of the time the bomb was detonated, Arthur would wire the seventy-five thousand dollars to Ramón's bank account in the Caymans.

"We won't be able to do a bomb every day," Arthur said, "but every explosion will be set to go off at exactly the same *time* of day."

"Why not random times?" Ramón asked. "Why would we give them a warning?"

"It's not a warning. It's a guarantee, a promise. A lot of people on airplanes are fearful because they know a crash is possible. But that fear turns to sheer terror when they know a crash is inevitable."

"How many bombs are we talking about?" Ramón asked.

"Not too many," Arthur said, avoiding the question. "When I sued the city of New York, all I asked for was a lousy five million dollars. Now I want to grind them to a halt. The economic backlash from these bombs will cost them billions. I just want them to feel the pain. Then we'll quit. Justice will have been served; Anna and Stefan Harmati will be avenged; I will quietly walk away, never to be seen or heard from again; and you, my friend, will be financially set for life."

It was a lie. Or maybe Arthur had actually believed it when he said it. But the media attention he got when the second bomb went off at precisely the same time as the first emboldened him. And once he learned that the woman who had put him behind bars was coming after him again, his mission became a crusade.

Arthur Harmati was more than a man hell-bent on revenge. He was insane. He was Napoleon on his way to Waterloo. Yes, he was smart, but he was an amateur, and eventually the NYPD would figure out that Arthur was the mastermind behind it all, the man with the grudge against the city. And the minute the cops came pounding on his door, he would fold. He would cut a deal. He would give up Ramón without a second thought.

That, Ramón realized, was what kept him up at night. *That madman is going to get caught, and he's going to take me with him.*

He looked down at the Sea to Summit dry bag on the floor. It had the next bomb in it, along with the tools and materials to put it in place.

Another seventy-five thousand was less than an hour away. And this one would be easy. He'd do it all under cover of darkness, and he'd be home hours before it blew.

He picked up the bag, stepped out into the warm July night, and looked back at the two-story red-brick house that had been his home for the past eight years.

He loved this place. He loved his cozy little basement apartment on this tree-lined block in Bayside. He turned and looked across the street at Marie Curie Park. The two-and-a-half-acre playground was always packed with happy kids, and he thought about the dozens who had adopted him as their pitching coach over the years.

He could never have afforded to live here if it hadn't been for Arthur's mother, Anna. One night at the restaurant, she introduced him to her friends the Castillo sisters, Estrella and Blanca. They owned a house on Forty-Sixth Avenue just off Oceania Street in Bayside, Queens. It had a beautiful remodeled apartment that was available for rent.

"Only twenty-five hundred a month," Estrella said.

Ramón held up both hands. "It sounds wonderful, but it's out of my price range."

Anna, who thrived on micromanaging other people's lives, smiled.

"There's another option," she said. "They need someone to help around the house."

"It pays twenty-five hundred a month," Blanca said.

And so Ramón became their handyman, mowing the lawn, shoveling the walk, and dealing with all the little electrical and plumbing quirks that were part of the charm of a house built in 1947.

He would miss this house, this neighborhood, those kids. But he had to get away. He'd spent hours online searching for his next home. He finally found it almost eight thousand miles away in Southern Africa. Botswana. The weather was warm, the crime rates were low, the economy was thriving, and Arthur would never find him. The NYPD might, but they couldn't do anything about it. Botswana had no extradition treaty with the US.

Today was Sunday. In a week, he would pack a single suitcase, get on an airplane, and start his life all over again.

But first, he thought, putting the dry bag in the trunk of his car, *I have another bomb to plant.*

CHAPTER 26

"HOW ARE YOU GETTING to Jersey from your place?" Arthur had asked when they were going over the logistics for the third bomb.

It was a loaded question, but Ramón was ready for it.

"At that hour, the fastest way is to take 495 to the Midtown Tunnel, then shoot across Thirty-Fourth Street and take the Lincoln Tunnel to Weehawken."

Arthur's jaw clenched. There were a lot of ways to get from Bayside to Weehawken, New Jersey, but as far as he was concerned, there was only one right way. And the route Ramón had suggested was definitely not it.

"*However*," Ramón said before Arthur could correct him, "Manhattan is going to be on high alert, and I'd have to drive past the Empire State Building, which will be on even higher alert. So I think I should go through the Bronx, take the GW Bridge out of the city, and then River Road to Port Imperial Boulevard. The cops won't be looking for a crazy-ass bomber on the Jersey side."

Arthur's jaw relaxed.

"You think you're the only one with a brain, Arthur?" Ramón said to his boss. Not then. But now, driving along River Road at 2:45 in the morning.

The two men had had a powerful relationship—one built on love and trust. But Arthur's obsession with revenge had eclipsed the bond of brotherhood. And Ramón's loyalty had evolved into a cold, crass business arrangement. The only thing that drove him now was the same desire that got him through his final days in Cuba: self-preservation.

La ciudad de las segundas oportunidades had given him the second chance he'd hoped for. Now it was time to move on.

He'd been to the Weehawken Waterfront Park and Recreation Center twice before: once in the daytime when it was thick with people, and once at three a.m., when it was deserted. Adjacent to the park was Henley Place, a condo complex for those who could afford seven-figure apartments with all the amenities and a spectacular view of the New York skyline. He scanned the buildings. Two lights were on, no one standing in the windows.

It didn't matter. Even if someone was watching, they were used to seeing people like him. He parked the car and found the app Arthur had installed on his burner phone.

Arthur trusted technology more than he trusted Ramón. This one was called What3words, and Ramón had to admit, it was rather ingenious. The developer had divided the entire planet into fifty-seven trillion three-by-three-meter squares. He opened the app, and a tiny What3words logo showed him the exact square he was in. He tapped it.

///chat.hero.pencil popped on the screen.

That's where he was.

"It doesn't matter if it's pitch black and the fog is as thick as molasses," Arthur had told him. "If you save your three words when you park, you'll always be able to find your car."

Even more important was the three-word square where he was told to plant the bomb. He typed the words Arthur had given him into the app.

///statue.busy.cook.

It was a mile away, on the other side of the Hudson River.

He removed the paddleboard from the trunk, walked down to the water's edge, connected the hand pump, and began inflating it. It took ten minutes to reach fifteen psi. He pressed his thumb down on the board. Rock solid.

The dry bag with its deadly payload was at his feet. He picked it up and strapped it to his back. Then he got on his knees, cuffed his ankle to the cleat at the tail end of the board, and shoved off.

He had started paddleboarding only two weeks ago, but Arthur convinced him he could do it. He secured his fishing pole, grasped the paddle, and stood up—shaky at first, but then he steadied himself and headed for New York.

The night sky was blue-black with a smattering of stars and a sliver of lazy moon that did little to light the way. He felt the weight of the bomb on his back—not just physically, but deep in his soul. He was on another mission for Arthur. More people would die. But . . .

But nothing.

Sleep helped him rationalize the choice he had made, but now he was wide awake, slicing through the calm waters, the lights of the city pulsing with life even at this hour.

He pushed his demons aside with memories of the first time his father took him out on his fishing skiff, *El Pescado*. Ramón was almost eleven, and it was finally his turn to learn the fishing trade as his four older brothers and sisters had done before him. He remembered sitting in the bow, gripping his fishing pole, praying to feel the tug of a tarpon. And he remembered his disappointment when, after two hours, he went home with nothing.

"*La próxima vez*," his father had said. *Next time.*

But there was no next time. Baseball consumed his life.

And now, all these years later, he was ready to pick up where he left off. Ten minutes into the journey, Ramón stopped, picked up his pole, and cast his line into the river.

"You never know who's watching," Arthur had said. "You might not see them, but if they can see you, you damn well better look like a fisherman. Just don't use a hook. The last thing we need is some dumbass fish chomping down and yanking you and the bomb into the drink."

So that was the routine. Paddle, stop, pretend to fish. Paddle some more, stop, and go through the charade another time. He could have made it across in thirty minutes, but following Arthur's instructions to the letter, he arrived at *///statue.busy.cook* sixty-four minutes after he left the Jersey shoreline.

An hour and a half later, he was back where he had started, his arms and shoulders on fire, his entire body depleted, his emotional gas tank on empty.

He dropped to the ground, turned the valve cap on the board, pressed down on the valve to release the seal, then closed his eyes and listened to the steady hiss of escaping air as his craft slowly deflated.

It was loud enough, and he was tired enough, that he didn't hear the rustling of the grass, or the snapping of the twigs as the footsteps approached and came to an abrupt stop ten feet from where he was stretched out.

But he heard the voice—sharp, high-pitched, and deadly serious.

"Police! Don't move!"

CHAPTER 27

RAMÓN FROZE, HIS BRAIN racing. The bomb was a mile away. The cops had nothing on him. But once they looked at his ID, they wouldn't forget him. He had to get back to the other side of the river and disarm it before they . . .

And then came the laughter.

"Fish police," the high-pitched voice said. "Not real police. I'm just pulling your legs."

Ramón turned to get a better look, but it was too dark.

"Ha, ha, ha, ha, ha," the man said. "Against the law to fish here, but I come every night. Not to worry. If cops lock you up, we be in same jail cell."

"Jesus!" Ramón said. "You scared the crap out of me."

"Oh, don't be old lady. It's funny. You think I'm cops? Cops don't care if you fish. They think it's stupid law. Some nights they come, they see me, they say, 'You catch any fish tonight?' And I say, 'No. You catch any crooks tonight?' We laugh. Laughing good for you. Keep you young. How old you think I am?"

The man held up a battery-operated lantern and turned on the light so Ramón could get a better look at him. He was small, Asian, wearing a white T-shirt and a pair of dark slacks. Not jeans, not chinos, but dress pants. He moved the beam closer to his face.

He repeated the question. "How old you think I am?"

"I have no idea," Ramón said.

"Make a guess. You be wrong, but make a guess."

He's seen me already, Ramón thought. Better to play the game. He studied the man's face. It was weathered, but his skin was still smooth. He had a full head of thick silver hair; his teeth were bright white and healthy. He was one of those rare specimens who got older without aging. He could be anywhere between sixty and a hundred.

"Sixty-two," Ramón said.

"Eighty-seven. My name Leo."

He extended a hand. Ramón instinctively kept his right hand at his side and fist-bumped Leo with his left.

"What I call you?" Leo chirped.

"Hector," Ramón said, pulling his oldest brother's name out of the air.

Leo shined his light on the paddleboard and Ramón's fishing gear. "You catch no fish tonight, Hector," he observed. "I catch four stripers. Good eating. You live somewhere here?"

"No, no," Ramón said. "Just passing through."

He looked down at his paddleboard. It had almost deflated, but it would still take four or five minutes to roll it up and pack it. Leo was eighty-seven, and despite his broken English, he was sharp. The more time he spent with Ramón, the more the old man would take in.

Ramón moved his left hand to his crotch and began to squirm. "Sorry," he said, "but I really have to pee."

"You come to right place. There's trees," Leo said, pointing. "And there's river."

"Thanks. I'll take the trees," Ramón said, turning his back and walking toward a thicket. By the time he returned, Leo had walked off.

Forget about packing. Ramón scooped up the board, the pump, and the rest of his gear and hustled back to his car. He didn't need the app to find it, but no sense telling Arthur that. No sense telling Arthur *anything*. All Ramón had to do was grab a few hours' sleep, drive out to Larchmont, wait for the boom at 11:59, and pocket another seventy-five thousand.

And then?

He had thought it through before he came to a decision.

One more bomb, and that was it. No sense getting greedy. One more bomb after this, and he would have earned three hundred thousand dollars in five days. Add that to the ninety-seven thousand he'd socked away in the Caymans over the past twenty years, and he'd have more than enough money to disappear without a trace.

Arthur would be furious, but he wouldn't quit. He would have to plant his own bombs. He'd get caught, of course. That was inevitable. He would try to cut a deal with the DA and give Ramón up. That was inevitable too. *But by then*, Ramón mused as he drove along River Road heading for the George Washington Bridge, *I'll have started a new life in a new country.*

He would get married, settle down, have kids, coach baseball . . .

His body shivered with joy. He tried to remember when his life held so much promise. And then it came to him. It was back in Cuba.

He was just a boy with dreams of fame and fortune. And ten fingers to make it happen.

CHAPTER 28

IT'S NEVER EASY to make sense of a senseless act of terror, but somewhere beneath the rubble, the fear, and the chaos left behind by the 11:59 Bomber, there was a clue that would link us to his madness. All we had to do was find it.

As the sun rose on that calm, clear Sunday morning in July, Kylie and I, along with almost a hundred other detectives assigned to the task force, were poring over all the data that been amassed since the carnage began three days earlier at the Wall Street subway station.

Our mission was two-pronged. The first prong is always our primary objective. Who is this madman? Where is he hiding? And how do we stop him before he takes another human life?

With the clock ticking on a possible third attack, we still couldn't connect the dots. We had his voice on tape saying, "I am going to destroy New York City the way it destroyed my family." We had his image on video strolling through Bloomingdale's, his weapon of mass destruction strapped to his back, and casually leaving it behind to maim or kill dozens of innocent people, whose lives meant nothing to him. We had successfully tracked him on his scooter ride from Fifty-Ninth Street, but we'd lost him in the Bronx. We knew he was using C4, but we had no idea where he was getting it.

For almost three days, a battalion of cops working around the clock had amassed stacks of information on this crazed sociopath, but we had failed to make sense of it.

"All filler, no killer," Kylie muttered.

And then, of course, there was the second prong of our investigation. What was his next target?

We weren't the only ones trying to figure that one out. Millions of rattled New Yorkers were asking the same question.

What is he going to blow up next?

Not only was it the burning issue across Manhattan, Brooklyn, Queens, the Bronx, and Staten Island, but thanks to social media, it had rapidly gone global.

And because there's never a shortage of people ready to exploit the misery of others to make a buck, there were gambling websites where you could bet on where the next mass murder would take place. And there was an ever-growing inventory of 11:59 merch, like the T-shirt of a glassy-eyed drunk sitting on the curb, his bottle of booze tipped to the sky, a giant mushroom cloud rising behind him, and a caption below that read, "I Got Bombed in New York City and Lived to Talk About It." And next to it was a winking smiley face emoji, in case you didn't get the joke.

Most New Yorkers don't find terrorism funny. The fear created by the bomber spread quickly throughout the city. Many people took shelter behind closed doors—if not for the entire day, then for a couple of hours on either side of 11:59, just to play it safe. Countless others left town, by car if they could, but within hours of the Bloomingdale's bomb, every car rental agency in the five boroughs had been picked clean. That left the buses and trains. In normal times, that was the easiest, smartest way to get out of town on a weekend in July. Now it was a last resort, and those who opted in felt that they were playing mass-transit roulette with their lives.

But that still left millions of other New Yorkers, who were not about to miss this perfect summer Sunday. They flipped the bomber a collective middle finger and flocked to the parks and beaches, where they felt safe or at least safe-ish, and they steered clear of confined spaces such as movie theaters, shopping malls, and transportation hubs like Grand Central Terminal or Penn Station.

The news media pounced on them, thrusting microphones and cameras in their faces and asking inane questions like "Aren't you scared to be outside?" Their answers were often more articulate and, no surprise, classically New York.

"No, I ain't scared. Are you?"

By 11:55 that morning, we were no closer to finding the bomber than we had been twenty-four hours earlier. Cates came in, and one by one we looked up from our desks and stared at the countdown clock: 11:56 . . . 11:57 . . . 11:58 . . . 11:59.

I held my breath as the seconds ticked off.

Silence. Silence. Silence.

And then our radios came alive with the two words that are reserved for only the most urgent transmissions.

"Priority Central!"

The cop making that call now had the attention of every person in the department, from the commissioner on down.

"Two-Four Precinct, Riverside Park Post," he said, identifying where he was calling from. "I have a confirmed explosion!"

I looked at Kylie. Riverside Park was barely on our radar. There wasn't anything of significance to blow up there. It didn't make sense.

"The bomb ripped a hole in the side of a Circle Line vessel currently traveling southbound on the Hudson River at approximately Ninety-Sixth Street," the cop reported. "She's still afloat but badly damaged, heavy smoke, and possibly on fire. Numerous persons jumping in the water."

Now it made sense. We'd been waiting for the bomber to hit New York. But this time, his target was a boatload of tourists in the middle of the Hudson.

The cop went on. He was professional, but I could feel the tension in his voice. This might just be the most critical radio call he had ever made. "Get me aviation, harbor, and FDNY vessels to the location! Notify the duty chief, One PP, the bombing task force, and PD on the Jersey side. Get me some help over here."

Kylie and I bolted from our chairs. "The Circle Line!" she bellowed as we ran down the stairs. "How did he manage to plant a device on one of the biggest tourist attractions in the city?" She said it again as we jumped in our car, only this time she peppered it with F-bombs.

I couldn't respond. All I could do was think about how millions of New Yorkers had underestimated him. After a subway station and a department store, they thought they'd be safe if they took to the outdoors. But they were wrong. Nobody was safe. Nobody.

CHAPTER 29

WITHIN MINUTES OF THE explosion, NYPD Harbor had lashed two tugs to the crippled sightseeing boat and was helping it limp to safety. At the same time, police boats from both the New York and Jersey sides of the river, along with civilian-operated pleasure craft, worked together to pull every swimmer out of the water.

The Riverside Park pier on West Seventieth Street was designated as the offload point. It was the perfect location for a massive rescue operation. The pier was wide and extended almost eight hundred feet from shore, which kept both the press and the public at bay.

By the time Kylie and I navigated across town through thick city traffic, the Circle Line vessel, its hull ripped open like a gutted fish and its framework groaning under the strain of a gaping wound, was securely docked. The bomb squad, which had scoured and cleared the pier for explosives, was already on board, searching every corner of the boat for secondary devices.

With TARU filming the entire evacuation, the passengers and crew were quickly offloaded. By some miracle, there were no casualties. The senior tour guide explained why.

"At 11:59, every last passenger was on the port side of the boat, scanning the shoreline. Like almost everyone else in New York, they had been watching the clock, hoping they might be lucky enough to get a glimpse of the next bomb blast as they circled Manhattan," she said. "I guess they did get lucky, because the bomb went off on the starboard side toward the stern. So yeah, we had injuries, but more from people panicking than from the actual blast."

And even though we doubted that our bomber had been on board, everyone who got off that boat was ID'd, photographed, and either taken to a waiting ambulance or questioned by one of the army of detectives who had been called to the scene.

"Kylie! Zach!"

We looked up. It was Nicole Merchant. Like Cheryl, Nicole is a department therapist, and for the past four days she had been working overtime. First the Wall Street station, then Bloomingdale's, and now she was on the front lines of the latest bombing.

"Nicole," Kylie said, "we've got to stop meeting like this."

"If it's any consolation, there were no fatalities," Merchant said. "But there are going to be a lot of scars. Some of these people are in shock, a few of them are Iraq War vets who are going through flashbacks, but every single person I've talked to has one thing in common: anticipatory anxiety. These bombings are taking their toll. And I'm not talking physical damage. That boat over there will go into dry dock and come out good as new in a few months. But these people aren't that easy to fix. They want to know why this is happening and when are we going to catch this lunatic." Merchant shook her head. "Sorry, I know you guys are working day and night. It's just that . . ."

She gave Kylie a quick hug. "We should all get back to work. I'll see you . . ." She stopped. "Strike that! Let's just go with, *Be safe*, and like you said, we've got to stop meeting like this."

Nicole turned and went back to work, but her words hung in the air. Anticipatory anxiety. The bomber was taking a bigger toll than most people realized.

As the rescue operation hit its stride, the NYPD brass, the mayor, and the governor arrived. There was little they could do that was hands-on. Their mission was more of a show of solidarity, a reassuring signal across departmental and political party lines that this assault on the people of New York was of the highest priority for the city's leadership.

And then another person showed up on the scene. Lieutenant Pete Peterson, our blowhard liaison to the press, and the man least likely to tear himself away from a leisurely Sunday unless there was something in it for him.

"Jesus!" Kylie said as Peterson crossed the yellow police tape and made his way down the pier toward the boat. "Look who he's got with him."

It was Nico Patrakis. I felt for Nico. He had lost his daughter, his wife, and his mother. But now that he'd offered a hundred-thousand-dollar reward and established his own rules of vigilante justice, his actions were not only hampering our investigation, they were bordering on criminal activity. Now he was back at another crime scene, and both he and Peterson had their phones in front of them, recording every detail.

"I can't believe that idiot," Kylie said, gaping at Peterson. "He's not only sleeping with the enemy, he's helping them break the law!"

We started moving toward the two of them, but before we could get there, Captain Cates stormed across the pier and intercepted them.

We backed off as Cates took command of the situation. We couldn't hear a word, but her demeanor with Nico was calm, concerned, yet unquestionably authoritative. He clearly appreciated the courtesy. Instead of barking back, which seemed to be his default setting when dealing with cops, he nodded graciously and walked back behind the tape, where he was pounced on by the media.

Then Cates turned her attention to Peterson. He had escorted a civilian into her crime scene without permission, and apparently without fear of repercussion. He had strolled casually past the yellow tape with his unauthorized plus-one as if his mother's state senate seat gave him total diplomatic immunity. It was a major breach, and he was about to find out that Captain Delia Cates was the wrong bear to poke.

Kylie and I had no idea what she said to Peterson, but from his body language during the harangue, and by the way he slunk off the pier, he'd think twice before he screwed with her again.

Cates strode toward us. "Lieutenant Peterson has assured me that every picture he took with his personal cell phone will be turned over to the case file and will not be released to the public media."

"Tough break for him," Kylie said, "because I heard that the press is paying beaucoup bucks for exclusive photos of an 11:59 Bomber crime scene."

Cates cracked a smile, but before she could respond, a squad car rolled down the pier, and Chief of Detectives Doyle got out.

"We just got a call from the chief of Weehawken PD," Doyle said to the three of us. "One of their detectives has a witness who saw someone paddle across the river and back again in the middle of the night. It's possible he delivered the bomb from the Jersey side and planted it out of sight and out of earshot of the security team that was guarding the boat on the dock in New York."

I looked at Kylie. We didn't say a word, but I knew that our minds were in sync. Crossing the Hudson to plant a bomb on a boat docked in New York sounded exactly like the kind of thing our bomber would do.

Cates was on the same page. "This could be the break we've been waiting for," she said to us. "Get on it."

"We're on the way," I said. Kylie and I turned and were about to double-time to our car.

"Detectives!" Doyle said. "Where are you going?"

We pulled up short.

"Jersey," Kylie said.

"Jersey's that way," Doyle said, pointing across the river as a Harbor Patrol launch pulled up to the pier. "Move it. Your ship just came in."

CHAPTER 30

"**WELCOME ABOARD,**" the captain of the launch said as Kylie and I stepped off the pier and onto the deck of the twin-diesel response boat. "Joe Keegan. That's my partner, David Porter. We're your ride. Wherever you want to go. For as long as you need us."

He didn't have to add 'compliments of the chief of D's,' but I'd bet the orders to put this boat at our disposal came directly from Harlan Doyle. I'd also bet that we didn't wind up with Keegan and Porter by chance. They must have been handpicked by the chief and were probably two of the top cops in the fleet.

"We'll be in Weehawken in about six minutes," Keegan said, handing us each a life vest. "Anything you need, just ask."

Kylie has never needed an invitation to ask questions, and I wouldn't have been surprised if she spent the entire six minutes asking things like what the weather was like last night, how bright was the moon, or how long would it take for someone to cross the river by paddleboard in the middle of the night, and were there any cameras anywhere that might have picked him up.

But she didn't say a word. As we pulled away from the dock, she quietly stepped to the front of the boat and stared at the water, the life vest dangling from one hand.

I caught her eye, and she gave me a look that I don't see often, but when I do, I totally respect it.

Give me some space. I'm wrestling with my demons.

I had no doubt which demon she was wrestling with. Spence. The man whose life she had saved more than once, the man who had disappeared two years ago, married another woman while he was still married to Kylie, was widowed, publicly threatened to kill Preston Balfour, was later found standing over Balfour's body with the murder weapon in his hand, and who, for better or for worse, was still her lawfully wedded husband.

That demon.

And she had six minutes to sort it all out.

It's the nature of the job. When you're the lead team assigned to solve the biggest mass murder case to hit New York City in decades, there's no time to grapple with your own personal problems. Kylie and I were up against a clock. Stop the 11:59 Bomber before he kills again.

I studied my partner as she stood in the bow, lost in her own silent world. Except for a gentle breeze from the Hudson tousling her hair, she was motionless. But I knew that beneath that stoic exterior, her brain was racing the same way she drives—dodging between options, swerving around doubts, and gunning toward a resolution.

I stepped away and gave her space. Then it struck me. If she could do it, why couldn't I? I decided to take the five minutes I had left to wrestle with my own demon.

Sylviane.

My feelings about her had been ping-ponging inside my head since the minute I learned that she was the mother of my child. I had loved her once, but now all I could feel was rage. Not only had she kept my son a secret from me, but she'd made a conscious decision to take that secret to the grave.

And now, twelve years after her death, not only was my life thrown into chaos, but Cheryl's was as well. Cheryl and I had just reached the stage of our relationship where we were quietly thinking about the next step. Neither of us had spoken the *M* word, but clearly marriage was the elephant in the room. And then suddenly, Cheryl had to deal with the fact that the man she was planning a life with just added a teenage son to the equation.

I leaned against the railing of the boat, closed my eyes, and inhaled deeply, trying to follow the simple breathing exercise Cheryl had taught me—four seconds in, hold for four, then let it out slowly for another four.

In theory, if you focus on your breath, you can ease into a state of meditation, but I was about as close to Zen as a monkey on speed.

I shut my eyes tighter and tried doing my breathing exercise one more time. Four seconds in, hold for four, then let it out slowly for another four. But as I exhaled, instead of tranquility, all I could feel was the incessant pull of the job.

I was about to give it one more try when the rumble of the engines cut to a hum, and I felt the boat settle into a gentle coast as Captain Keegan eased off the throttle.

I opened my eyes. And as I watched the Jersey shoreline draw closer, my cop brain kicked into overdrive, and the instant replay of three dead women on a bloodied subway platform pulled me back into the moment.

I had a killer to catch. My personal demons would have to wait.

CHAPTER 31

TWO COPS FROM WEEHAWKEN PD met us at the dock. Art Husted was the detective who found the witness. His boss, Captain Mark Hellinger, tagged along. Not because there was anything he could add. His role was strictly political. The 11:59 Bomber was the most wanted criminal in a city of nine million people. If Husted's witness helped us crack the case, a lot of the limelight would shine on Weehawken. Hellinger was there to take notes for the chief of police, the mayor, and probably the state house.

I doubted that he'd have anything exciting to report. Big cases like this one get a lot of unsolicited help from other law enforcement agencies. Most of them fizzle out fast. That's because when a well-meaning cop stumbles on something that sounds promising, instead of taking the time to dig deeper, they call us. Kylie and I show up, start asking the tough questions, and usually wind up shooting the cop's hypothesis full of holes.

It's all part of the grind of a homicide investigation.

I got right to it. "Tell us about your witness," I said to Husted.

"His name is Li Qiang Ngo, but everybody calls him Leo. He used to wait tables in a local Chinese restaurant, so I've known him since I was a kid. He retired about twenty years ago. Loves to fish. He sells what he catches to the locals. If they can't afford it, he lowers the price until they can. He's well into his eighties, spends a lot of time here in the park, but he keeps to himself, so most people barely notice him. But Leo sees and hears everything. And if he sees something dicey, he lets me know about it."

I couldn't help smiling. "You have an eighty-year-old CI?" I said.

"He's closer to ninety than to eighty," Husted said. "But he's definitely got all his marbles. So when Leo says he saw something, I pay attention. Anyway, as soon as I heard about the explosion, I shot right down here. I thought they might be ferrying the wounded over to the hospitals on our side. Also, I wanted to film everybody who showed up, on the off chance that the perp might come here to get a look at his handiwork. I'll send you the footage."

"Good thinking," I said. "Thanks."

I glanced over at Kylie. This guy was sharp. My attitude shifted from "expecting zilch" to "maybe he's onto something."

"The explosion drew a huge crowd," Husted told us. "It was like 9/11 all over again. Pretty upsetting. And then I see Leo. He gives me a nod, and I pull up on the hill. Everybody is looking toward the city. Leo jumps in the back of my car and tells me he saw a guy paddleboard over to the New York side at about three a.m. I'll let him give you the details, but it sounded credible, or I wouldn't have called."

"Let's go talk to him," I said.

"He's waiting for us in the Chart House restaurant," Husted said, pointing at the building fifty feet from where we had docked. "Leo has been my eyes and ears for years. He doesn't want people seeing him going in and out of a police station, so we always meet off campus. As soon as he told me what he saw, I called my friend Hans Nielsen, the general manager of the restaurant, and asked if he could find a quiet space for us to talk to Leo. And if I know Hans, he's got Leo sitting in a cozy little spot, and the old man is eating like the emperor of China."

The four of us entered the Chart House. The place was packed, and as soon as we stepped into the vast dining room, it was obvious why. Dappled sunlight shone through a wall of high windows, and a spectacular view of the Hudson River unfolded before us, framing the New York City skyline like a postcard.

"Worth the trip to Jersey," I said.

"And the food gives the view a run for its money," Husted added.

Before we could even get close to the hostess's station, a tall, distinguished man with an accommodating smile approached us.

"Hans Nielsen," he said, leading us away from the main dining room and toward a flight of stairs. "Your table is right this way."

He escorted us to a small private dining room, where our witness was waiting. As soon as we entered, Leo stood up. Husted had said he was close to ninety, but he could have passed for sixty.

"Thank you for lunch, Mr. Nielsen," Leo said with a slight bow. "The mac nut mahi and mango sticky rice was excellent. I give you five stars on Yelp."

The two men laughed. Leo had obviously been a guest of the management before.

"Anytime, Leo," Nielsen said, and left the room.

Husted introduced us, and Leo got down to business.

"This morning, almost three o'clock, I see car park on Henley Place," he said. "Driver inflates paddleboard, straps dry bag to his back, takes fishing pole, pushes board into water, and gets on. He's no good."

"What do you mean 'no good'?" Kylie said.

"Clumsy. Almost fall off board. I think why is amateur fishing in Hudson in middle of the night?"

"Did he see you?"

Leo smiled. "Nobody see Leo unless Leo want to be seen."

"Could you see where he paddled to?"

"He went straight, straight, straight, and then too dark to see."

"What do you mean, 'straight, straight, straight'?"

"Come, look," Leo said, holding up his cell phone. It was opened to Google Maps.

"Here is Henley Place, where he park his car," Leo said, pointing to the map. "Here is where he goes in water. Then he goes in straight line, and then he disappear in middle of river."

Leo stopped to let us take it all in. But we were way ahead of him.

"And where does he wind up if he keeps going straight?" Kylie said.

Leo smiled at Husted and gave a nod of approval. He appreciated a smart cop.

He zoomed out of the map till we could see the New York side of the river. "Straight, straight, straight take him here."

He held up the phone so we could get a closer look. *Here* was Pier 83 at West Forty-Second Street—home of the Circle Line sightseeing boats.

I looked up at Husted. His encouraging nod back at me was silent copspeak for *Wait. It gets better.*

"You said he left his car on Henley Place," I said to Leo. "Did you see him come back?"

"He come back four thirty. No fish. No surprise. He had cheap piece-of-crap freshwater pole—too small for Hudson River. I think this man fishy, but he is not real fisherman. We talk maybe a minute; then he say he has to pee, so goodbye. I go home. Then when boat have explosion, I tell detective what I see. Get free lunch. That's all."

"What did he look like?" I asked.

"Tall like you. Spanish—maybe Puerto Rican, maybe Mexican. I don't know."

"Do you think you could describe him to a sketch artist?"

"Yes. Brown skin, look like Spanish person, talk like Spanish person."

It's called the cross-race effect. People have trouble seeing facial nuances in races other than their own.

I gave it one more shot. "Was there anything about his face like a scar, or a tattoo, or anything that was unusual or different from other Spanish faces?"

"No. Regular Spanish face."

"Okay," I said. "Thanks."

"But hand," Leo said. "Right hand. Very different."

"What do you mean?"

Leo held up his right hand, pressing his thumb and index finger against his palm so all we could see were the remaining three fingers.

"Right hand only have three fingers—two missing."

I looked at Kylie. It felt like we had hit the jackpot. I turned back to Leo.

"Three fingers?" I said. "Are you sure?"

Leo gave me a benevolent smile, no doubt deciding that I wasn't nearly as smart as my partner.

"Yes, Detective. I am very sure," he said. "Man with three fingers stick out like sore thumb."

CHAPTER 32

BY LATE AFTERNOON, we had a sketch of the three a.m. paddleboarder. A patient and talented police artist can do wonders to jog a witness's memory, and the final drawing was a lot more detailed than Leo's original description. In addition to the suspect's face, we got a drawing of his right hand. It wasn't pretty, and I wondered if the missing fingers were brutal reminders of the occupational hazards of his profession.

We circulated the sketches to the task force, and then Kylie and I started searching databases. You'd think it would be easy enough to find a three-fingered perp. You'd be wrong. For starters, even though Leo was positive our suspect had two missing fingers, we opted to cast a wider net, so we put "missing one or more fingers" in the search criteria.

Add to that the fact that every single one of our databases has millions of records, which meant that no matter how narrow the parameters, we were going to get a staggering number of hits. I don't know how many people in the criminal universe are shy a digit, but even if it's just a fraction of 1 percent, that still would leave us with thousands of records to sift through.

The sheer volume of data at our command is a testimony to the far-reaching technical capabilities of modern police work. By the same token, it was daunting to realize how labor-intensive it would be to figure out if Leo's lead was even valid.

Around nine p.m., with another long night of very little sleep ahead of me, I got a call from Sergeant St. Claire at the desk.

"There's some wise-ass kid down here to see you and MacDonald," he said.

"What makes you think he's a wise-ass?"

"He said his name was Martin Scorsese."

"Tell him that after all these years, *Goodfellas* is still his best movie, but *The King of Comedy* is a vastly underrated masterpiece."

"No can do, Zach. *Goodfellas* is in the top five, but *Mean Streets* is epic."

"I wish I had time to set you straight, Sean, but there's a bomber on the loose, so just send the kid to the squad room."

In less than thirty seconds, Martin Scorsese, who also goes by the name Theo Wilkins, came bounding upstairs, his face an amalgam of boyish enthusiasm and grown-ass-man determination.

"Man, am I glad you guys are still here," he said.

"We're in a rut," I said. "We're here a lot. Where've you been?"

"Okay, yesterday after I left you at the lab, I went straight to the New York Public Library."

"Which branch?" Kylie said.

"The main one. Forty-Second and Fifth. I took a selfie with one of the big marble lions outside. Did you know they have names?"

Kylie ignored the question. "Did *you* know that those lions and that building could be a priority target for the bomber?"

"Yeah, I know. But there were cops everywhere. I felt totally safe."

"So did the people on the Circle Line, and you saw what happened to them," Kylie said.

Theo shook his head. He hadn't tracked us down so he could get a lecture on his blissful disregard for a serial killer on the loose. He took a deep breath and leveled a steely gaze at Kylie.

"Patience and Fortitude," he said, his voice filled with the gravitas of a seasoned philosopher.

"Patience?" Kylie shot back. "That ship sailed two bombs ago! Oh, and fortitude? You think I need a pep talk from you on how to do my job?"

"Calm down, Detective," Theo said, a smug grin spreading across his face. "Patience and Fortitude are the names of those two lions."

Kylie put her hand over her mouth, but she couldn't hide the smirk. The kid was good, and he knew it. She tossed me a look that said, *Go ahead, you deal with him.*

"All right, let's get back on track here," I said. "What was at the library?"

Theo perked. "Access to foreign newspapers. It's amazing what they have in print, on microfilm, online—"

"Foreign like where?" Kylie said, gearing up for round two. "Someplace fun?"

He shrugged. "More squalor than fun."

"Jesus," she said. "What is it about squalor that fascinates documentarians?"

"No, no, no. I'm not working on a film," he said. "I'm on a mission."

"A *mission*?" she said, denigrating the word as she said it. "And what's that?"

And then, with the artistry of an eighteen-year-old Martin Scorsese, Theo completely turned the conversation inside out and sideways.

"I'm on a mission to get Spence out of jail," he said, the enthusiasm returning to his face, his voice, his very core. "He didn't do it, Kylie. And I know who did."

CHAPTER 33

THEO IS A DREAMER. His documentaries may be based in reality, but his eighteen-year-old head and heart are in la-la land.

"*You* know who killed Preston Balfour," Kylie said, her tone rife with doubt.

"Well, I can't *prove* it," Theo said, his bravado barely dampened. He grinned and added, "Yet."

Kylie rolled her eyes, and we moved the conversation to an interview room. As soon as the door was shut, she gave Theo her least skeptical smile and said, "Go ahead. Enlighten us."

He opened his laptop. A photo of a man popped up on the screen. He was about forty, wearing medical scrubs. A girl, about six, was sitting on his lap. They both had deep-olive skin and rich, dark coffee-brown eyes. Their features, especially their smiles, were identical.

"His name is Dr. Kunal Sarin," Theo said. "That's his daughter, Kavya. She had nothing to do with it. She's just in the picture."

"And what makes you think Dr. Sarin murdered Balfour?" Kylie asked.

"He had motive, means, and opportunity. Plus, I've got forensics."

"*Forensics?*" Kylie said. "You mean like in the cop shows? Wow! This is getting exciting."

"Let's start with motive," Theo said, ignoring the dig. "Sarin grew up in a dirt-poor neighborhood in Mumbai. Remember the kid in *Slumdog Millionaire*? Sarin's life was like that. But he pulled himself up, went to college, and graduated from medical school at the top of his class. He could have had a high-paying job at any hospital anywhere, but no, he decided to go back to the people he was raised with. He takes a job in this clinic. It's a total shithole—overcrowded, underfunded, the equipment is outdated—but for tens of thousands of people, it's their only hope. Little by little, he started to make a difference."

Dr. Sarin sounded more like a saint than a killer, but I didn't want to interrupt. Theo can't just tell a straight story. Even if he's recounting his latest trip to Starbucks, he has to make it cinematic.

"One night, Sarin is doing emergency surgery on a factory worker who got tangled up with a piece of heavy machinery," Theo said, lowering his voice for dramatic effect, "when—*pfft*—the power goes out! It happens at the clinic all the time. They have a backup generator, but this time it fails. Sarin and his team try to work by flashlight, manually pumping oxygen, but without power, all the life-support systems shut down, and the patient dies.

"Sarin is crushed. It's bad enough to lose a patient on the operating table, but when the patient dies because the hospital's infrastructure is crumbling, it's devastating. That night, Sarin went home and told his wife it was a losing battle. He was ready to give up and settle for one of those cushy jobs in a real hospital. I can only imagine what a heartbreaking scene that was. But, of course, it wasn't in the movie."

"What movie?" Kylie snapped.

"Hey, give me a minute, will ya? I'm trying to establish motive here. I'll get to it."

Kylie looked at her watch. "No rush, kid. We're here all night."

"Now, where was I?" Theo said with the inflection of a world-class ballbuster. "Oh, yeah . . . in the *movie*, when the factory worker dies, the doc completely falls apart. He leaves the clinic, goes to a bar, gets shit-faced, and winds up getting arrested on a drunk-driving charge. He spends the night in jail, and by the time his wife bails him out, he's decided to give up medicine. But she convinces him to keep going. It's his mission.

"Cut to a few months later. A man comes into the clinic with his wife and daughter. The wife has been vomiting for days. Sarin treats her; it's an easy fix. But as the family is leaving, he spots a lump on the little girl's neck. He examines her. It turns out to be a cancerous tumor on her thyroid. He tells the parents that their daughter needs surgery immediately. But the father balks. Money is tight. Even in this low-rent clinic, it's way out of this guy's budget. Sarin says the girl can't wait, and offers to do it for free.

"During the surgery, the power goes out again. The backup generator kicks in, sputters, and shuts down. Once again Sarin is trying to save someone's life with nothing more than a flashlight and a prayer. But this time, it's different. The girl's father is an electrician. He races to the rooftop where the generator is, and while the medical team in the OR is doing all they can to keep the kid alive, he finds the problem, fixes it, and Sarin finishes the operation successfully.

"The next day when the dust has settled, Sarin has an idea. There are a lot of people who can't even afford the bare-bones health care they need, so they never even come to the clinic to be examined. But what if, instead of paying in cash, they could pay with services? Barter. He starts contacting the tradesmen in the community—plumbers, masons, carpenters. He offers to give their families the medical expertise they need in exchange for their skills in upgrading the infrastructure. Within a year, Sarin has turned the hospital around, one tradesman at a time."

"Stop!" Kylie said. "Where the hell did you get all this detailed information? And don't tell us it was the library."

"Well, some of it came from the library," Theo said, "but most of it I got from watching the movie."

"Oh, right," she said. "The *movie* again. Is this the part where you finally tell us what movie you're talking about?"

"It's called *The Healing Exchange*. It's the story of Dr. Kunal Sarin and the Niramaya Clinic in the slums of Dharavi in Mumbai, India," Theo said.

He paused because that's what gifted storytellers do when they have your undivided attention. Finally, he gave us the kicker.

"And it was written, produced, directed—*and stolen from Dr. Kunal Sarin*—by the late Preston Balfour."

He flashed us a triumphant smile. "And there you have it, ladies and gentlemen. The motive."

CHAPTER 34

NEITHER KYLIE NOR I said a word. It was a lot to process, and Theo knew it. He folded his arms across his chest and waited.

I finally broke the silence. "I remember at the screening, you told me that Balfour's first two movies tanked but his third one made money. Is this film about Dr. Sarin the one?"

Theo nodded. "Yeah. The critics were kind of lukewarm on it, but audiences liked it. It earned out enough for Shelley Trager and his partners to put up the money for *Last Call in Barbados*."

"And Balfour stole Dr. Sarin's story the same way he stole Spence's?"

"The exact same MO," Theo said. "He met Sarin on a train from Delhi to Mumbai, struck up a conversation, and knew right away that the doc's story had the potential to be movie gold. After that, he latched on to Sarin, hung around the clinic for weeks on end until he had a solid outline for the screenplay. Then he started dicking around with it, changing the facts, twisting the narrative, distorting the truth. It wasn't enough that Sarin was a hero, a model husband and father, a dedicated doctor. Balfour had to give him a tragic flaw."

"Why?" I said.

"Because tragic flaws sell movie tickets. A character who is too perfect is unrelatable. But give him an Achilles' heel, and audiences invest in him. Think about it. What's Superman without kryptonite? So Balfour decided that Sarin's kryptonite would be booze. Do you remember I told you that the night the factory worker died, Sarin wound up in jail on a DWI?"

"It's kind of hard to forget," Kylie said.

"Exactly. But it's all Hollywood bullshit. The real Dr. Sarin doesn't drink. Not now. Not then. Not ever," Theo said. "But in the film, Balfour turned Sarin into a full-blown alcoholic, performing surgeries while drunk, in and out of rehabs, using hospital funds to feed his addiction—which is totally ridiculous, because you don't have to steal from your employer to buy a bottle of booze. Even at the end of the movie, where Sarin has turned the hospital around, Balfour leaves you with the feeling that his recovery is rocky and his next bender is right around the corner."

"Why would Balfour—"

Theo didn't wait for me to finish asking the question.

"Because he's a scumbag who steals people's stories and dramatizes them for the sole purpose of getting as many asses in movie theater seats as he can. And he doesn't give a flying f—"

"Calm down," I said.

Theo exhaled slowly and then took several deep breaths.

"Sorry," he said, his emotions reined back in. "It just kills me how guys like Balfour don't care how many lives they destroy to get to the top. He knew he could make more money if he took the story of a gifted surgeon and added a Jekyll-and-Hyde spin. He painted a picture of Sarin as a reckless alcoholic, and that's the image that stuck in people's minds. And Sarin's not the only one who got hurt. Once that movie came out, almost every major benefactor cut ties with the Niramaya Clinic."

"You didn't get all that background information from just screening the movie," I said.

"Of course not. I talked to people in the industry who worked on Balfour's films. Now that he's dead, hundreds of them have opened up on social media about how much they hated him. And he's the cadaver of the day on half a dozen true-crime podcasts. He screwed a lot of people, Zach, but nobody suffered more than Dr. Sarin. The man has been disgraced."

He went back to his laptop. "My first thought was that maybe Sarin hired someone to kill Balfour," Theo said, tapping on the keyboard. "But then I found this."

He clicked on a link, and a head shot of Dr. Kunal Sarin popped up. Below him was a headline that said, "Fund the Fight: A Campaign to Sustain Community Health."

"Sarin is doing his best to fight back," Theo said.

"What do you mean, 'doing his best'?" I said.

"Think about it. People saw a movie where Sarin is a hopeless drunk. Now he's on a fundraising tour, saying, 'Hey, guys, that director is full of shit. I'm not really an alcoholic. Any money you give me really will go to the hospital. Trust me.'"

"Tough sell," Kylie said. "Especially when there are dozens of other good causes that don't have the stigma attached."

"I know, but that didn't stop Sarin. Right now he's on a tour across the US and Canada to restore his good name and to raise money for the clinic. And he's pulling out all the stops—putting on a major dog-and-pony show to attract big crowds. Remember the little girl with the thyroid cancer—the one who almost died on the table during the power failure?"

"Who could forget that touching cinematic moment when her father repaired the generator and started the whole concept of tradespeople bartering their services for health care?" Kylie said, her voice thick with exasperation. "This better be going somewhere, Theo."

"Relax, I'm getting there. Anyway, her name is Priya Sharma. She's fourteen now, a brilliant student with her heart set on going to medical school, and she credits Dr. Sarin with inspiring her to become a physician so she can go back and help her community. She's on this tour with Sarin. I caught a couple of her videos on YouTube, and let me tell you, the kid is a total charmer, and the donations are, like, five times higher than Sarin would ever get on his—"

"Theo!" Kylie snapped. "We don't have time for the entire epic production! Land the fucking plane."

"Fine! The first stop on Dr. Sarin's tour was Thursday night in the city with the largest Indian population in the United States, which, in case you're not up on the latest census data, is . . ." He paused, trilled his tongue dramatically, and unleashed a loud verbal drumroll. "Right here in Gotham."

"Jesus," Kylie said. "You're telling us Sarin was in New York the night Balfour was murdered."

"Not just in New York, but at the Triangle Loft on Hudson Street, which is less than two miles from Balfour's apartment."

CHAPTER 35

"THEO," KYLIE SAID CALMLY, "you know for a *fact* that this Dr. Sarin from India was a ten-minute cab ride from Balfour's apartment on the night of the murder."

"Yeah, he was. Really," Theo said.

"Are you *sure*?"

"Positive. I triple-checked. At seven p.m., he spoke to about a hundred and fifty people, many of them from the Indian community. He was there for a couple of hours, but he still had plenty of time to slip out quietly and pay Balfour a visit. Would you like to hear my take on how it went down?"

"You're on a roll," I said. "Keep going."

"Sarin never planned to kill Balfour," Theo said. "I think he was in New York, knew where Balfour lived, and went there in the hopes of . . . I don't know . . . getting him to make some kind of public retraction of all the lies. Balfour told him to fuck off, Sarin snapped, grabbed the kitchen knife, and that's when Spence walked in."

"Well, thank you for that, Detective Wilkins," I said, actually impressed with his thinking.

"Also, don't forget that Sarin had just flown over from India," Theo said. "That's why there were traces of *Sida cordifolia* in the blood sample that Chuck Dryden showed us. I told you I had forensics."

"Whoa, whoa, whoa," I said. "Slow down, kid. A billion and a half people live in India. Deciding that the traces of *Sida cordifolia* Chuck found at the crime scene belong to Sarin is not forensics. It's wishful thinking. The DA only deals in hard, cold, irrefutable facts."

"Okay, but still, if your job is to prove that the case was investigated fair and square, doesn't all this make it sound like there might be another viable suspect out there?"

"To you, maybe," I said. "But you just told us that hundreds of people hated Balfour. And the first thing a prosecutor will say to that is, 'That may be true, but how many of those people were found in the room with him, with the murder weapon in hand?'"

"So none of this helps?"

"Not in court," Kylie said, "but it gives us a path we can explore in our investigation. The first thing we can do is talk to Selma Kaplan at the DA's office and tell her we'd like to show Spence a photo array to see if he can identify Dr. Sarin."

"He can't," Theo said. "I already showed him the picture."

I could see the hope drain from Kylie's body. "You . . . you *showed* Spence the picture?" she said. "The one with Sarin holding the kid?"

"Yeah. I went to see him at Rikers this afternoon. He said it might be the guy he wrestled with in Balfour's apartment, but he's really not sure. I knew you were busy, so I thought I'd be saving you time. Why? What's wrong with that?"

"*Everything* is wrong with that! There's a procedure to asking a witness to identify someone. We—and by that, I mean sworn officers of the law—have to show the witness pictures of six people, same general physical description, all of them poker-faced, no expressions, not smiling at the camera, and definitely not sitting there with a sweet little girl on their lap."

"So I screwed up. We can find another picture of Sarin, and you can show it to Spence with five other guys."

"We can't."

"Why not?"

"Because once you show somebody a picture and they don't positively identify it, you can't go back and say, 'Remember that guy we already showed you? Here—try again.' You only get one shot, Theo. You took that shot, and it's over. At this point, Spence could swear on his mother's life that Sarin is the killer, but it would be inadmissible."

"Okay, so why don't you question Dr. Sarin? He's on a six-city tour. Philadelphia, Washington . . . hold on." His fingers flitted across the keyboard as he kept talking. "And . . . sent! I emailed you his schedule. Tomorrow, he'll be in Chicago. You can fly there, and—"

"Theo!" Kylie said, cutting him off. "Sarin may be our guy, but once we've got a tainted identification procedure, the DA's office is not going to authorize us to take a bus to Jersey to question him."

She buried her face in her hands for a solid fifteen seconds. When she removed them, her usual badass-cop, I-got-this-under-control look was gone, replaced by a vacant, dry-eyed stare that radiated sadness and defeat.

Theo has loved and admired Kylie ever since he was a kid of about six. I'm sure he's never seen her this low, and he was crushed that he was the cause of it.

"I'm sorry, Kylie," he said. "I'll make it up to you."

"Oh, God, no!" she said. "That means you're going to do something. I know you mean well, but this is a police investigation. You cannot do anything. You cannot be a part of it. You hear that?"

"I hear it," Theo said, "but I don't understand it. So the DA won't pay your way to Chicago. I've got money. I'll pay for it. Why do you keep saying you won't go?"

"I didn't say '*won't* go.' I said, '*can't* go.' Without the DA's approval, wherever I go, I have zero authority as a cop. All I am is a desperate wife trying to muddy her husband's case by creating reasonable doubt."

"That sucks," Theo said.

"Well, I'm glad that you and I finally agree on something." She checked the time on her phone. "Now, if you'll excuse us, Zach and I have to find a madman who is systematically blowing this city into little pieces, and he's not going to stop until we catch him."

She stormed out of the interview, leaving Theo sitting there, shell-shocked and crestfallen.

There was nothing I could say or do to make him feel any better, so I just nodded at him, said, "I'll catch up with you later," and followed Kylie out the door.

"I can't believe it," she said when we got to our desks. "He may be onto something with this Dr. Sarin guy, but he has completely destroyed our chances of getting Spence to ID him."

"He's a kid," I said. "He meant well. He just didn't know the ground rules. He made a mistake."

"And that mistake is going to keep Spence locked up," she said.

"Maybe for a few more days or a week," I said. "But if Sarin did kill Balfour, you and I will nail him."

"How, Zach?" she snapped. "How?"

I didn't have an answer, so I kind of shrugged and said, "Patience and fortitude, Kylie. Patience and fortitude."

CHAPTER 36

ONCE AGAIN RAMÓN couldn't sleep.

It wasn't just that he had two bombs stashed under his bed. Funny how fast you could get used to shit like that.

It was the damn notebook he'd found that was haunting him. *Notebook* was putting it mildly. It was made in Italy, bound in rich dark-brown leather, with a broad strap across the front that wasn't intended to keep people out. It was simply there to make a statement. Gentleman's journal.

It was Arthur's, of course. Arthur was a Wall Street guy. He worked in a world where billions of dollars could be made or lost in a heartbeat. He knew better than most people that the ability to execute a trade milliseconds faster than your competitor was the ultimate advantage. His very livelihood depended on cutting-edge technology.

But he didn't trust it to be part of his personal life.

"If it's on a computer, if it's in the cloud, if it's in binary code, it can be hacked," he had told Ramón. "The only way to keep your private stuff private is to write it down on paper and hide it in a secret spot. That way, even if the Russian Mafia and the Chinese cyberpunks break into your house, you still have time to eat it."

It took a while, but Ramón had finally found Arthur's secret spot. The notebook was organized, detailed, and, of course, extremely thorough. The tome had a title: *Operation 11:59*.

Ramón instinctively knew that it wasn't an arbitrary number. There was always a method to Arthur's madness, and when he finally explained the significance behind that exact time, it was all Ramón could do to keep himself from saying, "You are one sick fuck."

The first section was filled with surveillance data. Arthur's notes showed that he'd considered half a dozen other subway stations before deciding which one to target. Every station had a list of pros and cons. Ultimately, one stood out. "Neglected work shed. Perfect!" he'd written on the page for the Wall Street station. And he'd been right.

Ramón knew that Arthur had scouted every location, analyzed every scenario, even created a damage-inflicted-to-risk-taken algorithm, but this thick, dog-eared Bible was beyond anything he could possibly have imagined.

He thumbed through schematics of bombs and recipes for destruction that looked as if they'd been lifted from *The Anarchist's Cookbook*. He flipped through the pages until he found the section he'd been looking for: TARGETS.

One of the first questions Ramón had asked after he agreed to be Arthur's instrument of death was, "How many bombs are we talking about?"

"Not too many," was the vague answer. Eventually, Arthur suggested that five or six might be enough to bring the city to its knees.

But the hit list in the notebook told a different story. It included Yankee Stadium, Radio City Music Hall, the Roosevelt Island tram, the Cloisters in Washington Heights, Lincoln Center, the Bronx Botanical Garden, and twenty-four more iconic locations, all carefully divided into categories: transportation, commerce, tourism, cultural, sports and entertainment, medical, and environmental.

Thirty targets in all, every one of them a mecca for tourists and a beloved landmark for New Yorkers. Ramón took pictures of every page in that section and put the notebook back where he'd found it.

Now, as dawn broke on the day he was scheduled to plant the next bomb, at the Museum of Natural History, he thought about the run-in he'd had with Arthur last night. Hell, it wasn't a run-in; it was a screaming match.

Arthur wanted him to plant the bomb in the Milstein Hall of Ocean Life so it could destroy the museum's renowned blue whale, suspended high above the exhibit floor.

"No," Ramón stated.

"*No?*" Arthur snapped. "You're a messenger. I don't remember giving you a vote."

"A *messenger?*" Ramón repeated. "That's not what you called me when you recruited me to put my ass on the line and avenge the death of your parents. Back then you reminded me that they gave me a job, a future, a life. You said I had become a brother to you. Well, listen to me, *brother*. I made three scouting trips to the museum. That whale is the most popular attraction in the whole damn place, and that room is always packed with kids."

"Collateral damage," Arthur said. "It goes with the mission."

"Bullshit! A bomb is a bomb, Arthur. You want an explosion to make your point? I can do that. But I'll be damned if I'm gonna bring ten tons of steel and fiberglass crashing down on a roomful of innocent children."

Arthur's face softened and slowly relaxed into a smile that smacked more of arrogance than of amusement. He ambled to the mahogany-and-marble wet bar and poured two glasses of wine. "Fine," he said, handing one to Ramón. "I had no idea you were one of those save-the-whales types. How do you feel about dinosaurs?"

"There are about a hundred of them on the fourth floor," Ramón said.

"So when I dial the phone number at 11:59 tomorrow morning, that's where the bomb will be?"

"Yes."

"Well, then, *brother*," Arthur said, raising his glass, "problem averted."

They drank, smiling at each other as the rift between them deepened.

CHAPTER 37

RAMÓN CAUGHT THE 8:24 from Bayside to Penn Station. It was a typical Monday-morning commute. Hundreds of strangers on a train, their faces buried in newspapers or smartphones, their minds and hearts wrapped in their little cocoons of silence and anonymity.

Ramón glanced at a few of them. No one glanced back. He checked the Scotiabank app on his phone and smiled. He had opened the account shortly after he started working for Arthur's parents.

"I love America," Stefan Harmati had told him. "But it's the same wherever you live—once they know how much money you make, they want as much as they can get."

Ramón didn't have to ask who *they* were. He came from a country where *they* had tortured him, *they* had mutilated him, and *they* would have murdered him if he hadn't been smart enough to escape.

"That's why Anna and I are in a cash business," Stefan had told him. "Cash you can hide."

"I live in a one-room apartment," Ramón said. "There aren't that many good hiding places."

Stefan laughed and then stopped when he realized Ramón wasn't joking. "You never heard of offshore banking?" he said.

A few months later, Ramón flew to the Cayman Islands. It took him two days to get up the courage to walk through the doors of Scotiabank.

A bank officer, Judith McField, welcomed him into her office and offered him tea and biscuits.

"Oh, no, no, no, thank you," he said, determined to set her straight. "I really don't have that much money to deposit."

"Oh . . ." she said. "In that case, I'll tell my assistant to bring the cheap biscuits."

She smiled mischievously, and Ramón melted. Fame and fortune had eluded him, but in that instant, he realized that this was all he really needed: kindness, understanding, respect, and the soft brown eyes of a woman who accepted him for who he was.

Two hours later, he walked out of the bank with his new-client packet tucked into a leather binder, seven thousand dollars in his secret account, and a dinner date for that evening with his new banker, Judith McField.

Twelve years later, thanks to his hard work, Judith's financial savvy, and his recent business arrangement with Arthur, Ramón's modest deposit was now up to 430,000 dollars. And shortly after 11:59 a.m., his little nest egg would cross the half-million-dollar mark.

Time to hang up my spikes, he told himself.

When the train arrived at Penn Station, Ramón went upstairs, stepped onto Seventh Avenue, and breathed in the magnificence and the misery, the grandeur and the grime, the dreams and the disappointments of the city. Arthur was at war with New York, but for Ramón, it would always be the life force that made his own life worth living.

"*Adiós, Nueva York,*" he said. "*Y gracias. Muchísimas gracias.*"

He took his final walk up Seventh Avenue, slowing his pace as he entered Central Park. When he got to the carousel, he sat down on a bench and waited for it to open at ten. Then he spent twenty minutes soaking in the image of happy kids on colorful horses galloping in and out of view as the tinny but infectious sound of calliope music filled the air.

He murmured a bittersweet farewell and moved on, paying a respectful visit to the statue of Balto, a Siberian husky and one of the celebrated lead sled dogs who crossed the Alaskan wilderness in a raging blizzard to bring life-saving serum to thousands stricken by a diphtheria epidemic a hundred years ago.

Then on past the Sheep Meadow to Bethesda Terrace, where he strode down the grand staircase and tossed a fistful of coins at the Angel of the Waters statue that graced the Bethesda Fountain.

It was 11:15 when Ramón finally emerged from the park, his clothes damp with sweat, eyes moist with emotion.

He crossed Central Park West, entered the Museum of Natural History, and set about his mission. At 11:51, he left the building and walked a hundred yards to the subway.

By 11:59, Ramón was on a speeding downtown C train, too far away to hear the explosion. But he knew that the bomb he'd planted would have destroyed the 122-foot-long fiberglass skeleton of the titanosaur.

It would be a great loss to the museum and a major blow to the city, which, of course, had been Arthur's goal.

But Ramón also knew that no one would be killed or injured in the blast. That had been *his* goal. And he had gone to great lengths to make sure he succeeded.

CHAPTER 38

AFTER THEO LEFT, Kylie and I worked through the night, each managing to grab a few hours' sleep. At eight a.m., we hit the streets, driving from one end of Manhattan to the other, the sketch of our prime suspect in hand. We were working under the assumption that if he was going to set off another bomb, he'd have to surface, and we might just spot him and catch him in the act of planting it. More than a hundred other cops were doing the same thing, cruising from one high-priority target to another throughout the five boroughs.

Kylie and I were down at Chelsea Piers on West Nineteenth when we got the call that the bomb had gone off at the Museum of Natural History.

The bomber had succeeded in scaring a lot of people away from venturing into New York at midday, so traffic on the West Side Highway wasn't as slow as usual. But even with lights and sirens, it took us eleven minutes to navigate the four miles to Seventy-Seventh Street and Central Park West.

By the time we arrived, the streets were clogged with emergency vehicles of every stripe, and five hundred or more people who had been evacuated from the museum.

A command center had been set up on the east side of the avenue. When we got there, Cates was waiting for us with Sean Thomas, the museum's head of security.

"The bomb went off in the Wallach Orientation Center on the fourth floor," Thomas said. "The good news is, there were no casualties. In fact, no injuries at all. The bad news is, we lost one of our most popular attractions. It took three years and I don't know how many millions of dollars to build the titanosaur, and now it's a pile of rubble."

"I'm not sure I follow," Kylie said. "If it's so popular, how come no one was injured in the blast?"

"That's the thing," Thomas said. "The room is never empty. You put a hundred-and-twenty-two-foot dinosaur right next to the café and the restrooms, and it's always jam-packed. This morning was no different. There were probably fifty, sixty people in there until about six or seven minutes before the explosion. And then—*bam*—the fire alarm goes off."

"There was a fire *before* the bomb?" Kylie said.

"And thank God for that," Thomas said. "The room started filling with smoke, and people bolted for the fire exits. Our emergency protocol went into effect, and we immediately ordered the evacuation of the entire building. The stragglers were still making their way out when the bomb went off, but by that time, the fourth floor had been vacated. I can't imagine how many would have been killed if it weren't for that warning."

"You think the fire was a warning?" Kylie said.

"It looks that way," Thomas said. "The fire department got here after the explosion, and they found the source of the fire. It was deliberate. Somebody lit a road flare in a trash bin in the men's room. Those flares can keep burning for thirty minutes, and there was plenty of paper to keep it going."

"And you think the bomber set the fire to empty out the room?" Kylie said.

"I'm a retired police lieutenant out of Albany," Thomas said. "It's not exactly NYPD, but the first thing that popped into my cop brain was that the odds of a *second* maniac starting a fire that clears the room out minutes before the bomb blows are infinitesimal. It had to be the bomber who started that fire."

"Makes sense," Kylie said. "What doesn't make sense is, why did he change his MO? Until now, he hasn't cared how many bodies he leaves behind. Why does he suddenly care enough to get people out of harm's way?"

She didn't expect a response, but Thomas pondered it for a few seconds. "I have a theory," he said, "but I doubt if it'll help you."

"Go for it," Kylie said.

"He's a maniac," Thomas said. "And maniacs are totally unpredictable."

My phone rang. I couldn't imagine anything more important than what I was doing right at that moment, but I took a quick look at the caller ID anyway.

It was Efrain Curet, the detective in charge of the team that was going through four months of CCTV videos in search of a man with three fingers on his right hand, who may or may not have planted the bomb that killed Nico Patrakis's family and three others.

I stepped away and took the call. "Tell me something good, Efrain," I said.

"Better than good, Zach. We got him ID'd."

"Hold on, Efrain. I'm putting you on speaker. Repeat what you said for Kylie and Captain Cates. Go ahead."

"We ID'd the bomber, Captain," Curet said. "Once we got that sketch, especially knowing that we were looking for a guy with three fingers, we started back at square one, going over the same footage we'd been through before. And this time, we saw something we'd missed on the first pass.

"Two nights before the subway bombing, a Hispanic man who fit the description the witness gave us entered the downtown side of the Wall Street station at 3:14 a.m. He was carrying a small black duffel bag in his *left* hand," he said. "As he approached the turnstile, he moved the bag to his *right* hand. Then, using his left hand, he dug into his left pants pocket and pulled out a MetroCard. He swiped the card with his left hand, went through the turnstile, put the card back in his pocket, and switched the duffel bag from his right hand back to his left."

"So he's left-handed," Kylie said.

"And with good reason," Curet responded. "He's missing two fingers on his right hand. Hold on, I'm texting you a close-up."

Seconds later, a picture of the hand popped on my screen. It was grainy, but no question—there were two nubs where his thumb and his index finger had been.

"Excellent work, Detective Curet!" Cates said.

"It gets better, Captain," Curet said. "Eight minutes after entering the station, he leaves without the duffel bag. We tracked his MetroCard. He bought it at a machine a week earlier using his debit card. His name is Ramón Reyes, and he lives on Forty-Sixth Avenue in Bayside, Queens."

"Fantastic," Cates said. "This is the break we've been waiting for."

"I wish we'd caught it sooner," he said. "I heard about the museum."

"We're there now," she said. "Send us a shot of his driver's license so we can compare it to the security footage at the museum."

"On it," he said, and hung up.

Cates, Kylie, and I stood there in silence, but I knew we were all thinking the same thing. We knew our bomber's name. We knew where he lived. But we couldn't just pop over to his house and arrest him.

Ramón Reyes was armed with weapons of mass destruction, and capturing him safely would require a monumental logistic undertaking involving ESU, the bomb squad, Aviation, Counterterrorism, the Strategic Response Group, the hostage negotiation team—as many as 250 cops in all. And every inch of the planning would be scrutinized, analyzed, and criticized by the top brass, right up to the commissioner himself.

Most importantly, it all had to be kept tightly under wraps, because if Reyes got even the slightest hint that we were onto him, he could . . .

I shook the thought out of my head. I didn't want to start imagining the damage he could possibly do. Our Albany cop, Sean Thomas, had summed it up perfectly.

"He's a maniac. And maniacs are totally unpredictable."

CHAPTER 39

RAMÓN GOT TO PENN Station in time to catch the 12:15 train back to Bayside. By one o'clock, he was home, in the shower, the water turned up as hot as he could tolerate.

He wished he could cry, but he couldn't. So he screamed. First, at his stupid younger self for incurring the wrath of the Cuban government. Then, at Arthur for using him all these years. Finally, he beat his fists on his naked body for becoming a weak, soulless *pendejo* who murdered innocent people so he could make enough money to escape to another part of the world and become a different worthless person.

He screamed until his throat was raw. No one could hear him, of course. The Castillo sisters were gone. Blanca had died a year ago, and six months later Estrella, who had advanced dementia, had been moved to a nursing home. They had no heirs, so they never bothered with a will. Ramón stayed and continued to honor the original agreement. He could live rent-free in the basement apartment in exchange for taking care of the house and the property.

But he knew that once he left the country, it wouldn't take long for people to see the overgrown lawn, the dead shrubs, and all the other signs of neglect. The more daring among them would pry open a window or force a door, and before long, the house would be taken over by squatters.

God bless them, he thought as he toweled himself dry and got dressed.

He'd leave them a bottle of wine and a corkscrew on the dining room table, along with a note that said, "I'm not coming back. Make yourself at home."

The doorbell rang. He smiled. *Kids*. It was baseball season. They needed coaching. He could use the diversion.

He opened the front door. It was Arthur. He looked ravaged. His clothes were rumpled and reeking, as though he'd slept in them, but his eyes were wide and bloodshot, the skin beneath them dark, sagging, as if he hadn't slept in days.

He stepped inside and quickly shut the door behind him.

"Hello, Ramón."

"Jesus," Ramón said. "Are you okay?"

"Never better. I know I look like dog shit, but that's because I've been up all night working on *this* little beauty." He hefted the black duffel bag in his right hand. "You'll need this for tomorrow."

"I appreciate it, but you really didn't have to make the trip," Ramón said. "I'm all set for tomorrow." He reached under the bed and pulled out an identical black duffel bag. "Did you forget?"

"I don't forget things," Arthur said, setting his bag next to Ramón's. "But I have been known to take a great idea and make it even better. I've decided to go big tomorrow."

"Two targets on the same day?" Ramón said.

"No. One target. Two bombs. Double the payload."

"Double? Is that . . . is that really necessary?"

"I deposited your money as soon as I heard that the bomb went off in the museum," Arthur said, ignoring the question.

"I saw. Thank you. Much appreciated," he said, giving his ego-starved boss a big, toothy smile.

"Do you think you earned it?" Arthur said.

Ramón's smile turned to stone. "Did I *earn* it?"

"You heard me. I paid you seventy-five grand. Did you earn it?"

"Did you ask me to plant a bomb in a high-priority target at a time when the entire city is on high alert? Did it blow? Did it do millions of dollars' worth of damage? You're damn right I earned it, Arthur. As far as I'm concerned, mission fucking accomplished!"

"Nobody died, Ramón. It seems that a fire alarm cleared the building minutes before the explosion. Some of the survivors are calling it a miracle. But I don't believe in miracles. And before you tell me that you didn't start the fire, fair warning—I'm not an idiot."

"Of course I started the fire," Ramón said. "Your beef is with the city, not its visitors, and definitely not its schoolkids."

"News flash, Ramón. Nobody gives a shit about a pile of dinosaur bones. The only thing that puts the fear of God into people's heads is dead bodies. The more bodies we pile up, the more seriously this city will take us."

"I'm pretty sure they're taking us seriously, Arthur."

"Do you know who I am, Ramón?" Arthur said, his tone thick with disdain.

"I thought I did."

"No. You only know who I *was*. You know the pathetic loser who went up against the establishment, seeking justice, and wound up rotting in a jail cell like a twenty-first-century Jean Valjean."

"And who are you now?"

"I'm the 11:59 Bomber. I'm all over the newspapers, the TV, the internet. They gave me a Wikipedia page. I've inspired T-shirts, coffee mugs, bomber jackets! Is that insane? The 11:59 Bomber bomber jacket! Wherever you go, people are talking about me, and do you want to know why, Ramón? Do you want to know why?" he repeated, his voice tinged with a manic edge. "Because I spread chaos, I instill fear, and I leave dead bodies in my wake.

"Chaos, fear, and dead people," Arthur said. "Camera crews show up at their funerals. The father of one of them is offering a hundred thousand dollars to track us down. What do you think of that, Ramón? A hundred thousand dollars!"

"That's a lot of money," Ramón said, his voice soft and, he hoped, calming.

"It's shit! It's chump change!" Arthur screamed. "I was thinking of calling him up—this Nico Patrakis guy—and saying it should be a million, asshole. *Ten* million. And I would have done that, Ramón, if there were fifty more dead bodies among the dinosaur bones. But no!

You let them go. You failed me. Even worse, you defiled my image."

"Arthur, I planted the bomb. I did what you paid me for."

"Well then let me make myself clear going forward. I am not paying you to plant bombs. I am paying you to make my point. Do you understand?"

"Yes," Ramón said. "I understand."

"At 11:20 tomorrow morning, you will drop both duffel bags down the manhole on St. Clair Place in Harlem. You know where it is, correct?"

"I've done three dry runs. At this point, I can pry the cover off, drop the bag, and pop the cover back on in eight seconds. Two bags will take me nine."

"Nine seconds to make a hundred and fifty thousand dollars," Arthur said with a malicious smile. "Nice work if you can get it."

Ramón didn't respond. *Nice work?* The sheer insanity of those words enraged him. Ramón knew it was anything but nice work. That manhole led to a sewer system. The two duffel bags would quickly make their way to the wastewater treatment plant a mile away under Riverbank State Park at the north end of Manhattan.

The plant workers underground would be killed instantly. But that wouldn't satisfy Arthur's body count lust. He knew that at 11:59 on a summer morning, the park above the treatment plant would be teeming with five hundred people, maybe a thousand—kids playing ball, families picnicking, sun worshippers on blankets, faces tilted to the sky. How many of them would be killed or maimed in the blast?

As devastating as that was, the collateral damage would be even worse. The explosion would send millions of gallons of untreated sewage into the Hudson River.

Ramón stared at Arthur. With just a few taps on a cell phone, that man—that maniac—had the power to turn New York City into an ecological disaster zone. Not just for a day. Not for a year. But for decades to come.

"Did you hear me, Ramón?" Arthur said. "Nine seconds to make a hundred and fifty thousand dollars. You good to go?"

Ramón didn't hesitate. "Yeah," he said. "I am definitely good to go."

CHAPTER 40

WITHIN MINUTES OF the time Ramón Reyes was identified as our bomber, a surveillance team was assembled to watch his house on Forty-Sixth Avenue in Bayside, Queens. *Team* is an understatement. It was more like a platoon—a broad array of dozens of detectives: male, female, young, old, Black, White, Hispanic, and Asian. They formed a microcosm of the neighborhood, walking or driving past his house, sitting in the park across the street, blending in with the locals until the locals finally called it a night around one a.m.

At the same time, tactical units were sent out to determine how best to keep Reyes's neighbors out of harm's way if he resisted arrest and things got violent.

ESU, along with the bomb squad, determined that six homes had to be evacuated—one on either side of Reyes's house, two behind him on Forty-Fifth Drive, and two more around the corner on Oceania Street.

The school year was over, but with the Marie Curie Middle School and its adjoining playground directly across the street from Reyes, barriers were set up closing off the area, and four community-affairs officers posted signs around the entire complex with an ominous skull and crossbones and a message that said *No Entry Until Tuesday 5 p.m. Rodent Control Pesticides Being Applied.*

Closer to home, detectives compared Efrain Curet's subway footage of the perp with the video surveillance pictures from the Bloomingdale's blast. It was a positive match. Same guy.

Another team drove to Jersey, tracked down Leo, our eighty-seven-year-old fisherman, and showed him a photo array. He immediately tapped on Reyes's picture. "That's him," Leo said. "Paddleboard man who can't paddleboard."

By three thirty a.m., a contingent of thirty vehicles had gathered outside the 111th Precinct on Northern Boulevard, less than half a mile from our target location.

Kylie and I were in a BearCat toward the front of the caravan. As soon as Reyes was apprehended and the location secured, we would transfer to an SUV with blacked-out windows and take him back to Manhattan for questioning.

Ryan Stockwell, chief of the Special Operations Division, was running the show, which meant he was the one who would be either hanged or heralded. A gifted tactician, he relished the opportunity to bring Reyes down.

At five a.m., just as the sky began to lighten, Stockwell hopped into the front of the BearCat and turned to me and Kylie. "Guess which asshole asked if he could ride with us in the lead vehicle? That boob from DCPI, Pete Peterson."

"He's a loose cannon who doesn't know the difference between public information and this-shit-stays-in-house," Kylie said.

"I'm *well* aware," Stockwell said.

"We were hoping he wouldn't find out about this till after the fact."

"He works at One PP," Stockwell said. "There's no way he wasn't going to be in on it. But at least he'll be out of the way. I put him in the rear with the gear."

He strapped on his helmet. "Buckle up," he said. "We're heading in."

He keyed his radio to confirm that everybody in the convoy was ready to move out.

"Blocker cars, in position?"

Eight cars were assigned to move in and block Forty-Sixth Avenue to keep it clear of pedestrian and vehicular traffic.

The team leader responded. "Blocker cars in position."

"Entry team, in position?"

The plan was for ESU to pull up on the sidewalk in front of Reyes's house. The loudspeaker on top of their BearCat would blast out an order for him to come out with his hands raised above his head. If he complied, it would be over quickly. If he didn't, the entry team would storm the house.

"Entry team in position."

"Bomb squad, in position?"

"Bomb squad in position."

"Aviation, in position?"

First came the response from the helicopter above us. "Aviation in position, but be advised that two news choppers just entered the area."

It was quickly followed by our eyes and ears on the ground twenty miles away at Floyd Bennett Field. "Aviation base to operation leader. Your entire operation just went live on both Channel Two and Channel Seven, and it's streaming on social media."

I looked at Kylie. She said exactly what I was thinking. "Peterson!"

"Ignore it," Stockwell said. "I don't care if the whole world is watching. It doesn't change anything!"

And then came the radio call that changed everything.

"Surveillance van to operation leader." The voice was urgent. "Two vehicles turning onto Forty-Sixth Avenue, approaching fast."

Our surveillance team had two cameras in place. One was tight on Reyes's house. The second was a wide shot that covered the entire block. Stockwell, Kylie, and I stared at the monitor. Two SUVs came tearing around the corner from Oceania and pulled up to the house. Eight doors flew open. Eight men got out, pistols and rifles in hand. It was Nico Patrakis and his army of vigilantes.

"Move in!" Stockwell ordered as Nico and his men made their way toward the house. "All units, move in, move in, move in!"

The convoy started rolling, but we were still almost half a mile away.

Stockwell, Kylie, and I were glued to the monitor as four of Nico's men shattered the glass on the front door and poured into the house.

Nico and three others ran down the stairs to the basement apartment, made short work of that door, and disappeared inside.

"They're going to kill Reyes. They're going to kill him before we get there," I said as we turned the corner onto Forty-Sixth Avenue.

I braced myself for the sound of gunfire from the house.

We were four hundred feet away. Three hundred. Two hundred, and still neither Nico nor any of his seven-man crew had fired a single round.

Maybe Reyes was hiding. I got my hopes up. Maybe we could stop Nico from making the biggest mistake of his life.

We were less than fifty feet away when the house erupted.

Smoke and debris shot upward, followed by a rush of flames. Shards of glass and bits of what was once someone's home shot outward, peppering the street with debris.

The blast seemed to warp the very air. Inside the BearCat, we all instinctively recoiled. The sound was muffled, but the intensity was unmistakable.

And then we watched in stunned silence as the entire structure crumbled, beams and bricks collapsing into a chaotic heap.

CHAPTER 41

ARTHUR WATCHED AS HIS TV screen flashed white with the explosion. The picture became a blur of motion as the Channel 7 news camera, which had zoomed in on the men entering the house, quickly pulled back to capture the full scope of the carnage—a smoldering mound where Ramón's house once stood, the morning sun casting stark shadows across the ruins.

"*Vaya con Dios, amigo*," Arthur said out loud, "but you were going to give me up either to the police or to Nico Patrakis and his Greek mafia." He thought about adding, "At least I took them down with you," but he knew that Ramón would see it for what it was—bullshit.

The truth was, Arthur had been ready to let go of Ramón for a while now. For all his so-called loyalty to the loving couple that took him in, Ramón had never really been committed to avenging their deaths. Arthur could still picture the look of horror on Ramón's face when he told him about his plan to blow up the city one piece at a time until the mayor begged for mercy.

Arthur had tried guilt-tripping him into cooperating. *You became a brother to me.* Even that hadn't worked. The only thing that motivated Ramón was money, and in less than a week Arthur had paid his *brother* three hundred thousand dollars for something that should have been done willingly out of love and gratitude.

"Where's your little nest egg now?" Arthur said to the TV.

"I've never seen anything like this before, Amanda," the TV news anchor responded.

"I don't think any of us have seen anything like this before, Jeremy," his partner said. "For those of you who just tuned in, we were alerted to a major police action that was taking place in Bayside. NewsCopter 7 was on the scene as dozens of NYPD vehicles gathered on Northern Boulevard."

"And I thank you for alerting me, Amanda," Arthur said to the screen.

He hadn't been sleeping well, and at four thirty that morning he'd gotten out of bed, his mind fixated on the two bombs that would blow up the wastewater plant and pollute the coastline from Manhattan to the Jersey shore and beyond.

He was on his third cup of coffee when the news bulletin from Channel 7 popped up on his Apple Watch. He turned on the TV and saw exactly what they were rebroadcasting now.

"We didn't know it at the time," Amanda explained, "but it now appears that the NYPD had tracked down the 11:59 Bomber and were about to raid—is that the right word, Jeremy? *Raid* his house?"

"Probably not, Amanda. I would just say that they were about to bring the suspect in for questioning."

Arthur laughed. "You're an idiot, Jeremy. They don't send an armed battalion to bring someone in for questioning."

"Whatever the word is," Amanda continued, "as you can see, at 5:03 this morning, two unmarked cars turned onto Forty-Sixth Avenue, pulled up to this modest red-brick house in Bayside, and eight men, who we assume were plainclothes NYPD detectives, got out of the cars, and with guns drawn they entered the building."

Arthur laughed even harder this time. He watched the replay of Nico and his thugs, who had just been upgraded to NYPD detectives, as they raided—correction, *entered*—the house so they could bring the suspect in for questioning.

"What you're about to see is shocking, brutal," Jeremy said.

"Not to everyone, Jeremy," Arthur said. "Not to everyone."

And then the house exploded again. Arthur inhaled the feeling. It was definitely better the second time. Especially when Amanda, in all her blissful ignorance, capped it with, "Our thoughts and prayers go out to those eight heroic police officers."

"It's a tragic loss for the entire city, Amanda," her co-idiot said, "but based on this latest development, it looks like this may just be the end of the road for the nefarious 11:59 Bomber."

"On the other hand," Arthur said, grinning as he turned off the TV, "the nefarious 11:59 Bomber may just drop by the station and blow you all to hell."

CHAPTER 42

WITHIN TWO HOURS of the blast, the original army of more than a hundred cops had tripled. The bomb squad scoured the property for more possible explosives, and ESU determined that there were no survivors and transitioned from rescue mode to recovery.

Eight, possibly nine, men were dead inside the demolished building. Four cops and two civilians caught shrapnel and were taken to Jamaica Hospital with non–life-threatening injuries.

Because debris from the explosion was found two blocks away, the perimeter of the crime scene was extended from five hundred feet out from Reyes's house to fifteen hundred, and teams of cops did a door-to-door canvass of the neighborhood, looking for anyone else who might have been injured.

Heavy equipment arrived to help the crime scene unit search the wreckage, and a forty-five-foot mobile command center that took up four parking spaces on Oceania Street became Red's temporary headquarters vehicle.

And that was just the beginning.

At seven thirty, Cates called Kylie and me into the THV.

"A hundred and fourteen people were assigned to the unit that gathered last night on Northern Boulevard," she said. "Despite my best efforts to keep him in the dark, Lieutenant Pete Peterson was one of them. We did a return roll call this morning within minutes of the blast. A hundred and thirteen people were accounted for. One man was MIA: Peterson."

There was no doubt in any of our minds. Pete Peterson was a dirty cop. We had no hard evidence, but the facts were damning.

"Twenty-three people were privy to every detail of the operation to take down Ramón Reyes," Cates said. "I would personally vouch for the loyalty, honesty, and integrity of twenty-two of them. As far as I'm concerned, Peterson is the only one who could have and would have alerted both the media and Nico Patrakis. If that turns out to be true, he not only compromised one of the biggest manhunts ever undertaken by this department, but his actions led to the deaths of eight men. Finding Peterson is my top priority.

"But," she added, "we need to keep this under the radar."

"Koprowski," Kylie said.

I nodded in agreement.

Within minutes, Detective Rich Koprowski joined us.

"This is sensitive," Cates said to Koprowski. "It doesn't leave this circle."

"Yes, ma'am," he said.

"I want phone records on every departmental and personal electronic device used by Lieutenant Pete Peterson from DCPI," Cates said.

I could see the question spring to Koprowski's mind: *Why are we investigating another cop?* But he was seasoned enough not to voice it. "Yes, ma'am," he said without hesitation.

"And don't bother calling Peterson's work cell phone," Cates said. "We've managed to track it down. It was in a garbage can on Forty-Fifth Drive along with his department radio. I'm calling Chief Novick at IAB to notify him that Lieutenant Peterson is now officially under investigation."

"On it, Captain," Koprowski said and left the THV.

"Next order of business," Cates said. "Ramón Reyes. He lived in the basement apartment, so it's going to take time to dig him up and identify the body. But until we do, we are still out there looking for him, and his photo has gone to the media.

"In the meantime, detectives have been talking to his neighbors. We're just starting to piece it all together, but it turns out he's some kind of a local hero. He was born in Cuba, became a professional baseball player, tried to defect, was caught, and had two fingers amputated from his pitching hand. He tried again and had better luck the second time. He managed to cross the border, made it to New York, and was granted asylum. He's been living here in Bayside for ten years, and he's a volunteer pitching coach for the local kids. They love him, and so do the parents. One of the dads gave us a video of Reyes teaching his kid to throw a slider. Take a look."

She tapped a button on the video console, and a shot of Reyes and a boy of about twelve popped up on the screen.

"The most important thing you have to know is the grip," Reyes said. "You hold the ball with your fingers off-center. You want your middle finger directly on top of the seam, and your index finger is—"

Cates stopped the video. We'd heard enough. Ramón Reyes spoke English with a thick Spanish accent.

"As soon as I heard this, I sent it to the voice analysis unit to compare it to the bomber's original 911 call," Cates said. "They can't always be sure when two samples match, especially since he ran the call through a voice changer. But they are one hundred percent positive that Ramón Reyes is not the same man who made the 911 call just before the Wall Street subway station bombing."

Not the same man. The words sucked out every ounce of optimism that had kept me going through the night.

"We don't know if Reyes is alive or dead, but we now know one thing for certain," Captain Cates said. "He has a partner. And I guarantee you, that man is out there right now, planning to set off another bomb.

"Trust me," she added with ironclad certainty, "this nightmare is far from done."

CHAPTER 43

"**THIS NIGHTMARE IS FAR** from done," Cates had said.

Most of the nine million New Yorkers who had been holding their collective breath for the past five days were of the same mind, only they summed it up in a classic Yogi-ism.

It ain't over till it's over.

At ten a.m., the mayor issued a statement: "The incident in Queens at 5:33 this morning is relevant to the investigation of the prior bombings. Minor injuries were sustained by several members of the public and the NYPD. However, contrary to reports on the media, no police officers were seriously injured or killed. This investigation is ongoing. The NYPD is working in conjunction with the FBI, ATF, and officials from the governor's office. We continue to urge the public: If you see something, call 911 immediately. Thank you."

Dozens of reporters peppered her with questions. She ignored them all.

"Classic political bullshit," Kylie said. "Translation: The bomber is still out there, folks. Don't say I didn't warn you."

By late morning, the temperature had soared to the mid-nineties and was on the verge of breaking a hundred. Kylie and I could have stayed cool and comfortable in Cates's air-conditioned mobile HQ, but we couldn't bear to deal with the constant stream of two-, three-, and four-star chiefs and very important ass-kissers from the mayor's office.

So we opted for the brutal alternative. We spent the morning under a stifling crime scene unit canopy, shirts clinging to our backs, bodies withered from exhaustion, hunched over our laptops, doggedly excavating the details of Ramón Reyes's life.

Without a body, we were operating on the assumption that he was still out there, and we were looking for anything that could help us locate him or his partner. You'd think that trying to find two perps would be twice as hard as finding one. But the reality is that the level of difficulty goes up exponentially when you're trying to find a second needle in a haystack.

Ramón Reyes was a ghost. No social media. No record of employment. Never paid taxes. Never voted. The little bits and pieces of his life that we could trace were on paper. And except for the purchase of the MetroCard that led us to him, there were no digital footprints of consequence that would help us dig deeper.

He had gone to great lengths to stay off the radar. And with good reason. The Cuban government had hunted him down, mutilated the hand that could have earned him millions, and probably would have executed him if he hadn't escaped. He wasn't going to give another government a chance to destroy his life.

At 11:40, all activity on the rubble pile at Forty-Sixth Avenue stopped, and "in the interest of prudence and in adherence with the department's safety protocols," as the clock neared 11:59, everyone working the crime scene was moved to a safe location.

It was the smart move to make, and it gave us a chance to talk to Chuck Dryden.

"Hey, Chuck," Kylie called out as our go-to crime scene analyst gingerly made his way off the mountain of scorched stucco and twisted metal.

Dryden, who usually hops to whenever Kylie calls him, was not in a hopping mood. He and his team had been searching the wreckage for more than four hours, methodically retrieving and tagging body parts.

Dressed head to toe in Tyvek, they couldn't stay out in the blazing July sun for long without coming off the pile and heading to the hydration station.

"Chuck," Kylie said, bearing down on him.

"Jesus, Kylie," I said, "give the poor guy a minute, will ya?"

She waited impatiently while Chuck unzipped the stifling coveralls and downed a bottle of Gatorade. He was opening a second one when Kylie decided she had waited long enough. "What can you tell us?" she said.

He gave her a tired smile, thought for a few seconds, and said, "The best-laid schemes o' mice an' men gang aft agley."

Chuck is an enigma. Sometimes he can be as boring as a PowerPoint presentation. But there are other times when he'll respond to a simple question with a weirdly esoteric answer like the one he just gave to Kylie.

Scarily, I've been working with him long enough to know what he meant.

The plan had been for us to arrest Reyes. Then Chuck and his people would analyze every inch of the house and its contents. But, of course, that didn't happen. Our best-laid schemes had totally gang agley.

"Robert Burns," I said, giving him a nod.

Chuck returned the nod and took another few swallows of restorative liquid and electrolytes.

"The captain is hoping we can recover Reyes's body in time for the six o'clock news," Kylie said. "What are the odds?"

Dryden shook his head. "We've got body parts, Detective MacDonald, but it's going to be days before we can make a positive ID on any of them."

11:59 came and went without incident, and twenty minutes later the recovery team went back to the pile.

About two hours later, a voice bellowed out from the rubble. It was calm but commanding. "I've got a device."

One of the bomb squad detectives, also enshrouded in Tyvek, held both arms high in the air. "Nobody key their radio," he yelled.

Everyone froze.

Somewhere in the rubble was a bomb that hadn't exploded.

Yet.

CHAPTER 44

WITHIN MINUTES, THE ENTIRE block was cleared, and Ed Campbell, a veteran bomb squad detective, made the long, lonely walk toward the device.

Cates, Kylie, and I, along with half a dozen top cops, watched him on CCTV from the command vehicle two blocks away. All transmissions—radio, video, air traffic, or anything else in the vicinity that could emit an electronic impulse—were suspended, because even the faintest signal from the wrong frequency might trigger the bomb.

The feed came from a camera crew positioned on the roof of a building a safe distance away. It wasn't perfect—the picture was a little grainy—but Campbell's every move was visible.

He was dressed in what he likes to refer to as his "work clothes"—a thirty-five-thousand-dollar, eighty-pound explosives ordnance disposal suit.

I've known Ed for years, but every time I watch him lumber slowly into the jaws of death, I wonder if he's made peace with the idea that those steps might be his last. I can't imagine what it takes to be one slip of the hand away from extinction while the rest of us hang back out of harm's way.

I once asked Ed if it was bravery, dedication, or sheer lunacy to do what he does.

"All of the above," he said, laughing off the question. "And I try to go easy on the caffeine."

He knelt down in the rubble, and the camera zeroed in on a cell phone crudely wired to a block of C4.

Nobody in the command post said a word, but I knew that everyone was thinking the same thing I was.

The previous bombs also had cell phone detonators, but they were now in a million microscopic pieces. The phone on the monitor just might be the holy grail. If we had it intact, it could lead us to the bomber.

Reaching into his pouch, Ed pulled out a pair of cutters specially designed to minimize static charge. His hands traced the wires back to the power source. The small rechargeable battery pack looked innocuous, but it was the heart of the beast—a tiny powerhouse ready to flood the circuit with enough energy to vaporize Campbell in a fraction of a second.

He isolated a thin red wire snaking from the battery to the cell phone. I held my breath as he hovered over it. And then . . . snip.

The phone went dark. The battery was disabled, but the blasting cap nestled into the C4 still held a charge. Until Campbell neutralized the energy in that cap, the bomb was still lethal.

He reached back into his pouch and pulled out a slim, insulated grounding rod about the length of his forearm. The rod was attached to a compact copper ground plate that glinted faintly in the sun.

He held the tip of the rod over the blasting cap, his hand steady despite the weight of the moment. Then, despite the grainy feed, we could see his lips move. There was no audio, but those of us who know him were familiar with the words.

"Love you, Diane."

It was part of his ritual. He said them every time. Because if things went sideways, he wanted the love of his life to know that his final thoughts were of her.

The rod touched metal. A spark crackled and leaped into the air as the life force was sucked from the blasting cap and drained into the copper plate. Campbell slowly extracted the cap from the C4, now just a harmless lump of Silly Putty.

He raised a hand in the air. The device had been rendered safe.

The reaction in the command vehicle was subdued. No cheers or high fives à la the techs at NASA after a successful touchdown. That's not our style. The feeling of relief that coursed through those of us who watched Ed Campbell successfully complete another mission was palpable, but it was short-lived.

As Captain Cates had reminded us earlier, this nightmare was far from over.

CHAPTER 45

THERE HAD, OF COURSE, been a safer way to disable the bomb. A robot could have placed it in a TCV—a total containment vessel—which would then have been transported to the bomb squad's demolition range at Rodman's Neck in the Bronx, where it would have been detonated under controlled conditions.

But Ed Campbell had risked his life because he knew that retrieving the cell phone in one piece could lead us to the madman who built it.

We doubted that our bomber would gift us with his fingerprints. He didn't. As for DNA, we swabbed and hoped for the best, but even if any were detected, it might be from the retailer who sold the phone or the factory worker who assembled it.

The real value of having the phone intact was that it could contain a wealth of digital forensics, including call histories, text messages, and historical GPS tracking data.

Under normal circumstances, we would plug the phone into a laptop and have all that information in a heartbeat.

But when a phone has just been disconnected from a block of C4, you don't just *plug it in*. The top priority is to turn it over to the bomb squad so they can determine beyond a shadow of a doubt that it made the explosives viable and lethal, because one day the DA's case against the bomber might hinge on that critical evidence.

We'd have to retrieve the data another way.

So we used the phone's IMEI. The international mobile equipment identity is the unique fifteen-digit code identifier given to every mobile phone. We ran the number and subpoenaed the carrier, InvisiTalk.

They were quick to cooperate—and just as quick to shatter our expectations.

There was no data, they told us. No call records. No history. The phone had been manufactured four years earlier, and it had never been turned on.

"Never?" Kylie said. "Clearly, this guy doesn't want to be found."

From anyone else, those words might have sounded like surrender. But coming from Kylie, I knew it wasn't defeat—it was a spark. The tougher the challenge, the more driven she gets.

We subpoenaed Nokia, the manufacturer. They didn't give us much, but at least it was something. The phone had been manufactured in Brazil and shipped to a wholesaler in Ottawa, who sold it to an electronics retailer in Toronto.

"Toronto!" Kylie said. "Did you hear that, Zach? Toronto!"

Not only had I heard it, but I saw the look in Kylie's eyes when she heard it. She didn't say a word, but I knew what she was thinking as I followed her to Cates's office to give the boss the news.

"He's smart," Cates said. "He knows that a four-year-old phone is harder to trace, but there's a good chance that the store has a record of who they sold it to. It's worth a shot to send a team up there."

"Zach and I will do it."

"Absolutely not," Cates said. "I need to keep you close in case something big breaks."

"It's a quick flight to Toronto," Kylie said. "We can leave now, interview the staff at the store, and be on the first flight back to New York tomorrow morning."

"I am not going to send my lead team out of the country to ask some phone store clerk the same questions that a dozen other detectives could ask," Cates said.

"But, Captain . . ." Kylie said.

Cates cut her off. "No buts. Decision made."

I stood up. "You're right, Captain," I said. "And if I had your job, I would make exactly the same decision."

Cates shot me a look. What was I angling for?

"Well, you don't have my job," she said.

"Yes, ma'am," I said. "But you've had ours. So I'm sure you remember what it feels like to be at the heart of the highest-profile case to come along in years, and there's nothing—*nothing*—you can do but sit on your hands. It's hard to imagine that our bomber took the trouble to go to Canada and buy a cell phone, and then stupidly gave the clerk his name, home address, and phone number so the cops could track him down when he starts blowing shit up. Of course, a dozen other detectives could do the interview. But it's a fucking lead, and if you want your go-to detectives to feel *remotely* useful, you'll put us on a plane to Toronto instead of letting us stare at four walls until the bomber sends us his next message at 11:59 tomorrow morning."

Silence.

Cates let her right elbow dig into the arm of her desk chair and rested her mouth and chin on the knuckles of her right hand. It's her classic Rodin's *Thinker* pose. And when she's in statue mode, everyone else gives her time to think.

I stood there, my back to the glass wall in her office. Somewhere along the way, my voice had gotten loud enough for the rest of the squad to wonder what the shouting was all about, but I doubted that any of them would look our way.

She lifted her head from her hand. "Go," she said. "Just make sure you get back before I have to explain to the chief of D's why I sent a couple of brain surgeons to operate on a hangnail."

Kylie bolted from the office before Cates could change her mind.

"Thanks, Zach," she said as we headed to our lockers to grab a go bag.

"Thanks for what?" I said, even though I knew exactly why she was thanking me.

Kylie was determined to catch the bomber, but she was also obsessed with proving that her husband was not a murderer. Two days ago, Theo had given her hope. His account of Preston Balfour turning the heroic Indian doctor into a reckless drunk was compelling and credible. But once Theo showed Spence the picture of Dr. Sarin, he destroyed our chances of ever getting a positive ID that would be admissible in court.

"So why don't you question Dr. Sarin?" Theo had said. "He's on a six-city North American tour."

I can still picture Kylie's reaction. "Now that we've got a tainted identification procedure, the DA's office is not going to authorize us to take a bus to Jersey to question him."

Theo was crushed. But he had emailed us Sarin's schedule. And tonight was the final stop on his tour. Toronto.

Kylie knew it. I knew it. But Cates didn't.

"You're probably thinking I lied to the boss," Kylie said. "But we are definitely going to Toronto to talk to the dealer who sold that cell phone."

"You didn't exactly lie. But you left out the part where flying to Toronto on the department's dime gives you a chance to interview the man who might take Spence's place behind bars. How do you think Cates is going to react to that when she finds out?"

"She'll be fine," Kylie said. "I'll just tell her we got lucky and were able to kill two birds with one stone."

"Birds?" I said. "It feels more like you're about to hurl that stone and kill two *careers*."

CHAPTER 46

WE CAUGHT THE SIX thirty Air Canada flight out of Newark.

"We need a plan," Kylie said as soon as we settled into our seats.

"I have a plan," I said. "I'm going to sleep until we land."

"It can wait five minutes. We need a plan for what we say to Dr. Sarin."

"*We?*" I said. "*We* are not saying anything. This is your circus, not mine."

"I thought we were in this together. You're the one who convinced Cates to let us go."

"Convinced? Kylie, there is no argument on earth that could ever persuade Delia Cates to send a team of first-grade detectives to another country for a routine interview that could just as easily be handled by a rookie cop and a true-crime podcaster. The only reason we're on this plane is because I reminded her that the best way to reenergize two cops who don't have *anything* to do is to send them off to do *anything*. And I'm happy to be doing it. But chasing down Sarin is all your idea."

"Fine," she said. "So am I wrong to try to help Spence?"

"It doesn't matter if you're right or wrong," I said. "It's who you are. Kylie MacDonald to the rescue. Wait, let me make your emergency my emergency. It's called codependency. If you ever want help with it, my girlfriend is a shrink."

"Thanks, and what do you think Cheryl is going to tell me? Look the other way and let Spence do twenty-five years in prison for a crime he didn't commit?"

"I have no idea what she would tell you, but she might start by reminding you that Spence walked out on you two years ago. You didn't know if he was alive or dead till he showed up Thursday night, tried to murder someone in front of a live studio audience, informed you that he married another woman while he was still legally married to you, and was charged a few hours later with the murder of the very same man he beat and threatened to kill. And then she might say something like, 'Are you sure you want to sacrifice your needs and put your entire career at risk by trying to rescue that man, because in my professional opinion, Mrs. Harrington, you are enabling your husband's aberrant behavior and shielding him from the consequences of his actions.'"

"Jesus, Zach, you sound just like Shane. He's pissy over the fact that I'm all caught up in this Spence thing."

That took me by surprise. But then I realized that I shouldn't be surprised at all. Shane Talbot is a lot like me. Easygoing—to a point. But if my significant other suddenly stopped paying attention to my needs so she could move heaven and earth to rescue the man who dumped her two years ago and who might, in fact, be a 100 percent bona fide murderer who deserves to spend the next quarter of a century behind bars, I might get a little pissy myself.

"Look," I said, "Sarin's fundraiser is from six to nine o'clock tonight. It'll be at least nine thirty before you and I get to this phone store, and by the time we're done interviewing the clerk—"

She cut me off. "If the question is, *Do I know what hotel he's staying at*, the answer is no."

"Then how and where do you expect to—"

"I called my friend Angela Watson at HIDTA, and I asked her for Kunal Sarin's flight itinerary." And before I could say anything, she added, "The man is a suspect in a murder investigation, so it was a perfectly legitimate request."

I nodded. It was. "And?" I said.

"Dr. Sarin is on an Air Canada flight from Pearson Airport to Mumbai at nine tomorrow morning."

"Well, you and I are on a flight from Pearson to Newark at six thirty," I said, "so odds are, we're not going to bump into him."

"No problem. I moved us to the nine thirty."

"We told Cates we'd be on the first flight out."

"*You* can be on the first flight out, Zach!" she snapped. "Tomorrow morning is my last chance to talk to Sarin before he flies to the other end of the world. So I guess that means I'll be late for work."

"And what do you plan on saying to Sarin when you get that chance?" I asked.

"That's exactly what I asked you five minutes ago when this whole insane interrogation-slash-psych-eval started. I still don't know the best approach. I was hoping you'd help me come up with something."

"No problem," I said. "How about something like 'I'm NYPD Detective Kylie MacDonald, and my husband was arrested for murdering a man who done him wrong, and it turns out that the victim also done you wrong, and this eighteen-year-old friend of mine came up with the bright idea that maybe you're the real killer. Not that he had any actual proof, but he's in the movie business, and you know how they tend to let those things slide. Now, I realize I am completely out of my jurisdiction here, but instead of going home to your wife and family back in India, would you mind hopping on a plane to New York with me, where I can lock you up, get my husband out of jail, see the look of sheer gratitude on his face, and chalk up another victory for dysfunctional relationships?'"

She didn't say a word—just gave me the finger and shifted her body so she was angled toward the window.

I slept until we touched down in Toronto an hour and forty minutes later.

CHAPTER 47

TWO TORONTO COPS WERE waiting for us at the airport. Henley and Weeks. Both male, both young, and both captivated by my smoldering blond partner.

What they didn't realize was that the smolder, sexy as it might appear on the surface, was rage. Kylie was furious at me, Spence, and Shane and ready to lock horns with any other asshole in her vicinity who peed standing up.

In general, Canadians are some of the nicest people on earth. I think it stems from the fact that they've been humbled by their merciless winters. Another time, another set of circumstances, and the four of us might have bonded. Fraternal Order of Police, and all that shit. But Officer Henley blew that to hell right out of the starting gate.

"You're going to Jane Finch, right?" Henley said, opening the car door for her with a quick wink and a sly smile that was well beyond the bounds of it's-always-nice-to-meet-a-fellow-officer.

"No!" Kylie shot back, leaving the word *dickhead* implied but unsaid. "We're going to Toronto Connected. It's a phone store." She yanked the door out of his hand. "Do you know how to find it?"

Henley responded with a nod and a gulp.

Officer Weeks, who seemed to enjoy watching his partner go down in flames, jumped in. "Yes, ma'am. Toronto Connected is at the Jane Finch Mall. We'll have you there in twenty minutes."

Kylie waved Weeks off and shut the door hard. "Then, let's go, Officer."

Kylie is thirty-seven years old and a seasoned veteran of the NYPD. These two Romeos were twelve or fourteen, or whatever the minimum age is in their country to wear a badge, carry a firearm, and push the buttons on the dash to make the lights spin and the sirens squall.

I probably could have warned them that she was never going to be dazzled by their witty banter or even their snappy uniforms, but I decided I'd have more fun if they doubled down and tried again to win her over.

It didn't take long.

"You probably think Jane Finch is a woman," Henley said, looking over his shoulder at Kylie as he pulled the cruiser away from the terminal.

Dead silence. Kylie's favorite weapon.

"She's not. I mean, it's not. I mean, Jane Finch is not a woman. It's a mall," Henley fumbled. "It's at the intersection of Jane Street and Finch Avenue."

Kylie turned up the silence with a cold who-gives-a-fuck look.

Weeks's turn. "I guess you're here about the bombings," he said.

Crickets.

"You don't have to say anything, but come on. Two NYPD detectives fly up here with questions for a low-rent phone store in North York. You think your bomber bought his cell phone detonators here in Toronto?" He laughed. "You don't have to answer that either."

We didn't.

"Makes sense," Henley said, giving it one last shot. "The store gets robbed a few times a year. Gangs just come in, grab phones, and go."

"They close at nine," Weeks added. "But the manager will be there as long as you need him."

"Thanks," I said, "Much appreciated."

And that was that until we pulled into a dated mall that was populated by fast-food franchises, hair salons, mom-and-pop shops, and at least three other cellular outlets besides Toronto Connected.

Henley parked the cruiser, Weeks assured us that they'd be at our disposal all night, and Kylie and I headed toward the store.

It was dimly lit, a Closed sign on the door. I could see the manager inside, sitting at a desk and tapping on his phone screen.

Kylie and I have a standing rule. No matter what shitstorm is driving us apart—and we've weathered our share—when we're interviewing a witness, we are in lockstep, an army of two.

I stared at Kylie. She glared back. The grudge from our flight still loomed over us like a gathering storm. The interview would have to wait.

"Well, that was a fun ride, wasn't it?" I said.

She cracked a smile—the first since we got on the plane. "Do you believe the fucking balls on that kid?" she said. "Coming on to me with that don't-worry-Mama-I-can-handle-a-cougar swagger?"

"And there was no way I was going to tell those frat boys not to poke the cougar. I figured the interview would go better if you vented your men-are-toxic-assholes wrath before we got here."

"Good call," she said. "It helped. A lot."

"Then you're ready to do this?" I asked.

"Lead the way, partner."

I knocked on the glass door.

Our latest shitstorm was officially on hold.

CHAPTER 48

THE MAN WHO OPENED the door for us could take fourth place in a Timothée Chalamet lookalike contest—late twenties, lean and reedy, with an artsy mop of hair and brooding eyes that were more poet than phone salesman. He wore tailored Topman jeans and black Converse high-tops that said *this is who I am*, and a crisp blue button-down shirt with the Toronto Connected logo on the pocket that said *this is who I work for*.

Kylie and I would have introduced ourselves, but he was way ahead of us. "Detective Jordan, Detective MacDonald, I was hoping it would be you. I'm Duncan Kirkpatrick. How can I help?"

"For starters, you can tell us what you mean by you were *hoping it would be us*."

"Once the TPS called and told me to stick around because a couple of New York City detectives were coming to ask questions, I figured it had to be connected to the 11:59 Bomber. I Googled everything about it. I just never thought the top two cops would fly all the way up here."

"We're not the top," I said.

"Close enough for me," he said. "You think he used one of our phones to—"

"Duncan," I said, "we appreciate how willing you are to help, but how about you let us ask the questions."

"Sorry. Ask away."

I gave him the IMEI number on the phone that had been wired to the block of C4 pulled from the wreckage of Ramón Reyes's house.

"Was this phone purchased here?" I asked.

The operative word was *purchased*. We needed a record of the sale, but once Officer Henley told us that the store was a popular target for thieves, we knew there was a chance that the phone could have disappeared without a trace.

Duncan typed the fifteen-digit code into his computer.

As soon as the results appeared on the screen, his face lit up. "Yes!" he said, pumping a fist in the air. "It was one of ours."

He paused. "Oh, shit."

"What's the matter?" Kylie said.

"It was me," he said in a near whisper. "I'm the one who sold it."

"That's okay," Kylie said. "You can help. What can you tell us about the buyer?"

He gave her a blank stare. "Nothing. I sold it four years ago."

"Think back."

"Detective, I sell tons of these burners. Tourists buy them because it's usually cheaper to pay as you go, avoid your carrier's roaming charges, and toss the phone before you get on the flight home. We also do a brisk business with folks who want to keep their private lives private. Straight cash, no ID necessary."

"And this buyer paid cash?"

"Yes, ma'am. Sixteen hundred and ninety-five dollars."

"*How much?*" Kylie said.

Duncan checked his screen. "Thirty phones at fifty dollars a pop, plus 13 percent tax. Sixteen hundred and ninety-five dollars—Canadian," he added helpfully.

"Wait," Kylie said. "Someone walked into your store and bought thirty phones? It sounds like they'd be memorable."

"Not as memorable as you'd think, Detective MacDonald. A lot of companies buy these throwaways in bulk and give them to their employees who are on the road. Last week, I sold five hundred to the city for use by domestic-violence victims. Heck, I bet you each have a mobile issued by the NYPD."

We did. I didn't bother telling him that ours were top-of-the-line iPhones, because for the most part, Duncan was right. The world had become glutted with cell phones that were as disposable as fast-food wrappers.

Our bomber knew that. Four years ago, when he came to this hole-in-the-wall five hundred miles from New York City, he bought *thirty* phones, completely confident that the clerk would never remember him. And he'd been right.

But even the smartest criminals make mistakes, and I was about to find out if ours fit the mold.

"One more question, Duncan," I said. "That cash sale for the thirty phones—do you have a record of the IMEI number for each unit?"

"Oh, yes, sir," Duncan said. "That's the law. I'll print them out for you."

I'll print them out for you. The words took my breath away.

"I hope this makes up for me selling that dude all those phones," Duncan said as he handed me the printout.

I wanted to scream, "Are you kidding? You just blew this case wide open." But I'm pretty sure he knew what he'd given us. You couldn't work in a phone store and not know how valuable those IMEI numbers were to the investigation.

"Thanks," I said.

"I'll be following the bomber case online," Duncan said. "Good luck."

If it were any other time, I'd have stuck around and made one last denial that our visit had anything to do with the bomber, but my mind was already racing to what I would do as soon as I got back to the squad car.

First, I would send the list to Cates, because once she had those IMEI numbers, she could track any one of those phones as soon as it was activated.

Next, I would make a call to the man who retrieved the phone that brought us to Canada. Because heroes like Ed Campbell deserve to know that they didn't risk their lives in vain.

CHAPTER 49

KYLIE AND I SPENT the night at an airport Hilton. Sarin was booked on an Air Canada to Mumbai at nine. We grabbed some coffee at Tim Hortons, and by six thirty we were waiting for him at his gate.

Kylie texted Cates to let her know that we'd be landing at Newark at eleven thirty. Had we come up empty-handed in Toronto, Cates might have come down on us for missing the first flight out. But once we sent her the list of IMEIs that could lead us to the bomber, she wouldn't have any trouble defending her decision to send us out of the country.

Her response: A thumbs-up emoji, followed by I'LL SEND SOMEONE TO PICK YOU UP WHEN YOU LAND.

"How do you want to do this?" Kylie asked.

"I don't know how *you're* doing it, but I'm just going to sit here and watch the drama unfold."

"Ha! You say that now, Zach, but the minute Sarin shows up, your blind loyalty to me will kick in, and you will—"

"My blind loyalty will kick in?" I said. "Is that code for my defective rescue gene?"

"Don't knock it, Zach. Some of my best friends are hopelessly codependent."

"Hey, we're partners," I said. "You know I'm not going to leave you high and dry. But I hope you also know that using the bombing case to get Cates to authorize this trip is way out of line, totally unethical, and . . . and . . ."

"Blatantly against everything you stand for," she said with a smile. "Yet here we are, so let's just get it done."

"Fine," I said.

"Thank you. Now let me tell you what I'm thinking. Sarin is traveling with an entourage. I figured I'd call him aside, tell him I was at his fundraiser in New York, while you distract—"

"Stop! No. This is not a sting. You're an NYPD homicide detective investigating the murder of Preston Balfour, and you want to ask him some questions."

"I'm a New York City cop in Toronto, Zach. He knows I have no authority here."

"You don't need authority. You're just having a conversation. If he walks away, the conversation is over. Play it straight."

I didn't have to add, "Or I'm not having any part of it." She knows how far she can push me.

"Are we good?" I asked.

She nodded.

"Who is he traveling with?" I said. "I'm sure your friend Angela Watson gave you a lot more than his flight number."

"Well, you know Angela. The woman is relentless in the pursuit of justice," Kylie said, pulling out a pad and flipping to her notes. "First, we have Priya Sharma, the girl who almost died on the operating table when the power failed. She's fourteen now and planning to go to medical school, and Theo was not kidding—she is totally charismatic. When Sarin speaks, people give money. When Priya speaks, they give a lot more money.

"She's with her father, Vikram. He's the electrician who inspired the whole services-for-medical-care barter system. Then there's Maya Desai. She's a consultant who specializes in high-profile fundraising campaigns. Her job is to make sure that the most generous people in the Indian community attend the events, and so far, it looks like she's been nailing it. And finally, there's Rohan Kapoor. He's the facilitator, travel arranger, first-to-get-up-in-the-morning and last-to-go-to-bed right-hand man to Dr. Sarin. Any questions?"

"Just one," I said. "Who's interviewing Sarin?"

"Me," she said. "I'll take the lead."

"I know you'll take the lead," I said. "The question is, *who* is interviewing Sarin? Detective Kylie MacDonald? Or Mrs. Spence Harrington?"

She didn't answer. I'd made my point.

CHAPTER 50

SARIN'S PLANE WAS SCHEDULED to leave on time at nine a.m. At 8:15, the flight started to board. But no sign of him or his traveling companions.

By 8:40, Kylie called her friend Angela Watson to make sure Sarin hadn't changed his plans.

"The good news," she said when she hung up, "is that all five of them have been at the airport since seven thirty. They checked in at the Air Canada Maple Leaf Lounge. The bad news is that by the time they get to the gate, I won't have much time to talk to Sarin."

"Would you like me to tackle you if you try to get on the plane to Mumbai?"

"Zach, it's not funny. This is our only chance—oh, shit, here they come."

The group of five were walking our way. Sarin, Priya, and a man of about forty were in the lead. Based on his age and the protective hand he had on the girl's shoulder, I assumed he was her father. The three of them were chatting, smiling, clearly in good spirits. No surprise. They were headed home after a successful trip. Maya Desai, the fundraising specialist, and Rohan Kapoor, the young facilitator, were a few steps behind them, both on their phones.

"Dr. Sarin," Kylie called out as they got to the gate.

The group stopped, and Sarin walked toward us. "I'm sorry," he said. "Have we met?"

"I'm Detective Kylie MacDonald from the New York City Police Department, and this is my partner, Detective Jordan."

"How can I help you?" he said, puzzled but polite.

"Preston Balfour," she said.

It wasn't a question. Questions are too easily dismissed with a quick yes-or-no answer. But just those two words, "Preston Balfour," were a minefield. We waited to see how Sarin would navigate it.

"I read about it," he said. "Somebody killed him. Dreadful."

"When was the last time you spoke to Mr. Balfour?" she said.

"We haven't spoken in years, Detective. And I'm sure you know why. It's no secret that Mr. Balfour's movie destroyed my reputation. My associates and I have been doing our best to undo the damage. I know nothing about his death, and I'm sorry you had to come all the way up here to talk to me."

"We're talking to everybody."

"The man shattered the lives of countless people in my country," Sarin said, the slightest edge creeping into his gentle manner. "Are you planning to talk to them?"

"Only the ones who were in New York the same time Balfour was murdered," Kylie said.

A sly smile crept across Sarin's face. Possibly because he thought the idea of a New York cop ambushing him in a Canadian airport was preposterous, or maybe he was enjoying the fact that Kylie was a worthy adversary. Then I decided, nah. Underneath it all, the good doctor was just a red-blooded man, and the roguish smile is our primal response when we meet a desirable woman.

"Dr. Sarin." It was the facilitator. The group was still waiting twenty feet away. "Time to board."

Sarin held up a finger, then waved them toward the gate agent. Translation: *I'll be right there. Get on the plane.*

They didn't budge. They just stood in unwavering solidarity.

"Detectives," Sarin said, drawing me into the conversation. "I understand you have a grave and difficult job to do. You are looking for someone who took the life of another human being. I appreciate that you came all this way, but I can assure you that I am not that person.

"I'm a physician. I've dedicated my life to helping others. I don't have to like them—and I certainly didn't like Preston Balfour—but I would never, ever harm him. I'm also a religious man, and my faith categorically forbids the taking of any life—not for love, not for money, not for honor . . ." He paused, his eyes meeting ours unflinchingly. "Not for anything."

Kylie and I are trained to spot a lie. We can detect a subtle shift in body language, a change in tone of voice or pitch, or an involuntary facial expression that signals dishonesty. But Sarin's demeanor was steady, his voice even, his message sincere.

"One final point, and then I must go," he said. "Do you see that young woman over there? Priya Sharma. One day to become *Doctor* Priya Sharma. She has chosen to follow in my path. I am humbled to be her role model, and there is nothing I would ever do to jeopardize her trust or tarnish the example I have set for her."

He gave us a quick head bow, wished us well on our mission, and joined his group. As I watched him stride confidently toward the jetway, my cop instincts kicked in, leaving me with one inescapable conclusion.

He didn't do it.

CHAPTER 51

BLIND FAITH CRUMBLES WHEN confronted with harsh reality, and after hearing Dr. Sarin's impassioned declaration of innocence, Kylie came to the same conclusion I had. It just took her a little longer.

We were on the flight back to Newark when she finally said what I had been thinking.

"I guess we're down to one suspect," she said. "Spence."

I didn't say a word. This was her ethical quandary to unravel.

She tilted her seat back and closed her eyes, and I knew where she was going to do the unraveling. It's a little corner of her mind where she stores her Spence baggage. I can only imagine what it's like in there. More than a decade of being lied to by her drug-addict husband, one horrific moment when she brought him back from near death with a shot of Narcan, not knowing where he was for two years, finding out he married another woman while he was still married to her, and now this—arrested on a murder charge with three eyewitnesses ready to testify that they saw him do it.

Damn right we were down to one suspect.

We both slept for most of the flight, and were on our final approach to Newark when we were awake enough to get back to the subject neither of us wanted to talk about.

"*If* he did it," she said. "I find it impossible to conceive that Spence is capable of that kind of violence, but *if* he did it, it wasn't murder one. Maybe it's what Theo said when he thought it was Sarin. Spence went to Balfour's apartment with good intentions. His sponsor told him to make amends. But Balfour probably laughed in his face. Spence snapped and grabbed the knife."

It was a baby step. Yes, she was considering the possibility that Spence was, in fact, the killer, but she was doing what she always did. Justifying his actions.

She went on. "I'm not saying he did it, but if he did, it definitely wasn't premeditated. He just went off the deep end. And once he realized those witnesses saw him, he had to come up with a cover story, so he did. He invented a likely suspect. And a damn good one.

"You heard what he told Detective Elliott. He said he wasn't sure if the guy he tangled with was white or Black, and when Elliott tried to pin him down, Spence said the man was kind of swarthy. He knew that Sarin's beef with Balfour was all over the internet, so he figured 'kind of swarthy' would be enough to motivate Elliott to start looking in Sarin's direction.

"But the eyewitness testimony was so overwhelming that Elliott didn't dig any deeper," she said. "I can't blame him. The evidence is pretty convincing. I'm not sure even the Warlock can convince a jury that there's room for reasonable doubt."

She let out a long sigh. "It doesn't matter. I'm not giving up on him. I just haven't figured out where we go from here."

"Wherever it is," I said, "I'm right there with you."

She leaned forward in her seat. "Something is going on over there," she said, pointing out the window as our plane touched down on the runway.

Four Port Authority cop cars with their lights flashing were parked on the edge of the taxiway. Next to them was an NYPD helicopter. I got a queasy feeling in my stomach and turned off airplane mode on my iPhone.

A dozen texts from Captain Cates popped up. Before I could read them, the pilot's voice filled the cabin. "Ladies and gentlemen, welcome to Newark. We are not yet at the gate, so please remain seated with your seat belts fastened. Will the passengers in seats 12-A and 12-C please come to the front of the plane. Everyone else, remain in your seats until we are parked at the terminal."

But we weren't going to the terminal. We had turned off the runway onto a parallel taxiway and stopped. The four cruisers and an aircraft passenger-stair truck headed our way.

I called Cates.

"We just got a hit on one of the IMEIs you gave us last night," she said. "One of those phones was activated on the boardwalk in Coney Island. There's a chopper waiting for you. You can be here in about twelve minutes."

"Is the bomb squad on the way?" I said as I made my way to the front. Kylie was right behind me, catching enough of the conversation to connect the dots.

"Yes, but they're forty-five minutes out," Cates said. "TARU has triangulated the signal: an eight-hundred-foot stretch centered on Luna Park. I've got an army of uniformed officers pouring in from every precinct in Brooklyn to clear the area, but it's a beautiful day in July, perfect beach weather, and it's almost lunchtime. There are more than a thousand people just in that potential blast area alone, and we've got to get them out of harm's way without causing a stampede."

The front cabin door swung open, and four Port Authority cops boarded the plane.

"Detectives," one of them said, "these two officers will take you to the chopper. We'll get your bags."

We followed the two PA cops down the stairs and ran toward the helicopter.

I looked at my watch: 11:38. The bomb squad wouldn't get there by 11:59.

Cates had twenty-one minutes to get more than a thousand people off the beach and move them to a safe location. And knowing New Yorkers, some of them would not go willingly.

CHAPTER 52

"HOW CLOSE CAN YOU get us to the boardwalk?" Kylie asked our chopper pilot as we flew over the Verrazzano-Narrows Bridge between Staten Island and Brooklyn.

"Normally, I could set you down on the sand dollar of your choice," the pilot said, "but the rotor wash on this Bell 429 can kick up enough of a downdraft to topple an entire row of porta-potties. And if you think that's a shitstorm, it's nothing compared to what would happen if I flew anywhere close to a device that's primed to blow. I'll get you as close as I can."

Five minutes later, we touched down in the outfield of Maimonides Park, home of the local minor-league heroes, the Brooklyn Cyclones.

An NYPD sergeant was waiting for us in a golf cart.

"Bobby Diehl," he said, pulling out as soon as we jumped on. "It's chaos. Our guys are out there yelling, 'Get off the boardwalk. Clear the beach. Go, go, go.' But this is Brooklyn, man, so a lot of these bozos don't budge. They just give us the finger. 'Why you kickin' me out? I didn't do nuttin.' And we can't scream 'bomb,' because then they'll kill each other in the stampede to get away."

Diehl was a classic Brooklyn cop—full of opinions, short on tolerance. We were definitely not in Toronto anymore.

"Look at this," he said, weaving the golf cart through the crowd. "Some people, especially families with kids, are leaving. I mean, how many bombs have to go off at 11:59 before you realize that a bunch of cops trying to evacuate the area at 11:48 may actually know what they're talking about? But for every person who's running away from the danger, you got just as many assholes with cameras trying to get as close as they can. If this bomber is looking for maximum casualties, he couldn't have picked a more willing bunch of victims.

"TARU pinged the center of the signal right here," he said, stopping the golf cart on the boardwalk in front of Nathan's original hot dog stand.

Despite the order to evacuate, people were still lined up waiting to order. "It gives new meaning to the phrase 'dying for a hot dog,'" Diehl muttered.

"Jordan! MacDonald!"

We turned. It was Brooklyn Borough Chief Trevor Stokes.

"Chief," I said.

"You have any idea where this maniac might have stashed the device?"

"Chief, we know what you know," I said.

"All I know is, it's 11:49. If this bomber sticks to his MO, in ten minutes there's going to be a loud bang, but a lot of these people won't hear a thing. At this point, I can't waste manpower arguing with the holdouts, so I have most of my guys looking for the device."

Kylie and I joined the hunt.

Chief Stokes assigned someone to give us a countdown every thirty seconds.

"Eleven fifty-two. Eleven fifty-two and thirty seconds. Eleven fifty-three."

At 11:55, Stokes told his command to vacate the area. A few of them did. But most kept looking, Kylie and me included.

At 11:56, Sergeant Diehl's voice rang out above the madness. "Detectives! We got it; we got it!"

We ran over to a trash bin where a uniformed officer was standing next to a pyramid of empty soda cans, which she had spilled onto the boardwalk.

The cop was young, breathing heavily, probably scared out of her mind, but she kept it together.

"I'm going through all these garbage bins, and I notice this one bag. It's clear, and I can see it's full of empty soda cans. Hundreds of them—every one worth five cents. Who walks away from a gold mine like that? I go to lift the bag, and I can barely get it off the ground. The cans are filled with screws and nails. So I cut the bag open, and look at this."

She bent down and pointed to a few dozen soda cans that were held together with clear plastic tape. At first, they looked as innocuous as the thousands of other multicolored cans that now littered the boardwalk. And then I saw what the young cop had seen.

At the very center of that seemingly innocent kaleidoscope of reds, blues, greens, and oranges was an almost invisible brick of clay, probably no more than two kilos. Once, it had been grayish white, but now it was painted to blend in with the cans of deadly shrapnel that said Coke, Pepsi, Mountain Dew, or orange Crush.

My eyes traced the wires that were protruding from the camouflaged C4 to a red, white, and blue Nokia cell phone. My stomach tightened. We'd found what we were looking for.

"11:57," the timekeeper called out.

Kylie dropped to the boardwalk and inspected the device. "Let me get to work," she said.

I stared at her. *Doing what?* I thought.

CHAPTER 53

KYLIE STUDIED THE DEVICE but didn't touch it. "It kind of looks like the one they pulled out of the rubble at Reyes's house," she said.

"*Kind of?*" I said.

"I'm new at this, Zach," she said. "But I'm pretty sure it's the same exact setup as the one Ed Campbell disarmed."

"Great. Now all we need is Ed Campbell."

"Well, he's not here, so I'm going to give it my best shot," she said.

"11:57 and thirty seconds," the timekeeper called out.

"I need to focus," Kylie said. "Now, get the hell out of here and take cover."

I dropped to the ground beside her.

"Don't be an idiot, Zach. You have a son!"

"And he's never going to have a father who saved his own ass while hundreds of civilians got riddled with shrapnel. Now, do you have any idea what you're doing?"

"No, but it's not rocket science. You got a block of C4 and a blasting cap wired to an old-model Nokia phone."

"Built by an amateur," I reminded her.

"Yes!" she said, as if I'd said something important. "I keep thinking this guy is smart. He is, but he's still a rookie at making bombs, so he probably doesn't have the chops to build in any fail-safes to keep us from disabling it."

Probably, I thought. *Probably.*

"11:58," the timekeeper called out.

"Look, Zach, I don't know shit about bombs," Kylie said. "But I do know that in sixty seconds, somebody is going to call this phone, which is going to send a signal through these wires, which will spark the blasting cap and we'll all be dead. The C4 by itself is stable. The blasting cap is the firing pin."

"So you're saying we should remove the firing pin," I said.

"You game?"

"Eleven fifty-eight and thirty seconds," the timekeeper called out.

"Let's do it," I said.

She handed me the C4 that was wrapped in soda cans filled with thousands of tiny, lethal missiles.

"I'm going to yank the blasting cap hard enough to pull it out of the C4 on one end and disconnect the wires from the phone on the other end, and then I'm going to throw it onto that clear section of the beach and hope it doesn't explode while it's still in my hand."

"Got it," I said.

"And I'm going to yank hard, so hold it like your life depended on it."

I hugged the device to my chest. Fear surged through every nerve ending in my body, and then a second emotion washed over me—one I never expected. Regret.

I should have told Theo I'm his father.

Kylie let her hand hover just above the tip of the blasting cap.

Our eyes locked.

And like Ed Campbell, she whispered three words, knowing they could well be her last.

"Love you, Zach."

Then, in one swift motion, she plucked the cap from the deadly plastic, ripped the wires from the phone, and sent them flying through the air to land on the sand.

It sat there. No spark. No ignition.

"The cap must have been a dud," Kylie said.

"11:59," the timekeeper announced.

The phone, which was still attached to the device cradled in my arms, rang. In a nanosecond, the blasting cap exploded. Sand flew in the air, leaving a gaping hole on the beach.

I stared at the scorched rim around the hole. "I guess it wasn't a dud," I said as I slowly eased the homemade bomb from my body and rested it on the boardwalk.

Kylie gave me a shrug. "Close one."

The phone rang again.

"I'll get it," she chirped.

She picked up the phone.

"You have reached the New York City Police Department," she said, her voice a menacing mix of anger, authority, and resolve. "It's 11:59, motherfucker."

CHAPTER 54

ARTHUR HAD BEEN STANDING outside the McDonald's on Stillwell Avenue, more than a quarter mile away from the bomb, when he dialed the number that would set it off.

"Play the part," his mentor at Rikers had taught him. "Even though you know nobody is going to answer, you gotta look like a regular guy making a phone call. You never know who's got eyes on you, so you always, always, *always* gotta play the part."

In this case, playing the part meant putting the phone to his ear as soon as he dialed. That's when he heard the ring.

The phone *rang*? The phone wasn't supposed to ring. What was *supposed* to happen was a loud explosion that shot everything within fifty feet of the blast into a billowing cloud of toxic black smoke.

The phone rang a second time. And yet, the sky was still clear. And the only sounds he heard were the traffic on the avenue, and the rumble of the subway as it pulled into the Coney Island station, mixed with the jibber-jabber of people enjoying a beautiful day.

Shit, shit, shit, he thought. *I programmed the wrong number. I called the wrong phone.*

And then the woman answered. "You have reached the New York City Police Department."

His knees buckled. There was a bench outside the McDonald's, and he managed to stagger toward it before his body collapsed to the ground from shock.

Did I call the police? How could I—?

"It's 11:59, motherfucker," the woman said.

Oh God! It's a cop, and she was expecting my call!

Dumbstruck, he hung up and powered down the phone.

They knew where the bomb would be. But how could they know?

Arthur's mind, nimble as it was, could never have reconstructed the circuitous path that led the cops to him. An unexploded device detected in the wreckage of Ramón's house. An IMEI that led them to a phone store in Toronto. An alert salesman who could provide them with the tracking numbers of every single phone he bought years ago. A global electronic sweep to alert the cops the second he activated the next deadly bomb. And hundreds of dedicated cops willing to put their lives on the line to stop him.

Instead, his paranoia led him down the most logical path.

Ramón ratted me out.

Somehow, he survived the explosion and got word to the cops—no, impossible. Ramón didn't know where or when I was going to plant the next bomb. And he certainly didn't know which phone I was going to use. Unless . . . unless . . .

The thought made him sick.

Ramón had the list. He had the numbers of all the phones. And he left it someplace where the cops could find it. His car. The dumb bastard left the master list of all thirty phone numbers in the glove compartment of his car. The cops were just waiting for me to turn any one of them on, and when I did, they pinged it.

"Well, guess what, Ramón?" he muttered, just loud enough that only he and his dead ex-partner could hear. "You failed again. You gave me lemons, and I'm making lemonade."

He walked to where he had parked his car on West Twelfth and jumped on the Belt Parkway, his mind feverishly trying to conjure up a scenario to get even with the New York City Police Department for ruining his day.

By the time he reached the Whitestone Bridge, the midday sun was glaring through the windshield, bouncing off the bright expanse of water below. Squinting, he reached for the faded old ball cap on the seat beside him.

His hand froze as his fingers brushed the frayed brim. *The hat*, he thought. That was the answer! His heart thudded against his chest, and his brain kicked into overdrive as it tried to turn divine inspiration into reality.

A horn blared. He had been so caught up in thought that he drifted out of his lane. He jerked the wheel hard as the woman in the car he'd almost hit gave him the finger and sped past.

He calmed himself and held the hat up to eye level. Once, it was a crisp, rich navy blue, but ten years of sweat and sun had left a greasy black ring around the crown and bleached it to a pale denim.

It was a patchwork of memories, the most vivid being the first time his father saw it. Stefan had just closed the restaurant for the night, and the two of them were sitting at a table in the back sharing a plate of apricot *palacsinta* and drinking steaming cups of strong, dark *fekete kávé*.

"Fancy-schmancy hat," Stefan said, studying the gleaming gold lettering and the oak tree crest embroidered on the front. "What does *LHC* stand for?"

"The Larchmont Heritage Club. I just joined."

"What was wrong with your Hungarian heritage?"

"Nothing. It's a country club. It was Gwen's idea. They have a golf course—"

"Since when did you become a golfer?"

Arthur laughed. "I'm not. It's a thing with these clubs. They also have a beautiful pool—"

"I thought your new house has a pool."

"It does."

"So why do you need two pools?"

"It's not about the pool. Gwen and I moved to Westchester to give our kids the best life possible. People up there measure you by the circles you move in. So we joined a club. Gwen convinced me that it's worth the money."

"How much money?"

Arthur grinned. He knew that if he ever said, "Two hundred and fifty thousand if they accept you; fifty thousand a year after that," his father would keel over.

"Trust me, Pop. You don't want to know."

Stefan pushed. "So what are we talking about? Like a thousand dollars a year?"

"Give or take," Arthur said. "But on the plus side, they have a beautiful restaurant. Once we settle in, Gwen and I will invite you and Mom to join us there for dinner."

"Give us plenty of notice. We'll starve ourselves so we can pig out and work off the money you laid out."

"It doesn't work that way, Pop. You pay to belong. The food costs extra."

He would never forget the look on his father's face. "Wait. You're paying money just to *join* the restaurant? And then you pay more for the food? Anna!" he yelled to his wife in the kitchen. "We're idiots! All these years running a restaurant, and we never thought of charging people just to *walk in*."

His father was gone now. His mother too. They were two farm kids who came to New York from the little village of Fehérgyarmat and built their dream—a restaurant where neighbors became friends, and every meal felt like home.

And then the city crushed their dream.

Tears streamed down Arthur's cheeks as he merged onto the Hutchinson River Parkway. "But don't worry, Pop," he said. "I'm making them pay. And I'll do it again tomorrow."

He slid the weathered old Larchmont Heritage Club cap onto his head and caught a glimpse of himself in the rearview mirror.

And then he laughed out loud thinking of the look on the old man's face if he ever found out that so far, that fancy-schmancy hat had cost him seven hundred fifty thousand dollars.

CHAPTER 55

"WE GOT LUCKY TODAY," Cates said at the tactical debriefing. "We located and disarmed the device despite the fact that the bomb squad was still en route. But we can't trust to luck. The bear has been poked, and he's pissed. So next time—and I promise you there will be a next time—we have to step up our game, because he will be stepping up his.

"The good news is that he has a stash of cell phones we can track. Hopefully, he'll be using one of those. If he does, we have to swoop down on that target as quickly as possible, and in full force. We'll have choppers and a response team standing by at three strategic locations. Each team will comprise personnel from the bomb squad, ESU, TARU, and detectives from Red. No matter where in the city that signal comes from, we can have the closest team in the air within seconds. Any questions or concerns?"

No hands went up. It was a solid plan.

"Good," Cates said. "The bomber's MO has been to activate the device as close to 11:59 a.m. as he can and still get out of harm's way. But just in case he changes his pattern, all three units will be ready by first light."

Kylie and I were assigned to Orchard Beach, affectionately known to the locals as the Bronx Riviera. The beachfront is over a mile long, and the weather forecast that morning promised a scorcher, which meant that by 11:59 as many as a hundred thousand people could be blanket to blanket to blanket. A section of the beach's eight thousand parking spots was cordoned off to be our staging area. Kylie and I were in the mobile command center by five a.m.

The probability that the bomber would activate his next device before eleven was slim. That gave us six hours to focus on our other priority: Who murdered Preston Balfour?

We started by accessing the body cam videos recorded from the moment the 911 call came in. Basically, we would be reviewing all the footage that convinced Detective Elliott to charge Spence with Balfour's murder. Technically, our mission was to confirm that Elliott had been right, but of course, our hope was to catch something he had missed.

We watched the first cops to respond enter the building on Baxter Street. As they charged up the stairs to the fourth floor, they passed people in the lobby who were either waiting for the elevator or just standing around doing whatever the cool kids do at eleven o'clock on a Thursday night in the lobby of a building in the trendy part of town.

I counted five people. Kylie counted six. Several of the lobby walls were mirrored, and I'm pretty sure that one of hers was a reflection, but it didn't really matter. The cops ran past them so fast that even after we scrutinized every face, at best all we had were five or six blurs of interest.

We'd seen the most damning evidence before: Spence standing over Balfour's body, the confirmed murder weapon still in his hand. We watched it over and over, frame by frame, but it never got any less damning. It was impossible to conceive of a jury of twelve men and women watching that video and walking away with reasonable doubt.

Less than ninety seconds passed from the time one of those police officers left their car until the time Spence was in cuffs, but it took us close to an hour to pore over each body cam video. There were fourteen in all, and the more I watched, the more I was convinced that Elliott had made the right call. Kylie was married to a murderer.

We still had five videos to review when Eddie Acevedo from TARU looked up from his laptop. "We've got a hit," he said calmly. "Device activated six miles from here. We're mobilized."

It was 11:29. We had thirty minutes.

"I didn't think he'd hit the Bronx," I said as we jumped into the helicopter.

"He didn't," Acevedo said. "The signal came from Westchester. We're the closest."

"Westchester?" Kylie said. "I thought his beef was with the city."

Acevedo shrugged. "His beef may be with the city," he said, "but his bomb is at the Larchmont Heritage Club."

CHAPTER 56

"A COUNTRY CLUB IN Larchmont?" Kylie said as the chopper lifted off. "It doesn't make sense."

The way she said it made it sound as if all the other bombings made perfect sense, but I knew what she meant. Our bomber was consumed with destroying New York. What made him suddenly change his MO and branch out beyond the five boroughs?

"Does he think we won't show up just because he planted a bomb outside the city limits?" Kylie said. "This is our case."

"Maybe not," Acevedo said.

Kylie turned on him. "What are you talking about?"

"Well," Acevedo said cautiously, knowing full well that he was going up against a world-class verbal combatant. "We're the NYPD. Larchmont has its own police department. Don't be surprised if they say, 'Thanks, but we got this.'"

"Eddie, think about it. You're the chief of Larchmont PD. Why would you turn down help from one of the premier bomb squads in the world?"

"Because they have a damn good one right there in their backyard. Are you familiar with the Westchester County Police Hazardous Device Unit?"

She wasn't. I wasn't. Eddie enlightened us.

"They're as good as it gets. I live in Mamaroneck. One of the dads in my kid's school is in that unit. They're not as big as we are, but they're just as well trained, and they've got everything they need: dogs, robots, top-of-the-line equip— holy shit," Acevedo said, slapping a hand to his head. "I think I just figured out why our bomber bailed on New York City and brought his bag of tricks to Westchester."

"Why?"

"Because when we land, there's nothing we can do that isn't already being done by the Westchester bomb squad. We're going to be standing around with our thumbs up our asses, just like the rest of the spectators."

And that's pretty much how it went.

As soon as Kylie and I set down on the golf course, Captain Tom Small, the bomb squad CO, made it clear. This was their turf, not ours.

Ten minutes later, a second NYPD helicopter landed, and Cates got out. The two captains talked. The conversation lasted less than a minute.

"He made no bones about it," Cates told us. "We are not invited to the party, but he did give me an update. All members and staff have been evacuated. The dogs have gone through the buildings, and there is no detection of any explosive components."

"Nothing?" I said.

"Nothing. Including C4," Cates said.

"Can we help with *anything*?" I asked. "Crowd control comes to mind."

There were a couple of hundred people standing on the golf course, most of them with their phones in front of their faces, recording the impending disaster for social media.

"First of all, that *crowd*," Cates said, gesturing toward the throng of rich and powerful socialites, "is not exactly controllable. Second of all, Captain Small decided it was smarter and safer to move them a thousand feet away from any possible blast than to have a horde of *very important people* storm the valet station waving hundred-dollar bills and screaming, 'Bring my car up immediately.'"

"It's 11:55," I said. "What's next?"

"Captain Small has the numbers of all the phones you tracked down in Toronto, and one of them is still sending a strong signal from inside the club," Cates said. "He's confident that his dogs got it right and there's no bomb in there, but he's not going to risk anyone's life this close to 11:59. So we wait."

We waited. 11:59 came and went. We kept waiting.

Finally, at twelve thirty, Small invited Cates and the two of us over to the staging area. "We're going in with a Triggerfish," he said.

A Triggerfish is a handheld device that mimics a cell tower. When a mobile phone connects to it, the Triggerfish can pick up the unique identifiers of that phone, and then a tech can home in on it within a few feet. It's like a Find My Phone app on steroids. NYPD has two of them, neither of which was able to make it to Brooklyn before 11:59. Having one here was a game changer.

At 12:36, two Westchester cops entered the Heritage Club. We could watch the video from their helmet cameras on a large flat-screen monitor set up in the staging area.

The lead cop had the Triggerfish. He entered the dining area and crisscrossed the room slowly, deliberately. He made his way to the kitchen, which looked to be fifty or sixty feet deep. He was almost at the far end of the room when he said, "It's here."

His camera scanned a wall of metal racks stacked with clean linens. We could read the labels as he moved past the racks. Tablecloths. Napkins. Runners. Waiters' jackets.

And then . . . "Got it," he said.

The signal on his equipment was as strong as it could get. The label on the rack said, *Chef's Coats*.

The second cop, the most experienced bomb tech on the team, moved in and scanned the stack of white uniforms with a handheld X-ray device.

"It's a phone," the tech said. "That's all I'm picking up. No wires. No explosives. Just a phone."

One by one, he removed the coats, dropping nine of them to the floor until we saw what we'd been looking for.

One of the coats had a cell phone sticking out of the pocket.

"Wait," the tech said. "There's a message taped to it. Let me get my camera closer to the phone so you can read it."

The camera moved in. The focus kept going in and out until it held, and we could all read the two strips of tape that were stuck to the screen.

The words were handwritten in block letters. And in case we had any doubt who the message was for, our bomber had written them in bright red.

NOW WHO'S RUNNING THE SHOW? TICK TOCK, MOTHERFUCKERS.

CHAPTER 57

ARTHUR HAD BEEN SITTING at the Heritage Club bar nursing a Diet Coke when he heard the sirens.

It was 11:34. The cops had picked up the signal on the detonator phone as soon as he activated it, and they were on the scene within minutes.

Good news, bad news, he thought. The good news was, he had figured the only way they got to Coney Island so fast was that they could track his phones, and this little experiment had proved it. The bad news was, his entire stash of Nokias was now useless.

The sirens grew closer. He had positioned himself at the bar so he could watch the cavalry pull up to the front of the club. Larchmont PD was first on the scene.

The cops poured into the dining room, Vern Hollister, the chief of police, in the lead.

The Heritage Club prided itself in always taking very good care of the local gendarmerie—donations to ensure that they had the best equipment, holiday gift baskets, scholarships for their kids, and, of course, invitations to charity galas, golf tournaments, and the annual Fourth of July clambake.

It was a mutually beneficial arrangement. The police knew exactly who buttered their bread, and as one of their biggest champions, Arthur was on a first-name basis with all of them, especially the chief.

"We need to clear the building," Chief Hollister bellowed without polite apologies for barging in. "We have a situation, and everyone—club members, staff, managers, *everyone*—has to leave immediately."

The cops broke into two groups. Some fanned out through the building to make sure no one was left behind, while the rest shepherded the crowd toward the golf course, where they would be out of harm's way, and to Arthur's delight, he would have a front-row seat for the festivities.

Next to roll up on the scene was the Westchester County Police Hazardous Devices Unit. Arthur had done his research. The WCPD was one of the few FBI-accredited bomb squads in the state that could compete with the NYPD.

Bringing up the rear were two NYPD helicopters. The first one had the two lead detectives. He had watched the Coney Island videos on Facebook and Instagram, and he recognized the blond immediately. She was the bitch who had disarmed his bomb and answered the phone when he tried to set it off.

Cates arrived on the second chopper. Arthur knew that by now, her minions had radioed her the bad news, and he watched her walk toward the top gun on the bomb squad with the practiced ease of someone who knew exactly where she stood—and where she didn't.

The exchange was brief and to the point. She and her team were benched.

The drama played out much the way Arthur had scripted it, and the finale, which he recorded for posterity, was even better than he had imagined. Cates had played it close to the vest the entire time, but she reeled like a wounded gazelle when the little love note he had sent her popped up on the monitor.

At heart, Arthur was a numbers guy, and having watched all that NYPD manpower and firepower get cockblocked, he couldn't help but run the mental math. The choppers, the gear, the trained specialists all just sitting there with nothing to do and no place to go—how many thousands of taxpayer dollars were being pissed away every minute?

The media would eat it up, and before this day was over, Delia Cates and her entire lah-dee-fucking-dah Red team would be dragging their high-priced, high-profile asses back to the city, while he and his cronies would be back in the Heritage Club toasting Vern Hollister and the rest of their local heroes.

He was about to saunter over to Police Chief Hollister and congratulate him on a job well done when the text came in.

> **Guess who's not dead?**

His stomach knotted. It couldn't be. He texted back.

> **Who is this?**

> **Your long-lost Brother. ¿Cómo estás, hermano?**

CHAPTER 58

ARTHUR'S MIND RACED. RAMÓN? No. Impossible. But who else could it be? Arthur was about to text back, but he stopped himself. It didn't matter if it was Ramón or not. He wasn't going to respond.

And then another text popped up.

> I guess you'd rather talk than type.
> Answer the phone or my next call
> is to NYPD. Ramón.

And then his phone rang. Arthur backed away from the crowd and moved toward the tree line before he answered. "Who is this?" he said.

"Come on, Arthur. It's your favorite eight-fingered pitcher."

"I doubt it," Arthur said. "He's dead."

"Is he? According to what I read online, the cops have identified eight bodies—Nico Patrakis and seven of his loyal followers. Unfortunately for you, I wasn't home when you decided to blow me to hell. *Yo soy Ramón Reyes, pendejo.*"

"Or you're one of those AI programs that can duplicate his voice."

Ramón laughed. "I almost forgot how your twisted brain works. You're right. Voices can be faked, but would AI know that your mother used to put her rings inside a Bustelo coffee can when she was cooking?

Or that you had a cat named Boglárka when you were a kid? Or that for the past five years, every time you go on a business trip to London, you're banging that antique book dealer from Notting Hill? Her name is Fiona Willoughby, and she thinks you're Michael Croft, an insurance underwriter who spends his days in a cubicle crunching numbers. Boring as hell, but it keeps her from asking too many questions."

How? How? How? Arthur thought as he moved deeper into the tree line. *Calm yourself. Just remember, it's not a problem if you can throw money at it.* "How much do you want, Ramón?"

"Glad you asked. A million dollars."

"Fuck you!" he growled into the phone.

"In that case, two million. Do you know how many of our little conversations I recorded?"

Arthur didn't say a word.

"Almost all of them," Ramón said. "Hold on. Let me play one of my favorites."

Ten seconds passed, and then Arthur heard his own voice.

"When I sued the city of New York, all I asked for was a lousy five million dollars. Now I want to grind them to a halt. The economic backlash from these bombs will cost them billions. I just want them to feel the pain. Then we'll quit. Justice will have been served, Anna and Stefan Harmati will be avenged, I will quietly walk away, never to be seen or heard from again, and you, my friend, will be financially set for life."

"As it turns out," Ramón said, returning to the phone, "you terminated our employment prematurely, so I am not financially set for life, but two million dollars will fix that. You have twenty-four hours to get it to me. And don't tell me you don't have it."

"You know I have it, but do you think it's just sitting around? I need at least a week to put that kind of cash together."

"I'll give you five days. If the money isn't in my account in the Caymans by then, I will post every last one of those recordings on YouTube. The cops will see it. Gwen will see it. And the kids who go to school with your daughters will see it. You shouldn't have tried to kill me, Arthur."

"I'm sorry."

"Add two million to that heartfelt apology, and all is forgiven. You have five days," Ramón said. "And before you try to calculate how far you can get in five days, just remember that you need a passport to leave the country. Don't bother looking for yours. It's in a safe place. I'll tell you where as soon as you wire me the money. *Adiós, amigo.*"

Ramón hung up.

"I have bad news for you, Ramón," Arthur said, talking into the dead phone. "You're not getting two million. You're not getting two cents. My parents have been avenged. But I really needed the five days to get even with the person who ruined my life."

He looked across the golf course until his eyes found Captain Delia Cates.

He put his phone in his pocket and smiled. The 11:59 Bomber's twisted brain was making plans to set off one last bomb.

CHAPTER 59

COPS THRIVE ON BUSTING each other's balls, so as soon as word of the bomber's latest kick to Red's collective nuts got out, the gloves came off, and a text chain dubbed *The Country Club Clusterfuck* spread through the department, picking up steam as more cops joined in to pile on the jokes.

Someone even took the time to Photoshop a picture of Kylie and me decked out in tennis whites, holding champagne flutes on the lawn of the club, with the caption NYPD RED: PROTECTING AND SERVING . . . MIMOSAS.

It was hard not to laugh. On the other hand, the brass at 1PP has zero sense of humor, so when the media exploded with headlines like "Heritage Club Hoax: NYPD Red-faced!" and "Tick, Tock, Laughingstock!" the backlash was swift, furious, and brutal.

Kylie and I were in Cates's office when the desk sergeant called. "Captain, there's a steaming-mad three-star chief headed your way."

Steaming mad was putting it mildly. Chief Doyle, who has always been one of our biggest supporters, was anything but supportive.

He stormed into Cates's office, and the three of us immediately stood up. Doyle shut the door, but the room is a fishbowl, and his voice was thunderous, so the entire squad could see and hear him tear us a new one.

"Do you have any idea how much this little debacle of yours cost the taxpayers?" Doyle bellowed.

Kylie and I had no idea. Truth be told, we didn't give a rat's ass. Our job is to save lives, not to balance the city's checkbook. But we knew better than to respond to the question.

The tongue-lashing continued. "You sent three of *our* helicopters and most of *our* bomb squad to a fucking elitist country club, leaving *our* people unprotected, and for what? So you could star in the *How Dumb Can Cops Look* show on social media?"

Another rhetorical question best left unanswered.

"Identify this fucking 11:59 cocksucker! Find him! And bring him in!" Doyle demanded, laying out the words as if this were a new concept that might finally motivate us to get it right.

He wrapped it up with "You can, you must, and you will! Am I clear?" It's not exactly up there with Vince Lombardi's halftime locker-room pep talks, but it's been his signature closing for over thirty years, so why mess with tradition?

We assured him that he was extremely clear, and he left. What we didn't say was that we were extremely screwed. The bomber had not only embarrassed the department, he had outgamed us.

As Kylie put it, "If we were playing chess, he just took our queen."

She was right. Twenty-four hours earlier, we had all his phone numbers and were waiting for one of them to light up. But he figured out that we were onto him, and sent us on a wild-goose chase, and we wound up being a source of amusement on a text chain. Even worse, we lost our biggest advantage. He would never activate another of those Nokia phones again. There are more than seven thousand lakes in New York State, and I figured that by now, those phones could be at the bottom of any one of them.

We turned to Captain Cates. She returned to her desk and went into her Rodin's *Thinker* pose. She sat there, elbow on the desk, mouth and chin on the knuckles of her right hand for a solid minute.

Finally, she looked up and scowled. "You heard the man," she said. "Find the cocksucker and bring him in."

Then her face softened into a half smile. "Don't take that little performance personally. Back in the day, Harlan Doyle was a legendary detective. Trust me, he knows what you're up against. But at this point, his office is one floor below the police commissioner's, and you know what they say. Your perspective changes as you get closer to the cross fire."

"I wish he would unleash some of that pent-up rage at the Larchmont Heritage Club," Kylie said. "They refuse to cooperate in our investigation. We asked for a list of their members. They were horrified that we'd even *think* that anyone connected to the club could have been involved. We asked for a list of tradespeople who come in and out of that back door, and again they said no. Nobody bombed them. Someone left a cell phone on a linen cart. Not a crime. They refuse to let their members' or their vendors' names be dragged through the mud. And if we try to subpoena their records, they'll fight us in court."

"And they'd put up a good fight," Cates said. "On any given day, their golf course and their dining room are ass deep in lawyers and judges."

"I hate to say this," I said, "but there's not much we can do until the bomber makes his next move. Till then, we'll just go back and comb through what we've already been through."

"Don't," Cates said. "I already have fifty detectives doing that, and I could pick up this phone and get fifty more."

"We can't sit on our hands, Captain," Kylie said.

"I agree. So do something productive," Cates said. "It's been a week since I asked you to investigate Preston Balfour's murder and make sure the department arrested the right man. Where are you on that?"

"We keep moving it to the back burner because of the bomber," Kylie said.

"Well, then move it to the front burner," Cates barked, making it sound more like a direct order than a gift. "If the wrong man is in jail, I want him out, and I want him out now."

CHAPTER 60

WITHIN MINUTES, KYLIE and I were in the conference room, scanning the body cam footage from the night of the Balfour murder.

"Number thirteen," Kylie said as we booted up the next-to-last video. "This one is going to be the charm."

She had said the same thing ever since video number three, but so far, we'd struck out a dozen times.

The squad car with officers thirteen and fourteen was the last to arrive, and by the time they got to the scene, Baxter Street was so jammed that they had to park on Canal, almost two blocks from Balfour's apartment.

Officer thirteen bolted from his vehicle and started running immediately, so most of the people he passed on the street were no more than a blur.

"It's like trying to read the bottom line of an eye chart from a moving train," Kylie said.

Suddenly, officer thirteen stopped. His partner must have called out to him, because when he turned, his camera picked up officer fourteen a few feet away. Body cams don't record sound for the first thirty seconds, so I didn't know what was said, but the image was so clear that when we zoomed in we could read the nameplate on fourteen's chest: RANDOWSKI.

And then the karma gods, or the universe, or whatever it is that always seems to watch over Kylie came through one more time. In the five and a half seconds that the body cam stopped long enough to stay in focus, a man entered the frame.

"That's him," Kylie yelled, freezing the image. "That's the guy!"

The man was about forty, average height, average weight, with skin that I would have said was tawny brown but which also would fit Spence's description of "kind of swarthy."

He was a civilian, so of course he wasn't wearing a nameplate. But we didn't need one. We'd met him a few days ago at the Toronto Airport.

It was Vikram Sharma, the father of the girl whose life Dr. Sarin had saved.

"It's Priya's father," Kylie blurted out. "We knew he was in New York that night, raising money for the Niramaya Clinic, but now we find out that he was walking away from the scene of the crime just minutes after the 911 call."

She enlarged the freeze-frame. "Remember Spence said he head-butted the guy? Sharma has a bloody cut on the bridge of his nose. Plus, when a cop is racing down the street, everyone turns to look at him. Even in the blurriest shots, you can see heads swivel to see what's going on. But look at this," she said, advancing the video by two seconds. "As soon as the cop turned toward him, Sharma's head began to look away. Zach, this is our guy!"

I don't jump to conclusions as quickly as Kylie does, but in this case it was more of a baby step than a leap. "It certainly looks like it," I said. "It definitely feels like it. But proving it won't be easy."

"I know," Kylie said, "but it shines a whole new light on the case. Sharma owed Dr. Sarin big time for saving his daughter. And then Balfour came along and destroyed Sarin's life. Sharma may well have been making good on a debt. That screams motive, and Charlie Elliott totally missed it."

"Whoa, whoa, whoa," I said, holding up a hand. "I agree that this is new evidence that might help Spence, but don't use it to crucify Elliott. He had three eyewitnesses who saw Spence standing over the victim with the murder weapon in his hand, plus fifty more who watched him kick the shit out of Balfour and threaten to kill the man. It's pretty damning, but Elliott still went by the book and reviewed all this body cam footage of hundreds of people in one of New York's most multicultural neighborhoods. You and I saw dozens of people of color who might fit Spence's description of *swarthy*, and the only reason we were able to pick out Sharma is because we got a good look at him in the Toronto Airport. Elliott didn't have that advantage, but I'll bet he's the kind of cop who will be crushed knowing he could have sent an innocent man to prison."

Kylie didn't say a word. She's never been very good at accepting criticism from me or anyone else. Even when she knows it's valid, I've never heard her respond with the classic six-word apology, "You're right. I'm wrong. I'm sorry."

The best I can hope for are the two words she finally managed to eke out.

"Duly noted."

CHAPTER 61

CATES AGREED THAT SHARMA was a person of interest, but when we told her we'd have to fly eight thousand miles to question him, her response was, "In that case, I am not interested. The two of you are not going anywhere until this bomber is off the streets and behind bars. But take the body cam footage to the DA's office. Maybe ADA Steckler will send an investigator to India."

As soon as Kylie heard the name of the assistant district attorney who was assigned to prosecute Spence, she groaned. Cops and ADAs work as a team every day, and over time the chemistry can become so comfortable that it evolves into more of a partnership. But we've also had to deal with our share of pricks like Harvey Steckler.

Fiftyish, divorced, humorless, he follows a rigid go-by-the-book code that clashes head-on with Kylie's bend-the-rules-but-get-it-done approach to law enforcement.

We got to Steckler's office by five thirty, and the dark scowl he gave us as we walked through the door reminded me of the way one narcotics detective described him years ago: "He looks like he was born constipated, and it only got worse over the years."

"Detectives," he said without any foreplay. "Despite the fact that we have an open-and-shut case on the Balfour homicide, I agreed that it was prudent to have a team make sure the cops who made the arrest covered all the bases. But now I find out that the lead investigator is the defendant's wife."

"My job, Counselor, is not to help the defendant," Kylie said. "It's to follow the facts wherever they may lead."

"That's all very noble, Mrs. Harrington, but the media will bury that quote on page twenty-seven, while the headline on the front page will say, 'Cop Wife Springs Killer Husband.'"

"Or it could say, 'DA Praises Top Cops Who Find Real Killer and Help Free Innocent Man,'" Kylie said. "Now, how about we show you what we found before you shoot any more holes in it."

We took him through the body cam footage. He stayed silent through it all. It was a good sign. At least he knew we had something. A full minute went by before he spoke.

"Here's how I see it," he said. "Detective Elliott arrived on the scene and found Spence Harrington, who had threatened to kill Preston Balfour earlier that evening, standing over the body with the murder weapon in his hand. And you want our office to cut him loose because you found a person of interest who was in the victim's neighborhood at the same time?"

He shook his head. "Not on my watch. I have enough evidence to convict Harrington right now. And I'm confident there is nothing in that body cam footage that Dennis Woloch can use to convince a jury that we have the wrong man."

Kylie snapped back, "Vikram Sharma is a lot more than a person of interest. He's an intensely viable suspect who has given up his personal life to raise money to make up for all the damage Balfour did to his community. Can you at least authorize a trip for us to go to India so we can question him as soon as we can wrap up this bomber case?"

"No problem," Steckler chirped. "First class, or would you mind flying coach?"

Kylie didn't utter a word, but she did a great job of screaming *Prick!* with her eyes.

"I don't know what world you live in, MacDonald, but I get scrutinized when I approve a trip to Hackensack, New Jersey. So no," he sneered. "It's the twenty-first century. Facetime the fucker."

"Great idea, Steckler," Kylie said. "I'll schedule it. It's always better when you give the suspect a few days to practice lying to put an alibi together."

"One more thing before you go," Steckler said, even though we gave no indication that we were going. "I just got the notification that your husband's attorney is going to subpoena the two of you to appear at the bail hearing Monday morning."

That blindsided us. But Kylie didn't bat an eye.

"You work for the city of New York," Steckler said. "And if I find out you shared this body cam bullshit with your husband's attorney before you shared it with this office, there will be hell to pay. As for you, Detective Jordan, do not for a minute think that I see you as a spectator. You are just as accountable as your partner."

My mind was racing. Kylie and I knew better than to tell the Warlock about Vikram Sharma before we told Steckler. Why the hell would he push for a bail hearing? The judge would deny bail in a heartbeat. I was still trying to figure out the Warlock's strategy when Steckler blindsided us a second time.

"And just so you know," he said, "this little bail hearing ploy is going to come back and bite Counselor Woloch in his ass. Because come Monday morning, I'm going to inform the judge that I'm ready for trial, and push for opening arguments by the end of the week."

We left the office and barely looked at each other until we were back on the street.

"If Steckler answers 'ready for trial' Monday morning, Spence is dead meat," Kylie said.

"I don't get it," I said. "Dennis Woloch is too smart to—"

The light bulb went off in my head. Of course. The Warlock was smart. But his client was an idiot. And if Spence pushed for a hearing, the Warlock would have no choice but to file for one.

Kylie was half a step behind me. "Spence!" she said. "He hired the best lawyer in the city, and then he decided to take charge and left Woloch with no time to prepare a defense. He has to be the dumbest fucking man on the planet."

I braced myself for the eruption. Rage. Fury. Wrath. The usual Kylie MacDonald response when she's forced to deal with idiots.

But it never came. She just shook her head and put her hand to her face.

And for the first time in a long time, she looked utterly defeated.

CHAPTER 62

I WOKE UP AT five thirty, when the first hint of a dismal gray dawn crept into my bedroom and let me know it was going to be a crap day.

My weather app confirmed it. Rain. And not the kind of magical Hollywood cloudburst that inspired Gene Kelly to sing, dance, and splash his way down a cobblestone street, decked out in a wool suit, snappy fedora, and pricey leather wingtips.

No, this was that uncinematic New York City rain that starts as a fine mist tinged with the smell of the streets, then shifts gears, turning into an unending blanket of wetness that snarls traffic and leaves anyone caught in its path soaked to the skin.

Kylie and I had planned to spend our day making house calls to the families of the bomber's victims. Our purpose was to update them with as much of our progress as we could and to assure them that they had not been forgotten. We don't leave until we feel we've replaced some of the despair with hope, and their parting words are invariably filled with gratitude.

But it's a two-way street. While we bolster them, they reignite us, and we walk away with a renewed determination to track down the source of their pain and bring him to justice. It's a solemn duty. The downpour only made it more heart-wrenching.

By day's end, we had crisscrossed the city and commiserated with six families who lost loved ones to the bomber. The first five ended on a positive note. But our final stop was a stark reminder that not everyone is interested in our compassion or our commitment.

Kostas Vassilakis, the man who lost his bride-to-be in the subway bombing, was a thirty-year-old venture capitalist, an entrepreneur with his eyes on the future. But his values were rooted in the traditions of his ancient Greek culture.

From the moment we entered his apartment, he was polite without being cordial, his demeanor an echo of the man who would have been his father-in-law, Nico Patrakis.

The first red flag came when Kylie pledged that NYPD was doing everything in its power to bring the bomber to justice.

"Yes," Vassilakis responded. "But justice comes in many forms, doesn't it?"

"It does," I said, jumping in. "And the best way to achieve it is through the law."

"And what about those who slip through the nets of your law?" he said. "What happens to them, Detective Jordan?"

"We do our best to ensure no one slips through," I said, resigned to the fact that I had already lost the battle and he was now just toying with me for sport.

"I'm sure you do your best, but sometimes the net needs to be tighter," Vassilakis said. And then he added, "Especially for those who betray their own. Wouldn't you agree?"

He stood up to let us know that the question didn't require an answer. The meeting was over.

As soon as we got back to the precinct, we went straight to Cates's office.

"Especially for those who betray their own?" Cates said. "He's not talking about the bomber."

"No," I said. "It sounds like he's talking about Pete Peterson. We know Peterson was dirty. He was after Nico Patrakis's hundred-thousand-dollar bounty, so he gave up Ramón Reyes's name and address to a band of vigilantes who were out for blood."

"Technically," Kylie said, "it wasn't Peterson's fault that Nico and his crew were blown to kingdom come, but Peterson didn't stick around to have that conversation. He ran. And for an old school, eye-for-an-eye hardliner like Kostas Vassilakis, that's betrayal."

"So not only has Vassilakis picked up the torch to hunt down the bomber, he's also out to get Peterson," Cates said.

"Looks that way," I said. "Any progress happen on dry land while we were out slogging through the muck?"

"We finally managed to subpoena the names of the members, staff, and visitors to the Larchmont Heritage Club," Cates said. "And since we released the picture of Ramón Reyes to the press, we've gotten more than five hundred calls from people who have seen him, and every one of them swears they can positively identify him."

"Amazing," Kylie said. "All this time, I thought Reyes was a loner. There's barely a trace of him in our databases. Who knew it would turn out he had more than five hundred close friends?"

"Is there any *good* news?" I asked.

"Our bomber didn't blow anything up today," Cates said. "That's about as good as I've got."

"I think we need a sit-down," I said.

Cates smiled.

Sit-down is code. To the uninitiated, it sounds like let's find a conference room and talk this through. But in copspeak, it means let's get the hell out of here and eat.

Uniforms usually grab a sandwich. Detectives get a knife and fork.

"We're going to Shane's restaurant on Bank Street at eight," Kylie said. "You want to join us?"

"I don't know," Cates said. "I had plans to stay here, beat myself up, and start thinking about my next career."

"Shane is a hell of a chef," Kylie said. "Can't that wait?"

Cates pretended to ponder the question. "Why not? I can do that tomorrow," she said. "Unless the chief of D's does it for me."

CHAPTER 63

A NIGHT OUT WITH good friends and good food was just what I needed. Okay, not *everything* I needed. I also needed sex. So did Cheryl. And as soon as we got to her apartment, we didn't waste any time getting to it.

It was fast, furious, and long overdue. We showered, put on robes, poured two snifters of Rémy, and adjourned to the living room to talk—also long overdue.

"You okay?" Cheryl said.

"Who's asking?" I gibed. "My girlfriend or the department shrink?"

"You spent the day consoling the families of the victims of a series of senseless tragedies, so for now this is Dr. Robinson asking. You okay?"

"Reaching out to the families has always been the toughest part of the job, but when it's done, I walk away thinking it's the most important. So I'm okay, but . . ."

I hesitated. The last thing I wanted to do was rehash my encounter with Kostas Vassilakis. But Dr. Robinson countered with a piercing don't-you-dare-stop-now look, so I gave it to her chapter and verse, including Vassilakis's barely veiled threat to find and kill Lieutenant Pete Peterson.

"Were you surprised?" she said.

"Actually, I was. I mean, when Nico swore vengeance, I got it. He was old school. But Vassilakis is a millennial. He's supposed to be all about startups and tech innovation, not driven by this old-world sense of retribution."

"His desire for revenge has nothing to do with his age. If Nico Patrakis gave him his blessings to marry his daughter, then this guy passed the ultimate test. I guarantee you that young Mr. Vassilakis has been immersed in Greek culture and tradition since the day he was born. You ever hear of Nemesis?"

"You mean like Batman and the Joker, Superman and Lex Luthor, Sherlock Holmes and Moriarty—"

She held up a hand. "Stop."

"Are you sure? I got plenty more nemesisisses, or whatever the plural of *nemesis* is."

"You're an idiot," she said. But she couldn't hold back the big grin that spread across her face, so I took it as a win.

"When I was in college," she said, "I took a course in Greek mythology. Nemesis was the goddess of retribution. She didn't just punish the wicked; she made sure no one could have too much good fortune without consequence. I bet anything that your guy Vassilakis has that concept deep-seated in his cultural DNA."

I held up my hand.

"What now?" she said.

"Sorry to cut you off, Doc, but would you mind taking the rest of the night off and sending my girlfriend back?"

She let out a long, pouty sigh, which I'm sure was meant to convey exasperation, but at this hour, with the cognac reawakening my libido, it came off as super sexy.

"Fine," she said. "Happy to dumb it down. Dinner was great."

"Now you're talking," I said. "Especially having Cates there. She's had the weight of the world on her shoulders for the past ten days. It was good to see her laughing."

"And she really connected with Theo."

"That kid has a way about him," I said. "And I'm not saying that because I'm his father, because I take zero credit. But Cates is the last person on Theo's list of cops to interview for the documentary he's shooting, and somehow, busy as she is, he persuaded her to give him an hour tomorrow."

"I agree. Theo has this genuine likability that wins people over. And you're spot-on when you say you deserve zero credit."

"I'm glad we could finally agree on something," I said.

"Now, at the risk of crossing the line from girlfriend back to shrink, did you notice anything off between Kylie and Shane?"

"You mean, did I notice that Shane barely looked at her, answered her questions with yes, no, or a shrug, and spent more time running back to the kitchen than he did sitting at the table? Hard to miss. Also, no big surprise. Kylie is obsessed with doing whatever she can for Spence."

"And Shane is doing what men do best when they stop feeling loved and adored," she said. "He's backing off."

"Just curious," I said, "but is there a Greek god for whatever is going on with the two of them?"

She thought for a second and then said, "That would have to be Flushius, the god of relationships going down the shitter."

I cracked up. "I have no idea if the shrink or the girlfriend said that, but this is why I love both of you."

She stood up and loosened the tie on her robe. "Well, in that case, why don't you follow the two of us into the bedroom and find out which one is grateful for the compliment."

CHAPTER 64

IT HAD BEEN a big decision, and Arthur couldn't have made it without one last trip into the city. He smiled and corrected himself. One *next-to-last* trip into the city. In the goddamn rain.

Feeding people had been his parents' passion, and their little Hungarian bistro on the Upper East Side had been their dream. They'd opened it back in that golden era when Second Avenue was dotted with cozy little family-run cafés serving home-cooked meals that reminded people of their roots.

Closing his eyes, he could picture it: warm, welcoming, soft lighting, polished wood, accents of brick, with framed black-and-white photos of New York in the fifties to commemorate Anna and Stefan's integration into American life.

He smiled at the memory of his mother chatting away as she rolled cabbage leaves, while his father stood at the stove pretending to listen as he stirred, tasted, fixed, and fussed over the day's offerings.

He could almost hear the jingle of the bells over the door, welcoming each new guest. Bells! They were so *not New York*, and yet they seemed to harmonize with the mingled scents of paprika and freshly baked bread, and the perfectly imperfect tables covered with hand-embroidered linen and set with the mismatched china they had collected over the years.

His father's cooking was the bedrock of the restaurant's success, but his mother was the heart. She welcomed each new arrival with joy and hugs as if they were stepping into her own home. So of course the sign outside read *Anna's Kitchen*—Stefan's tribute to the woman who gave the place its soul. It was gone now, snuffed out by a heartless city. He stood on Second Avenue in the steady rain, staring at the sprawling, unwelcoming CVS Pharmacy that had swallowed his parents' legacy and replaced it with the soulless chill of twenty-first-century commerce.

It was a painful journey, but one he'd had to take. And now, at two fifteen on that Sunday morning, sitting at his workbench in the shed, his final fuck-you to the city assembled, wired, and primed to wreak havoc, he sat back and looked up at the handwritten message his father had given him when he was sixteen years old.

Tudd, mikor kell tartanod, és mikor kell bedobnod a lapjaidat. Despite his parents' wishes, Arthur had never gotten the hang of their native tongue, so of course he had no idea what the hell it meant.

"Hey, Pop," he had said. "You realize I only speak English and *un poco español*. But I'm going to take a wild guess and say it's another nugget of wisdom from one of your Hungarian heroes. Who is it this time?"

A shrug, a grin, and then his father's trademark devilish *gotcha* wink. "Kenny Rogers."

"Kenny . . . the country singer? *That* Kenny Rogers?"

"He's the best, isn't he?" his father had said, enjoying the moment and reveling in the fact that he was one step ahead of his favorite sparring partner.

Stefan Harmati was not your typical farm boy from Fehérgyarmat, Hungary. Leaving behind the spirited yet soulful folk music of his youth, he fell in love with the twangy truth-telling of country, and over the years he became a full-fledged, card-carrying shitkicker. And Kenny Rogers was his number one, all-time favorite.

"I thought Kenny Rogers was from Texas," young Arthur parried. "But now that I know his soul is from Budapest, would you mind translating?"

"You've got to know when to hold 'em. Know when to fold 'em," Stefan said.

"I see," Arthur said. "So apparently, Kenny found out about my ongoing feud with Vice Principal DeLuca to get them to change the stupid dress code, and his best advice is to accept defeat and cut my losses."

"Bingo," his father said. "I know DeLuca. He doesn't make the rules. He doesn't give a shit if they're right or wrong. He's just the pit bull who enforces them. You're applying to colleges next year. You push him too far, and instead of saying Arthur Harmati is a principled young man who has the courage of his convictions, he might just decide to flag you as a troublemaker. You're out of aces, kid. *Sétálj el.* Walk away."

Instinctively, Arthur knew that his father was right, but his teenage bravado forced him to look for a loophole, an angle, any way to turn the fight in his favor. There were none, and in the end, he decided, "Fuck the dress code." It stung, but when college applications rolled around, his record was spotless and his recommendations were glowing.

He hadn't won. But at least he hadn't lost.

"Well, Dad," Arthur said out loud to his dead father, "you were right back then, and I hope you're right now, because I'm following your advice out the window."

He gestured at the bomb he'd spent hours crafting. "I'm out of aces. It's time to fold 'em."

CHAPTER 65

KYLIE AND I MET for breakfast at Gerri's Diner. Gerri Gomperts, the wisecracking owner who loves to come to our table and meddle in our lives, both personal and professional, didn't even come out of the kitchen. Instead, she sent us something we hadn't ordered: a stack of pancakes in the shape of a heart.

On the outside, Gerri enjoys playing the stereotype of the classic New Yorker. Opinionated to the bone and quick to tell you what she thinks of you whether you want to hear it or not. But this morning, we were reminded of the total sweetheart she is on the inside, and she pulled it off without saying a word.

At seven a.m., we were on our way to Cates's fishbowl office when we saw her through the glass wall.

"Captain, my captain," Kylie trilled to me. "Look at what she's wearing."

I know nothing about fashion, but my trained detective's eye could tell that the boss was not dressed for work.

"Zara," Kylie said to me, summing up the stylish gray-blue pantsuit, the tailored shirt, and the definitely-not-for-chasing-perps high heels in a single word that meant absolutely nothing to me.

"Excuse me, ma'am," Kylie said as soon as we entered Cates's office. "But what did you do with my commanding officer?"

Cates, who can take a jab as well as dish one out, laughed. "Last night, I made the mistake of asking Theo what to wear for the video he's shooting with me. He looked me over, thought about it, and then dropped his voice real low and said, 'Cop glam.'"

"And you nailed it, girl!" Kylie said.

I didn't say a word. All I could do was think, *That's my boy.*

"We kind of figured that if any of the five hundred calls to the tip line panned out, you would have flashed us the bat signal," Kylie said.

"We're up to seven hundred," Cates said. "Most of the callers are from Queens, where Reyes lived, and they're positive they're going to crack this case wide open by telling us he was a pitching coach. So far, we've got no leads, but I've got twenty detectives chipping away at the list."

"And now you've got twenty-*two* detectives," Kylie said.

"I know you're ready to get out there," Cates said, "but I need my two lead detectives as close to home as possible. There were a dozen or so calls from right here in the Nineteenth. Why don't you chase those down."

"On it, boss," Kylie said as we made for the door. "See you on the red carpet."

The list of tipsters from the 19th, along with the transcripts of what they said, were on our desk. One by one, we ran the callers through our database. Three of them were Upper East Side doormen, two were regular callers—residents of the nursing home on East Seventy-Second Street—one was a building superintendent, and then . . .

"Holy shit," Kylie said. "Look at this."

The caller was Petra Westfield. Her address on Sixty-Fifth Street between Park and Madison was a four-story town house.

I ran her and gave Kylie the top line.

"She's fifty-five years old, married to Paul Westfield, the CEO of Westfield Construction Group, and her social status is about as far from Ramón Reyes as you can get."

"And she called in Reyes?" Kylie said.

"She called a little before midnight on Thursday. The only thing she said was, 'I know Mr. Reyes. He did some work for us.' Detectives reached out to her twice by phone. No answer. So they went to the house. No Mrs. Westfield, so they left their cards, but she never called back."

"The fact that she called in with a tip on Reyes is interesting," Kylie said. "The fact that she seems to have changed her mind and doesn't want to talk is even more interesting. Let's call her."

"You dial," I said. "The detectives that left her messages were men."

Kylie called from her cell. "I got her voicemail," she said. "And that, Detective Jordan, is all I need."

She waited for the beep and, in her best I'm-a-cop-and-I-mean-business voice, said, "Hello, Mrs. Westfield, this is NYPD Detective Kylie MacDonald. We got your message that you have some information about Ramón Reyes, and since we haven't been able to reach you by phone, my partner and I will drive over to your house. I'm sure you're a busy woman, so if you're not at home, we'll be glad to park outside. We'll be in a white car with blue letters. You can't miss it. Happy to wait for you. This is a major case, and we need all the help we can get."

She left her phone number and hung up.

"Zach, this woman called the tip line, got cold feet, and now she's avoiding the cops. Which means the last thing she wants to see parked in front of her ten-thousand-square-foot twenty-eight-million-dollar-according-to-Zillow brownstone is the po-po. Five bucks says she calls back in less than five minutes."

Before I could answer, Kylie's cell rang. She gave me a big grin. "Wow. She's even more nervous than I thought."

She took the call and put it on speaker.

"Detective MacDonald. How can I help you?"

"This . . . this is Petra Westfield," a shaky voice said. "You, um . . . you called me. How can I help?"

"Thanks for getting back to me, Mrs. Westfield," Kylie said, her voice oozing with courtesy, professionalism, and respect. "You called saying you had some information on Ramón Reyes. How do you know him?"

"I can't talk on the phone," Westfield whispered.

"No problem," Kylie said. "My partner and I can be at your place in less than ten minutes."

"Oh, no, no. That wouldn't work. I'm . . . I'm hosting a dinner party tonight, and the caterers are here. It's too hectic."

"No problem," Kylie repeated. "I can send two uniformed officers to bring you to the precinct. I promise we won't take long."

"Oh, no, no, no, no."

"Ma'am," Kylie said, her voice sharp, civility gone, "this is a police investigation. We have to talk to you now. Is there a place where you'd like to meet?"

Silence, but I could picture the panic in her eyes, her brain searching for an answer.

"You know the gazebo in Central Park at Sixtieth and Center Drive?"

"One of my favorite spots," Kylie said. "And very private."

"I can meet you there in fifteen minutes."

"Perfect," Kylie said, and hung up.

"Nicely done," I said.

"Yeah, but if she'd waited another thirty seconds before she called back, I would have taken you for five bucks."

CHAPTER 66

THE GAZEBO PETRA WESTFIELD chose for our meeting place is a popular wedding venue. Made of rough-hewn logs and covered in vines, it sits at the crest of a hill and has a sweeping view of the park. And since we'd seen pictures of her online, she was easy to spot. Tall, slender, walking a large dog who heeled at her side as if it were gearing up to compete at Westminster.

"Oh. My. God," Kylie said. "Zach, do you see what she's wearing?"

"Didn't we just establish the limitations of my fashion sense in Cates's office? But I'll give it my best shot. Stripey summer frock, probably ran her forty, fifty bucks at Target," I said, knowing I'd missed by a mile.

"You're an idiot. It's a Brunello Cucinelli Monili shoulder-belted midi dress," further expanding my words-I'll-never-use lexicon. "That little *frock* costs about five grand at Bergdorf, and she's wearing it to walk the damn dog."

"Damn dog?" I said. "Now look who's an idiot. That, my unenlightened friend, is a Bouvier des Flandres, and she probably spends more on feeding, grooming, training, and boarding it whenever she jets off to the Maldives than on a dozen of those Bruno Coochy-Cooty dresses."

Mrs. Westfield hesitated as she approached us. "Are you . . ."

"Detective MacDonald," Kylie said. "And my partner, Detective Jordan."

Our database had told us that Petra Westfield was fifty-five, but with her perfect hair, perfect teeth, and well-toned athletic body, she could easily have passed for twenty years younger.

"Thank you for meeting me here," she said. "I don't have a lot of time. I told my husband I was walking Lulu. He doesn't know I'm talking to you, and I don't want anyone else to know either."

"The only way your husband will find out is if you tell him. We have no intention of doing anything that would compromise your comfort and safety," Kylie said. "So, please, tell us how you know Ramón Reyes."

Westfield let out a sigh of relief and lowered herself to the rustic bench. She gave the dog a slight nod, and Lulu settled down at her mom's designer sandals.

"We met when my son was in third grade. Bryce took to baseball at a young age. He's a pitcher, a really good one, so we signed him up with one of those private programs where the kids get to travel and play against teams all around the state. One of his coaches saw that he had a lot of potential, so he suggested we get him some private lessons to sharpen his skills. Bryce worked with Ramón for four seasons. We would have done more, but Ramón moved out of the city."

"Do you know where he went?" Kylie asked.

"I have no idea. As soon as the restaurant closed, he just disappeared."

"What restaurant?"

"Anna's Kitchen. It's where he worked. My husband and I ate there from time to time, and when we found out Ramón was a pitcher in Cuba, we hired him. Bryce is now a senior at Arizona State—a starting pitcher for the Sun Devils—and to this day, he says Ramón was the best coach he ever had."

"Let's get back to this restaurant. What did Ramón do there?"

"It was a mom-and-pop place, so Ramón would do whatever Anna asked. Worked in the kitchen, bussed tables, and . . ." She ended the thought with a shrug.

"And what? Every little detail helps," Kylie said with a smile.

"Well, sometimes he would deliver. You know, takeout."

"Right. Takeout," Kylie said. "Thank you. You've been helpful, Mrs. Westfield."

"Please, call me Petra."

Kylie gave her a second smile. "Just one more thing, Petra."

"Sure. What is it?"

"Did you ever see Ramón Reyes socially?"

Westfield stiffened, her body tensed, her fists clenched. The dog sat up immediately, putting her bulk between us and her owner, her eyes on full alert.

"Socially?" Westfield sputtered. "I don't understand what you mean."

"Mrs. Westfield," Kylie said, her warm woman-to-woman tone shifting gears. "You're doing your best to look calm and relaxed, but clearly you are anything but. Instead of meeting us in your home, you lied to your husband about why you were going out, and quite frankly you seem terrified to be talking about a man you had a passing relationship with ten years ago. So let's cut to the chase. Has he contacted you?"

"Oh. God, no. When he moved, I changed my cell phone number. I don't want him to . . ." She closed her eyes and took a deep breath. It didn't help. She was trembling now.

"Look, when I heard that Ramón might be connected to these bombings, I felt like I should call."

"And you did," Kylie said. "Close to midnight. But in the cold, sober light of day, you had second thoughts. Listen to me. My partner and I are not remotely interested in your private life. We are trying to find Ramón Reyes. And if you had more than a passing relationship with him, he might see you as a safe harbor and reach out to you for help."

"Oh God, I never even *thought* about that. Do you think I'm in danger?"

"Ma'am, right now, everybody in this city is in danger until we find Mr. Reyes. If you know anything that can help us do that, you have to share it with us now."

And then the dam burst.

"I don't know what I was thinking," she said through the tears, her hands stroking the dog to let her know everything was all right. "It was a rocky time in my marriage. Ramón was so sweet, so gentle. I can't believe he would hurt anyone. Do you think I should leave town till you catch him?"

"That's your decision," Kylie said. "If you do, we need to be able to reach you. And if we call, you need to pick up . . ."

Kylie stopped in mid-sentence, letting the words hang, because Petra Westfield could easily finish it on her own. *You need to pick up, or else the next call we'll make is to your husband.*

"I swear to God I don't know where he is," Westfield said.

"Do you know anyone who might?"

She shrugged. "Maybe Anna."

"And who is Anna?"

"Anna Harmati. She and her husband owned the restaurant, and I know that Ramón adored them. They took him in when he came to America. If he's in touch with anybody, it would be Anna or her husband, Stefan."

"Do you know where we can find them?"

"The restaurant closed years ago. I have no idea where they'd be." She looked at the delicate rose-gold watch on her wrist. "My husband is expecting me."

"Understood," Kylie said. She scribbled something on her notepad, ripped off the page, and handed it to Westfield. "This is my number. Put it in your cell phone, and call me if Reyes contacts you."

Westfield stared at the scrap of paper. "I'm confused," she said, holding it up. "You say this is your *personal* number?"

Kylie nodded. "You can call me twenty-four seven."

"But it says Tatiana at Bottega Veneta. I don't understand."

"I figured if your husband should happen to look at your phone, he'd ignore the name of a salesperson at a high-end department store. But if it said Detective Kylie MacDonald, NYPD Red, he might decide to ask you a few questions you'd rather not answer."

Westfield smiled, her face radiating gratitude. She stood up, and the late-morning sun illuminated her face perfectly, as if Kubrick himself had lit the scene. She was agelessly beautiful with piercing blue eyes and the smooth, flawless skin of a Disney princess.

Up close, however, I could see the stress we had brought down on her, and I had no doubt that by the time she went to bed tonight, an army of wrinkles would be storming the castle.

CHAPTER 67

"THIS IS HUGE," Kylie said as we made our way to the address on Second Avenue where Petra Westfield told us Anna's Kitchen had been.

Huge was an understatement. Until now, we'd encountered only people who had known Ramón Reyes casually or, in most cases, barely at all. But now we had the names of people who had hired him, treated him like family, and would know either where he was or at least where he went when the restaurant shut its doors. For ten days, we'd been groping our way in total darkness. And now suddenly, the lights clicked on and we could see a path that might lead us somewhere.

Usually, when a restaurant in New York goes belly-up, another one grabs the space, taking advantage of the commercial-grade ventilation and gas lines that the previous owner paid to install. And sometimes, they'll even scoop up any equipment that was left behind.

But Anna's Kitchen was gone, erased as if it never existed—just another little slice of neighborhood charm gobbled up by the insatiable Pac-Men of corporate America.

"I doubt that anyone inside this CVS will even have heard of a little Hungarian restaurant that was here ten years ago," I said. "But we know someone who will."

"Hackie," Kylie said.

"Bingo." I looked at my watch. "And it's a little after eleven, so we know where to find him."

"Marisha's," Kylie said. "Let's pay him a visit."

Hackie is a cop. His real name is Harold Kidd III, one of the few cops I know with a Roman numeral after his name. But his mother started calling him Hackie from the day he was born. She swore she had no idea where the word came from. She just liked the ring of it, the smile it put on her face.

And Hackie was happy to stick with it, because his real name made him sound like a trust-fund baby when, in fact, he was just another blue-collar kid who grew up in a factory town in Jersey, dropped out of college after a year, and finally found his calling with the NYPD.

He's a beat cop, a foot soldier, a throwback to the days when a strapping six-foot-four presence in a blue uniform was a welcome sight and a reassuring constant in an ever-changing neighborhood. Those days are gone, replaced by cops in marked cars. But thirty-five years later, Hackie is still chewing up shoe leather, pounding a beat along Second Avenue between Sixty-Fifth and Eighty-Sixth Streets. He knows every doorman, every penthouse dweller, every soda can collector, every dog walker, every nanny, every shopkeeper by name. And they all know him as Hackie, the mayor of Second Avenue.

People trust him, respect him, and some are even willing to tell him things they wouldn't tell anyone else. Over the decades, he's become the keeper of the neighborhood's unspoken truths, and his low-key approach to resolving minor squabbles before they become 911 calls has made him an invaluable asset to the precinct.

He is also a creature of habit, taking his lunch break every day at eleven a.m. at Marisha's.

To say that Marisha Lunde makes sandwiches would be like saying Taylor Swift sings songs. The woman is in a league of her own, famous for her home-baked bread, mind-blowing meatloaf, and a half dozen other secret family recipes that have made her a lunchtime legend on the Upper East Side and beyond.

She opened up shop decades ago in a hole-in-the-wall on Second

Avenue between Seventy-Sixth and Seventy-Seventh, and despite the demand, the little culinary gem still only has six tables. The one in the rear was reserved for her good friend Officer Kidd.

Good friend is a relative term. In truth, the depth of their friendship has always been a matter of speculation among the locals. It was a nice touch of irony that while the two lunch companions knew everything about everybody in the neighborhood, none of us had a clue what was going on between them.

It was still early, but the line at Marisha's waiting for takeout was already twenty deep. By noon it would triple, but Marisha had a crew of five behind the counter. The sign overhead read, "It's not fast food. It's great food fast."

Kylie and I gave her a quick wave and headed to the back. There's an unwritten code at NYPD. If a cop has staked out a place to eat and claimed it for his own, other cops steer clear. It's more than territorial. It's about respect. If Hackie had been eating lunch at his desk, we wouldn't think of sitting down uninvited. Same thing here.

He spotted us immediately and grinned. "NY-fucking-PD Red," he said. "What could you two rock stars possibly want from an old dinosaur like me?"

"Apologies for barging in," I said, "but we're scrambling to run down someone who left this neighborhood a million years ago, and you're the last dinosaur standing."

"Technically, I'm sitting. But if this is about the bomber case, grab a seat."

"It's all about the bomber," I said.

As Kylie and I each pulled up a chair, Hackie looked over at Marisha. "It's all right. They're not eating."

Neither Kylie nor I took it personally. Hackie was old school to the core.

"People around here are afraid to leave their goddamn apartments to buy groceries," he said. "Anything I can do to help catch this bastard, just ask."

"What can you tell us about a long-forgotten restaurant, Anna's Kitchen?"

"Long gone, maybe," he said. "But not forgotten. Anna and Stefan Harmati were the best. Salt of the earth. He was a food wizard, and she was one part trail boss, one part den mother, one part Mother Teresa."

"And what about Ramón Reyes?" Kylie said.

Hackie reached into his rear left pocket and pulled out a memo book holder. I can only imagine how many notepads he'd filled over the decades, but the weathered leather holder was the same one they issued him in the Academy back when Kylie and I were still in grade school.

He flipped it open. "You mean this guy?" he said. "I've been carrying his picture around ever since you put it out there. Don't you think if I recognized him, I'd have said something?"

"We just got information that he worked at Anna's Kitchen," I said.

"Bullshit. If this guy worked for Anna, I'd have—"

He stopped cold, leaned back, then pounded the flats of both fists on the table. His drink toppled and crashed to the floor.

"Fuck, fuck, fuck!" he said, pounding again and again and again.

He held up a hand to Marisha and the line of customers at the front of the store. It was as good an apology as they were going to get.

"Ray-Ray," he said, his entire being ready to spontaneously combust, but his voice back to a respectable decibel level.

"Ray-Ray," I repeated.

"Anna and Stefan had a worker in the kitchen," Hackie said. "He never came out when I was around, so one day I asked Anna what's the story on this guy. She said he was from Cuba. Told me he got caught trying to defect, and the Cuban gestapo, or whatever you call them, tortured him, mutilated him, and seeing a big dude like me in a blue uniform scares the living crap out of him. She said, 'Hackie, there's no law that says you have to meet every single person in the whole neighborhood. Trust me, Ray-Ray is the sweetest person in the world. He's just terrified.'"

"And you believed her?" Kylie said.

"Hey," Hackie said, "if Anna Harmati asked me to cut a deck of cards and then stand back because as soon as I cut, the king of spades is going to jump out of the deck and spit in my eye, I'd believe her. The woman was a saint. If she vouched for somebody, I took her word."

"And all these years, you knew there was a guy working there, but you never laid eyes on him?"

"Never. I respected the situation, and it wasn't just for Anna. I felt for this poor guy. It's kind of like a dog who's been kicked around and abused all his life, and he finally gets rescued. But he's still afraid of his own shadow. Anna asked me to give Ray-Ray his space, so I did."

"And she called him Ray-Ray?" Kylie said.

He nodded and shook off a laugh. "I didn't pick up on it when you released his name, but now it all adds up. RAY-mone. RAY-iss. It's just like Anna to call him Ray-Ray."

"She and Stefan are our next stop. Can you tell us how to find them?"

He shook his head. "They're dead. Ten years now. Maybe more. The two of them died on the same day. They had a joint funeral. The mass was at Saint Monica's. The whole neighborhood came out. It was so crowded, we had to detour traffic off of Seventy-Ninth Street."

"They died together?" Kylie said. "Do you know the details?"

"You want me to tell you what it says on their death certificates? Or you want the unvarnished truth?"

"We can track down the death certificates. We'd rather hear the mayor of Second Avenue tell us what really happened."

"The fucking city of New York is what happened. It was that goddam Second Avenue subway nightmare we all lived through. First it killed their business, and then it killed the two of them."

Echoes of the bomber's first phone call came roaring back in my head.

"I am going to destroy New York City the way it destroyed my family."

CHAPTER 68

"YOU REMEMBER THE MUCKING station?" Hackie asked.

That was all it took. "Jesus," I said, throwing my head back and staring up at the tin ceiling tiles that added yet another touch of home to the cozy little dining nook.

In a split second, it all became clear. Maybe not crystal clear, but at least we had dots to connect, bread crumbs to follow.

Beginning in 2007, the residents of the Upper East Side had to endure ten years of misery while the city carved out nearly two miles of tunnels under Second Avenue. From Sixty-Eighth Street to Ninety-Fifth, storefronts disappeared behind scaffolding and construction barriers, leaving them invisible, inaccessible, or both. Revenues plummeted, and almost half the shops and restaurants failed or were forced to relocate.

The only way to get rid of the millions of tons of earth they dug up was to build a four-story monstrosity where conveyor belts dumped soil and rock from below into waiting trucks on Second Avenue. The mucking station.

For years, the unrelenting hell choked the avenue, cut traffic to a crawl, and clobbered small businesses.

"Anna's Kitchen was in the worst spot of all," Hackie said. "Directly behind the mucking station. They never had a prayer."

"What happened to the Harmatis after they went out of business?" Kylie asked.

"They were never the same after that. Most days I would stop by their apartment." He put both hands to his temples, shook his head, and exhaled long and heavy. "*Apartment*," he repeated, spitting out the word. "It was a goddam overpriced typical Upper East Side shoebox in a four-story walkup on Seventy-Third. They should have moved back to their old neighborhood, but they didn't have the money, and even if they did, they didn't have the will to start over again.

"So they were stuck there, half a block from what used to be their whole world—their pride and joy, their . . ." He dug down to find the right words. And then, anger be damned, "Their fucking *place* in the neighborhood, only now it's covered in muck from below and pigeon shit from above. Still standing, but dying a slow, agonizing, and, for Stefan, humiliating public death.

"Anna did her best to put on a brave face, but Stefan—it was like the poor guy just aged overnight. Some days, Anna couldn't even get him out of bed. He stopped eating. He stopped *cooking*. Do you know what it means when a man who lives to feed others stops cooking?"

Of course we knew. Cops meet a lot of people who simply give up on life.

"Six months after the restaurant closed, Stefan had a heart attack. Anna called 911, but you remember what happened to response times during the subway construction. Traffic didn't move. EMS had their sirens screaming, but there was no place for the cars, the trucks, or the goddam sixty-foot articulated buses to go.

"Anna calls 911 again, desperate, pleading. They say they're doing the best they can. But by now the poor woman is desperate, so she decides to drag Stefan down the stairs and maybe try to hail a cab on Third Avenue. He died on the second-floor landing. A neighbor heard the commotion and came out to help."

Hackie wiped a hand across his eyes. He'd told this story before, and it never got any easier. "Anna looked up at the neighbor, grabbed her chest, struggled to speak, managed to get out a few words in Hungarian, and collapsed. By the time EMS got there, they were gone. Both of them. Just like that."

Hackie was drained. Done. And both Kylie and I knew enough to give him back his private time. We stood up.

"Thanks," I said. "We can't begin to tell you how much you've done to help us solve this case. Now that we know about the Harmatis and their connection to Reyes, we can dig into the database and—"

"Fuck the database," Hackie said. "Call the son."

"What son?"

"Anna and Stefan had a son. I met him a couple of times. He was nice, but . . ."

"But what?"

"Let's just say he was Wall Street nice. You know the type. They're nice to anyone who can do something for them, make money for them. If that ain't you, you're invisible. And you know me, Zach. Big, loud, hard to miss, and impossible to ignore."

"And yet the guy never gave you a *hello, how are you*, so you decided he was an asshole," I said.

"Hey, who among us is perfect?"

"What's his name?" Kylie asked. "I've never been accused of blending into the woodwork. Maybe he'll notice me."

"His name is Arthur Harmati, but hell, girl, of course he'll notice you," Hackie said, giving her a practiced wink. "You've got something he wants."

"Well, I'm betting that he's got something *we* want," Kylie said, winking back. "Answers."

CHAPTER 69

"ARE YOU THINKING WHAT I'm thinking?" I said to Kylie as we double-timed it back to our car.

"If it's halfway intelligent, I probably thought of it before you," she said, not breaking stride. "If you recall, only one of us graduated at the top of our class at the Academy, while you graduated somewhere in the middle."

"Sixth out of a thousand isn't exactly the middle," I said.

"Maybe not for you, but for me the middle is everyone from two through nine-hundred-and-ninety-nine. Get to the point, Zach. What are you thinking?"

"The name Arthur Harmati definitely does *not* ring a bell."

"Well done, Grasshopper," Kylie said as we got to the car. "That picture of Ramón Reyes has been all over the media for five days, and yet we haven't heard a word from Mr. Harmati. Granted, he has no use for anyone who can't butter his biscuit, but Reyes was practically family. Anna took him in, adored him, protected him. I guarantee that Arthur and Ramón not only knew each other, but they had to spend time together, bonding over stuffed cabbage, chicken paprikash, and their mutual love for Anna and Stefan."

"And yet, Arthur Harmati," I said as I typed his name into the car's laptop, "never reached out to NYPD to say something like 'Hey, you know that madman you're looking for? We're like bros, man.'"

I stared at the laptop as the first gut punch popped onto the screen. "Oh, Jesus. Arthur Zoltan Harmati sued the city of New York for five million dollars, blaming the deaths of his parents on gross negligence caused by the construction of the Second Avenue subway."

"'I am going to destroy New York City the way it destroyed my family,'" Kylie said. "I guarantee the city offered him twenty thousand in nuisance pay, and he turned it down. So he went to court, got the traditional judicial finger, and went home without any cash or prizes."

"If you're trying to impress me with your deductive reasoning, you failed," I said. "The guy who finished a thousandth in our graduating class could have figured that one out. Guess what happened after the judge tossed his case."

"Enlighten me."

"Arthur beat the shit out of the judge. Give me a minute." I scrolled down. "No surprise. He did six months at Rikers."

I kept scrolling. And then another gut punch. Kylie didn't wait for me to speak. She leaned over to get closer to the screen.

"The apprehending officer was Lieutenant Delia Cates," Kylie said. "Zach, we've got to check this guy out. Run him through the DMV."

I typed *Arthur Zoltan Harmati* one more time. His current driver's license popped up on the screen. Knockout punch. "He lives in Larchmont."

"Oh my God, Zach!" Kylie thundered. "He lives in *Larchmont*. Quick, open up the list of members of the Larchmont Heritage Club."

I did. He was right there in the top ten. Arthur Harmati, Finance Committee chair.

Kylie pounded the dashboard. "It's him. He's our guy. Arthur Zoltan Harmati is our bomber." She started the car. "We're going to Larchmont," she said. "Let's get eyes on him immediately, call Cates to put together a team, and bring this maniac down."

We were on Third Avenue speeding uptown when I got Cates on the phone. I put her on speaker.

"Boss, Arthur Harmati. Do you recognize the name?"

"Why, yes, Detective," she said. "As a matter of fact, I am here with Theo right now. He's quite the young documentarian."

Kylie looked at me and pulled the car into a bus stop.

"Captain," she said. "Harmati lives in Larchmont. We're on our way up there now."

"He won't be home, Detective MacDonald," she said, her voice cold, robotic.

"Cap," Kylie said. "I don't understand."

"Arthur Harmati is in my office right now," Cates said. "And he has a bomb strapped to his chest."

CHAPTER 70

"GO, GO, GO, go, go!" I yelled.

Kylie was way ahead of me. She flipped on the siren, cut across four lanes of Third Avenue, hung a left on Eighty-Sixth, and tore through a red light to head back downtown on Lex.

"I should have told him. I should have told him," I said to one of the few people on earth I had shared my secret with.

"Don't think about it," Kylie said as she weaved around the idiots who didn't get out of our way fast enough. "Theo is with Cates. You know her. You trust her. She will not let anything happen to your son."

"Your son. Your son who has no idea that you're his father," the punishing voice inside my head berated me. *"What the hell were you thinking that you made a decision not to tell him?"*

"Whatever is going on in your head, get rid of it," Kylie said, smelling the fear that had gripped me. "You're a cop, and you're trying to stop a madman. That's your focus. That's your mission. Do your job and trust that Cates will do hers."

By the time we got to Sixty-Ninth Street, it was blocked off as hundreds of cops from every corner of the city swarmed to the scene to evacuate everyone in harm's way and to clear the avenues for emergency vehicles.

A uniform moved the barricade, we drove to Sixty-Seventh, and Kylie and I jumped out of the car and ran past a growing army of responders—ESU, EMS, the hostage negotiation team, the bomb squad—all wearing heavy vests and Kevlar helmets, and many of them with long guns taking up position along the street and on rooftops. A stream of cops, detectives, and civilians from the precinct, along with tenants and staff from the nearby apartment buildings, were being shepherded to a makeshift safety area in the Park Avenue Armory, a medieval fortress that had been converted from a military facility to an art museum and performance space.

Kylie and I ran toward the precinct. Nobody stopped and asked, "Where do you think you're going?" That's the advantage of having a partner who is known, recognized, and respected departmentwide.

"Zach! Kylie!" It was Detective Rich Koprowski. He met us in the middle of the block, just outside the precinct.

"Rich," I yelled. "What happened? How'd he manage to get up to Cates's office?"

"It's insane. A call came in to the main line. It's One PP. The caller tells the operator that the chief of D's wants to speak to the desk sergeant, and he wants him now. McGrath scrambles off the desk, races over to the phone, and the voice tells him to hold for Chief Doyle."

"How long was McGrath on hold before he realized Doyle wasn't calling?" Kylie asked.

"He didn't even think that. He waited a few minutes, figured the chief had something more important to do, and told the TS to give him a shout if and when Doyle called back."

"And nobody was covering the desk?" I said.

"Of course somebody jumped on the desk as soon as McGrath walked away," Koprowski said, "but do you know what it's been like around here? We've got a hundred revolving detectives on loan from Tottenville to Spuyten Duyvil. And when a guy wearing a suit walks in, flashes a shield, and grunts hello like he's not thrilled to be here, you don't make his day any worse by asking him to pull out his ID. Hey, it was a total fuckup, but this guy is good."

"Jordan, MacDonald." It was Chief Doyle. "Suit up."

We threw on heavy vests and helmets and followed him inside.

The building was empty, eerily quiet, cleared of all personnel not critical to the mission at hand.

"This old relic was built in the eighteen hundreds, back when buildings were designed to last," Doyle said. "God forbid a bomb goes off on the third floor, it's going to do a lot of damage, but this old brick shithouse isn't going to collapse, so the command center is situated right here on the first floor. The kid who was filming Cates set up his camera in her office. His monitor and his tech were behind a wall on the third floor, so TARU rewired it and moved it down here."

We entered a thick-walled room. I knew everyone there but didn't bother to say hello. My eyes lasered in on four monitors. Three of them were wired to the department internal security cameras. One was trained on the stairway, recording every person who came and went. Another had a wide shot that captured most of the workspace. The third was a picture-perfect shot of the fishbowl. Theo's camera was on a tripod in the center of the room, pointing at Harmati, Cates, and Theo. Harmati had been wearing a suit when he walked past the desk, but now his jacket, tie, and shirt were draped over a chair, revealing a multipocketed mesh photographer's vest, loaded and wired for destruction. The detonator, a black cell phone, was in his right hand.

The fourth monitor was the feed from Theo's brand-new Sony camcorder that he wouldn't stop raving about.

I looked at Cates. She was still wearing her suit jacket. "Is she armed?" I said.

"Negative," Sergeant Nathan Torrence from TARU said. "She gave her gun to one of her detectives to lock up before she started the interview."

"How about Harmati?"

"If he has a weapon, it's hidden," Torrence said. "He doesn't really need one. That phone in his hand is another old Nokia. We can't pick up a signal, so it's not from the batch he bought in Toronto, but it's perfect for the job. He told Cates he rewired it so that all he has to do is press one of the reliable old-school buttons on the keypad, and it's over."

"Can you jam the phone?"

"Way too risky."

I looked back at the monitor. The three of them didn't move, didn't speak. "Is there sound?" I asked.

"Oh, yeah. Clear as a bell. And it's closed-captioned."

"Cates knows how to get somebody to open up. Why isn't she engaging him? Building a rapport?"

"He put her on a timeout. Told her to keep her mouth shut for five minutes. He set his watch."

"And then what?" I said.

Torrence looked up at me. "He didn't say, Zach. But my best guess is, it just gets him another five minutes closer to 11:59."

I looked at my watch. My son had fifteen minutes to live, and I was powerless to save him.

CHAPTER 71

"SHIT." IT WAS CHIEF Doyle. He was staring at his cell phone. "Just what I suspected."

"Sir?" Kylie said.

"I was hoping ESU could take him out with one bullet to the head," Doyle said. "Kill him before his brain could tell his finger to push the button. But no. That same glass was used in the office of the CO of the range at Rodman's Neck. I had them pull a panel and put a round through it. The trajectory was thrown off way too much for it to be an effective shot."

Silence. And then the alarm on Harmati's watch went off.

"Can I talk now?" Cates said.

"I've heard enough of your bullshit, Delia," Harmati said. "*Sorry the city killed your parents, Mr. Harmati, but how about that new Q train? Upper East Side to Times Square in less than fifteen minutes. At least your mom and dad didn't die in vain.* But I am a little curious about this kid shooting a movie in your office." He turned to Theo. "What's that all about, kid?"

"Theo," my son said. "And that's a loaded question, sir."

Harmati grinned. "Arthur. And what makes it a loaded question?"

"I think it's pretty obvious that I think Captain Cates is the kind of cop who can serve as a role model for women, especially women my age. It's just as obvious that you don't. As long as we have a few minutes, I'd like to hear your side of the story."

Harmati laughed out loud. "A few minutes! Good one." His face turned cold. "The city killed my parents. I was trying to get justice, and she stopped me."

"Translation," Cates called out. "He was beating the shit out of an eighty-year-old judge. I just made it a fair fight."

"*Judge*," Harmati said, spitting out the word. "He was a puppet of the regime, whose only job was to throw out valid lawsuits so the city doesn't have to pay for all the lives they've destroyed. If he's not too old to do that, he's not too old to get his face beat in."

"This is getting interesting," Theo said. "How did the city kill your parents?"

"It's not important now," Harmati said.

"Bullshit. You set off all these bombs to get people's attention. You've got mine. I'm a filmmaker. I want to hear your story."

There was an audible gasp from the group of seasoned cops who were glued to the monitor. "Jesus H. Christ," Doyle said. "The balls on this kid!"

Harmati was just as impressed. He looked at his watch. It was 11:47. "I'll give you the short version," he said.

"Can I film it?"

Harmati looked at him. His face said it all. *I'm going to blow this place up. What good will filming it do?* "Look, kid . . ." he said.

"Theo."

"Theo," Harmati said. "The cops are already filming this."

"The cops are filming you blowing up a police station. Did they film anything about the city killing your parents? And even if they did, do you think they're going to put it on YouTube or take it to Netflix?"

"I made a video at home. My wife will find it."

"Cool. What editing program did you use? What's on the B roll? How about the titles, the music—"

"Whoa, kid—Theo. Who am I, Spielberg? It's a home video."

"I get it. I'm sure you have a riveting story, but it's not enough for people to hear it. They need to *feel* it. I can make that happen. What were your parents' names?"

"Anna and Stefan."

Theo held up his hands like a director framing a shot. "The City that Killed Anna and Stefan Harmati," he said, setting the stage, pulling Arthur into the moment. "You sit in that chair, let me get behind my camera, and I will get you to tell your parents' story so that it doesn't die with you."

Harmati motioned Cates to sit on the floor, and then Theo, gifted beyond my wildest dreams, pulled a raw, unfiltered videotaped confession from Harmati—rage, grief, and the shattered pieces of a man who had lost his soul. In seven minutes, he didn't just get Harmati to talk. He got him to *bleed*.

It was masterful. I knew it, every hardened, heard-it-all-before cop in the room knew it, and so did Harmati.

"We done?" he said.

"One last question, Arthur."

"Lay it on me."

"11:59? I know it's significant, but . . ."

"But it's just another little piece of my parents that the city buried with them," Harmati said. "That day when my father had the heart attack, my mother dialed 911 at 11:02 a.m. It took fifty-seven minutes before the ambulance showed up and the paramedics pronounced both of them dead. Do the math."

"11:59," Theo said. "And . . . cut."

"Now, get the fuck out of here, Theo," Harmati said. "Take your movie and go win an Oscar." He looked at his watch. "Make it quick. You got five minutes."

Theo came out from behind the camera. "No."

Harmati stood up sharply. "What do you mean, no?"

"I mean I'm not going and leaving you here to die."

"Well, then you are a minority of one, kid. Right now I am probably the most hated man in the city, maybe the country, maybe even the world. And you want me to stick around so I can spend the rest of my life in prison?"

"No. I want you to stick around and finish what you started. The city didn't think twice about destroying your parents' restaurant. The city didn't take a nickel's worth of responsibility for their deaths. You think everybody hates you? I'll bet every bankrupt storeowner who sees this film will cheer you on. Yes, you'll be in prison, but do you really think Anna and Stefan want you dead? I guarantee you they are rooting for you to stay alive and do what you can to change the system so it doesn't keep fucking over more people like them."

"Wow," Arthur whispered, the single word a rare tribute that seemed to resonate throughout the deserted station house. "You are one in a million, Theo, but I'm done. I'm staying. You're going."

Theo folded his arms across his chest. "No."

"Theo!" It was Cates. She looked up at him from the floor.

"Stay out of it, Cates," Theo snapped.

"It's *Captain* Cates, and this piece of shit deserves to die. If he takes me with him, so be it. It's the job I signed up for. But you didn't. Now, get the hell out of my office. That's an order!"

"An order? I don't work for you, and I'm tired of the fucking police and this fucking city telling me how to live my life. That shit ends today. This is between me and Arthur."

The cops in the room were spellbound. This nineteen-year-old kid had managed to turn Arthur around in some kind of a reverse Stockholm syndrome. And now he was standing up for Arthur, taking his side.

"Are you looking at this?" Chief Doyle said. "This kid just slid into the role of good cop, and Cates, fucking pro that she is, caught it, jumped in, and she is bad cop from hell."

"Three minutes," someone called out.

I couldn't speak. But the voice in my head was screaming. *Run, Theo, run. You did the best you could. He said you could go. Please, just go. There's something I desperately have to tell you.*

"We're out of time, kid," Arthur said. "You gotta go. I'm not giving you an order. I'm asking you a favor. Do for my parents what I couldn't."

Theo let out a deep breath and gave in. "Yes, sir." He offered up his outstretched right fist. "To justice."

Arthur reached out his left hand and fist-bumped the young man who would carry his message.

"To justice," he repeated.

Theo detached the camcorder from the tripod, set it down, and methodically collapsed each leg one by one, his movements smooth, unhurried. He gripped the heavy metal frame in one hand, adjusting his hold as he gathered his gear.

Then, in a single explosive motion, he twisted to the left, coiled his body like a spring, and with all the ferocity of an Olympic hammer thrower, spun around and slammed the heavy metal tripod into Harmati's ribs with a sickening crack.

Air burst from his lungs in a guttural hack. He flailed, the phone flying from his hand as he clawed at his sides gasping for breath that wouldn't come.

Cates dove on top of Theo as ESU stormed the room, a cop grabbing each arm as Harmati buckled in pain. Another two took trauma shears, cutting the vest on each side and deftly lifting it over his head. Then they cut the rest—pants, shirt, socks, underwear, and dragged him naked and screaming out of the room.

Two floors below the chaos, I ran to the bathroom, slammed the stall door, buried my face in my hands, and totally lost my shit.

CHAPTER 72

IT TOOK ME TEN minutes to pull myself together. The first person I saw when I stepped out of the bathroom was Chuck Dryden.

"Zach," he said, "the bomb squad is upstairs and I'm here with my team to photograph, dust, swab, record, and preserve every inch of the crime scene, so the chief of D's moved the party next door to the firehouse. How about that young Theo? Amazing. What a stellar kid."

"Yes, he is," I said, and hustled over to FDNY Engine Company 39 and Ladder Company 16, who have shared a building with NYPD's 19th Precinct for over half a century. As is their custom when we are guests in their house, they greeted us with hot coffee and freshly baked cookies.

I got there just in time to see the stellar kid shaking hands with none other than the top cop himself, Colin Radcliffe.

"Zach," Theo said as soon as he saw me come through the door. He strode over, arms outstretched. "We got him."

"*We?*" I said, grabbing him. "There was no *we*, kiddo. It was all you." I pulled him close, and then, as much as I wanted to hold on to him, I let go, keeping it to a respectable bro hug.

Kylie came up behind me. "You okay?" she said.

"I am now," I breathed.

The firehouse was noisy, filled with an energized crew of people, all recapping the drama or celebrating the outcome as we waited for the powers that be to fill us in on next steps.

And then Delia Cates walked through the door. In a heartbeat, the crowd went silent as she looked around for the unlikely hero who had just saved her life. But Theo spotted her first.

"Captain!" he yelled, and the two of them ran toward each other like in one of those sappy movie reunion scenes at a small-town train station. They hugged each other, overwhelmed with emotions that few people will ever experience in their lifetime. The crowd responded with cheers and applause.

"All right, folks. Bring it in, bring it in." It was Chief Doyle.

Everybody settled, and Kylie, who knows Doyle well, gave me an eye roll. The chief was about to give one of his famous Oscar acceptance speeches where he thanks everyone and goes on too long because there's no band to play him off.

"I honestly don't think I can find the words to express how proud I am," he began.

And then, despite the supposed limitations of his vocabulary, he spent the next five minutes thanking everybody from the bomb squad to HNT, ESU, the police officers from all corners of the city who had evacuated everyone so quickly and efficiently, and the men and women of the 19th Precinct and the way they handled this situation.

And then he moved on to Cates and the gifted young lad who just gave us all a master class on hostage negotiations. "And, Theo, I personally invite you and will absolutely recommend you," he said, "for employment with the greatest police department in the world." Applause, applause.

The chief went on. "A search warrant was obtained and executed even before the bomber was apprehended, and I've just received word from Westchester County that the work shed where the bombs were built has been located and all hazardous materials removed safely.

"But," he added, "we still don't know if there are any other bombs out there, and we don't yet have a location on Ramón Reyes. However, the search warrant turned up several fictitious IDs that had been created for Reyes, and it was determined that he used one of them to fly from

Washington, DC, to Frankfurt, Germany, three days ago. From there, he boarded a train to Prague. We doubt that's his final destination, but until we are positive that New York is no longer under threat, we will continue to be vigilant, and the identity of our young hero will be withheld from the public, and he will have around-the-clock police protection."

He looked at Theo for a smile and a nod of appreciation. He got the smile, followed by a polite question. "Sir, when can I get my footage back? I want to start editing."

Laughter from a roomful of people who spend their days choking on red tape and have witnessed evidence like Theo's film disappear into a bureaucratic black hole never to resurface again.

"Ignore them," Doyle said. "Son, you have my word that at some point your film will be back in your possession, but right now we need to keep it pristine to ensure a successful prosecution."

I had seen Theo pick up on the words "at some point," so he had to know that the chief was making a promise that the DA wouldn't let him keep. But when he smiled and gave Doyle a grateful thumbs-up, I realized he had only pretended to fall for the bullshit, because his precious footage was already safely stored in the cloud.

Kylie, Cates, Doyle, and the PC left the firehouse to share the good news with the throng of reporters who had gathered outside the precinct, while Theo and I slipped away unnoticed in a big red fire truck.

Cheryl was waiting for us at her apartment. The TV was on but muted. "Pick a channel," she said. "Every one of them is talking about Arthur Harmati, investment banker turned mad bomber, Captain Delia Cates, intrepid head of the elite NYPD Red team, and an unidentified civilian who was in Cates's office when Harmati walked in with a suicide bomb strapped to his chest."

She unmuted the TV.

"According to Chief of Detectives Harlan Doyle," the newscaster said, "the brave civilian who helped Captain Cates subdue the bomber is currently under twenty-four-hour police protection, and his identity will not be released until the department has all suspects connected to the bombings—and that includes Ramón Reyes—in custody."

"Well, this brave unidentified civilian needs a nap," Theo said.

"Your room is ready," Cheryl said.

She had converted her dining alcove into an office. Theo had stayed there before, and he was happy to crash on the IKEA sleeper sofa.

"I'll be wearing Beats, so feel free to talk about me," he said, closing the door behind him.

As soon as he was out of earshot, Cheryl, who misses nothing, said, "Your eyes are red."

"It's either because of all the damn pollen in the air or the fact that I locked myself in a stall in the precinct bathroom and cried like a baby."

"I can't imagine what you were going through," she said.

"I couldn't stop thinking about how close I came to losing him. The whole time he was in that room with Harmati, I cursed myself for not telling him I'm his father."

"And now that you have another chance?"

"Kylie and I were subpoenaed to testify at Spence's hearing tomorrow. But first thing Tuesday morning, Theo and I are going to drive out to Montauk, and I'm finally going to make good on that fishing trip I bailed on."

"And you are going to tell him that you're his father," Cheryl said.

"Yes, Dr. Robinson," I said. "I am. I promise."

That was the plan. But like so many of my plans, that's not what happened.

CHAPTER 73

THE COURTROOM WAS PACKED. No surprise. In just a short time, Spence had transformed from obscure TV writer to producer of a hit show to one-half of the Harrington–MacDonald power couple. And now, after a two-year disappearance that was shrouded in mystery, he was an accused murderer whose cop wife had just played a key role in tracking down the man who terrorized New York. This wasn't just another Monday morning down at the courthouse—this was the Super Bowl Sunday of bail hearings.

"All rise!" the court officer announced loudly. "The Criminal Court of the City of New York is now in session. The Honorable Judge Laura Russom presiding."

"We're screwed," the Warlock had told us when he learned that Judge Russom had been assigned to the case.

The statement caught both of us by surprise. Russom was one of the most respected judges in the system. Younger and hands down more attractive than her peers, she had a reputation for being fair, open-minded, patient, and, perhaps because of her Savannah, Georgia, roots, truly gracious.

"I thought you liked Judge Russom," Kylie said.

"I do—when I have a case, or at least a solid game plan," Warlock said. "But your control freak of a husband forced this bail hearing, and now I'm saddled with it."

"So what are you going to do?"

"I have no idea, Detective. What does one do when one shows up to a gunfight armed with nothing more than a butter knife?"

"Ninety-nine-point-nine-nine-nine percent of them run like hell," Kylie said.

His face lit up. "Yes, they do! But the fearless few," he said, underscoring the words with a wink that assured her she was included in that elite group, "look for a whetstone to sharpen that knife."

With that, he gave us a wave of the hand, said, "I'll see you Monday morning," and took his leave.

And now it was Monday morning.

The judge settled into her chair and cut to the chase. "Counsel for the defense, please proceed with argument for bail."

Tall, angular, with a full head of white hair that played perfectly against his warm Good Neighbor Sam blue eyes, the legal legend that was Dennis George Andrew Woloch stood up.

Everyone in the courtroom, especially the prosecutor, knew that his sorcerer-like ability to win hearts and change minds had earned him the nickname *Warlock*. But he never did the same thing twice. All eyes were on him, waiting for his latest gambit.

He rose to the occasion.

"Your Honor," he said, "the prosecution is concerned that if you grant bail, my client will pack up and leave the country. Talk about not seeing the forest for the trees. Nothing could be further from reality. May I suggest that we all take a step back and ask, why did my client uproot his idyllic life in Barbados and come to the US in the first place? He is here on a mission, and the only two words that will get him back on a flight to Bridgetown are not 'Bail granted.' They are 'Mission accomplished.'

"Imagine this, Your Honor. You are an upstanding citizen. You have led a perfectly exemplary life. Your reputation is beyond reproach, and suddenly, you are hit with the news that someone has hijacked that reputation, created a movie that grotesquely reinvents your life story, and is days away from releasing that . . . that horror film to the public, destroying every shred of good, erasing every ounce of decency, eradicating every achievement, every act of human kindness that should be your legacy.

"Imagine that kind of soul-crushing gut punch coming at you out of nowhere. That happened to Spence Harrington, Your Honor. He did not hesitate. He flew to the United States to rectify this gross injustice, and I can assure you that he is not leaving this country, this city, or these proceedings until his good name is restored and justice is served.

"Your Honor, I know the difference between a bail hearing and a lawyer's lame attempt to prejudice the court by going into defense mode before trial. And so I will stop here and respectfully request that bail be granted so that Mr. Harrington can remain in New York and finish what he came for. And that is to meet with the studios who own the egregious film, and work with them to correct it so that when it is finally released to the public, it will portray his life as it was lived.

"Thank you, Your Honor," he said, his voice a reverent whisper that somehow echoed into every corner of the hushed courtroom.

Woloch gave the judge a slight, respectful head bow and slipped into his chair.

As soon as he sat down, every head turned to Judge Russom. No amount of vowed impartiality could hide the look in her eyes. She was impressed. Witchcraft can do that to a person.

Kylie nudged me and gestured over to Harvey Steckler. Despite the pricey suit, the starched white shirt, and the perfectly knotted two-hundred-dollar Paul Stuart tie, the man looked as if he'd just been run over by a fully loaded thirty-ton garbage truck and was just lying in the gutter, waiting to be tossed in the hopper.

"Top that, Harvey," she whispered.

CHAPTER 74

"MR. STECKLER," THE JUDGE said. I may be kidding myself, but it felt as if she too wanted to say, "Top that."

Steckler shuffled some papers that were on the table in front of him. It was a stall. Whatever argument he had in his bag of tricks had just been rendered useless by the Warlock. Painting Spence Harrington as a flight risk was no longer going to cut it with the judge. He stood up, took a deep breath, and grabbed for his next-best idea.

But, of course, the Warlock had set him up to grab wrong.

"Your Honor," Steckler said, "the reason that counsel laid forth for why Mr. Harrington would remain in this country is the very same reason why he came here with a vengeful obsession to kill Preston Balfour."

The Warlock stood up slowly. Hands hopelessly outstretched, he gave the judge a weary sigh. "Your Honor," he said, "I just double-checked my calendar, and it says right here, 'Bail hearing.' And yet, it sounds as if my learned colleague is trotting out his opening remarks for a murder trial."

Russom could not hide the grin. "Noted," she said. "Mr. Steckler, what does *your* calendar say?"

I could almost see the flop sweat. "Apologies, Your Honor," Steckler stammered. "If I could just have a moment with cocounsel."

"A moment?" Russom said, reinforcing her reputation for being fair, patient, and gracious. "If you need some time, I'd be happy to grant you a brief recess."

Before Steckler could respond, the doors at the rear of the courtroom opened, and the last people I ever expected to see stepped inside.

"Holy shit," Kylie said, pounding my shoulder. "I can't believe it."

I couldn't either. Dr. Kunal Sarin and Vikram Sharma, the two men Steckler had stonewalled us from interviewing, were now standing at the top of the center aisle, looking lost, as if they had just shown up for jury duty.

A court officer, Jimia Avery, hustled over to get them seated.

Sarin said something to Avery, who pointed in our direction. Kylie and I scooched over and Sarin joined us. He beckoned to Sharma, but the man didn't move. His face sagging with exhaustion, eyes wide with fear, he held his arms up to the judge and said, "I am here to confess."

This is New York City. Our judges have seen it all. It's not unusual for someone to stumble into a proceeding and announce that the CIA is following them and they want to enter witness protection.

Russom didn't respond. She just nodded her head at Avery. For many court officers, the fascination of the job wears thin over time. But not for Jimia Avery. She loved the drama enough to attend Brooklyn Law School at night and was only a year away from taking the bar exam.

She put a hand on Sharma's shoulder. Whatever she said calmed him. He seemed about to leave when Spence, who had been sitting at the defense table talking to Warlock, turned around and caught sight of the man standing in the center aisle.

Despite having his ankles shackled, Spence jumped up.

"That's him!" he yelled. "That's him. That's the guy!"

Sharma turned to him. Their eyes met, and Spence snapped. Without thinking, he tried to lunge in the other man's direction, but his feet couldn't cooperate, and he crashed to the floor.

Judge Russom banged her gavel. "Court officers, remove the defendant from the courtroom."

They were way ahead of her, two of them lifting Spence to his feet and shuffling him out the side door.

The judge now turned her attention back to the cause of the disruption, who still stood his ground.

"And you, sir, what is your name?"

"Vikram Sharma."

"Well, Mr. Sharma, I am holding you in contempt."

The look in his eyes told me he had no idea what that meant.

"Officers," Russom ordered, "remove him from my courtroom."

Avery cuffed Sharma, who stood there and looked up apologetically at Judge Russom.

"I am very sorry," he said. "I'm a simple man. I know nothing about how to do this."

"For the future, Mr. Sharma, you should know that you cannot address this court unless you are a witness in this case."

Sharma looked at her, confused. "But I am more than a witness," he said. "I did it. I killed Preston Balfour."

Sharma's confession ricocheted off the walls and ignited the crowd. Russom tried to restore order, but after three bangs of her gavel, she opted for a simpler solution: Get the hell out.

But not without hostages.

"Counselors," she commanded Steckler and Woloch. "My chambers. Now!"

"And you two," she barked at Kylie and me. "Don't even think about leaving this building. Officer Avery, make sure they join the party!"

CHAPTER 75

JUDGE RUSSOM SAT BEHIND her desk. The rest of us stood.

She glanced at her watch. "It's 11:09. And that *fucking shitstorm* that disrupted my court is currently my problem," she said, now that we were behind closed doors and she could finally unleash the hellfire she had kept hidden under all that public Southern charm.

"By 11:15, it will be your problem. *But,*" she warned, "it won't be your *biggest* problem."

She lowered her voice. "I will."

She gave us a hint of a smile, but not the kind you want to see on the face of an angry judge.

"Are we clear?" she said.

We were clear.

Russom focused her gaze on Kylie. "Detective MacDonald, as soon as those men entered the courtroom, one of them zeroed in on you and Detective Jordan and joined you. Who is he?"

"His name is Dr. Kunal Sarin, Your Honor."

"You're not on the witness stand, Detective. I'm not going to spoon-feed you the questions. Cop to judge, tell me what I need to know about Dr. Sarin."

"Several years ago, he was the subject of a film by Preston Balfour. It should be a heartwarming story of one man's sacrifice and dedication, but Balfour decided to give the doctor some . . ." She pretended to grope for a phrase that wouldn't sound damning, but, of course, she was doing just the opposite.

"Let's just say he gave Dr. Sarin some *marketable perversions* because, as we all know, that's what sells tickets. The movie was a financial success for Balfour, but the shameful picture he painted of Dr. Sarin not only destroyed the man's personal reputation, but the funding for his clinic dried up. Balfour was about to do the same thing to Mr. Harrington when he was murdered."

I could see Steckler's jaw clench. The details of the trial were unfolding right here in chambers, and he was powerless to object.

Kylie went on. "When the cops arrived at the scene, they saw Harrington, covered with the victim's blood, defensive wounds on his arms and wrists. He swore that he had struggled with and disarmed the real killer, but how many times have we heard that before? Plus, there were three eyewitnesses who saw the defendant standing over the body with the murder weapon in his hand. The investigating officers found nothing at the scene to suggest a second man, so they made the arrest and closed the case.

"Knowing that the defense could use that decision to convince the jury that Mr. Harrington was yet another victim of the department's *inability to conduct a thorough investigation*, my partner and I were tasked with making sure nothing was missed."

"And was there?" the judge asked.

"Big time, Your Honor. The first thing we learned was that Dr. Sarin and his entourage were in New York at a fundraising dinner for the clinic on the very night that Balfour was murdered. He immediately became a person of interest. We tracked him down in Toronto, but in the brief conversation we had with him, despite the fact that he had a compelling motive, our best instincts said he didn't kill Balfour."

"And what about Mr. Sharma?"

"He is the father of Priya Sharma, the young girl whose life Dr. Sarin saved. It was one of the more memorable events in the film, and both father and daughter are so grateful, they have been traveling with

Dr. Sarin to help him regain the public trust and raise money for his clinic. We only saw Mr. Sharma in passing at the Toronto Airport. But we don't forget faces, and when we were going through the police body cam footage on Friday, we saw him again. As the cops were responding to the 911 call, Sharma was a block away from Balfour's apartment, walking away from the murder scene."

"Excellent police work," Russom said. "And what did you do with that information?"

"We brought it to ADA Steckler and told him we wanted to pursue the lead and question Mr. Sharma. As you know, we can't do that by setting up a video call and giving him days to concoct an alibi. We wanted to fly to India, show up unannounced, and hit him with questions he wouldn't have time to prepare for. But ADA Steckler said there wasn't enough evidence to warrant the expense."

"So you called Dr. Sarin and persuaded him to show up at the bail hearing with Sharma in tow," the judge said.

"Absolutely not, Your Honor," Kylie said. "I did call Dr. Sarin Friday night. It was Saturday morning in India. He is a man of integrity, and I asked him to reach out to Mr. Sharma and try to get enough information to convince the District Attorney's Office that our taking a trip to India was warranted. We spoke for less than five minutes. He never called back. Seeing those two men walk into your courtroom this morning was probably a bigger shock to me than it was to you. I haven't spoken to Dr. Sarin since he sat down next to me, and I still haven't been able to put all the pieces together."

The judge turned to the Warlock. "Mr. Woloch, you're rather well known for your courtroom showmanship. Did you mastermind that little piece of theater?"

"No, Your Honor. My . . . *specialties*, if you will, are convincing jurors to see things my way, which I will tell you is not always as easy as it may appear, and making prosecutors look like knuckleheads, which, I must admit, is pretty much a walk in the park. However, I have never done, and I would never do, anything to demean, insult, or embarrass the court. You have my word on that, Your Honor.

"And," he added, "as an officer of the court, I am appalled that the district attorney refused to follow up on the valuable information these two detectives brought to light on Friday afternoon. You saw the shock and horror on my client's face when he finally came face-to-face with the man he saw murder Preston Balfour on that fateful night. I apologize for my client's outburst, but that might have been avoided if Mr. Steckler had not chosen to ignore vital evidence provided by Detectives MacDonald and Jordan. His decision has not only derailed the pursuit of justice but also undermined the integrity of these proceedings."

I know my partner. She would have liked to grab Dennis Woloch and hug him. She had wisely decided not to throw Steckler under the bus, knowing that if she did, he'd screw us the next time around. But the Warlock happily—and deftly—did it for her.

"And that leaves you, Mr. Steckler," Judge Russom said.

"Your Honor, the detectives did show me footage of Mr. Sharma, but at the time it seemed circumstantial, and based on the evidence we already had on the defendant, it seemed hardly worth spending the taxpayers' money to fly to India to ask a man who just happened to be in the area—"

"Spare me your logic, Mr. Steckler. I will be following up with your chief, and if I find out that any impropriety occurred on your part, I am going to be recommending sanctions against you with your office. You'll not only lose your job, but after what occurred in my courtroom this morning, I will see to it that you lose your license to practice law. You have until Friday morning to undo this confluence of poor decisions, properly and thoroughly investigate the charges against Mr. Harrington, and either validate or dismiss the confession made by Mr. Sharma.

"At nine a.m. on Friday, you and Mr. Woloch will appear before me prepared to address and resolve this fiasco. Detectives, I'll be saving a front-row seat for you, and this time we will be locking the courtroom doors."

She checked her watch. "It's 11:15. This is no longer my problem. Mr. Steckler, are we clear?"

I looked at Steckler. He was as clear as a dead man walking can get.

CHAPTER 76

KYLIE AND I FOLLOWED Steckler back to his office. He was about five paces in front of us on the phone, barking orders. Top of the list was, "Get this guy Sharma out of holding and into an interview room. No! I don't have thirty minutes. Just drop whatever the fuck you're doing, and get him now!"

"What a guy," Kylie said. "Top of his class at charm school."

News travels fast in the halls of justice, and by the time we got out of the elevator on Steckler's floor, the other ADAs had heard he was about to self-destruct, and gave him a wide berth.

When we got to his office, there was a note stuck to his door. He ripped it off, but not before Kylie and I could make out the two words scrawled in black marker: FIX IT!

It was unsigned, but clearly it was a message from on high. Bosses avoid texts, preferring to communicate their lightly veiled threats by untraceable Post-it notes.

Steckler's phone rang as soon as he sat down.

"No! No!" he said, loud enough to let people in the adjoining offices know he was still a force to be reckoned with.

I had no idea what response he got from the other end, but whatever it was only enraged him more. He squinched his face, contorted his body, raised his voice, and went into a full-blown middle-aged tantrum. All to no avail.

"Fine!" he bellowed. "Get them both up here now!"

"Problem?" Kylie asked as soon as he hung up.

He gave her a cutting look. Of course there was a problem. And Kylie and I had precipitated it by finding Sharma on the body cam footage and then making a whole big deal about it.

"This guy Sharma who *confessed*," he said putting the word in air quotes. "He waived his right to an attorney, but he won't sit for an interview unless his pal can be in the room with us."

"His pal?" Kylie said. "You mean Dr. Sarin?"

"Yeah, that one."

"In case you missed it in the judge's chambers, Dr. Sarin saved Sharma's daughter's life. Since then, the man has done all he can to express his gratitude. My best guess is that he not only trusts Sarin, he wants to make sure he doesn't say anything that will further damage the doctor's reputation."

"Whatever."

Ten minutes later, we were all in an interview room. Sharma had been Mirandized, and Steckler began asking questions.

"Why did you come here today?"

Sharma looked at Sarin. He had already explained that to the judge. He didn't expect to be asked again. Sarin gave him a nod. It was okay to answer.

"I killed Preston Balfour. I did not mean to, but I did."

Steckler rolled his eyes and leaned back in his chair. "And I'm sure you've rehearsed a nice little story about how it all went down. But first answer one question. Who put you up to this? Was it her?" he said, pointing at Kylie.

Sharma turned to Sarin and said a few words in Hindi.

"May I speak?" the doctor said.

"Your buddy here isn't, so you might as well," Steckler said.

"Mr. Sharma is a simple man. Nobody put him up to this. Unbeknownst to me, he went to Balfour's apartment that night to try to convince him to at least donate some of the proceeds from his film to the clinic. But Balfour was drunk when he got there—"

"Stop!" Steckler said. "This shit is useless. I've already got a dubious confession. But he's the one who's got to give me the details, not you. Tell him to start answering my questions. In English."

"He won't."

"He . . . ? Jesus H. Christ." He turned to Sharma. "Look, pal, this is my show. If you won't talk to me, then why the hell did you come here?"

"I came to confess to a murder," Sharma said, "but I refuse to confess to you."

"And why not?"

Sharma looked straight at Steckler, his voice soft but firm. "I came to America to offer something of great value—my freedom. I am willing to sacrifice it for the doctor who saved my child, for the honor of keeping an innocent man free, for my daughter's future, and for the truth.

"But you, sir—you regard my decision as if it's worthless, as if the truth I am ready to speak is just another lie. I will not dishonor my confession by offering it to someone who holds no respect for what it costs me."

Steckler reeled. I wondered if he had visions of the message on his door that said, "Fix it!" and suddenly realized that he might not be able to. He groped for a comeback. Whatever it was, I knew it would not be an apology.

Kylie stepped in before Steckler could throw more gasoline on the fire.

"Vikram," she said, her tone warm yet filled with the gravity of the moment. "I not only respect your decision, I am in awe of your courage and your commitment. Would you be willing to share your story with me?"

A wave of relief and gratitude spread over Sharma's face. "Thank you, Detective MacDonald. I would be honored."

CHAPTER 77

KYLIE LOOKED UP at Steckler. She didn't say a word. It was his call, and I seriously wondered if he was capable of making it.

Years ago, I was at a bar with a bunch of cops and lawyers. We had just lost a case that should have been a slam dunk, because the ADA who was calling the shots put his monumental ego ahead of the smarter, humbler road to victory.

Three or four rounds into the evening, Garrett Billings, the elder statesman of the group, raised his glass and said. "To arrogance. Long may it continue to get in the way of justice."

And now, watching Steckler pout under the weight of his own arrogance, I couldn't help but think that history was on the brink of repeating itself.

But Kylie was not about to let that happen.

"I could use some water," she said to Sharma. "Can I get you some?"

"Yes, please," he responded.

Kylie motioned toward the door, and Steckler and I followed her out.

"Harvey," she said, getting two bottles of water out of a vending machine, "we're down to our last two options. So tell me, would you like me to proceed, or would you rather explain to the judge that a suspect who wanted to confess to a murder flew back to Mumbai because your gut told you he didn't really have anything worth listening to?"

Fear triumphed over ego. Steckler caved.

"Do what you have to do," he said.

We followed Kylie back into the interview room. She handed Sharma the water, and he drank gratefully.

"In your own words," Kylie said, "please tell me what happened that night."

"It was the first night of our fundraiser in America, and I was so proud of my daughter," Sharma said. "Her speech on behalf of Dr. Sarin and the clinic made people laugh, made them cry, and most of all, it convinced them to help. By the end of the night, they had donated even more than we expected.

"Priya has done so much, and I thought, what have *I* done? Carry luggage? Set up chairs? Bring food to those who are doing all the hard work? I knew Balfour was in New York to talk about his new movie. I thought, surely by now he understands how much he has hurt Dr. Sarin, and he would be willing to help. He had been so kind to everyone when we first met him, so I thought maybe that part of him still exists. I knew where he lived, so I decided to pay him a visit and ask if he would give us just a small portion of his profits to help the people of Dharavi get their medical facility back."

He looked at Sarin. "It was foolish. I'm sorry."

The doctor was about to respond, but Kylie waved him off. "This is very helpful, Vikram. What happened when you got to Balfour's apartment?"

"I rang his doorbell from the lobby. I thought he would ask who it was, but he didn't. He just pressed the buzzer and said, 'Apartment 4B,' like he was expecting me. When I got upstairs, he opened the door, and the first thing I saw was his face. It was bruised, discolored, with a bandage over his left eye, like he had just been in a fight. He was also quite intoxicated.

"I'm sure he had no idea I was in New York, so he was very surprised to see me. More than surprised. Outraged. Angry. As soon as he saw me, he screamed, 'What the hell do you want?' I had prepared a little speech in my head, but my mind went blank, and all I could say was one word. Reparations.

"That made him even angrier. He flew into a rage. He said, 'First Harrington, and now you? Did you two parasites plan this together?' That's the word he used. *Parasites*. At the time, I had no idea what he was talking about, so I asked him who Harrington was. That only incensed him more.

"He called me a bloodsucking slumdog, and he started swinging at me wildly. I didn't want to return the blows, because he was too drunk to defend himself, so I pushed him away, and he fell to the floor, slamming against this rolling kitchen trolley. One of the wheels snapped off, and everything that was on it—glasses, bottles, a pot of coffee, everything—crashed to the floor. I tried to leave, but he staggered to his feet with a knife in his hand."

Sharma put one hand over his eyes and face. "You know the rest."

"I don't, Vikram," Kylie said. "I really don't. Only you know the rest. Please share it with me."

"He wanted to kill me. I didn't just imagine that. He said it. 'I'm going to kill you.' He lunged at me with the knife in his right hand, but I was able to grab his wrist with my left, and I started flailing at him with my right. The floor was wet, and I went down. Balfour fell on top of me. He still had the knife in his right hand, and I somehow managed to keep him from stabbing me.

"But then, he took his left hand and pressed his thumb to my windpipe. I struggled, but I couldn't breathe. I could see the darkness closing in around me. And then . . ." He closed his eyes. "I reached up until I was able to grab his wrist with both hands. And with every last ounce of strength in my body I drove his right arm—and the knife—into his chest.

"He released his grip on the knife, and I pulled it out. My brain was numb with fear, but I knew what to do. I stood up, ran to the door, opened it, and there was a man. I had no idea who he was. I know now that it was Mr. Harrington. His eyes took in everything—Balfour lying on the floor bleeding, me with a bloody knife in my hand—and he tried to take it from me. I fought back, but at this point I was no match for him. I dropped the knife, and as soon as he went to retrieve it, I ran out the door, down the stairs, and out of the building."

"Did anyone see you?"

"I don't think so. My clothes were covered with blood. But fortunately, they were dark—black trousers, navy blue kurta—so I didn't stand out. By the time I got back to the hotel, the blood had soaked through to my undergarments and my skin. I showered, tied my bloody clothes up in separate bags, and walked ten blocks, burying each bag in the trash cans of random apartment buildings. The next morning, we left New York."

"And did you tell anyone what happened?" Kylie said.

"Tell anyone? No. This is not something you share. This was my shame and mine alone to bear. But then Saturday morning, Dr. Sarin told me that the police had a video of me from that night, so I told him everything. That's when he told me that Mr. Harrington was going to be punished for my crime. I was horrified. I knew he had been arrested, but I knew he hadn't done anything wrong. I couldn't understand how an innocent man could go to prison for a murder he didn't commit. So I came here to tell the truth and to accept the consequences."

He drank the last of his water. "That's all. That's everything."

Steckler nodded to me and Kylie, and we followed him out the door.

"If that's *all*," Steckler said, "if that's really *everything*, I can't charge him."

"Why not?" Kylie said.

"He has no way to corroborate his story," Steckler said. "Forensics has established that the only viable DNA they found belongs to Harrington and Balfour. Sharma *conveniently* trashed his blood-stained clothes, so there's no proof he was actually in Balfour's apartment that night. All he has is a story."

"But why would he make up a story that would only put him in prison?" Kylie said.

"Don't be naive, MacDonald. You heard him. His daughter has done so much to raise money for Sarin, and he feels like he's done nothing. He wants to help. So he comes back to New York, spins this yarn, and it's a damn good one. So good that I would probably accept a plea of self-defense and he'd get a couple of years. And in return, your husband would pay Mr. Sharma whatever the going rate is for copping to a murder that he didn't commit."

"But the judge—"

Steckler held up a hand. "The judge charged me with getting to the bottom of it. I did. Have you ever been to India? Do you know how many millions of people walk around barefoot, in rags, begging for pennies? So this guy is maybe one step above that, but I guarantee he hasn't got a pot to piss in. He's doing it for the payday."

"Oh, my God," Kylie said. "Oh, my God. That's it. That's it."

"What?" Steckler said.

"Shut up," Kylie said. "I'm not done here."

She charged back into the room, and we followed.

"Vikram," she said. "A few more questions, if you don't mind."

He nodded.

"You said there was a lot of blood, correct?"

"Yes. Mine, but mostly his."

"And it splattered all over your clothes."

"Head to toe. I had to wash my hair several times when I showered."

"And you threw your clothes away."

"Reluctantly, but I had to. Like I said, I put each article of clothing in separate bags and deposited them in various trash cans along Hudson Street."

"I see. And where did you dispose of your shoes?"

"My shoes? That was impossible. I only own two pair. My work boots and my Peshawari chappals. But the boots were still at home in Dharavi. If I had thrown my shoes away, I would be barefoot for the remainder of the trip."

"That makes sense," Kylie said. "And where are those shoes now—the ones you were wearing the night you were forced to struggle with Mr. Balfour to defend your life?"

"They are right here," Sharma said, pointing at his feet.

All eyes went to Sharma's aging brown sandals, the style rooted in tradition, the leather weathered by time, worn down from years of walking the unpaved streets of Dharavi, stained by rain and mud, every crease holding a story of journeys taken, roads traversed, and maybe, just maybe, a silent witness to tragedy in a room eight thousand miles from home.

"May I have them, please?" Kylie said.

She grabbed a pair of nitrile gloves from her jacket pocket and slipped them on, and Sharma handed her his shoes.

She set one down and turned the other in her hands, slowly examining every inch of the worn leather. She held it up to me and pointed at a dark-brown, almost black stain that had seeped unevenly into the leather.

"What does that look like to you, Zach?" she said.

"No question. And I don't need a microscope. It's blood. Dried blood," I said.

She held up the other shoe. It was obvious now. I pointed at several spots. "Blood. Blood. Blood."

"Mr. Steckler," Kylie said, "I'd like to send these shoes to the lab forthwith. I think they are going to give you all the corroboration you need."

CHAPTER 78

"THAT'S ONE PAIR of magical shoes," Kylie said once we were on our way back to the precinct. "They have the power to save Spence's ass—and burn Steckler's."

She was right. Steckler's decision to dismiss the body cam footage of Vikram Sharma as irrelevant had been a colossal mistake. If Spence turned out to be innocent—and it looked as though that was where things were headed—Steckler would be bozo of the day from one end of the city to the other.

And since shit floats, his boss, and his boss's boss, would also be covered with the stink. So the District Attorney's Office went into immediate damage control mode.

Before the shoes had even left the building, the DA himself was on the phone, calling in favors. Priorities were shifted, resources were reallocated, overtime was approved, and instead of waiting two, three, or more weeks, the results of the blood analysis were released thirty-six hours after they arrived at the lab.

Sharma had been telling the truth. It was his blood that had been commingled with Balfour's. His confession that he was the killer and that Spence had been the wrong man in the wrong place became front-page news. And the hero—the man who saw the possibility of an injustice and prevented it from happening—was none other than the asshole who caused it in the first place: Harvey Steckler.

In a brilliant display of media manipulation, the district attorney praised Steckler for pursuing every avenue to continue to investigate the case, even though multiple witnesses had identified—correction, *mis*identified—Spence.

"Eyewitness testimony alone is not a reason to prosecute someone," the DA said at a press conference. "Perceptions are fallible. People can become disoriented by the stress of being at the scene of a crime, followed by the unfamiliarity of being caught up in the drama of a police investigation. I certainly don't fault the witnesses. I would rather focus on the tireless efforts of Assistant District Attorney Steckler and his team for leaving no stone unturned, and for their efforts that resulted in an innocent man regaining his freedom."

It was a masterful piece of self-preservation, but it was pure bullshit. The police commissioner knew it, but as long as the DA didn't lay the blame on NYPD, he didn't say a word. The Warlock knew it, which is why he volunteered to defend Sharma pro bono. Not only were Kylie and I confident that he would convince a jury that the humble, hardworking, loving father had acted in self-defense, but he would rake his favorite knucklehead prosecutor over the coals and have a grand time doing it.

And, of course, Laura Russom also knew that the district attorney's tribute to ADA Steckler was, as she said to her court clerk in private, "pure twaddle." But the esteemed Georgia judge was above petty departmental politics, and her heartfelt apology to Spence when she exonerated him that Friday morning could not have been more gracious.

And speaking of apologies, shortly after the charges against Spence were dropped, Charlie Elliott, the veteran cop who had arrested him, walked into our office.

"In keeping with tradition," he said, "I made sure to show up unannounced. But in an effort to add a little class to my appearance, I brought a gift. It's my way of saying thank you."

He handed us a box that said *Tai Pan Bakery*.

"You're welcome," I said. "But what are you thanking us for?"

"Some people are asking me how I feel about you guys making me look bad," Elliott said. "But you didn't. You made the system look good. Every cop makes mistakes. And when a man is locked up for a minute because I made a mistake, it's a minute too long. If you hadn't dug out the truth, and I found out years from now that I put an innocent man in prison, I wouldn't be able to live with myself. So thank you.

"Fair warning, though," he said, just a hint of a smile in his eyes. "There are two dozen mooncakes inside that box. Before you even finish half of them, you'll be begging your captain to transfer you downtown so you can get your hands on these little treasures of the Fifth Precinct every day."

He let the smile blossom into a big-ass grin, congratulated us on a job well done, and left. The man was a class act.

It was late afternoon, and Kylie and I were still wading through the morass of paperwork that comes with the job when Cates called us into her office.

"I just got off the phone with the PC," she said. "Pete Peterson is in custody. He was arrested in Saranac Lake, about two hundred miles north of the city. He rented a cabin through a local real estate agent, paid cash, used a fictitious name, and wasn't even close to being on our radar."

"But . . ." Kylie said, her face lighting up with the prospect of a fun story about the downfall of a man who definitely had it coming.

"But he couldn't stop being Pete Peterson," Cates said. "Last night, he was at the local pub and tried to pick up the bartender. Apparently, she was not impressed, so he confided to her that he was an undercover cop on assignment for the NYPD. She didn't buy it, so he doubled down and told her he just got off that big New York City bomber case. She still didn't believe him, so he showed her some of the crime scene photos he took at the museum, along with his shield, and then, of course, the traditional closer of all asshole cops who are trying to impress girls."

"His gun," Kylie said.

Cates nodded.

Kylie looked at me. "This dude's got moves, Zach. You should take notes."

"This time, the bartender was impressed enough to check out his story," Cates said. "She went online, found his picture, but it said his name was Pete Peterson, which was not the one he'd been using. So now Mr. Cool turns out to be a stranger in a small, close-knit town, who is clearly a liar and who is carrying a concealed weapon. You can imagine what happened next."

"The bartender saw the error of her ways, they're now engaged, and the three of us are invited to the wedding," Kylie said, clapping her hands like a little kid.

It's not easy to get Delia Cates to break character and burst into peals of laughter, but that did it.

"She called the locals, they called us, and Peterson will be back in the city tomorrow morning. Now, get out of my office," Cates said, still chuckling.

By seven p.m., we had wrapped up our paperwork and were faced with something we both thought we might never see again: the weekend off.

"You're finally going to get some time to spend with Shane," I said as we headed down the stairs. "You going to go away or stay in the city?"

"Both," Kylie said. "I'm staying in the city; Shane left for Vegas tonight. He got an offer from one of the big casinos to open a restaurant on their property. He'd be crazy to say no. It's a once-in-a-lifetime opportunity, but it means he'll have to move to Vegas for at least a year. He wants me to go with him."

"So go," I said. "The department will give you a year's leave of absence."

"That was option one, but I decided against it," Kylie said. "I'm going with option two."

"And what's that?" I asked as we got to the first floor.

"My husband is back in New York. After what went down these past few weeks, he had no trouble convincing Shelley and the other production companies to shitcan Balfour's movie. Spence still owns a bar in Barbados, but he's decided to hang around Silvercup Studios for a while, kick some ideas around with Shelley, and see where it goes."

"Good for him," I said. "What kind of ideas? Movie? TV? Another cop show?"

"He didn't say. But Spence and I are having dinner tonight, so . . ." she said without any attempt to hide her excitement. "We'll see where it goes. How about you?"

We stepped out into the evening. The city pulsed around us, its frantic, chaotic, unique-in-the-world rhythm restored as if the 11:59 Bomber were just a bad dream. New York was back to normal, whatever the hell that is.

"Me?" I said. "I'm going straight home, setting my alarm for four a.m., and I'm finally going to be able to get on the road, drive out to Montauk, and go fishing with my son."

CHAPTER 79

THEO AND I WERE on the road by four thirty Saturday morning. I told him I hadn't slept well the night before, which was true, and I asked him to drive. Then I told him I was going to try to catch a nap on the way out to Montauk.

But that was a lie. I couldn't sleep. My mind was racing, trying to come up with the best way, the best time, the best words to tell him that I was his father. Call me a coward, but it was easier to curl up in the passenger seat with my eyes closed than to try to make small talk, when all I could think about was preparing for the biggest talk of my life.

Somewhere along the way, I finally did doze off, and I didn't wake up until we came to a stop and Theo turned off the engine.

I opened my eyes. We were on a country road. To my left was an old wooden windmill, a silent sentinel from another era, its original function long vanished, its new role to proclaim the locals' proud history.

To my right was a cemetery, the grass a lush green, its tombstones weathered by the centuries, surrounded not by stately stone walls or wrought iron detailed with intricate scrollwork, but by nothing more than a four-foot-high wooden picket fence. It was all very Eastern Long Island quaint.

"Where are we?" I asked.

Theo, armed with information as always, couldn't wait to enlighten me. "The South End Burying Ground, the oldest cemetery in East Hampton. Some of the residents have been here since the sixteen hundreds, and it's the final resting place for socialites; artists; shipwreck victims; an accused witch; Lion Gardiner, the first English colonist to settle in New York; and finally, saving the best for last, Sylviane LeBec Wilkins, my mother."

I felt my stomach tighten. "What are we doing here?" As soon as I said it, I regretted it.

"I'm sorry," he said. "It's just that you were asleep, and the cemetery is on the road to Montauk, and I couldn't just drive by and not pay my respects."

"No, no. *I'm* sorry. It was a dumb thing to say. I'm glad you stopped."

"Cool. Then come say hello to her."

"Are you sure?"

He gave me a grin. "I don't have any flowers. I've got to bring something. You're the best I can come up with on such short notice."

We walked through the graveyard. It was tiny by New York City standards. Minuscule but welcoming. A community of adventurous souls who came here hundreds of years ago and never left.

"Here she is," he said.

The headstone was simple and unassuming. Blue pearl granite with her name, the two dates that marked her lifespan, and a single inscription: *Son esprit danse toujours dans la lumière.*

"'Her spirit still dances in the light,'" Theo translated. "Let me tell her you're here."

He turned to the grave. "Maman, this is Zach Jordan. He's an amazing detective, part of this elite squad, NYPD Red. He has this way-cool partner, Kylie MacDonald, and the two of them catch the baddest of the bad. Zach is also an incredible guy."

He paused. "But you already knew that, didn't you?" he said.

I heard what he said, but I couldn't make sense of it.

"Anyway, Zach has been crazy busy these past few weeks, so I'm sorry it took so long, but here we are, finally—the three of us, together at last."

I could barely breathe. The walls closed in. The tears welled up.

"By the way, Maman, Zach and I are the same height, and I think I have his eyes, which is pretty cool. But I'm definitely smarter than he is. I can tell by the look on his face that right now he is totally gobsmacked."

"How . . . did you . . ." I stammered. "I . . . I only told Kylie and Cheryl, and I know they would never say a word. How did you . . ." I shook my head. Gobsmacked was an understatement.

"It's actually pretty easy. Once I figured it was you, I waited for you to toss an empty water bottle in the trash. I took it to a lab—"

"Theo, I'm a cop. I know how DNA testing works. I took one of your toothbrushes."

"Ha! I knew you knew. Why didn't you tell me?"

"Because you already have a father. Travis. I didn't want to ruin that relationship."

"Dude, you don't know Travis. He will always be the dad who raised me. I love him. Nothing can change that. But I promise, he will be over the moon to know I found my real father."

"That's great to know, but let's hold that for another time and get back to the question I was trying to ask. How did you even suspect that . . ."

"That you're my father?" Theo said. "You can say it."

I said it. "I am your father. I loved your mother. I never knew she was pregnant, but now I do, and I couldn't be happier. And yes, you are smarter than I am. So could you please tell me how you figured it out?"

"I was about ten years old, and I took all my mom's old photos, digitized them, and put them together as a video with a music track— the whole thing. It's twelve minutes long, and some days when I really miss her, I watch it. It's not the real her, but it's something."

"Wow, I'd love to see it."

"Oh, you will. My mother had a ton of friends, so I have no idea who some of those people are. But you know me. If I don't know somebody's story, I make one up. There was the guy in the *Pulp Fiction* T-shirt who was positive he'd have been a better Vincent than Travolta, the girl with the butterfly necklace who steals toys for her cat from Walmart, and, of course, there was you."

"I'm on the video?" I said.

"A couple of times. I didn't make the connection when I met you, but a few weeks ago, I was looking at it again, and I see this guy I call Lance, and I was like, *Holy shit, that's Zach!*"

"Are you serious?" I said. "You had pictures of me at eighteen and you called me *Lance*? That's about as unflattering as—"

"Wait, wait, wait, wait," Theo said. "It's not that bad. Every picture of you with my mom, you have that look."

"What look?"

"Lovestruck. Smitten. Like Romeo with Juliet. Gatsby with Daisy Buchanan. Sir Lancelot with Queen Guinevere. You became Lancelot du Lac. Lance for short."

"Is it too late to give me any other name in the world besides Lance?"

He smiled. "I think I've got one you might like."

As soon as he said it, I knew what was coming next. Before he could even say it out loud, the dam burst and, tough New York City cop that I am, I started sobbing.

And then the young man who just by chance stepped into my life a few months ago wrapped his arms around me and whispered in my ear.

"How about *Dad*?"

CHAPTER 80

IT WAS SUPPOSED to be one of the happiest days of Ramón Reyes's life.

It was day number forty-nine of his fresh start in Botswana. And 49 had been his jersey number when he pitched in the Cuban National Series. Everyone knew that 7 was lucky, and 49 was 7 times 7. It couldn't get any luckier than that. But it did. When he woke up that morning, the clock said 7:07.

"*Gracias, Dios,*" he said out loud.

"Who are you talking to at this hour of the morning?"

He rolled over, and there she was. Judith McField. His trusted adviser. His secret keeper. His reason for being. His true love. And soon to be his wife and the mother of his child.

"I'm thanking God."

She smiled. She didn't have to ask what he had to be thankful for.

A few days ago, they had moved into their new home on Acacia Grove Lane, on the outskirts of Gaborone.

The two of them had fallen in love with the house as soon as they set eyes on it. A modest little cottage made of sun-dried red bricks, with a high thatched roof, a spacious living room, a small modern kitchen, and two bedrooms, every inch of it filled with light, air, and hope.

They made love, showered, dressed, and settled into the little breakfast nook off the kitchen, where they sipped rooibos tea; shared bowls of yogurt, wild honey, and chunks of mango, papaya, and watermelon; and gazed in awe at the distant flat-topped acacias that changed colors with the rise and fall of the sun.

At 8:30, Judith left for her job as a finance officer at the Savannah Conservation Alliance, an NGO dedicated to wildlife protection in Botswana.

At 8:45, Ramón drove to Gaborone Hardware Supplies, where he found a fifty-two-inch heavy-duty ceiling fan to replace what Judith called the "dinky-ass, slow-as-molasses pinwheel" they currently had in their bedroom.

At 11:30, with the fan now whirring in place, he stopped at the barbershop for a haircut, then met his new friend Tshepo Molosi, a mechanic at the local garage, for a quick lunch of johnnycakes and ginger beer at a food stall in the market.

At 2:15, he was outside the schoolyard. There wasn't much call for a baseball coach in Botswana, so he'd been coming by every afternoon to watch the kids play soccer until he felt confident that his ability to motivate young athletes, help them improve their technical skills, and teach them to work together as a team would soon lead to a job.

At 5:40, Judith came home. Dinner was almost ready: baked salmon, jasmine rice, roasted asparagus. He poured two glasses of Hamilton Russell Chardonnay. They talked about their day and all the good ones that lay ahead.

At 5:58, Ramón's phone chirped with a text.

> Hope you're enjoying your new life. It ends in one minute.

Ramón sprang from his chair. "Run!" he said, grabbing Judith's hand. Judith pulled away. "Where? Why? What's going on?"

"I'll explain later. Just run. Please."

They made it as far as the kitchen. Eight thousand miles away,

Arthur Harmati sat on the edge of a steel cot in a grim Rikers Island cell, a contraband phone in his hand, smuggled in through the usual channels.

A slow smile crept across his face as he watched the modest little house on Acacia Grove Lane explode in flames.

Worth every penny of the fifty grand he paid to make it happen.

It was 5:59 in Botswana.

11:59 in New York City.

ACKNOWLEDGMENTS

I dedicated this book to Detective First Grade Danny Corcoran, NYPD (ret.). I named the hero of *Snowstorm in August* after him. And yet, I still cannot thank him enough.

I met Danny ten years ago, while I was researching *NYPD Red 4*. He answered all my questions and then—smart as he is—made the rookie mistake of saying, "If you need any more help, give me a call." I've been calling ever since, and my books have been better for it.

The 11:59 Bomber is pure fiction, but thanks to Danny Corcoran, every step Zach and Kylie take to bring him down is grounded in real NYPD procedure.

In case you somehow missed the dedication, Danny has become my friend, my anchor, and my partner in crime.

In a world ruled by algorithms, social trends, and attention spans measured in seconds, getting a book into the hands of people who want to read it is no mean feat. It takes a rare mix of instinct, strategy, and timing, and that's what Laura Russom brings to the table. She's always testing new ideas and finding smarter pathways through the noise, all with the singular focus of connecting books with the people most likely to love them.

If you're holding this book in your hands, there's a good chance that Laura is the reason you knew it existed. I'm lucky to have her on my team, and even luckier to call her a friend. And if the name Laura Russom rings a bell, that's no coincidence—she's Judge Russom in the book. Southern charm, sharp instincts, and zero tolerance for posers. Art imitating life.

And then there's Michael Carr—my editor, my challenger, and the guy who won't let me get away with anything lazy. He doesn't just clean up the mess; he helps me see what's missing, what's bloated, and what needs to hit harder. Our process isn't always smooth, but it's always worth it. Every time we go a round or two, the book comes out tighter, sharper, better.

Thanks to Hans Nielsen, general manager of the Chart House in Weehawken, New Jersey, for opening up his world—and his restaurant—to help me get the setting right. Thanks to Bill Neill for sharing his experience from the Second Avenue subway project and helping me understand just how disruptive and far-reaching that mess really was. And thanks to Steve Norcia, who gave me a crash course in how country clubs actually operate—politics, protocol, and all the other stuff that doesn't show up on the website.

And to the readers, librarians, booksellers, bloggers, podcasters, content creators, and anyone who ever recommended one of my books to a friend, thank you! Some of you spread the word quietly, one reader at a time. Others, like my ardent supporter Dennis Diamond, go big. Either way, you're the reason the stories travel.

Thanks, as always, to Anthony Goff and the entire team at Blackstone Publishing, most especially Stephanie Stanton, Sarah Riedlinger, Josie Woodbridge, Anne Fonteneau, Bryan Barney, Sean Thomas, and Courtney Vatis. Thank you to my overqualified assistant, Bill Harrison; my multitalented designer, Dennis Woloch; and my grace-under-fire web team at Xuni.com, Maddee James and Riley Mack. And to Mel Berger—my agent, my advocate, and the steady hand who's had my back every step of the way.

And, of course, to my family: Emily, Adam, Lauren, Zach, Sarah, and Jim, who are in unanimous agreement that I'm much better at writing than I am at micromanaging.

And finally, to Aunt Pearl, who read every word I wrote, skipped past the swearing, and told me to keep going—because, in her eyes, the world needed more good books. I think she'd say this is one of them.

EXCERPT FROM
DON'T TELL ME HOW TO DIE
BY MARSHALL KARP

Read the first twelve chapters of the character-driven novel readers are calling a slow-burn thriller—emotionally explosive and impossible to put down.

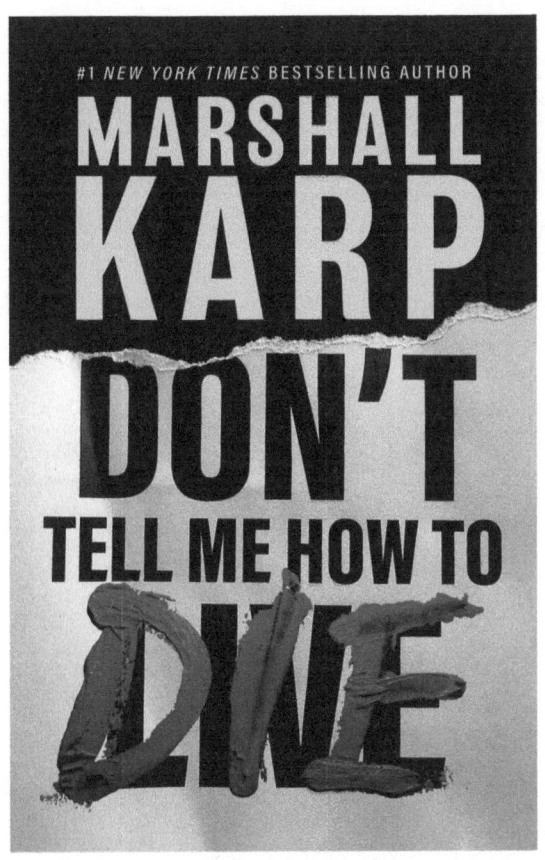

REAL READERS. RAVE REVIEWS.

"I've never read a book that left me so utterly speechless. Marshall Karp deserves a standing ovation for crafting such an incredible story."
—GRAY

"Big kudos to the author for making me feel our female MC's pain so viscerally."
—MARISHA

"HOLY CRAP!!! THAT ENDING!!!!"
—HOLLY

"A domestic thriller that'll wreck your sleep and ruin your social plans (in the best way possible)…It had me laughing, crying, and questioning how anyone could come up with a story as intricate as this."
—LAURA

"This will be one of the best books of 2025. No doubt."
—SUSAN

"Just when you think you have the story figured out, Karp pulls the rug out from under you."
—CHANTELLE

"I was nearly crying in the first half. Then the last third has my jaw on the floor. How often does that happen in a mystery? I'll tell you, not often."
—ALLYSON

"You will cry, you will be on the edge of your seat, and you will be totally astounded…This is going to be one people will be talking about for years."
—BARBARA

"This book deserves INFINITY STARS."
—BRIE

"Twists and turns that left me dropping my jaw and literally pontificating out loud."
—CORINNE

"Completely unpredictable…*No one is as they seem.*"
—KIANNA

"I devoured the book in under 48 hours!!"
—MADELEINE

"This book is a roller coaster…My jaw was consistently on the floor."
—KATELYN

"This book had me completely glued to my Kindle. If I wasn't reading it, I was thinking about it."
—STEVIE

"A gripping read…[Karp]'s officially made it onto my favorite authors list!"
—JULIE

"Wow! Wow! Wow!…Such a wild ride—five big stars!"
—LIKESTOTRAVEL

"A roller coaster of emotion, mystery, and rich storytelling that keeps you hooked…This one is a must-read!"
—BRITTNEY

"An emotional, compelling read that stayed with me long after I finished."
—ANGELA

PROLOGUE
THE ANGEL OF DEATH

ONE

THREE MONTHS BEFORE THE FUNERAL

At six feet eight, 360 pounds, Irv Hollingsworth was not only the biggest TV weatherman in Heartstone, New York; his larger-than-life personality and his flair for showmanship had made him the most popular in the county.

Which is why instead of reporting from a warm, dry studio that watershed June morning, Big Irv, dressed in bright yellow waist-high waders and a matching XXXXL slicker, was broadcasting live from Magic Pond during a torrential downpour.

"I'm here at Heartstone Medical Center," he said, letting the rain lash his face for effect. "The hospital has been operating on auxiliary power for the last twelve hours. And I do mean operating. I spoke to the chief surgeon, Dr. Alex Dunn, and he told Channel Six that despite this nor'easter, it's business as usual inside.

"But outside is a whole different story." The camera panned to take in the rest of the medical center's campus. Big Irv slogged across the muddy grounds to the swollen edges of Magic Pond, which had crested far beyond its banks.

"Normally, this is where hospital workers and locals would be sitting around enjoying their morning coffee," he said, stopping at a partially submerged bench, its seat lost beneath the murky waters. "But as you can see, Magic Pond has—"

And then, as if the media gods had come down to help the big man claim his place in broadcasting history, she appeared on camera. A woman. Floating face down on the surface of the pond.

For a second, maybe two, the only sound that could be heard was the white noise of the rain hammering on the water. Then Big Irv regained his composure and heralded her arrival with two words. Probably not the same two that most people would choose, but Irv was a TV pro. He knew what would resonate.

"Good Lord," he said in a reverent hush.

Within seconds, the internet's lust for the bizarre kicked into high gear, and the video of the hulking man in a yellow rain slicker gently guiding the sad remains of a woman in a lavender sweat suit to shore spread like a virus on steroids.

Within minutes, Big Irv, a local celebrity here in Heartstone, would be seen by millions of people around the world. I'm the mayor of Heartstone, and I'll bet that the mayor of Helsinki saw the poignant footage before I did. It's the curse of social media. Death and bad weather course through the ether with the speed of light.

As Irv's star was rising, mine was rapidly sinking. Thirty hours of relentless rain had left my town with roads that were submerged, trash pickups that were suspended, power lines that were down, and emergency services that were stretched to the limit.

My inbox was also flooded. The emails were split between my being woefully unprepared or deplorably unresponsive. Either way, I expected the front page of the *Heartstone Crier* to be a photo montage of downed trees, mud-caked basements, and disabled cars in three feet of water. The headline might not say "This Mess Is All Mayor Dunn's Fault," but society needs a scapegoat, and I was the obvious front-runner.

And then came the coup de grâce. Chief Vanderbergen called.

"Minna Schultz is dead," he said. "Her body was found floating in Magic Pond."

Immediately, my instincts as a former prosecutor for the DA's office kicked in. "Foul play?" I asked.

"The ME isn't here yet," the chief said.

"But *you* are," I said. "What's your take?"

"There's no obvious signs of trauma, but let's face it, the woman had enemies."

Enemies was an understatement. Minna Schultz had destroyed a lot of people's lives over the years. Most of them would probably show up at her wake just to make sure she was really dead.

"Of course we can't rule out suicide," the chief added.

"Absolutely," I said, although I doubted it. Anyone who ever met Minna would know that she wouldn't have the common decency to whack herself.

"One more thing, Mayor Dunn. The Channel Six weather guy discovered the body while he was on the air. The video has gone viral."

"Shit," I muttered. "So we're talking media frenzy."

"Yes, ma'am."

"I'll be there as soon as I can," I said, ending the call.

"Madam Mayor," a familiar voice said.

I looked up, and there she was, standing in my doorway, a dripping-wet pink umbrella in one hand, the tools of her ugly trade in the other.

The Angel of Death.

She was blond, in her early thirties, and still holding on to her kick-ass high school cheerleader body and flawless skin. Her name was Rachel Horton, and like the six other phlebotomists who had come before her, her job was to draw my blood three times a year to make sure I hadn't contracted the same fatal disease that killed my mother.

It had been a medical ritual for me and my sister Lizzie for over a quarter of a century. But this was the first time one of those smiling bloodsuckers ever showed up in my office unannounced.

"Rachel," I said. "Whatever it is, I have no time for you."

She flashed me a perfect smile and held up her blue soft-sided medical tote bag. "I only need a minute, Mayor Dunn," she said, as perky as a Girl Scout delivering a box of Thin Mints. "Dr. Byrne needs some more blood."

"What did he do with the blood I gave him last week?"

"He said the lab screwed up," Rachel said, capping off the ominous news with yet another sunny smile that was so genuine I realized I'd misjudged her. Rachel was not the Grim Reaper. She was more like one of those lovable yellow Minions, gullible enough to believe that the lab actually bungled a routine blood test.

The lab screwed up. I've been married to a surgeon long enough to know medical malarkey when I hear it. It's a classic doctor ploy. Rather than tell you straight up that your first set of test results looks suspicious, they give you the healthcare equivalent of "the dog ate my homework."

But I knew the truth. My white blood cells were amassing the troops and were hell-bent on killing me just like they killed my mother.

"Make it fast," I said, sitting back down at my desk.

"You'll feel a little prick," the sweet young thing said to me with a straight face, which never fails to make me wonder if she gets the sexual innuendo. She stuck the needle in my vein, and I closed my eyes.

It was a Thursday. I would have to wait till Monday before my hematologist made it official, but when you have a fatal disease hanging over your head for twenty-six years, you learn to arrive at your own medical conclusions before your doctor has the clinical proof and the balls to tell you what you already figured out.

I was dying.

"What's so funny?" Rachel asked.

I hadn't realized I was grinning, but I had to admit that my entire morning was rife with macabre humor. I was only a few weeks past my forty-third birthday, and I suddenly realized that I was going to be spending my forty-fourth with Minna Schultz. In hell.

Yeah, hell.

I'm a fairly popular mayor and a rather well-liked human being. On paper I look like a shoo-in to be ushered through the Pearly Gates and into the Kingdom of Heaven by St. Peter himself. That's just because I've been able to hide the truth from the rest of world.

But I can't hide from God, so I had no doubt that when my time was up, I was destined to spend eternity burning in hell for my sins.

TWO

Rachel removed the needle, put a piece of gauze over the vein, and taped it to my arm. "There you go," she said. "You survived another one."

Survived, I thought. Interesting choice of terms.

She zipped up her bag and gave me a cheery "Have a good one."

I wasn't having a good one when you got here, and I'm certainly not going to have one now, I thought, but I opted for, "You too. Close the door on your way out."

Minna Schultz would have to wait. I went to my laptop and typed into the Google search bar: *How often do labs screw up blood tests*. Google, always trying to stay one step ahead of me, immediately gave me some options to finish my question: *in cats, in dogs, in criminal cases, in early pregnancy*.

"This is not a good day to test me, Google," I said, banging out the words *in humans* on my keyboard.

I got ninety-six million results. I scanned the first few till I found an encouraging number. Labs make twelve million mistakes a year.

Yes, but out of how many, I thought, trying to decide if twelve million was a life raft. I was about to explore Google's credibility quotient by typing in *How many dogs a year actually do eat homework*, when my cell phone rang.

I looked at the caller ID and burst out laughing.

It said JIFFY ESCORT SERVICE.

My husband, Alex, the absolute love of my life, knows how to make me laugh. One of his favorite pranks is to sneak into my phone and change his name in my contacts. Today his timing was off. I stifled the laugh and answered the phone.

"I heard," I said, throwing on my coat. "I'm on my way."

"I'm at the pond," he said. "How are you holding up?"

How was I holding up? I wanted to take him in my arms and say, "You run the damn hospital. Can you find out if some klutz in the lab spilled their Red Bull all over my last blood test, or am I a dead woman walking?"

But nothing sours Alex faster than a whiny patient having an "I know I'm going to die" episode. I let it go.

"It's going to take us at least a week to get back to normal," I said, "but I managed to get the County Environmental Commission to send two generator trucks, so I have the equipment I need to keep our little shitstorm from overflowing into the Hudson River."

"Great. You can play that up when you run for reelection."

Reelection. More dark humor. God was working overtime today.

"What's going on at the pond?" I asked.

"A few dozen people braved the storm in the beginning, but the rain is finally starting to let up, and the crowd behind the yellow tape is starting to build."

"Tell Chief Vanderbergen to take pictures. They're all suspects."

"I doubt it. I saw the body. No sign of trauma. I don't think we're looking at a homicide, Maggie."

"Suicide?" I said.

"Not my call," he said. "That's for the medical examiner to decide."

"Alex . . ."

"What?"

"How are *you* holding up?"

He let out a long exhale. "Minna Schultz has been a roadblock to everything we're trying to do here at the hospital. That's over now, but I would feel a whole lot better if we beat her in court. This . . . this just leaves a stain on the whole project."

"If she did commit suicide, that would be her motive," I said. "She knew she couldn't win, so rather than lose publicly, she decided to piss all over your victory on her way out."

"You sound like a lawyer."

"A lawyer in desperate need of a hug," I said. "I'll be there in ten. Love you."

"What an incredible coincidence," he said. "I love me too."

It was a tired old line, but it always made me smile.

I hung up, looked down, and it caught my eye. The gauze bandage that Rachel had taped to my arm.

I peeled it off and tossed it. But I couldn't ignore it. It was a graphic reminder that I had been getting ready for this day for more than half my life.

The first time I found out I was a candidate for an early grave, I was seventeen. You'd think it would have destroyed me. Just the opposite. It was the perfect excuse to break away from my poster-child-for-teenage-excellence image. I was still president of my class, snagging straight As, going to church on Sundays, and rocking the SATs with a 1500, but once Dr. Byrne told me I had the markers for a fatal inflammatory blood disease, I developed an instant case of the fuck-its.

Sex, drugs, alcohol, rule-breaking, risk-taking? Fuck it. If I was going to die young, I was going to live life as hard as I can.

Of course, I couldn't compete with my best friend, Misty Sinclair, a one-woman wrecking ball who'd call me and say, "Let's crank shit up to eleven and break off the knob." But I ran a pretty strong second. Because, hey . . . what the hell did I have to lose?

And then I met Alex Dunn, and suddenly I had an anchor in the insanity of my life. Three years later, when I gave birth to Kevin and Katie, my Mommy genes kicked in, and I found a purpose beyond the adrenaline rush of survival.

Dying young was no longer all about me. It was about them. What would happen to them if I died?

The more I ruminated about it, the more obsessed I became with their lives after my death. It was not a random obsession. My shrink confirmed what I already knew. It was PTSD.

When my mother died, I watched in horror as women circled my grieving father like hammerheads on a feeding frenzy. And when the wrong woman stepped in to take my mother's place, the consequences were devastating.

I refused to let the same thing happen to Alex and my kids. I know it sounds insane, but the idea I'd buried in the darkest recesses of my brain became a priority as soon as the Angel of Death with her little pink umbrella showed up at my door.

I was going to spend my last remaining days on earth searching for the next Mrs. Dunn. I might not find her, but I would die trying.

PART ONE
WOMEN WITH CASSEROLES

CHAPTER 1

TWENTY-SIX YEARS BEFORE THE FUNERAL

I've had twenty-six years to contemplate the fact that a ripe old age might not be in the cards for me. But my mother was caught completely by surprise. She thought she still had half her life ahead of her when the doctor blindsided her with the diagnosis—hemophagocytic lymphohistiocytosis. They call it HLH because it's impossible to pronounce. It's also impossible to cure. But they don't tell you that.

"There are new advances in chemotherapy every day," Dr. Byrne told her. "They may not be the wonder drug we're hoping for, Kate, but they can slow down the spread. They can buy you time."

Time. That was the magic word. Time to impart more of her life skills to her teenage daughters, time to allow her husband to come to grips with his impending loss, time to savor the familiar warmth of her countless friends.

She knew that the ravages of chemotherapy could steal the very time it was supposed to deliver. But her doctor was optimistic, her 24/7-support group was deep and unwavering, and she knew that everyone at St. Cecilia's parish would be praying for a miracle.

"I've decided to go ahead with the chemo," she told us at dinner that snowy December night. Six months later, she told us how much she regretted that decision.

I remember that day vividly. It was the start of the summer between my junior and senior year in high school, and I was in the kitchen of our family restaurant cracking lobster claws for the lunch special.

It was a mindless job, which gave me the opportunity to use my brain to focus on something much more important—coming up with a killer essay for my college applications. Would it be better, I mused, to write about something global like the technology revolution, or should I stick to the tried and true—a personal challenge I've overcome, and how it shaped my—

"Yo, Maggie, what the hell are you doing?"

I looked up. It was my sister Lizzie.

"What does it look like I'm doing?" I said. "I'm prepping for Chef Tommy."

"Sure you are. I'm tempted to tell Grandpa Mike to change the blackboard from creamy lobster bisque to extra crunchy, but I don't want to spend the whole day giving the Heimlich maneuver to people who are choking on soup."

She reached down into the bowl of lobster meat I'd been filling and started picking out the shells I'd been absentmindedly tossing in.

"Sorry. I was deep in thought."

"You daydreaming about Van again?" Lizzie asked.

"No. My *Vantasies* are strictly a bedtime thing. I was trying to work out an idea for a college essay."

"Well, you better work fast. Applications are due by December thirty-first, and—oh my God—it's June twenty-fourth already. You're running out of time!"

Lizzie is my Irish twin, born 314 days after me. She's also my fiercest competitor, my biggest pain in the ass, and my dearest friend. I love her beyond words, which is appropriate since I hardly ever come right out and say it. She, in turn, expresses her affection for me by busting my chops on a regular basis.

She clutched her throat with both hands and began to gag. "I can feel the pressure building. If only you had been elected president of next year's senior class. Oh, wait—you were," she said, relaxing the choke hold. "Problem solved."

"You know how many class presidents apply to college?" I said, picking out the last of the rogue shells. "I'm not that unique."

"You could be if you wrote about how you miraculously managed to get elected despite living your entire life in your younger sister's shadow."

I was working on a comeback line when we both heard the throaty growl of the Harley Electra Glide as it barreled up Pine Street.

"Here comes Dad," I said.

"Sucking the serenity right out of the neighborhood," Lizzie added.

Dad's motorcycle roared into the parking lot and stopped at the reserved space next to the kitchen door.

Chef Tommy banged a metal spoon on an empty soup pot three times, and everyone in the kitchen—me and Lizzie included—yelled out in unison, "God bless Black Monday."

It's the standard homage whenever my father arrives at the restaurant—kind of like playing "Hail to the Chief" for the president. There's a long story behind that ritual, and it gets recounted every year at the Thanksgiving feast for our employees and their families.

The back door swung open, and Finn McCormick charged into the room. He's a big man, six feet four, barrel-chested, with a full head of thick hair that shook loose when he removed his helmet. He peeled off his leather jacket and yelled, "What's cooking?" to the kitchen crew.

It's a far cry from his past life with his preppy haircut, conservative suits, and monthly commuter ticket to his job as a stockbroker on Wall Street. That's the life that ended eleven years ago when the market crashed.

"Good news, girls," he said, spreading his arms wide. "You are done. Get out of here."

"Are we fired?" Lizzie said. "Or did Child Protective Services finally catch up with you?"

That got a belly laugh. "You wish," he said. "But alas, it's only a brief reprieve. Your mom wants me to give you the rest of the day off and send you home."

"Is she okay?" I said.

"Hard to say. What woman in her right mind wants to spend the day with her teenage daughters?" He flashed us a wide grin. "Just kidding. She seemed downright chipper all morning. Oh yeah—she's fixing lunch, so she told me to tell you not to eat here."

"Don't eat at McCormick's," Lizzie said. "Good advice."

Another big laugh from my father. Which of course was Lizzie's mission in life. Early on she had decided she wanted to be a doctor, and ever since she read about the healing powers of laughter she became the family stand-up comic commando, bombarding us with one-liners every time any of us had so much as a sniffle.

My mother, of course, had a lot more than a sniffle.

"Dad, are you sure she's okay?" I asked again.

"She looks better than she's looked in months," he said. "Besides, you know your mom. If she wasn't okay, she wouldn't want you guys around."

"That's great news, Dad," Lizzie said. Then she turned to me. "Especially for you, Lobster Girl."

"What do you mean especially for me?"

"*How My Mother Beat a Rare Blood Disease*," she said. "It's got all the makings of a great college essay."

CHAPTER 2

Lizzie got her driver's license when she turned sixteen in March, and the four-year-old Acura Integra that had been all mine for ten months now belonged to both of us. We can barely share a bathroom, so we politicked for another car. But our parents' logic, which basically boiled down to "you go to the same school—just work it out," prevailed.

"I'm driving," Lizzie said when we got to the parking lot.

"Fine," I said. "But that means I'm in charge of the radio."

"Oh God, you're going to play that annoying shitkicker music, aren't you?"

"I won't know till I'm on the road. Make a decision," I said, jangling the keys in front of her.

"This is why we each should have our own car," she said, snapping the keys out of my hand.

She got behind the wheel, and I started rifling through the CDs.

I pulled out a Garth Brooks album, popped it into the CD player, and turned up the volume.

The pub is only three miles from our house, but it was enough time to make her sit through four annoying shitkicker songs.

There was a lime-green Honda Civic hatchback with a mashed right rear fender parked in front of our house.

"Nurse Demmick is here," I said as Lizzie pulled into the driveway.

Marjorie Demmick is the school nurse at Heartstone High, a friend of my mother's from church, and one of a small platoon of women who have been there for her during her illness.

We were just getting out of the car when Marjorie, who always looks like she's in a hurry, bustled out of the front door of the house.

She's short, plump, with beautiful ivory skin, and a head full of tight red ringlets. "Hello, girls," she called out in a squeaky voice that would be adorable for a character in an animated movie, but is extremely grating in real life. "Enjoying your summer vacation?"

"We are indentured servants at an Irish pub," Lizzie said. "Can't wait till September. How's Mom?"

"Well, I just spent some time with her, and this is the best I've seen her in months. She even put on some makeup today. I couldn't stop telling her how beautiful she looked. And now she's puttering around the kitchen like . . . like . . . like . . ." She pursed her lips and looked up at the sky, grasping for an analogy.

"Julia Child? Martha Stewart? Betty Crocker?" Lizzie ventured.

"Oh, that's so funny," Marjorie squealed. "You girls are so smart."

"But you think she's doing well," I said.

"Oh yes. Look, I'm only a school nurse, but I think her treatment is working. And I'll bet now that you two are here, she is going to get even better."

Nurse Demmick was like a walking, breathing Hallmark card. I've never seen her anything but upbeat and positive.

We thanked her for stopping in, said goodbye, and opened the front door. The intoxicating aroma hit me immediately.

"In the kitchen," my mother called out in a singsong voice. "I hope you're hungry."

The kitchen smelled like the inside of a Cinnabon. Mom was just taking a pan out of the oven. She set it down and turned around.

Nurse Demmick was right. My mother looked beautiful. She was wearing a flowery pink summer dress, her strawberry blond hair was tied back in a ponytail, and her face, which had been drawn and tired for months, had a rosy glow. I didn't know if it was from the makeup or the medical treatment, but I didn't care. I hadn't seen my mother looking this good in a long time.

Lizzie inhaled the sweet fragrance that had hit us when we walked in and would seduce passersby on the street if we left the windows open. "Cinnamon swirl raisin bread," she said. "What's the occasion?"

My mother, who has never been the type to pull any punches, smiled. "I'm vertical—an occasion definitely worth celebrating. When was the last time we had a mother-daughters picnic?"

If she had asked that question when we were seven and eight years old, the answer probably would have been last weekend. But once we became teenagers, picnics at the park were replaced by volleyball team practice, homework, babysitting, and talking incessantly with other girls about boys.

"Everything is packed and ready to go," she said, pointing to an ancient handwoven picnic basket that was sitting on the countertop. "All I need is ten minutes to make the Monkey Paws. Then we're going to Magic Pond."

"I'm driving," Lizzie said.

"*I'm* driving," my mother corrected. "We're taking the Mustang."

The 1996 red Mustang GT convertible was my father's gift to my mother on her fortieth birthday the year before. It had less than two thousand miles on it when she got sick and couldn't leave the house. Dad started it every week and would drive Mom to her doctor appointments in it, but Lizzie and I had never been behind the wheel. It was *Mom's Wheels*.

"Chop, chop," Mom said. "Wash up, so we can get this show on the road."

"I've got the bathroom first," Lizzie said, bolting toward the stairs.

"You look fantastic," I said to my mother, giving her a gentle hug.

"You should have seen me when I was your age. Boys were dropping like flies."

She turned back to the oven, popped the golden-brown loaf out of the pan, and expertly drew a knife across the center. Steam lofted up from the fresh-baked bread.

"Perfect," she said. "I've had a wonderful morning, and it's going to be a glorious afternoon."

And it was.

Until the four words.

CHAPTER 3

During my mother's illness, my father had lovingly washed and waxed the Mustang, so when Mom backed it out of the garage for the first time in months, the bright red car gleamed in the afternoon sun like one of those vintage fire engines that roll up Waterfront Avenue every Fourth of July.

The top was down, the shiny black boot snapped snugly in place, and with her mixtape already queued up in the cassette player, Mom made it clear that she was not only behind the wheel; she was also in charge of the music.

While Mom was packing the picnic basket, Lizzie and I had tried to guess what the first song on the tape would be.

"Slam dunk," Lizzie said. "'Love Will Keep Us Together.' The Captain and Tennille. It's Mom's go-to song."

"Too predictable," I said. "That first song is not going to be about the music. I know Mom. We're on our way to Magic Pond for the first time since we went ice-skating in December just before she got sick. She's going to want to come up with something that's totally about the moment."

"Spare me the logic," Lizzie said, "and cough up a song title."

"'Teddy Bear's Picnic.'"

"From when we were in *kindergarten*?" Lizzie said, like it was the dumbest idea in the world. But then she shrugged because, on second thought, it was just the kind of crazy sentimental thing my mother might do.

Lizzie and I played Rock-Paper-Scissors to see who would ride shotgun. I won. She climbed in back, and I settled into the soft leather bucket seat up front.

Mom pulled the Mustang onto the street, and the moment we'd been waiting for arrived. She tapped a button on the cassette player, and the warm whiskey voice of a Texas shitkicker erupted from the speaker.

Lizzie clapped both hands to her cheeks, looked up at the sky, and yelled, "Oh my God." Not because it was the country music she hated but because the choice was so inspired. She leaned over and kissed Mom on the back of the neck.

And as we drove down Crystal Avenue on that glorious summer afternoon, the four of us—Lizzie, me, Mom, and Willie Nelson—sang about the joys of being on the road again.

Ten minutes later we arrived at Magic Pond, found a quiet shady spot to spread our blanket, and walked over to the water's edge.

The pond is large by city standards, a two-acre freshwater ecosystem where birds, frogs, plants, bugs, and people coexist in quiet harmony. I inhaled deeply, and a sense of serenity washed over me as I studied the reflections in the water—the trees, the clouds, and of course, the seven-story hospital complex that loomed above it all.

Magic Pond is not part of a city park. It is the centerpiece of Heartstone Medical Center. The story of how that came to be is a hodgepodge of fact, fiction, and folklore.

This is what I know to be true. In 1872 Elias Majek, a young brickmaker from Germany, immigrated to America and settled in the Hudson Valley, where the soil was rich in clay deposits.

His timing was perfect. As immigrants teemed into New York City by the hundreds of thousands, the demand for bricks to raise the metropolis to new heights skyrocketed. And by the dawn of the twentieth century, Elias and Eleanor Majek were the wealthiest couple in the county, living in a forty-two-room mansion looking out at lush gardens, abundant fruit orchards, and their magnificent freshwater pond.

In 1912, at the age of seventy, Elias sold the brickyard and celebrated his retirement by taking Eleanor on a long-overdue vacation. They sailed across the Atlantic aboard the luxurious ocean liner *Mauretania*. It was a far cry from the passage he had made forty years earlier, when he came to America in the steerage compartment of an ancient steamer out of Hamburg.

They spent the next month touring Europe in grand style, but Elias was saving the best for last. He had a special surprise planned for their trip back to New York, and on April 10, 1912, the happy couple arrived in Southampton on the southern coast of England for the maiden voyage of the world's largest ocean liner, White Star's queen of the seas—*Titanic*.

Five days later Elias perished in the frigid waters of the North Atlantic when the unsinkable ship hit an immovable iceberg.

Eleanor was one of 705 passengers rescued from their lifeboats by the RMS *Carpathia*. A year later she contracted tuberculosis. It's at this point that the story of the Majek legacy becomes shrouded in mystery.

It's been said that Eleanor's doctor gave her less than six months to live. She spent much of that time sitting by the pond, reading, drawing, or writing in her diary. But instead of dying, her health improved, and she survived for another nine years.

When she died in 1923, she bequeathed her property to the people of Heartstone with the stipulation that her home be converted into a hospital. She also requested in her will that the pond not be reconfigured or altered in any way in order to preserve its magical restorative powers.

Over the decades the hospital doubled and tripled in size, and then doubled again. And Majek Pond became Magic Pond as generations of people trekked to its banks to pray for speedy recoveries, healthy babies, or medical miracles.

And now my mother, my sister, and I stood on the shore, ready to entrust our most fervent desires to God, Jesus, and the ghost of Eleanor Majek.

Mom unsnapped the brass clasp on the cracked leather change purse that had belonged to her mother. She plucked three pennies from the pouch and gave one to each of us. One by one we closed our eyes and tossed the coins into the water.

"Now let's eat, drink, and be silly," my mother said.

We sprawled out on the blanket; Mom opened the picnic basket and passed out the Monkey Paws. It's the name Grandpa Mike gave to Grandma Caroline's peanut butter, honey, and banana sandwiches on fresh-baked cinnamon swirl raisin bread.

I was starved and attacked the gooey, chewy treat. Lizzie began wolfing hers down as well. Mom poured three cups of strawberry lemonade from a Thermos and nibbled at her sandwich.

"I have a surprise," she said. "You know all those pictures I have in shoeboxes that I've been threatening to sort through one of these years?"

I stopped eating as she reached into the picnic basket and pulled out a thick photo album bound in bright green fabric. *The McCormick Family* had been carefully inked on the cover in Mom's perfect Catholic schoolgirl handwriting.

"Ta-da!" she said, setting it down on the blanket.

Lizzie opened it to the first page, and there were four black-and-white shots of Mom, Dad, and the Harley Electra Glide, each one taken in a different location.

"These are from 1979," Mom said. "Your father and I went to the biker rally in Sturgis, South Dakota. It was our last big road trip—thirty-five hundred miles—and I was pregnant with Maggie at the time. I don't know what I was thinking."

"Sounds like the poor kid got bounced around a little," Lizzie said.

"More than a little. It was almost all interstate, but I had to make a lot of pee stops, and some of those side roads were bumpy as washboards."

Lizzie drummed on the side of her head with both fists and smirked at me. "Well, that explains a lot," she said.

Mom turned the page, and there was an artfully arranged cluster of pictures of me as a baby.

"Oh, there's the little darling now," Lizzie said.

I put my hand over the pictures. "Stop," I said. "What's going on?"

They both stared at me.

"What are you talking about?" Lizzie said.

I ignored her, closed the album, and slid it to the side. "Mom . . . what's going on?"

She kept staring at me, stone-faced.

"Maggie, what the hell are you doing?" Lizzie said. "Mom's finally having a good day, and you're ruining it."

"I'm sorry. I'm not used to Mom having good days lately, and I'm trying to ask her if it's real."

"I don't get it," Lizzie said.

"She got sick in December, and she kept getting sicker, and then she wakes up one day in June, and like Cinderella, she's all dressed, and her hair is done, and we drive to Magic Pond for a picnic, and now all of a sudden there's a family photo album, which has been on her bucket list for years, and I just want to know what's going on. Is this real, or does the Mustang turn into a pumpkin at midnight?"

Lizzie didn't say a word. She was wrestling with my logic, and I could see in her eyes that my questions were starting to make sense.

She turned to my mother for answers.

Mom just looked at us. Well, she didn't exactly look. She kind of squared off, sizing us up, like we were about to get in the ring and go fifteen rounds.

And then she said them.

Four simple words that she uttered only once. Yet of all the hundreds of millions of words I have heard before or since, those are the four that will forever be burned into my soul.

I have written them in the margins of countless notebooks, screamed them into caves and canyons so I could hear their taunting echoes, traced them onto frosty car windows and steamy shower doors, and ached as I watched them trickle down into trails of tears.

Four words.

How strong are you?

CHAPTER 4

Life is filled with defining moments—those pivotal points in time where your entire world can change in a heartbeat.

By the age of seventeen I'd had a few, but none that I couldn't handle. It's not just that I was lucky or blessed, which admittedly I was, it's more that when things don't go my way, I have this unique ability to turn them around.

My father calls it Irish grit. Mom said it was a gift. Lizzie has a different take. She says, "The only reason everything works out exactly the way Maggie wants is because she's an obsessively compulsive micromanaging control freak."

Harsh. But not without merit.

This time was different. I knew from the look in my mother's eyes that this would not be something I could fix. I didn't know exactly what she'd say next, but I knew that this picnic in the park would not have a happy ending.

How strong was I?

"Very," I lied, my mouth dry, my breathing shallow.

"And I'm stronger than Maggie," Lizzie said. "Ask anybody."

Mom smiled. She'd always been so proud of Lizzie's bravado. She took a deep breath. "It's not working," she said.

"What?" Lizzie said. "What's not working?"

"The transfusions, the new chemo, the brilliant doctors . . . hundreds of people praying for me . . . nothing is working."

"Don't give up," Lizzie said. "It's only been a few months. The next round of transfusions is going to do it."

"There is no next round. This past one was a Hail Mary. It didn't work, and there's nothing left to try. Dr. Byrne had a long talk with me yesterday. I'm out of options . . . and I'm almost out of time."

"I don't understand. You seem so healthy," Lizzie said, her fists clenched, her body taut, determined to reverse Mom's news with irrefutable logic. "You're baking bread. You're driving the car. You look fantastic."

"It's all smoke and mirrors. Dr. Byrne put together some kind of concoction with vitamin B-12, antioxidants, and God knows what else, and Marjorie Demmick came over this morning, gave me a shot in the ass, touched up the outside with a little blush, added some pink lipstick, and presto change-o, I look like a million bucks. But Maggie was on the right track. The Mustang won't turn into a pumpkin, but by tomorrow morning I'll look like two cents."

I felt the tears welling up. "Why would you do this?" I said. "This whole . . . charade? Why did you get our hopes up?"

"I made a big mistake." She reached across the blanket and put one hand on my knee, the other on Lizzie's arm. "I never should have put myself through all those medical procedures hoping for a miracle. I should have spent these past six months with you. I can't get any of that precious time back, so I asked Dr. Byrne if there was anything he could do to give me one more joyful day with my daughters. This was supposed to be it, but you caught me. I am so, so sorry. I wasn't trying to get your hopes up. I was trying to give you one last final happy memory."

"Dad came into the restaurant all excited this morning," I said. "He was going on like you'd turned the corner. He really thinks you're getting better, doesn't he?"

Mom nodded. "Your father is the world's worst poker player. If I told him the truth, you'd have read it in his face, and I wanted one last sunny afternoon with you before you found out. I'll tell him tonight. The big man is going to crumble. He's going to need you to help him get through this." She shook her head. "No, it's more than that. You're all going to need to help each other."

Lizzie got to her feet. "But first I need a group hug."

We helped Mom get up, and the three of us embraced for a solid minute. No tears, just silence, each of us wrestling with her own thoughts.

"I'm writing you each a letter," my mother said when we finally let go. She lowered herself to the blanket, and Lizzie and I dropped down next to her. "I started writing them back in February. You know what they say—'hope for the best, but plan for the worst.'

"I'm glad I started when I did, because I didn't realize how much I have to tell you. I'd been planning to spread it out over the next forty or fifty years, but now the best I can do is a crash course. I tried to think about all the important advice a mother can give her daughters. Things you can't learn in books. Or worse yet, there are dozens of books on the subject, every one of them with their own point of view, and I wanted to make sure you had the wit and wisdom of Kate McCormick before you made any life-altering decisions."

"I hate to break it to you, Mom," Lizzie said, "but if your letter to Maggie has any good advice on the virtues of remaining a virgin till her wedding night, you're too late."

That broke the ice. Mom howled in laughter. I poked Lizzie in the arm, but I didn't care. I was pretty sure my mother had already figured it out. And I was also confident that she hadn't shared her suspicions with my overprotective father.

I have no idea how many times the three of us have been to Magic Pond together, but the next two hours were the best ever. First, we went through the photo album, and page by page, with Mom giving us a hilarious running narrative, we watched ourselves grow up.

And then we talked. No subject was off-limits. Thinking back, I realize that we asked my mother a lot of questions about her past—her childhood, her achievements in school, and of course, everything she could possibly tell us about her relationship with my dad from the first day she met him.

Her questions to us focused on the future. She asked about our plans, our dreams, and so many of the other parts of our lives she knew she wouldn't be here to watch unfold. To this day, I wish we could relive that moment, and give Mom better answers. Lizzie knew she wanted to become a doctor, and eventually she did. But all I could tell my dying mother at the age of seventeen was that the University of Pennsylvania was my first-choice college.

I never got the chance to tell her that I married a wonderful man; had two beautiful, intelligent, healthy children; found a challenging career that brought me joy and would make her proud; and that my life was purposeful, productive, and relevant.

But there are times, especially when I'm alone in my private little attic hideaway rereading her handwritten eighteen-page letter to the teenage me, that I feel she is up there with me, and she not only knows what I've accomplished but she also knows I couldn't have done it without her inspiration.

At about three o'clock that afternoon, Mom started to fade. The magic elixir Nurse Demmick had given her was starting to wear off.

"You're looking tired," I said. "Why don't we pack up and go. We can talk more later. Dad's going to bring home dinner."

"Okay, but let's stay five more minutes," Mom said. "There's one more thing on my mind, and I can't talk about it at home."

"Lay it on us," Lizzie said.

And then my mother dropped the second bomb.

CHAPTER 5

"This is about your father," my mother said. A smile bloomed on her face at the mere mention of him. "He's only forty-three years old, and that man is tough as nails. He's going to live at least another forty-three years—probably more.

"But . . ." she said, and then paused, choosing her words carefully. "But he's not going to want to spend all that time alone."

"Don't worry, Mom," Lizzie said. "Maggie and I will be there for him. We promise." She turned to me for confirmation.

"I don't think that's what she's saying, Liz." I looked at my mother. "You know we'll be there for him, but that's not what you're talking about. Right?"

"Right. Let me try it again. Lizzie, your father will grieve when I'm gone. You all will," she added quickly. "I know how difficult it will be, but when the initial pain lifts, and I promise you it will, you and Maggie will move forward in the very same direction you were headed—college, a career, marriage, a family . . ."

We nodded, still not sure where this was going.

"It won't be the same for your father," she said. "Years ago, he and I charted a course from our twenties all the way into old age. We had plans; we had dreams. Nothing exotic. Just the simple things most married couples think about—retirement, a house on a lake, travel. But when

I die, a lot of those dreams will die with me, and with the path to his future gone, I'm afraid he'll be rudderless . . . lost at sea."

Lizzie looked lost herself. I knew Mom had something important to say, but she was treading so lightly that it was hard to connect the dots.

"I spoke to Father Connelly," she said. "The church has support groups to help people get through their loss. There's one specifically for teens."

"We'll be okay, Mom," Lizzie said. "Maggie and I have each other."

"That's your choice, but tonight when I talk to your father, I'm going to ask him to please go to some of the meetings for widows and widowers. Father Connelly told me it's the best way for him to cope with his loss. I know he will miss me something fierce, but eventually I know he'll come out on the other side and be ready to find a life partner to share the second half of his life."

"*A life partner?*" Lizzie said. "You mean a *stepmother.*"

We were no longer treading lightly.

"No. You're not five years old. You don't need another mother to take my place, but your father will need another woman to make him feel whole again, and I want you to promise me that you'll support him, maybe even help him choose the right person."

"Eww," Lizzie said. "You want us to find Dad a girlfriend?"

My mother laughed. "Trust me, sweetie, the girlfriends will find him. I know you think of him as Daddy, but in the grown-up world, Finn McCormick is a successful, funny, lovable, sweet hunk of a man. He goes to church, volunteers for school functions, and he's the magnet that draws people into the restaurant. I guarantee you that once he is single, women will flock to him like stray cats to an overturned milk truck. The problem is, he's not going to know how to handle it."

"Mom, women flirt with him all the time," I said. "They see the wedding ring, but they have a couple of glasses of wine, and they get all playful. Don't worry. Dad knows how to handle them."

"He won't once I'm not there to come home to. And they won't be *playful*. They will know that he's lonely and vulnerable, and let me tell you, some of these women are predators. I know. I've seen it firsthand."

"You've seen women hitting on Dad?" I said.

"No, nothing like that. Forget it." She waved me off.

"No. I'm not forgetting anything. What did you see?"

Mom sat there organizing her thoughts. Finally, she said, "Did you know Bernadette Brennan? She used to come into the restaurant all the time."

"Yes!" Lizzie said. "Didn't she die?"

Mom nodded and crossed herself. "Last year just before Thanksgiving. I went to her wake. I never told anyone this story before, but I was standing on the receiving line, and Rita Walsh was in front of me. She was wearing a flower print dress with a Queen Anne neckline, which struck me as a little bit out of season for November and maybe not the most delicate choice for a wake. But, hey, she works in the women's clothing department at Macy's, so who am I to tell her how to dress?

"Anyway, when she gets up to the front of the line, she kind of sidles up to Leon Brennan—that was Bernadette's husband—and she flashes him more than a little bit of cleavage. And the poor man—his wife is dead, but he isn't, and he can't help it. He takes a good look. And then Rita starts in with, 'Oh, Leon, I'm so sorry about Bernie. She was so wonderful. After this is all over, I'm stopping by, and I'm bringing you a nice, hot home-cooked dinner.' And then he said something, and I couldn't hear him, but Rita gives him a little laugh and strokes his hand, and says, 'Oh, Leon.'

"Can you imagine? Right there in the funeral home with Bernadette laid out in a box, not even in the ground yet, and that . . . that tramp is coming on to the poor dead woman's husband. It was none of my business, so I forgot all about it until four o'clock this morning when I woke up with my mind racing.

"I always knew that recovering from this disease was a long shot, but I kept telling myself I could beat it. Now that I know I can't, I woke up thinking about your father standing there at the wake, shaking people's hands, thanking them for coming, and there's Rita Walsh flashing her tits and offering to come over with a pan of baked ziti."

"That's not going to happen," Lizzie said. "Mrs. DiMarco told me that Rita and Mr. Brennan are getting married."

"Married?" Mom said. "That's insane. The woman is practically the same age as his daughter."

"The daughter is four years younger," Lizzie said. "Mrs. DiMarco told me. Then she said Rita's a gold-digging bitch, and she feels terrible for her friend Bernadette, and she wishes she could talk some sense into Mr. Brennan's head, but she doesn't think he'll listen. Then she asked me what I would do."

"What did you say?"

"What I said to her was I don't know. But what I said to myself is I wonder if Mrs. DiMarco, who is divorced, feels sorry for her dead friend, or does she feel sorry for herself because she has the hots for Mr. Brennan, and Rita beat her to the punch."

Mom leaned over and hugged Lizzie. "Child, you are wise beyond your years."

"I guess we know why you couldn't talk about this at home," I said.

"Oh God, please don't tell your father about this. I realize it's a terrible burden to put on you girls, but if I can't be around, I'll die happier knowing the two of you will be there to love him, and watch over him, and . . . and . . ."

Lizzie finished the sentence for her. "Keep the bitches from digging their claws into him."

The words hit my mother like a gut punch. But they were exactly what she needed to hear. I could see the tension visibly drain from her body. A smile crossed her lips, and her eyes welled up. "Thank you," she said.

It was a moment I will never forget. Twenty-six years later, I would relive it. Only this time, I would be the woman who was dying, and the thought that I would be leaving the man I loved to the mercy of a calculating band of ziti-baking, husband-hungry predators would make my imminent death all that more difficult to accept.

CHAPTER 6

"You didn't tell me we were having company for dinner," Mom said as Dad came through the door with Victor, one of our busboys, both their arms laden with food.

"Don't worry. He's not staying," my father said. "It's just the four of us, but I didn't know what you were in the mood for, so I brought some of everything. Meat loaf, baked salmon, pork chops, colcannon, mac and cheese . . . a whole bunch of veggies that I'm sure nobody will eat, plus Chef Tommy made your favorite—an orange pound cake, and I've got a quart of vanilla ice cream. I wound up with so much damn food that I couldn't get it all on the bike, so Victor followed me in his car. Thanks, kiddo. I'll see you tomorrow."

Victor nodded shyly, gave Mom a quick hug, and hurried out the door.

"Finn, are you nuts? There's enough food here to feed a village," my mother said.

"Hey, lady," he said, wrapping his arms gently around her. "If you don't like it, call Pizza Hut. Girls, get the food on the table, while I kiss your mother and tell her how beautiful she looks."

Dinner was bittersweet. It had been a long time since we'd done this as a family, and Dad was overjoyed. "So . . . tell me all about your outing to Magic Pond," he said.

Mom, cheery and upbeat as ever, launched into all the fun stuff—the ride in the Mustang, the picnic, the photo album, and of course, the ritual tossing of the coins into the pond and hoping for medical magic.

"Well, you better go back there often," Dad said, "because clearly Eleanor Majek's magic is working."

Lizzie and I put on our best game faces, knowing what was to come.

Years later, the two of us named it *The Last Supper*, because there was enough food to feed Jesus and all twelve apostles, and because it was the last time the four of us ever sat down at the table together.

After dessert, Lizzie and I said we were going out, and we'd be home around ten.

"No drinking and driving," came the knee-jerk Dad reaction.

"Chill out, Dad," I said. "We're just connecting with some old friends. We're not going to drink."

"And Maggie can barely drive," Lizzie said, laughing as we went out the door.

Technically, we had told the truth. We weren't going to drink. But we had said nothing about smoking a little weed. We'd also left out the fact that our old friends had been born in the middle of the eighteenth century. Caleb and Birdie Heartstone, who founded our fair city, were currently residing in the cemetery that bore their name.

I drove there, parked the car, and we walked along a path till we got to Caleb and Birdie's mausoleum, our favorite spot to toke up.

I lit a joint, and we passed it back and forth, not saying a word, just leaning back against the stone crypt, looking up at the darkening summer sky, and quietly self-medicating our anxieties away.

Lizzie finally broke the silence. "You high yet?"

I never know how I'm going to react to weed. I guess it's the luck of the draw, depending on what my friend Johnny Rollo is dealing that day.

"Definitely getting there," I said. "But it's not the kind of high where I'm flying and everything gets trippy. It's more just this soft, mellow glow washing over me."

"That's the little ganja faeries massaging the cannabis receptors in your brain," Lizzie said. "I read it in a medical book."

"Don't make me laugh," I said. "I'm dealing with serious thoughts here."

"Like what?"

"Like how ironic it is that this afternoon Mom tells us she's going to die, and right after dinner we head straight for the graveyard."

"That's not irony, Mags. It's more like we don't have a lot of choices. We can't exactly smoke dope at home. This is the go-to place for kids to get stoned or hook up. Did you and Van used to get it on back here?"

"Just quickies and BJs, but it's way too creepy here to have great sex and then curl up naked together and go to sleep. Van had his dad's fishing cabin for that."

"You think Van is having sex now?"

"No. I think he's the only marine in South Korea who is remaining celibate so he can come back home in three years and marry his high school girlfriend. I may be a romantic, but I'm not an idiot. Van is nineteen years old, for God's sake. I read in *Marie Claire* that men hit their sexual peak at nineteen. Women don't get there till around thirty-five."

"So, what you're saying is that right now the guy you're being faithful to is on the other side of the world banging some middle-aged Korean woman."

"You're an idiot," I said. "But you're a funny idiot."

"Have you cried yet?" Lizzie said.

"No. I've cried a lot since Mom got sick, but not since . . ." I paused, thinking back to that afternoon. "I got weak in the knees as soon as she said those words. *How strong are you?* I mean, I knew what was coming next."

"Me too. I haven't cried yet either. I keep thinking about Dad. Dating! What did Mom say . . . 'Women will flock to him like stray cats to an overturned milk truck'? It's funny—Mrs. DiMarco said the same thing about Mr. Brennan, except she said, 'Honey, those hags were bringing him food, baking him cookies . . . they were all over him like flies on cow flop.'"

"You think Dad is going to remarry?" I said.

"Probably. It's what men do. Women not so much, or not so fast, but men . . . Do you want to hear something really disgusting?"

"Sure."

"Do you know Beverly Reidy? Brown hair, glasses, kind of a science nerd, but I like her. I sit with her at lunch sometimes. Her mother died last year, and guess who her father started banging pretty soon after the funeral?"

"I give up."

"The mother's *sister*. Beverly's aunt. Beverly came home early from school one day because she was sick. The father's bedroom door was shut, but she could hear the two of them in there banging their brains out. She ran out of the house and came back a half hour later. The dad and the aunt were in the kitchen having coffee and looking all normal and shit, but now every time Beverly sees the two of them together, she says her skin crawls. She's at the point that she wants them both out of her life."

"You're right," I said. "That's disgusting. I hope you're not planning on sharing that with Mom."

"You're an idiot," she said. "And you're not even a funny idiot."

I smiled. I love my sister. Even her trash talk makes me happy.

We lit up a second joint and sat there painting scenarios and conjuring up what-ifs. We made a list of women who might go after our father once he was single, and we split them into four groups—gold-digging predators, horny bitches, clueless losers, and Mrs. Doubtfire, who could come to work for us as a housekeeper, but she could never replace our mother, because underneath the wig, the makeup, and the padding was a penis.

We were that stoned.

We drove home hoping to slip quietly into the house and go directly to our rooms, but Dad was sitting on the porch steps.

Lizzie and I got out of the car, and he stood up. The radiant, joyful, smiling life force we'd had dinner with was gone. He stood there, head lowered, shoulders slumped, heartbroken.

He let out a long, low, stifled wail and spread his arms wide. Lizzie and I ran to that familiar safe space, burying our faces in his chest, hugging him, clinging to one another, and the three of us stood there sobbing, bracing ourselves for the loss of the woman we loved most in the world.

CHAPTER 7

Mom still had a few good days left in her. One by one, she reached out to her closest friends, and one by one, they came to the house for brief farewell visits. That first weekend she chatted with them in the garden, but with each new day her rapid downhill slide was clearly visible, and by midweek she was relegated to welcoming her visitors from her bed.

Even so, she insisted that life at 811 Crystal Avenue remain as close to normal as possible. She forced Dad to go to work. He half-heartedly went in for the busy times, but most nights after the dinner rush, Grandpa Mike and the rest of the crew at McCormick's held down the fort till closing.

Lizzie and I alternated shifts. One of us would go into work, while the other would sit at home with Mom. Dr. Byrne came by every day, and when Mom finally became too weak to do the simplest things for herself, a hospice nurse came in to help.

On July 3, 1997, I knew it was the beginning of the end. It was my turn to stay with her, so Lizzie and Dad reluctantly went to handle the heavy Fourth of July weekend crowd at the restaurant.

Mom slept most of the day. About 6:00 p.m. she woke up looking a little better than she had in days.

"Call Dad," she said. "Tell him to come home. And bring Lizzie."

"What's wrong?" I said.

"Nothing. I've been thinking about something, and I finally feel good enough to try it."

Fifteen minutes later my father pulled into the driveway on his Harley, my sister right behind him in the Acura.

"What's wrong?" he said, sitting on the edge of the bed and taking Mom's hand.

"Nothing. I feel almost human, and there's something I want to do."

"Name it."

"I want to take one last ride."

"Please don't say *last* ride. But sure, let's go for one *more* ride. I'll pull the Mustang out of the garage."

"No," Mom said. "I want to go on the bike. Like the old days."

"Honey, are you sure you're in any condition to ride around on a motorcycle?"

Mom smiled. "The only thing I'm sure of, Finn, is that I want *one more ride*. And it's now or never."

He smiled back, but I could see his blue eyes glistening with tears as he stood up and lifted her out of bed.

He carried her to the living room, and Lizzie and I helped her dress for the adventure.

"I don't think I can handle leathers and a helmet," she said. "See if you can find me a cardigan and some kind of kerchief to cover what's left of my hair."

Five minutes later, wearing a pink nightgown, a gray sweater, and a red, white, and blue bandanna tied up in a headscarf, she was ready.

Dad wanted to carry her, but she wanted to get to the bike on her own two feet.

"Okay," Dad said, "but you are definitely not sitting behind me holding on for dear life. You're sitting in front, and I'm behind you, making sure you don't fly off."

"Ooh, I love it when you get all macho biker boy with me," she said.

He kissed her and helped her onto the Harley. Then he got on, his beefy body shielding her, his arms keeping her safe.

Helmets are mandatory in New York, and I picked his up from the driveway and tried to hand it to him.

"Not this time, kiddo," he said. "Now you and Lizzie get in the car and follow us."

"Where are you going?" I said.

"That's up to your mom. Where to, love?"

"Finn, my good man, I'd like to go back to a place we haven't been to in eighteen years."

"And where might that be, my lady?"

Mom turned, and I could see a small twinkle in her eyes, a mischievous smile on her face.

"1979."

CHAPTER 8

Dad rolled on the throttle, and the Harley roared to life.

He pulled out of the driveway, not at rocket speed, but with the measured grace and style of Morgan Freeman driving Miss Daisy to the market in her 1949 Hudson Commodore Custom Eight.

Mom sat up tall in the saddle, gazing out at the road ahead, then slowly turning her head to take in the homes on either side.

"Oh my God, she looks so regal," Lizzie said as we followed them in the Acura. "Like the queen of bloody England."

Evening was beginning to streak the sky with color. Some of our neighbors were out—having drinks on their porch, watering their lawns, playing ball in the street. They'd probably ignore a passing motorcycle, but when one is trundling along at fifteen miles an hour, and the biker chick in the driver's seat is wearing a pink nightgown, people stop what they're doing. They look. They smile. They wave.

And Mom, like the queen of bloody England, waved back. *Noblesse oblige*.

A mile from the house, Dad came to a roundabout, pulled the bike into the right lane, and turned onto Throop Avenue.

There was only one stop along Throop worth visiting: Heartstone High School.

Dad drove onto the campus and stopped at the edge of the

four-hundred-meter oval track. It was a quiet Sunday summer evening, but there were still at least a dozen people out there jogging.

"Hallowed ground," Lizzie said, gazing at the painted white lines and the rich brown cinder track.

Hallowed indeed. It's where my parents met.

We'd heard the story a thousand times. They were teenagers. Heartstone High had their annual track-and-field meet against six other schools in the county, and one of the biggest events of the afternoon was the women's sixteen-hundred-meter relay race.

The first runner for Heartstone stumbled out of the starting block, and the Hawks were dead last after the first lap. The second girl picked up some distance, and then the third did the same, but by the time the anchor got the baton, the Heartstone fans knew it would take a miracle to win.

Coach Williams had that miracle in her back pocket—Mary Katherine Donahue, a freshman in a field of juniors and seniors. Nobody knew the girl back then, but today her name is in the record books—one of the fastest runners ever to burn up a high school track in the state of New York. She had started that last leg a daunting twelve meters behind the leader, but she broke the tape half a step in front of the pack.

The Hawks fans went wild. One of them, a burly sophomore, climbed out of the stands, made his way down to the field, and waited for the school's newest rock star to come over to the sidelines.

"You were amazing," he said, extending a hand. "I'm Finn McCormick."

The poor girl was exhausted, dripping with sweat, her thick red hair twisted in a damp, limp knot behind her. "Mary Katherine Donahue," she said. "Call me Kate."

They've been inseparable ever since. And now they'd returned to the scene of that first handshake.

"Uh-oh," Lizzie said.

There was a large green-and-white sign at the edge of the field spelling out the regulations for anyone using the facilities. *No tobacco, alcohol, or other controlled substances allowed. No food or beverages allowed. No bicycles, skateboards, rollerblades, or strollers allowed.*

Dad guided the bike up to the sign.

"If you want to get technical," I said, "it doesn't say anything about middle-aged couples on Harleys."

Even if it had, I'm sure my father wouldn't have cared. He pulled the bike onto the track.

"Wait a minute," I yelled. I turned to my sister. "If they're gonna do this right, they're gonna need a soundtrack."

I grabbed the box of CDs, dumped them all on the floor, and scrambled through them till I found the one I needed.

I stuck the disc in the player and hit the play button. Trumpets blared, and the very same inspirational music that lifted Rocky Balboa as he ran up those steps in Philadelphia filled the air and spilled out onto the field.

Dad pumped one fist high in the air, gripped the throttle with the other hand, and revved the engine.

I expected him to putt-putt around the field at about the same speed as he went through town. But I was wrong. The song echoing across the field was called "Gonna Fly Now." And that's exactly what Dad did.

He flew. Gunned it. Chunks of heavily rolled, carefully tended stone and cinder flew in all directions as the Electra Glide barreled down the track.

Later that day I cornered him and asked what he was thinking when he went tear-assing around the oval like that.

"It wasn't my idea," he said. "I thought she'd be happy with that first little cruise through town, but when we got to the track, she said to me, 'You better haul ass around this track, Finn McCormick. I want my last ride to be on a real motorcycle, not a goddamn parade float. I want to feel the wind in my face, and my heart pounding in my chest. I want to feel *alive*.' So, I kicked it."

Boy, did he kick it. I don't know exactly how many laps they took around that track, but every time they whizzed past us, I got a brief glimpse of intense joy on my mother's face that I hadn't seen in months.

And then the cops showed up.

CHAPTER 9

A Heartstone PD patrol car rolled onto the field and pulled across the running track.

"This just in, folks," Lizzie said, holding an imaginary microphone to her mouth. "The cops have finally caught up with the bizarre biker gang who have been terrorizing the neighborhood. They're setting up a roadblock now."

Two uniformed police officers stepped out of the car, and as Dad sped around the track for the umpteenth time, they flagged him down.

He skidded to a stop.

Lizzie killed the music. "Quick, Magpie," she said. "Bail out before they spot you. I don't care if I get busted, but it will look bad for the president of the senior class to be caught playing DJ while her parents destroy school property."

"Thanks for the offer," I said, "but right now I'm not the president of anything. I'm the daughter of that crazy Irishman, and if they throw him in jail, they can lock me up too."

The two cops walked over to the bike. One was blond and in her midtwenties. I'd never seen her before. But I recognized the older one. Kip Montgomery had known my parents since high school. And when Kip, his wife, and their three kids came into the restaurant for dinner, Dad would always send over dessert on the house.

I was about thirty yards away, but it looked like he gave both Mom and Dad a friendly small-town police officer hello. Then Dad got off the bike, and he and Kip walked off to talk in private. Dad did most of the talking. Finally, Kip took out his radio.

"This is serious, folks," Lizzie said. "Officer Montgomery is calling for backup."

"Shut up," I said. "Dad's coming."

My father ambled over; a grin spread across his face. "Get back in the car and hang tight," he said.

"Excuse me, sir," Lizzie said, thrusting the fantasy microphone in his face. "Elizabeth McCormick, *Heartstone Crier*. Can you tell our viewers what the bleep is going on?"

Dad belly-laughed. "Don't worry, kiddos. It's all good."

He walked back to Mom, and the two of them powwowed. Then he scanned the gathering crowd of gawkers, spotted a trio of twelve-year-old boys on bicycles, and signaled them to come over.

The kids responded with a classic "*Who us, mister?*" look on their faces. But he beckoned again, and they decided to find out what he wanted. Pretty soon their heads were nodding vigorously. Dad reached into his pocket, dug some cash out of his wallet, handed it to them, and they raced off.

"Ma'am," the inquiring reporter said. "Can you tell our audience what the hell that was all about?"

"It's Dad," I said. "Don't ask."

Five minutes later, two motorcycle cops and two more squad cars joined the group. Dad revved up the Harley, rolled over to us, and said, "Follow me."

"Where are we going?" I said.

"That's up to your mother," he said. "But wherever it is, we've got ourselves a police escort."

The turret lights on all three cop cars went on, flashing red and blue against the graying sky. And with the biker cops clearing the traffic along the way, the motorcade moved out smartly.

First stop on the journey was St. Cecilia's, where my parents got married. The three kids on bicycles must have been the advance team, because by the time we pulled up to the church Father Connelly was standing outside, along with two of the younger priests, and some of the staff from the rectory. There were hugs, kisses, and blessings, and then off we went again.

The convoy proceeded along High Street at a leisurely pace—about twenty miles an hour. Mom, who'd had her thrill ride for the day, didn't complain.

"Next stop, Main Street," Lizzie said.

She was wrong. The procession hung a left on MacDougal, a two-lane thoroughfare that skirts the business district and is peppered with gas stations, fast-food outlets, chain drugstores, car dealerships, and not much else.

"What the hell is here?" Lizzie said.

I had no idea. And then one of the motorcycle cops stopped traffic, and the entourage crossed the road and turned into a strip mall.

"Holy shit," I said, looking at the Chinese restaurant nestled between a Staples and the Sew Rite fabric store. "Dragon Heart."

Lizzie gave me a blank stare.

"It's where Mom and Dad were having dinner when her water broke, and she went into labor with me. They never got to finish dinner, so Mr. and Mrs. Lum delivered it to the hospital the day after I was born."

A white-haired Chinese couple was outside waiting for us. Mrs. Lum had a silver tray with an assortment of appetizers on it. Dad popped a dumpling in his mouth. Mom took a mini egg roll, thanked the Lums profusely, and held on to it. I was sure she'd pass it to Dad as soon as we were out of sight.

"Next stop has *got* to be Main Street," Lizzie said.

It was. And from the reception we got, our three young town criers had done their job well. It was as if all of Heartstone had dropped what they were doing so they could make way for the lady in the pink nightgown. Cars pulled over and honked their horns as we rode by. People shouted from windows, and almost everyone at the outdoor cafés that lined the block stood up and gave us a standing ovation.

We drove past the firehouse, where a dozen firefighters hooted and saluted as their electronic message board flashed *HFD loves Kate McCormick.*

And then we turned onto Pine Street, where the sidewalk in front of McCormick's was packed with customers, waiters, and kitchen staff. In the middle of them all was Grandpa Mike, arms high, a flag in each hand—one red, white, and blue; the other green, white, and orange.

Loud pipes howled as twenty of Dad's biker buddies roared out of the parking lot to join the celebration, and the caravan, which had started out with a single motorcycle and a chase car and was now a joyous mob, wended its way to Crystal Avenue, where the whole neighborhood was there to welcome us home.

Someone set off a string of firecrackers, which may have been for Mom, or it might just have been some kid getting a jump on the Fourth of July. People who knew our family well called out her name, pumped their fists in the air, and many of them—big, strapping men included—dabbed at their eyes.

Our police escort stopped just past our house, and the cops got out of their cars and off their bikes as Dad pulled into the driveway.

He lifted Mom off the Harley and turned her to the crowd. She looked exhausted, but exhilarated. She waved, threw kisses, said thank you over and over, and finally, Dad carried her inside the house and upstairs to her bed.

She kissed us all, told us she loved us, went to sleep, and never woke up.

CHAPTER 10

My mother had done her research on the downside of dying at home. A week before she passed, she sat down with the three of us and gave us our marching orders.

"Rule number one," she said with the same sense of urgency she'd had when we were kids, and she taught us about stranger danger. "Once I'm gone, do *not*—repeat, do not—call 911. A lot of people do, thinking that the cops will help them transport the body. But what happens is that the first ones to arrive are the paramedics. They're on a mission—save lives. So even though I'm dead as a mackerel, they will start pounding on my chest and cracking my ribs . . ."

"The hell they will," Dad said, jumping in.

"Let me finish. Pounding my chest and cracking my ribs, which will quickly escalate into a fistfight with my husband. *That's* when the cops will show up."

Dad acquiesced. "So, you want us to call the funeral home first."

"No. First call Dr. Byrne. He and I discussed this. The law says you need a physician to sign off on the cause of death. He'll come right over and fill out the paperwork. Otherwise, the state of New York will ship me off to the morgue for an autopsy to figure out what killed me. Whatever you do, please do not let them cut me up."

"What if we get an offer from a medical school willing to pay big bucks for a fresh cadaver?" Lizzie said, her face completely deadpan.

Mom clapped her hands and shrieked with laughter. "Oh God, I am so going to miss this shit."

"How do you think I feel?" Lizzie said. "I'm losing my best audience. Maggie barely *understands* most of my cryptic banter."

I was jealous of my sister's innate ability to deal with death so matter-of-factly, but I loved her for how effortlessly she could keep Mom smiling during those final days.

My mother and I were a lot alike. We needed to be in charge. So, while she still had the strength, she dragged Dad to Kehoe's Funeral Home to pick out her casket, her dress, the flowers, the Mass card, and whatever else Mr. Kehoe had on his extensive, expensive checklist.

Mary Katherine Donahue McCormick passed peacefully at 3:27 a.m. on July 4, 1997. My father was holding her hand when she took her final breath, but he didn't leave her side to wake me or my sister until seven. His excuse: "The next few days won't be easy on any of us. I figured you'd need your sleep."

Dr. Byrne was a man of his word. He came immediately, filled out the death certificate, and stayed until Mom was on her way to Kehoe's. No autopsy—the top box on her checklist.

Grandpa Mike arrived after eight o'clock Mass, and his eyes teary, his voice shaky, he announced, "I put a sign in the window and hung the bunting over the front door. Then I poured Kate her last drink, set it on the bar, and locked up. Just like I did with Grandma."

It was only the second time since he opened the place on St. Patrick's Day 1965 that the lights at McCormick's had gone dark.

News of Mom's passing spread quickly, and by 2:30 p.m. the first hot home-cooked meal made its way into our kitchen—chicken divan, delivered by a neighbor, Josie Henson, early forties, three kids, recently divorced.

Lizzie and I had been told what to expect. "You may get a few who bring flowers, or wine, or pastry," Mom said. "But the ones on the prowl will come with Corningware, Pyrex baking dishes, or dutch ovens—anything they have to come back for a few days later.

"I can hear them now," she said. "'Just stopping in to pick up my dish, Finn. How are you holding up? Let me know if there's anything I can do for you.' It won't matter what he says. They'll keep coming back."

She was right. They came in droves. It didn't matter that Dad owned a restaurant. They just kept showing up with food as if the poor man didn't know where his next meal was coming from.

Grandpa Mike called them "women with casseroles." But, of course, he was from back in the day, when a girl might get lucky with some baked tuna, noodles, and mushroom soup topped with crumbled potato chips. But the vultures of the late nineties had ramped up their culinary skills.

Some of the meals bordered on gourmet, like Isla Cantor's Moroccan couscous with tender chunks of lamb, topped with golden raisins and slivers of almonds; or Nikki Conklin's buttery quiche laced with goat cheese, arugula, and prosciutto; and my favorite, Jill Sawyer's lobster mac 'n' cheese, which Lizzie and I polished off in one sitting.

It was a competition with Dad as first prize, and by the end of the week Lizzie and I calculated that there were between eight and twelve contenders. It was impossible to get an exact count because some of them were so subtle we couldn't tell if they were in play or just good-hearted friends.

We trusted none of them. So, when Andrea Tursi showed up, her Dow Chemical boobs cascading over the top of a scoop-neck sweater, we watched her make a beeline to the kitchen, check out the competition, and swap the name tag on whatever crap she brought with Deborah Roelandt's signature chicken and dumplings. Then she headed straight for the golden ticket—my father.

"She's exactly the kind of calculating bitch Mom told us to keep an eye on," Lizzie said, putting the name tags back where they belonged.

Each night, we would transfer all the entries to Tupperware, wash all the dishes, and return them the next morning. We were pretty sure most of the women knew what we were up to. We didn't care. We were on a mission. We dubbed ourselves the Casserole Patrol.

The wake was a two-day affair that snarled traffic along Brandywine Avenue for a quarter of a mile on either side of the funeral home. I knew Mom was popular, but as Lizzie put it, this was more than people paying their respects. This was Wake-a-Palooza.

The lines snaked around the block. My father wore the brand-new black suit and tie Mom bought for him. Pinned to his lapel was her tiny gold claddagh ring, a symbol of their love, loyalty, and friendship. For hours on end the three of us stood dutifully next to the casket as more than five hundred people filed in to clasp our hands, hug us, and softly speak words of sympathy and condolence.

The funeral Mass was at St. Cecilia's on a warm summer Friday morning. Any number of people would gladly have been honored to eulogize my mother. But she made it clear that she only wanted her husband and her two daughters.

Dad went first. The man has the soul of a poet and is blessed with the Celtic gift for storytelling. For twenty minutes, working without notes, he mesmerized the room as he recounted the tale of their romance from the day they met on a high school running track to their final night on the back of a Harley.

He was brilliant—the quintessential loving, grieving husband—and my first thought as he stepped down was how proud Mom would be.

Then Lizzie put it all in perspective for me. "We're doomed," she said. "After that tribute, every single woman in the whole damn church is going to want to scoop him up."

Lizzie was next. She introduced herself as Mom's favorite *bad daughter*, and in her own devilishly sweet way, she put the F-U-N in funeral.

And then it was my turn.

I still have a vivid image of sunlight streaming through the stained glass as I stepped up to the pulpit to deliver my eulogy. I looked down at the sea of black dresses, somber faces, and anxious eyes, and I wanted to run. Then I looked down at the white casket with a spray of red roses, and I heard my mother saying, "Breathe. Repeat if necessary."

I breathed. And the words flowed.

"My mother's favorite place in the entire world is less than a mile from here. You all know it: Magic Pond. She loved to remind her daughters that she's been taking us there since before we were born. I remember as a little girl tossing stones into the water, and wondering why some go straight to the bottom while others hit just right, and their ripples travel across the surface, transferring energy as they go.

"That same thought crossed my mind this week as hundreds of you came to the wake, and again this morning as I look out across this sanctuary, and I see her family, her friends, her neighbors, her restaurant family—both staff and customers—her book club, her garden club, her biker buddies, her three high school teammates from that historic five-thousand-meter relay, her coach, the ladies of the Christmas committee, our mayor, our school bus driver from Heartstone Elementary, doctors and nurses who cared for her during her illness, and at least a hundred people I hardly know, but whose lives were touched by my mother.

"Some people can live a hundred years and barely have an impact on the world. But the life force that was Kate McCormick for forty-one short years on this earth still lives on in this room. We are the many ripples she left behind."

I'd written everything down on index cards before I spoke, and I still had two cards left to read. But as I gazed out at the crowd, at the women with tissues to their eyes, and men with heads bowed, I knew I had said just enough.

I stepped down and walked to the front pew. Dad stood and hugged me. Lizzie squeezed my hand. As soon as the three of us settled back in our seats, the choir director stood, and forty-eight men and women in magenta robes rose as one.

The crowd was probably anticipating one of Father Connelly's go-to hymns, like "Alleluia! Sing to Jesus" or "Amazing Grace," but he was merely officiating. Mom was running the show.

The organ came to life—not a somber chord, but a driving gospel rock beat. The choir began swaying, clapping, and oohing. Two of the singers thumped tambourines, and for the next five minutes, that requiem became a joy fest as the choir, and eventually every man, woman, and child in that church, stood and sang "Ain't No Mountain High Enough."

No dirges for Kate McCormick. This was her love song to my father. This was the send-off she wanted, and she'd planned every inch of it.

The only thing she knew she couldn't control was the parade of women who would come by to comfort my father as soon as she was in the ground.

Thanks for sampling *Don't Tell Me How to Die*.

Maggie Dunn is one of the most compelling, complex characters I've ever created. These opening chapters give you a glimpse of who she is—and what she's willing to do. But if you think you know where this is going—buckle up.

What lies ahead isn't just a twist. It's a full-on emotional, psychological gut punch of a ride.

Don't Tell Me How to Die starts as one woman's mission to protect her family . . . and turns into a slow-burn thriller packed with betrayal, heartbreak, revenge, and murder—with twists you won't see coming, right up to the final five-word sentence that'll hit you like a truck—and stay with you long after you've turned the last page.

Marshall Karp